Keith Dixon was born in Yorkshire and grew up in the Midlands. He's been writing since he was thirteen years old in a number of different genres: thriller, espionage, science fiction, literary.

He's the author of eight novels in the Sam Dyke Investigations series and two other non-crime works, as well as two collections of blog posts on the craft of writing.

When he's not writing he enjoys reading, learning the guitar, watching movies and binge-inhaling great TV series. He's currently spending more time in France than is probably good for him.

THE HARD SWIM

A Sam Dyke Investigation

KEITH DIXON

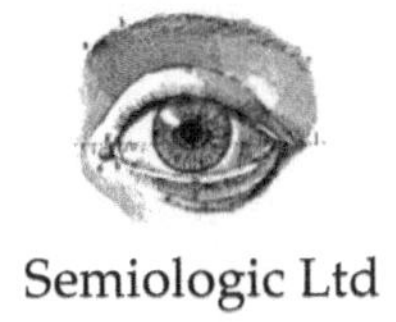

Semiologic Ltd

COPYRIGHT

THE HARD SWIM

FIRST FRIDAY

HE HAD WANTED to take her with him, but now he would have to kill her.

There were too many people around and they were too close. And they were all translators – they could call for help in over twenty languages.

Connell Steele, who was not without a sense of humour, grinned to himself. Although the concept of evil was one in which he didn't believe, he recognised that others would think it a wicked act to kill someone so obviously undeserving.

But at this point in his career he didn't care. His experience had taught him that everyone had an agenda and it was not his job to understand this woman's. He was being paid a fee and, most of the time, he told himself that that was all the moral indemnity he required.

The Conference of European Translators was being held for the first time in the Mansion House of Edinburgh Zoo, a grand Victorian pile that stood at the top of contoured grounds like a stern overseer and looked down on a wide and unexpected collection of exotic animals. Conferences were held most days in the Mansion House unknown to the gaggles of visitors who wandered around the zoo below.

The target had arrived an hour previously and had engaged in a raging and bitter argument with a uniformed guard in the entrance foyer. The guard had been sufficiently cowed – or pissed-off – that he had made a phone call, glancing suspiciously at her all the while from beneath his peaked cap. The target had then spoken to the stiff-looking woman who had arrived, striding purposefully in a pencil skirt across the lobby, and had eventually been allowed to walk up to the Mansion House itself, accompanied by the guard.

Steele had thought he saw an attitude of triumphalism in her body language – a kind of strut that infected her gait, probably without her knowing. Steele had been party to many covert observations and thought he was passably expert at sizing up the mental landscapes of those he observed.

The guard had dragged one of the delegates out of the evening meal – a thin man with long hair who, to Steele, looked like a filing clerk with ambition. The target had spoken urgently to him for two minutes and then, with the conversation apparently concluding amicably, she had been allowed by the guard to go to the bar, where Steele now observed her attentively.

From his position in a dark corner of the room, beneath an oil painting of a bearded, crimson-cheeked Victorian, Steele watched the target drink her rum and coke. She looked pleased with herself, sitting at one of the tables by the large picture window and smiling from time to time, her hand clasped over the tan leather handbag that had never left her side.

Obviously that was where she kept the asset.

Steele shifted in his seat and felt again for the wire in his blazer pocket. Its loop was cool and firm against his fingers. He glanced around the bar. Pairs, trios and larger groups of men and women from a variety of nationalities were sitting talking in umpteen languages. The Conference had attracted almost two hundred delegates from more than twenty countries, ready to discuss areas of translation that seemed to his reading of the programme both obscure and pathetic.

But that was all right. Now he knew whom the target had spoken to he could act on the first objective. Still thinking of himself as a military man – despite everything that had happened to him – he liked objectives that linked together into a plan. His particular skill, he told himself, was to be flexible around those objectives so long as the ultimate outcome was achieved. Lately he'd been thinking a lot about karma and what it meant to someone in his profession. If it was true that the sins he committed on this earth would be sent to revisit him, then he was in for a rough ride in his next incarnation. But until that journey came to pass he would do the best he could to live a purposeful life. Whatever that purpose turned out to be.

Without moving his position, he watched as the target stood to leave the bar. She would have to walk through the gardens towards the path that led, further down, to the glass doors of the foyer and main exit.

She smoothed her navy-blue skirt with pale hands. Above the skirt she was wearing a cream blouse with pockets on the front. She was tall, about five-nine, with neatly-shaped light brown hair. Too thin for Steele but he supposed she was attractive in a refined way. French genes.

She picked up a short black jacket from the padded chair next to her and put it on, then reached down and picked up the handbag containing the asset, looping its long strap crosswise over her shoulder. One final look around the room, then she headed for the glass door that led out of the bar and into the garden.

Connell Steele finished his drink, looked quickly at his watch as though he'd remembered something urgent, then followed, trying to suppress an anticipatory, vulpine grin.

CHANTAL BRESSETTE STOOD outside the bar of the Mansion House for a moment and let her eyes grow accustomed to the night.

The air had a March chill and she wrapped her arms around her chest. From where she stood, the Members' Garden stretched ahead of her and when she raised her gaze she could make out the vague rise and fall of the Pentland Hills, outlined like a gently rumpled quilt against the last of the evening light.

She smiled with satisfaction. The day had been long and difficult, but at least she had managed to make an appointment with Duhamel, the translator. Lunch-time tomorrow. It felt as though she had achieved something against her expectations – a success to counter her usual dragging fear of failure.

She prided herself on her independence, especially after the death of her father two years ago, but there were still times when the risks she took surprised even her. Taking a day off work to come on this kind of opportunistic venture was in many ways typical of her conduct, but each time she did something like this she experienced two contradictory thoughts – first, that she had to do adventurous things or die; secondly, that she must be insane to compromise the comfortable life she was building for herself.

She stepped down from the doorway of the bar and began to pick her way along the gravel path, feeling the stones like individual invitations to pain through her thin canvas shoes, the din from the bar receding behind her.

She knew that there was a bus-stop outside the Zoo that would take her back into town and she quickened her pace, looking forward to treating herself to a nice meal in one of the city's excellent restaurants. The path was not particularly dark here, but she was still surprised when a figure stepped from the shadows and stood directly in her way.

Chantal stopped abruptly, her weight rising slightly onto her toes because of her momentum on the downward slope. The figure had resolved into the shape of a man of average height and weight, his hair cut tight to his head, curly in a way she associated with rather well-off sons of the aristocracy. She couldn't see his features clearly, even when he spoke.

He said, 'You'll come with me.'

He wore a dark blazer over dark trousers, a white edge of cuff protruding from the jacket. His voice had been without an accent that she could place. He seemed real enough on the path, casting a sharp-edged shadow, but his presence was light, almost insubstantial, as though he had been aggregated from stray atoms and had no real weight. His face was still indistinct but she sensed a depth of calmness in him, as though he knew how this was going to play out.

Chantal had never liked men who thought they knew what she was going to do – their presumption was almost as insulting to her as if they had leered at her body.

'Who are you? More security? I have permission to be here.'

'I'll have the bag, please. Don't make me take it.'

Now a spike of fear ran down Chantal's spine and she gripped her handbag more tightly. Realising her mouth had gone dry, she swallowed to put some saliva on to her tongue before she spoke again.

'Get away from me or I'll scream.'

He seemed almost amused. 'Scream all you want. There's no one to hear.'

'Take my purse. In the bag. That's all the money I have.'

Now she thought she saw a glint in a dark eye. He reached out a hand.

'Ah, but it's not the money I'm after, is it, darling?'

He took a quick step forward and stretched his right hand towards her cheek in an almost sensual gesture, then curled the fingers around her head, covering her mouth and twisting and pulling her off-balance, tilting her backwards towards his chest. His left hand reached round and pinned her arms to her body.

Chantal felt herself toppling helplessly backwards, then being pulled relentlessly into the shadowed area beyond the edge of the path. The man's strength and sudden physicality compared to his appearance of slightness came as a shock to her. He had a strong male smell that he was trying to hide with a sweet deodorant, but it didn't work.

She found herself staring up at the sky as he dragged her back with him, the twigs and dead wood in the shrubbery crackling underfoot in a series of dry explosions. She tried to bite the fingers that covered her mouth but the man wore thick padded gloves and her teeth didn't penetrate. The gloves tasted obscurely of chalk.

She kicked backwards against his ankles but he was moving so quickly that she found she had to use her feet to stay upright instead, her thin shoes not finding any purchase on the matted undergrowth. There was a noise emanating from somewhere close and she was embarrassed to realise that she was snorting through her nose.

It seemed impossible that no one had heard them, but at the same time she knew that it was happening so fast that her life might be over in another second ...

Then abruptly, from behind her, there came a sound reminiscent of a metal bar hitting a rubber tyre, and the grip on her mouth fell away.

Unable to find her balance quickly enough, she fell backwards with a small cry. Her arms flew out and she waited to hit the ground.

But she was caught by two large hands which absorbed her weight gently and then pushed upwards, restoring her to an upright position. She stepped forward and turned, raising her fists in a useless gesture of protection or aggression – she was unsure which. She heard herself breathing hard as she drew in the air that the man had denied her.

A different man was standing before her – taller, heavier, his dark hair straight and longer than her putative kidnapper. His features were also in shadow but seemed square and strong, and his presence was also definitive, as though you could never mistake this person for anything but a man.

Her attacker lay flat on the ground, his body as crumpled and deformed as an empty potato sack. She looked back at the man who had intervened to help.

'Who are you?'

'My name's Sam Dyke, and I'll be your rescuer today.'

IN A WEEK'S TIME, Sam Dyke would wonder whether he had become involved in the whole business simply because of the woman's haircut. In the bar twenty minutes ago it had caught his eye because its short, sculpted shape contrasted with the slightly lank Oxford bluestocking look sported by everyone else – female *and* male. He had little interest in clothing or hairstyles, but he had found himself glancing at her from the end of the bar. It was her hair to begin with and, as he looked more intently, he saw that she had the kind of restrained beauty that you didn't notice at first. He had known beautiful women whose allure was evident at once in the lift of their lips, the smooth curve of flawless skin across their bones, the delicate shape of their ears. This woman seemed to be holding it back, hiding it beneath a downturned gaze, a leg crossed at the knee, a smile that was turned inward and not meant for others. And she had a lithe slimness that reminded him of Laura, though her reaction to the crowd in the bar was warmer than Laura's would have been, who tended to dislike the encroachment of other people.

This realisation had surprised him because it was not how he typically thought of Laura, who from the beginning had seemed willing to take him at face value and be open to him on his own terms. Perhaps that was changing – as was the whole relationship, he thought wryly.

This line of thought had been placed on hold when he had seen the young woman stand, put on her jacket, pick up her bag and leave.

And almost immediately he'd seen the other man feign a look at his watch and follow her out. From the first there had been something about the man that triggered an alarm in Sam's subconscious. It was a combination of his deliberate lack of attention to the woman while she had been seated, the weightless ease with which he now rose from his chair, the keen purpose in his gaze as he followed the woman through the tall glass doors and into the dark gardens beyond.

Sam knew that his impulsiveness was a trait that brought him more trouble than reward, more grief than praise. But he liked to think of it as a direct link to an instinctual knowledge of how things worked. His managers had often said, using the new jargon, that he had little 'emotional intelligence'. But on the other hand his experience had taught him that his first perceptions of situations were often correct.

So when he saw the man leave the bar he had put down his warm Guinness at once and followed, hesitating only at the door because the man was still standing on the small patio outside.

He had watched the man keep his position and observe as the woman started down the path to the exit. He seemed focused and calm with the stillness that Sam had seen in trained military personnel who made themselves inhabit the terrain before acting.

Having evidently made his decision, the man had then cut across the lawn and sliced through the woods, moving quickly to head the woman off lower down the path. Sam had followed at a distance, the sound of his own passage masked by the other man's movements. The man hadn't been particularly stealthy, probably thinking that the woman had neither training nor an expectation of what was about to happen.

Sam had been close enough afterwards to see the confrontation on the path. He had seized a handy fallen branch from the floor, took two quick steps and aimed it crunchingly at the back of the man's head. It had made a satisfying contact and would leave a nasty bruise.

Now the woman was staring at him wildly, her oval face flushed as a result of the choke-hold the man had used, her feet slightly apart as if ready to run, her hands slowly moving to rest claw-like over the top of her handbag. The physical exertion of the last few moments was now emphasising her beauty, exaggerating the fire in her eyes, the delicate tendons of her neck and the high colouring of her cheeks. And despite what he'd just done, Sam felt mildly embarrassed, especially after he introduced himself with a line that he regretted immediately.

She said, 'What's going on? Who are you?'

Sam took a step back and lowered his arms. He had already dropped the branch, which lay on the ground between them now like an unexploded bomb. She glanced down at it, then up at him. There was a look of mistrust in her pale blue eyes for which he couldn't blame her, but it was likely that time was short.

'We shouldn't have this discussion here. One second.'

He bent down and went through the fallen man's pockets. He took out a wallet.

'Look. One VISA card, in the name of John Smith, three hundred pounds in cash. No other ID. A phone.' He pressed a few keys. 'No names or numbers in the address list, so it's probably a throw-away. What's this?' He had pulled out a length of glinting wire held between two wooden pegs. He held it up to show to the woman. 'I'd say this was a professional job. You're lucky he didn't use it on the path.'

He turned the man over on to his front and used the wire to tie his hands behind his back, knotting it by using the wooden handles. He took off the man's gloves and laid them to one side, then turned him on to his back once more.

'He'll do himself more damage trying to get out of that. He'll have to wait till his friends find him.'

'Friends?'

'Doubtful he's acting alone. Grab his feet and we'll pull him further out of the way. He won't come round for a while.'

He bent down and took the man beneath the arms, then looked up at the woman, who hadn't moved.

'Come on, we haven't got all night.'

The woman stared at him for another moment, then turned on her heel and walked back to the pathway. Sam heard her clicking insistently down the tarmac. He took a firmer grip of the man and pulled him deeper into the wooded edge of the path.

Sam stood and jogged to catch up with the woman, who didn't stop walking. Her gaze was fixed steadily on the exit as if unwilling to be distracted from her intention of leaving. He wondered how she had managed to recover so quickly from what had happened to her. She was young but had a kind of poise and self-possession that he had seen before in professional women who worked in male environments. That didn't mean that she wasn't affected.

He said, 'Look, you'd do well to listen to me. We should report this. I'll come with you to the police. Or we can just tell these security guys on the doors and let them take care of it.'

'I can't get involved.'

'The police take a dim view when attacks like this aren't reported. What if he does it to someone else?'

The woman stopped now and looked at him fiercely.

'You said it yourself. He's a professional. You said he had friends. He was after me, not any stray passer-by.'

'And why are you so important?'

'I'm not. I don't know what he was after.' She started walking again, obliging Sam to catch up.

'You're not a very good liar.'

'I'm not lying.'

'Right. Your hands are trembling. You're very pale. Your voice is a bit shaky. But you haven't screamed or had a crying fit like someone who's just been attacked. You have some idea of what's going on here but for some reason you don't want to tell me.'

She stopped again. The glass doors of the foyer were now forty yards away, glinting dully. She stared ahead, apparently fixated by them. He wondered why she was lying to him.

She said, 'You're not a translator, are you?'

'Not exactly.'

'Then what?'

'I have a card that says I'm a private investigator, but that makes it sound very glamorous. Which it isn't. Well, not most of the time.'

'And you just happened to be here, at the right time to stop that man from ... doing whatever he was going to do?'

Sam hesitated.

'I've been working.'

'On what?'

'I can't tell you.'

'Goodnight, then.'

She turned away.

'Wait ... '

The woman stopped and looked back at him impatiently. 'I thought you said we should get out of here quickly.'

'I was paid to serve papers on a guy at the conference.'

'And?'

'I had only one chance to serve him. Tonight. He'd decided he didn't want to visit his wife while he was here.'

'Why?'

'Because he'd found a replacement model in Geneva.'

'You're right.'

'What?'

'It's not glamorous. It's squalid.'

'A simple thank you would have done.'

She glanced at the heavens. 'Thank you. Now please leave me alone.'

'That's not a good idea. I repeat, that guy won't be here by himself. There'll be others somewhere, waiting to hear from him. If he doesn't check in by a certain time they'll come looking.'

The woman glanced around then turned to look back up towards the Mansion. 'Will they be in the zoo?'

'Probably not. Either he was going to finish the job in the woods or find a way to smuggle you out. He may have needed a distraction or help from outside the zoo. We should get away from here as quickly as we can. Incidentally, did I mention my name was Sam?'

'Yes.'

'And you are ... ?'

'Hard to say, isn't it?'

She glanced down the path towards the low building that housed the entrance foyer. 'Can we go through there together?'

'Yes, or my name's not Sam Dyke. Did I mention that?'

THEY PASSED THROUGH the darkened foyer without the two guards even looking at them, engrossed in their own conversation, and stood outside at the head of the steps that led down to the busy main road. Buses and cars boomed past, heading either for the airport and its constellation of hotels or in the opposite direction, towards the glowing centre of Edinburgh.

The air was cool and windy away from the protection of the trees inside the zoo and the woman shivered. She looked pale now that he could see her more clearly. Her blue eyes had taken on a violet tint under the orange street-lighting and as far as he could tell she was without lipstick.

He wondered when he'd become so interested in women's make-up.

He took her arm and pulled her quickly down the dozen steps, his boots clattering noisily, her pumps completely soundless, then turned left when they reached the pavement, walking briskly towards the Holiday Inn where he'd taken a room earlier in the day. There were no cars parked on the road but in his estimation that didn't mean they were any safer.

He was aware that the demands of his job meant he was likely to see dangers and difficulties where there were in fact none. This sense of caution was at nonstop war with his almost obsessive need to act. He wondered briefly whether he was over-dramatizing what had happened in the zoo, but then recalled the behaviour of the man he'd knocked out. He'd moved with forethought and alacrity once he'd decided on his course of action. In his manner there'd been no sign of hesitation or fearfulness, as you might expect with a casual mugger. That led Sam to believe that there was a deliberate intention behind the attack. The man's lack of real identification was also suspicious – even alarming. It suggested the involvement of an organisation or a team of some kind with access to resources.

You didn't create fake identities unless you had something much larger to hide.

He'd made no plans for that night other than to relax before heading home the next day, but changing plans was never a problem for him anyway. Despite this, he felt himself becoming frustrated with the girl's stubbornness. It was as though she believed that withholding her identity and intentions would protect her, like an animal who refuses to look you in the eye in the hope that you'll fail to notice it. But if he was to help her properly he'd need a lot more information than she seemed willing to give.

He considered for a moment whether he should just abandon her. Laura had told him that his desire to protect other people, especially women, was a kind of misplaced paternalism that continually put him in harm's way. Intellectually he knew this was true – as much as any psychological assessment of his confused thinking could be – but he found it hard to prevent himself intervening when he saw potential injustice.

If she told him to go away and leave her alone, that was another matter.

As they walked he held her thin wrist and realised he was pulling her faster than she wanted to move.

Slowing down, he said, 'Where are you from? Are you visiting or do you live here?'

'Do you have to pull so hard?'

'We have to get out of the light. We don't know who's watching. Are you certain you don't want to tell the police?'

'You can drop me off in town if you've got a car. Or I'll get a taxi.'

'Did you hear a word I said in the zoo?'

'God, you're touchy ... I'm staying at the Radisson in the town centre. I've brought an overnight bag.'

'Anything you wouldn't mind losing?'

'My only Gucci bag and you want me to leave it behind? I don't think so. Where are we going, anyway? You do realise I haven't agreed to any of this.'

'Any of what?'

'Whatever this is. Your taking over my life as if I can't look after myself.'

Sam halted and she almost collided with him. 'You're right. Here I am, trying to be helpful, and I haven't given a thought to your feelings. How do you feel?'

'Don't be sarcastic. Where are you taking me?'

'To my lair, of course.'

He had let go of her wrist and now she threw up both hands with exasperation.

'I think it's a perfectly reasonable question in the circumstances.'

'The problem is, the circumstances aren't reasonable. Look, I'm a little prone to seeing worse-case scenarios, I'll grant you that. I'm not exactly Mr Happy. But if I were in your paper-thin shoes right now I'd be wanting to get out of the area as quickly as I could. I don't know what you've got but it's obvious that some rather nasty people want it.'

'And you know that just because a grinning prat in a blazer tried to mug me?'

'I hope you're not questioning my years of experience.'

'How many years?'

'What?'

'How many years have you been doing this? Private investigating.'

Sam looked at her and couldn't help himself smiling. 'Nearly four.'

'Four!'

'Plus ten working for the government.'

'Oh ... okay. So where are you taking me?'

'Just come and you'll find out. It'll be a nice surprise.'

She looked down at the pavement and took a deep breath. 'All right. I'll have to trust you, won't I? Am I doing the right thing?'

Sam said nothing but took hold of her wrist again. In truth he didn't know what to say that might make her feel comfortable. When he became task-focused his attentiveness to the feelings of others became of secondary importance. That was something else that Laura had told him. He sometimes thought that if Laura didn't talk to him, he wouldn't know anything about himself or his motives. He wasn't sure whether that was a good or a bad aspect of his self-development.

Or 'Journey', as Laura sometimes called it.

He turned left and started up the winding incline to the Holiday Inn's entrance which, oddly, was positioned to the rear of the building. A taxi appeared suddenly beside them and swished past on its way to deposit a fare at the hotel's entrance.

He noticed that the woman was now keeping pace with him up the incline and didn't seem out of breath. He was reminded that he'd thought of her as lithe when he'd seen her in the bar. Evidently his instincts were still good, though the time and place in which he exercised them was sometimes suspect.

He went through the hotel's glass doors and steered her to the right, away from the chest-high Reception desk and into a small lobby harbouring a bank of three lifts. A group of small Chinese women standing in the lobby looked up at them and smiled knowingly, their lined faces crinkling like brown paper. Sam let go of the woman's wrist. His life was complicated enough without being perceived as a seducer of young women.

ONCE INSIDE THE lift she said, 'The only people I know called Sam these days are women.'

'Good Yorkshire name.'

'You don't have an accent.'

'I moved away.'

'Where?'

'Crewe.'

'Wow, you went upmarket.'

'I'll add snob to your list of attributes.'

'You're making a list?'

'You should see it. Getting longer all the time.'

At his room he went straight to the wardrobe, retrieved his rucksack and started gathering his things. He was pleased that he was an essentially tidy person and the room was not a total mess.

The woman stood in the doorway but didn't cross the threshold. Sam turned and looked back at her. For the first time she seemed hesitant, as though becoming aware of what had taken place only a few minutes ago.

It was another opportunity to demonstrate his sensitivity.

He said, 'You're thinking you don't know me, you haven't got a clue what happened out there, and this could all be some kind of elaborate set-up just to get you back to my room.'

'Crossed my mind.'

'Dream on. Here … ' He took a business card from his wallet and handed it to her. 'That's my address. I live with a nice woman called Laura and have a son from a previous marriage who stays with us from time to time. Now get inside and close the bloody door.'

She put the card in her jacket pocket and said, 'A girl can't be too careful.'

But she was smiling as she stepped through and shut the door behind her. The room was functional – a wide bed, a desk in the far corner with plugs for power and internet connection, a small glass-topped table and chair. A door led to the bathroom. Like all modern hotel rooms it was stifling hot, even though there was a gap where Sam had left one of the windows slightly ajar.

Sam had placed his rucksack on the bed and was now organizing the space inside it prior to packing. Through the window you could see the lighted hotel car-park rising up towards the wooded slopes of the zoo beyond, as though concrete civilization had encroached on the wilderness but could stretch no further. Sam noticed her looking.

'That's the monkey house up there. You can see them swinging around during daylight.'

As if she hadn't heard, the woman said, 'I'm Chantal Bressette.'

Sam paused and stood up from the bag. 'Well that's not Yorkshire.'

'French father. I was born over here, though.'

There was a change in the atmosphere. It was that moment when a relationship begun by accident, and likely to be provisional, becomes personal.

Sam stuck out his hand, which she reached towards and shook with a kind of artificial forcefulness, making a game of it. Then she turned away again as though unwilling to watch him handle his personal effects.

He said, 'Are you sure you're all right? What you've just gone through would terrify most people.'

'Well my heart's still thumping and my mouth's a bit dry.'

Sam pointed to the bathroom.

'Help yourself to some water while I carry on.'

She crossed to the bathroom and he heard what sounded like miniature fireworks going off as she took the crinkled plastic wrapper from the complimentary mug. She came back in with a cupful of water, cradling one elbow in her other hand while she watched him work, folding and packing a shirt and some papers. Then she lifted the cup and swallowed, her neck muscles moving silkily beneath her skin. Sam had found himself watching her from the corner of his eye – her physical movements had a kind of grace that was compelling.

It was as though a ritual had been played out and Sam felt able to be pragmatic again. 'We have to leave Edinburgh as quickly as we can. That man was not messing about. If you don't want to go to the police we have to get you out of here and then think where you can go that's safe.'

'But I've made an appointment to meet someone tomorrow. I can't just leave.'

Sam hoisted his rucksack on to his back and zipped up his leather jacket. 'I thought I was clear. Whoever that guy represents, they're serious. They're not amateurs. He's probably already out of the restraints and contacted his partners. Your room may well be under observation, assuming they know where you're staying.'

He had been watching her expression grow more alarmed as he told her the hard truths. He had spoken deliberately to provoke a response. In his mind she had assumed the position of client and he had a duty of care towards her now. He added, 'You sure you don't know what they're after?'

Chantal Bressette avoided his eyes and shook her head in a way that told Sam she was still lying.

THE PROCEDURES HAD worked, of course.

Having missed his half-hour check-in, Steele became the object of a grid search. Not that the formality was necessary. His subordinates, James and Nate, had worked their way through gate security with their official IDs and Steele was already upright and waiting in the shadows of the path for them. He seemed so angry that neither man could look him in the eye. They hadn't worked together for long but already the younger men were aware of Steele's temper when thwarted. He acted as though he was always in control but they saw what an effort it was for him sometimes.

James had carefully unwrapped the garrotte from Steele's wrists, twisting open the taut loops of wire with the delicacy of a bomb disposal expert. Steele had stared ahead silently, uncomfortable with the fact that another man was touching him.

Once free of the wire loops, he retrieved his phone, thought for a moment and then punched in the number for Clifford, the fourth member of the team, who had been tasked to watch the target's hotel. They had been tracking her since she had left Manchester with a brief to see who else she spoke to, then retrieve the asset using whatever means necessary.

Steele forced himself to be calm as he waited for the phone to be answered.

Clifford came on after two rings and Steele said, 'The target is probably coming your way.'

'You missed her?'

'Third party interference. There could be two of them turn up so watch yourself.'

When he'd finished, James looked at him, his face specked with the acne that he still hadn't outgrown. It made him look younger than he was.

James asked, 'Who was it got in the way?'

'Never saw him. Didn't hear him, either. Which means he knows what he's doing.'

'Will you tell the boss?'

Steele allowed his irritation to show. 'Of course I'll tell the boss. He's waiting on us to do our job, so let's just fucking do it, OK?'

They were standing on the pavement outside the zoo by now. Nate had gone to fetch the car and the square black VW Touareg pulled up before James could reply. Steele climbed into the passenger seat, brushing a last leaf from his pants leg. When he touched a hand to the back of his head he could feel a bruise beginning. An hour ago everything was going smoothly. That would teach him to be complacent, he thought.

From behind the wheel, Nate asked, 'Where to?'

'Give me a minute.'

Nate nodded and drummed his fingers on the wheel. Unlike many men in his trade he was physically distinct – tall and thin, his glossy black hair cut into spikes, like a cartoon character; a face that was mobile and friendly and sported a single diamond pin in his left earlobe. Steele knew that James had been educated at a minor public school and sounded like it, whereas Nate was originally from the north east and still bore a trace of a Geordie accent.

What they had in common, usefully, was that neither remorse nor guilt formed any part of their psychological make-up.

Finally Steele said, 'Drive into the town centre and get as close as you can to the woman's hotel.'

'Right you are.'

The Touareg glided out of the bus lane and edged between the cars streaming into Edinburgh.

Steele began to consider what he would say to Blake. He'd never failed a project before so he didn't have a repertoire of apologies to use. Of course he could keep quiet about it, despite what he'd told James. But that wasn't good enough. It wasn't ethical and didn't reflect the kind of relationship he thought he had with the boss. They had agreed when the relationship began that they would be honest with each other because both had experience – in their different worlds – of lies or half-truths getting in the way of success. In a team you had to be honest as a way of staying focused. The corollary of that was that there would be no blame from either man. Situations changed and fortune changed with them. You shouldn't blame the man if the situation had made achievement difficult or impossible. You regrouped and re-focused your attention.

That was the theory, anyway. It had never been exposed to the demands of the real world. Until now.

He took out his phone and dialled Blake's number. It was answered on the third ring, and Steele heard classical music being played in the background, growing fainter as Blake moved away from his party guests, or whoever they were, to take the call in private. As usual, he spoke without preamble.

'Did you get it?'

Steele's mouth was dry. He swallowed and licked his lips. 'Someone made an intervention. We don't have the asset yet.'

There was the slightest hesitation as Blake reconfigured his thinking. 'But you know where it is.' His deep, authoritative voice resonated down the connection.

'We're tracking it. Give me another hour.'

'No hurry. We don't know how important it is but now we know what she was doing up there I would like to get my hands on it anyway, before she tries something else. I'm tired of waiting for her to make a move. We must assume by now that no else knows. You'll do a good job, don't worry.'

'Thank you, sir. I have to go now.'

The connection was closed immediately, leaving Blake's voice resonating in Steele's head. He had always complimented Steele and made him feel good about what he did and how he did it. It was one of the reasons Steele was so loyal – and now felt so guilty because he had failed to achieve an objective.

The Touareg had made its way into central Edinburgh and up on to the Royal Mile. Tourists still crowded the pavements, though fewer of them than earlier in the day. They walked around with their heads tilted back to look at the architecture, or stared blankly at shop fronts like visitors to an exhibition of modern art, unsure what they were seeing.

Nate manoeuvred the vehicle until it was parked on the incline below the pale bricks and curved tower of the Radisson hotel so they could look back up towards it.

Disdain dripping from his voice, James asked, 'How many kilt shops do they need?'

Nate followed James' glance.

'Kilts and haggis. A cultural goldmine.'

'Coming from Gateshead, you'd know.'

Steele said, 'Shut up. Where's Clifford?'

'We passed him back there. Dark blue Toyota.'

Steele called the other man. 'Anything?'

'Nothing in or out. I can see front and side doors from here. What do we do?'

'We'll take this. You get back to the train station. That's how she came in – perhaps that's how she'll go out.'

'What do I do if I see her?'

'Tell me. Then go after the asset. I'm going back to the first location when we're done. I have to talk to a translator, test his vocabulary.'

CHANTAL SAID, 'One of the cars is leaving.'

Since learning her name, Sam had begun to think of her as French even though she spoke with a standard middle-class

English accent. After all, if her parents hadn't wanted her to exude Frenchness, why had they given her a French name?

'Changed shifts – more manpower in the new car. They probably think we're in the hotel.'

They were sitting in the bar of the Bank Hotel, across the width of a narrow street from the Radisson. From the window they had spotted the lone man in the Toyota and the arrival of another three in the black Touareg.

Chantal was becoming edgy.

'How am I going to get my stuff? Who are these people and why don't they leave me alone?'

Sam had already questioned her closely on the taxi drive from the Holiday Inn. She had no connection to any kind of governmental agency, was not even a civil servant, and was a totally honest citizen of the United Kingdom. Not a terrorist nor an illegal immigrant. Not an activist for any kind of political party. Not a journalist on the trail of a juicy story. Not the mistress of a cabinet minister – or a cabinet minister herself.

Despite all the negative replies to his questions he thought she was still keeping something from him. And it was connected to her presence at the translators' conference, because whenever he asked why she had been there she became evasive and looked away. All she would say was that she had something that needed translating, but it was personal and of no importance to anyone else.

In the meantime, he couldn't very well leave her to deal with these people herself. He didn't know their agenda, but he knew enough to see that it probably wasn't beneficial for the woman. There were at least four men in the team and they looked young, fit and competent. The fact that they had found and released the first man and come to the hotel so quickly told him that they were both organised and had resources.

Also, that they had been shadowing the woman for long enough to know where she was staying, but were willing to give her some leeway so they could uncover her destination.

He placed his orange juice on the table and stood up, glancing out of the window at the vehicle containing the three men.

'Have you got your hotel key with you?'

'Yes, why?'

'Let me have it, please.'

She dug the plastic keycard and its paper wrapper out of her purse and laid it on the table. Sam picked it up.

'Stay here and don't step outside. I won't be long.'

Her eyes grew hard. 'You're not calling the police, are you?'

'No, I'm not. I'm going to get your bag.'

SAM KNEW THAT none of the men could recognise him so in theory there was little danger. He hoisted his rucksack on to his shoulder, crossed the street, and entered the Radisson through the front door.

The foyer was empty except for a Chinese couple who were consulting maps as large as tablecloths and chattering to each other. Chantal's room was on the fourth floor. Sam held her key prominently in his hand, assumed the proprietary air of someone who belonged in an expensive hotel, crossed the foyer and took a lift to the third floor. Then he found the stairs and walked up to the next floor and pushed open the door that opened on to the corridor, peering cautiously both ways.

Nobody in sight.

In her room he quickly gathered her toothbrush and paste, a small bag containing toiletries, and a crumpled mackintosh from the wardrobe. Her Gucci overnight bag was in the bottom of the wardrobe, out of sight. It seemed to be made from snakeskin, with long textured handles and some kind of gold padlock contraption, currently unlocked, to keep its contents private.

He laid it on the bed and saw a problem – it was bigger than his rucksack. There was no chance that he could stuff her bag inside his. He swore. He didn't want to be seen exiting the hotel carrying more than he'd entered with. It might just alert them if he was seen carrying a bag that was obviously a woman's.

But he had an idea. He picked up both bags and closed the room door softly behind him as he left. He walked to the lift and went down to reception, then found the concierge, an older man with thinning red hair wearing a uniform that seemed at least a size too big for him.

The concierge raised his face expectantly, as though eagerly awaiting the next bizarre task that a hotel guest might have in mind. His eyes were dark and alert in a face that had inhaled too many cigarettes, the upper lip lined, the cheeks raw and tight over the bones.

Sam swung the Gucci bag up on to the concierge's desk, where it landed with a cushioned thud.

'Hi. Can I ask a favour?'

The man's eyes focused into an intent squint. 'Yes, sir?'

'My girlfriend's having a drink next door, in the Bank.'

'Oh, aye.'

'I said I'd fetch her bag from the room but I've just had a call and I've got to get back to the office. Do you mind just walking it across to her? She's in on the left, near the window. Short pale brown hair. She'll recognise the bag when she sees you. I'll call and tell her you're coming.'

'Aye, I can do that right enough. What room were you in?'

Sam told him and showed the room keycard and its paper wrapping. 'Thanks a lot. She's only here for the day and I don't want to see the look on her face when I tell her the office wants me back.'

The concierge gave him a look of empathy, as though he too were a fellow combatant in the ongoing battle to mollify the female sex, then seized the bag and came out from behind his desk.

'You go along, sir. I'll take care of it for ye.'

'Let me call her first.'

He walked away from the concierge post and dialled Chantal's number, which she'd given him in the pub. She answered and he told her to look out for someone delivering her bag. Then he turned back and nodded to the concierge, who gave him the thumbs up.

Sam watched him go, then made his way to the exit that led on to the side-street.

Glass doors led out to a small enclosed area where a couple of cars were parked. The air seemed to have turned colder in the fifteen minutes he'd been inside and he pulled up the zip on his leather jacket, then hoisted his rucksack so that he was carrying it over his right shoulder with his right hand, raising it so that his face wasn't visible from the street.

Up the slight incline to the High Street, he watched the concierge cross the road looking purposeful, the Gucci bag gripped firmly in his small hand as though it were the most important thing he'd ever carried. It may well have been the most valuable.

Now for the tricky bit, Sam thought.

He waited around the corner until the concierge had returned, now bag-less, and vanished through the front entrance of the Radisson. Then he walked up the steps to the Bank Hotel and stood inside the door until Chantal noticed him. She had been looking through the bag and now grinned. He waved her over.

'I'm going to find a cab and stop it right outside the door. When you see it, run straight down the steps and get in.'

'Will that work?'

'It's dark, there's a lot of people about. But probably not.'

'They're professionals.'

'You're learning.'

STEELE HAD FELT the frustration building in him for ten minutes now. He pushed it down by thinking of his house on Anglesey, down near the beach. He had a 12-foot windmill dinghy that he'd finished off himself from the bare-bones kit. He liked to take it out when he could, lean back into the wind, keep the sail taut.

Sometimes he'd take a little Coleman stove and eat down on the beach itself, fry up something he'd caught or maybe a steak, plain food but good when cooked outdoors with a breeze in your face.

The house itself was old – the roof needed repairing and a couple of outhouses should have been knocked down thirty years ago. Inside there was a small bedroom and a study upstairs, just one big kitchen-diner downstairs, with a shower-room through a door into an extension that had been added only ten years ago. Prior to that there was an outside toilet and you sat in a tub in front of the wood-burning stove for your monthly wash.

He liked the fact that there was more wood in the house than brick and that he could say something in the kitchen and be heard in the bedroom. That was all the space he needed. Women had always baffled him, so there had never been one close enough to necessitate a bigger place. His views had been formulated many years ago, when he was still in his teens, and they were not about to be changed now, after twenty years of going his own way.

If he ever found a woman he could talk to like a man, about practical matters, it might be different.

He was frustrated because there was nothing he could do. They couldn't find the woman and they didn't know who had interfered. It would be a man – but who? She hadn't arrived in Edinburgh with anyone and hadn't met or talked to a single person when killing time in the shops that afternoon. But someone had had the skill and the balls to see what was happening to her and do something about it. Steele didn't mind admitting that he was baffled. But mostly he was frustrated.

James spoke to him from the back seat.

'Boss.'

Steele turned and followed his gaze. It was heading towards seven-thirty now and the tourists had thinned out considerably, though there were still a few pedestrians entering the pubs and restaurants that were scattered around this section of the city.

So when a taxi pulled up outside the Bank Hotel it had caught James' eye ... and as they watched, they saw a slim, brown-haired woman come out of the hotel and run quickly down the steps and through the taxi's open door. She carried a large overnight bag over her shoulder and her tan handbag in her other hand.

Steele said, 'Clever. Must have found a way around Clifford and she's been hiding out.'

Nate raised his chin to point.

'There's someone in the taxi. The back door was opened but not by the driver.'

'So her little helper is still around.'

'Do I follow?'

'Yes, go straight down then turn when you can. Don't turn here.'

Nate gave him a look as if to say he would never have been so crass, then pulled away slowly. The taxi had already moved off in the opposite direction. Nate took a right on St Mary's Street by the Worlds End pub, but turned again immediately in the wide junction and back on to the High Street. The taxi was moving quickly away from them and had turned right.

James said, 'They're going back to the station. Idle sods. It's only a five minute walk.'

They followed as the taxi crossed North Street and turned left on to Princes Street, then left again for the entrance into Waverley Station. Steele dialled Clifford.

'Where are you?'

'On foot, near the overhead timetable. Have you got her?'

'They're in a taxi coming your way.'

'It's still busy here. What do you want me to do?'

Steele agonised for a moment. 'Just follow. I'll send Nate with you. Get on the train – she's bound to be going home.'

'You got more translating to do?'

'Go firm, you understand? Just watch the taxis. And try to get a fix on the man with her. A picture would be good.'

'Ooh, I get to use my spy-cam.'

STEELE ENDED THE call and told Nate to stop on the down ramp to the station. The taxi they had been following turned left at the bottom, heading for the drop-off point.

He signalled Nate to get out of the driver's seat and said, 'You heard. Follow them.'

Nate glanced at James in the back seat, making him complicit. 'That's all? We followed her up, we follow her down. Wasted trip, then.'

'The long game. We don't know who her mate is yet so best be careful. If you get the chance, and it's easy, take the asset. But don't reveal yourself unless you're certain of the outcome.'

Nate nodded and set off at a trot down the ramp. He wore a long raincoat and its tails flapped behind him as if snapping at his heels.

James climbed out of the back seat and stood by the passenger door. After a moment Steele climbed out, brushed past him and walked round to take the driver's seat. James got in beside him. Steele smelled again the lotion that James applied to his face, an astringent medical odour. A car parped its horn impatiently as it went by.

Steele said nothing. He was engaged in a fierce effort to control his emotions. Nate's comments had sparked in him the kind of self-doubt to which he wasn't generally prone but which, in the past, had rendered him as helpless as a lost child. He didn't like the way this was going. He didn't like variables. He didn't like uncertainty.

Especially when he wasn't responsible for creating it.

CLIFFORD WAS FEELING on edge. He hadn't seen his team since lunchtime, when the tasks had been distributed, and he felt as though he was being sidelined.

All he'd had from Steele were isolated bulletins and questions barked at him without any context. Now the situation had changed with the introduction of this other player, and Clifford felt exposed.

Moreover, he thought the station was weird. He disliked railway stations anyway – too noisy, too busy, too ... changeable. He liked things to stay as they were once he'd got a handle on them. People as individuals were all right, he could manage that. But people *en masse* were a different matter. Crowds were emotional, herd-like. They didn't play to what he saw as his strength – the ability to be the rational, calming presence in any group, especially among the kind of aggressive jokers he often found himself partnered with. People who took risks because they didn't understand the notion of consequences. The types who grew absurd moustaches and tattooed their necks to try to earn some kind of kudos amongst other 'hard men', the ex-military crowd he had been working with for the last two years.

He'd served in Humint in Afghanistan before transferring out as soon as he could, largely because he couldn't take the antagonism between the British and American commands, which did nothing but make his job more difficult.

He had wanted something more spicy, where he had more say in the decisions that were taken and had more personal impact on the outcomes.

And here he was, still waiting for orders while not knowing what was going on.

Edinburgh Waverley was particularly odd because taxi traffic drove right through its centre. You came down a long ramp to a small roundabout and turned left to arrive at the taxi rank drop-off point. Then you turned and came back to the roundabout and drove up the ramp to the exit. There was a pedestrian crossing point just before the roundabout, so if people wanted to cross, the taxis had to stop until the flow of pedestrians abated enough for the next taxi to squeeze through. Nightmare.

And it was big. A straight row of platforms in the main concourse – fifteen? Twenty? But you could go up a metal staircase to walk to further platforms, or just cross the road that the taxis turned on to reach another pair of platforms that seemed to go out at right-angles to all the others.

The whole place was like a Victorian factory – huge, echoing, grandly metallic and full of people doing things he didn't understand.

Weird. And difficult to watch.

But at least you could see the taxis clearly when they stopped. He had climbed the staircase leading to yet more platforms and from the top of the steps he could see each taxi as it came in and disgorged its passengers. Thirty seconds had passed since Steele had told him the target was on the down ramp but her taxi had yet to show up.

His phone buzzed. It was Nate.

'Where are you?'

'Top of the stairs looking at the taxi rank. You?'

'Outside the waiting room. Wave for the cameras.'

Clifford glanced around and saw Nate looking up at him. 'Anyone got a clue what we're doing? Licking our balls or what?'

'If that's your personal preference.'

'I heard it was yours, but not your own balls.'

Before Nate could reply, Clifford said, 'Got them,' as the target stepped out of the latest taxi to arrive.

A big man climbed out after her and gave the driver some cash, then took the target's arm and led her away. He had a rucksack over his shoulder and carried what was evidently a woman's overnight bag in his right hand. She carried her tan handbag. Neither of them glanced at him as he shielded his face with his mobile phone, some fifteen feet above their sight-line.

'The man's about six-one, black hair, black leather jacket, well-built.'

'I see them.'

'How do you want to do it?'

'Boss said to watch them on to the train, grab the asset if we can. Oh, and don't fuck up.'

'That's my Plan A shot.'

'Back to Plan B then.'

'As usual.'

They grinned at each other across the concourse in a way that Clifford, later, realised was an indication of their lack of seriousness about this job, and which in turn proved to him that they were sorely lacking leadership.

NATE WALKED AWAY casually as the target and her friend headed towards the double doors leading into the bustling café hall. They weren't talking and seemed intent, like lovers who had argued and were each harbouring their own thoughts.

He strolled across to the newsagents and stood just inside the door, looking back. He imagined himself as someone who worked in advertising or journalism, someone creative who took an interest in the people around him and in the arty magazines on the shelves. It helped him to build his own cover story, even if it was provisional and likely to change within the hour. He felt more credible if he could see himself as others might.

Although Friday night was wearing on, the concourse was still busy with arriving travellers and those commuting home for the weekend. The smell of grilled meat came to him from the Burger King franchise away to his right. He saw Clifford walk into the café hall, still apparently on the phone but almost certainly miming.

Nate bought a newspaper then walked slowly back towards the café hall, reading the front page.

Inside the hall he saw the target and the man, who he'd decided to call Black Jacket, sitting in the Costa Coffee seats, though they didn't have drinks on the table. Clifford was sitting on one of the waiting benches behind them, now looking as though he was playing a game on his phone.

Abruptly, Black Jacket and the woman stood up and walked further into the hall, towards the ticket office. Clifford glanced up but stayed in his seat, so Nate concluded it was his turn to move.

He followed them casually, still reading the newspaper, an idle traveller passing time until his train arrived. At the last minute, the target changed direction and went into the ladies toilets and Black Jacket turned suddenly and stood outside the door, facing out with his arms folded like a bouncer. He wore his rucksack on his back but the woman had taken her large bag inside with her. Nate had no option but to carry on past.

As he drew level with the door, Black Jacket leaned over and said, 'You're busted. Give it up.'

Nate looked up from his paper as if disturbed from an engrossing story and smiled dimly.

'Sorry?'

The man looked at him, his dark eyes glittering.

'You talking to me? Or to your pal over there with the trendy phone?'

Nate shook his head as if wondering yet again at the odd people to be found in the modern world. He lifted his paper to carry on reading and walked on, the back of his neck burning. He forced himself not to turn around.

When he did, Black Jacket was gone, and so was Clifford.

SAM FELT THAT at last he was beginning to take charge of the situation.

He had never been analytical, preferring to rely on action to produce consequences rather than try to predict outcomes beforehand. He had learned that he was unable to commit to plans because of a fundamental mistrust of the predictability of human behaviour.

He preferred to base his actions on instinct and risk-taking.

Now he'd separated the two men he could at least deal with one of them. The one who had been playing with his phone was fair-haired and seemed chunky, but whether it was with fat or muscle Sam hadn't been able to tell. The tall one with the spiky hair had looked the likelier candidate, being slightly built, but Sam would simply observe who followed him when he made his move and take it from there. Chantal would be safe inside the ladies toilet until he called her out: there were too many people around – and too many police officers – for the men to try anything stupid.

He'd seen the black car turn in behind them when they'd left the Bank Hotel and had assumed that the fourth man – the one who had driven off when the other three turned up – would go to the station because that's where Chantal had arrived earlier that day. It was commonsense that she'd have a return ticket. So the black car with three men had followed them, but only one man had got out of the car and come down the ramp.

When their taxi had stopped for pedestrians to cross at the bottom of the ramp, Sam had seen the man, who had been running, suddenly slow himself to a casual walk and take out his phone. He would have been sent to back up his colleague already in the station and was probably phoning to find out where he was.

The car behind him had swung out and driven away.

That suggested to Sam that the men were only going to follow them now, especially as the one he'd knocked out wasn't one of those currently in the station. He would have been sure to participate if anything more serious had been planned.

He pushed off from the wall and moved rapidly out of the hall. He sensed the second man standing up behind him but didn't turn.

Out in the concourse he walked quickly to one of the stairways leading up to the overhead gantry that in turn led to other platforms and to outside exits. He took the steps two at a time and turned left at the top.

Then he stopped dead and bent down, as if tying his laces.

Within moments he heard steps running up towards him in pursuit, heavy footfalls on the metal staircase. As the man reached the top, Sam stood and turned back, rounding the corner, thrusting his weight forward.

His chest collided with the chasing man, and in an instant he had extended his arms and spun the other round, hooked a foot around his ankles, and pushed.

A look of surprise and immediate fear traversed the man's features, but then he was turned and gone, crashing in a headlong fall past two startled travellers who skittled rapidly out of his way.

Sam waited for the man to stop in his descent and for a group to form around him, then walked down the stairs peering into the concourse as though searching for someone and giving only a momentary glance at the collapsed man. He passed two police officers in luminous waistcoats as they ran towards the commotion.

INSIDE THE CAFÉ hall he saw that the first man, the one with the spiky hair, had gone. Probably made himself scarce so that he wasn't caught up in any questioning. Smart move.

Sam walked to the ladies toilet, pushed open the door and shouted Chantal's name.

She came forward clutching her bags, her expression hopeful, and Sam hustled her out quickly.

She asked, 'What happened?'

'I've made them reconsider.'

She opened her mouth to ask more questions but seemed to realise that he was in no mood to reply.

In his transit across the concourse he had identified the platform for their train. Manchester via York. They had ten minutes.

They found the platform and walked alongside the train towards the far end. The platform was nearly empty, except for a man and a woman with two children in tow.

Sam walked as far down the platform as he could before choosing a carriage, then stood aside and allowed Chantal to climb up first. He stood on the platform watching until the train made its beeping sound and the doors began to close, then climbed in and found her sitting at a window seat, iPod buds already in her ears. The train jolted and the station began to move past their window.

He touched her hand and said, 'I should be sitting down to chicken with snow peas in Sampans Chinese restaurant in the Holiday Inn.'

She pulled a bud from one ear.

'But instead you've done something much more worthy.'

'You mean I've pissed off a bunch of very dangerous men.'

'You can handle it.'

'Thanks for the confidence. Now are you going to tell me what it's all about?'

She looked at him steadily for ten seconds, then reached inside her handbag. She pulled out a small book about the size of an old Letts diary, covered in cracked brown leather.

'I think they were after this. I don't know what's inside it, and neither do they. But it seems to be rather important.'

JAMES WAS WAITING for him in the car, his face eager in the dashboard light.

'Did he say anything?'

'Fucking academic. Knows everything, understands nothing. She told him she had something to translate that he might find exciting. As if anything French could be exciting. That was all.'

'You believe him?'

Steele turned his head. 'Why not? I'm a representative of the British Government, aren't I? Why should he lie to me?'

James had moved across to the driver's seat while Steele had been inside. Steele thought he probably wanted to feel he was contributing something other than sarcastic commentary to the evening's events. Nate had told them what had happened to Clifford and that he'd been able to follow the target and her protector on to the train.

James was probably itching to get involved too and acting as chauffeur was the best he could manage.

James put the car into gear and moved off slowly, focusing on his driving, his moonscape skin showing its bumps and hollows as the vehicle went in and out of shadow.

The Holiday Inn car park was almost empty and the overhead lamps bounced a hard white light from the concrete. Steele leaned back and considered for a moment. He felt tired and bereft of the energy needed to motivate both himself and the others. That indicated to him that his commitment to this enterprise was waning. When he knew his mission brief and believed in it, he had all the energy in the world.

He couldn't let those feelings leak out, however. He shifted in his seat and sat more upright.

'Drive south. They'll be going via York. We can make up good ground if we go straight to Manchester. She had a boyfriend, didn't she?'

'Jack.'

'Indeed.'

'You think he might know something?'

'She's a modern girl. Has a mobile phone and everything. Be odd if she didn't tell him about all this la-di-dah. Any more word from Nate?'

'He said Clifford texted him from hospital. He's got a broken nose. A few bruises.'

'Dumb fuck. He must have got too close.'

James said nothing and reached forward to switch on the GPS unit. Steele thought he should try to interpret his body language to see if there was any implied criticism in it. But then he decided he couldn't be bothered.

Steele settled back in his seat for the long drive. He had some thinking to do. He had waited for the translator in the foyer of the Holiday Inn until he'd returned from the gala meal in the Mansion. Fortunately the man had finished early. Being French he'd probably eaten at lunch and didn't need a big meal. Steele had followed him into the lift, followed him out into the corridor and waited for him to enter his room. He'd then walked down the corridor and knocked on his door, introducing himself with a false name and pushing effortlessly into the room.

A few pointed questions had revealed that the man, Duhamel, had nothing to add. The target had said nothing meaningful to him, but Steele still had to work hard on himself to avoid sliding his knife into the man's thin ribs. He reminded himself that while easy to achieve, that kind of casual atrocity would earn him no points with Blake at this stage in the game. Maybe later, if things became complicated.

THEY WERE OUT of Edinburgh and on the A702 heading for Biggar when James spoke again.

'Boss, what's the end state here?'

Steele opened his eyes and moved his tongue in his mouth. It felt like a piece of liver and his mouth tasted foul. The road was dark and the countryside he could make out in the headlights was grim. He was in no mood for philosophy.

'What did I say to you, Spratt, when we got together on this little jaunt?'

James' surname was Pratt but it had been swiftly replaced in every team he'd ever worked with.

'Need to know only. The quickest way to get us all in trouble is for everyone to know everything.'

'And do you think I've revised that view in the last half hour?'

'No, boss, of course not.' He risked a quick glance at Steele's profile in the dashboard lights and saw Steele's eyes staring at him, unmoving. 'But this is a specialised job. Anyone can see that. I just thought I might be able to add more value if I knew where it was all heading.'

Steele said, 'Add more value? Add more fucking value? Jesus, do you all go on management courses these days? Do they tell you about teamworking and leadership and all that bollocks? Listen, I have my orders and you have yours. I'm the intermediary and you're the fucking tool. I'm the carpenter and you're the hammer. Get it?'

'Got it.'

'Good.' He glanced at James again. His lips were thin, his eyes staring straight ahead, unblinking. 'The target has got an asset. Our superior wants that asset. We can use any and all means to achieve that objective, but no word must leak anywhere about our activities.'

'So the guy you've just seen ... '

Steele looked sideways at him, considering what to say. How far was it possible to push sprogs like this? He didn't want to antagonise Blake by questioning his judgement but next time round he'd ask if he could pick his own team. He could stick a pin in the Yellow Pages and find a better bunch.

In the end he punished James by not replying. He looked forward again and saw that they were entering Biggar, its single-storey houses flicking past the car's windows.

He said, 'Let's find a fish and chip shop or something. I'm Hank.'

'What?'

'Hank Marvin. Starving. Jesus.'

James blushed and slowed the car, his lack of experience of military life and its jargon highlighted once again.

Steele smiled inwardly and began to think about Jack, waiting for them in Manchester.

GIDEON BLAKE SAT in front of his computer screen and eased the knot of his tie away from his neck. He was a solid man whose body, he noticed, was beginning to push against the constraints of his clothes – belts, collars, even shirt cuffs. The result of too much sitting and too much social eating. Even his face was turning soft, his cheeks beginning to drop and an extra chin manifesting itself beneath the original. When he had the time he would start exercising again, he told himself. But he had been telling himself that for the last ten years. There was never enough time and probably never would be.

He could hear the laughter of his guests downstairs, ably guided and steered by his wife. Fiona was a powerful woman in whom he had complete trust, especially when it came to positioning him in the social set to which his role at the Ministry was suited.

The word was perfect – 'role'. It was a part he played, a mantle he assumed, as a way of keeping the family name in trust for the next generation. As his father had done for him, so he would do for his children, Jemima and Ross.

Of all the lessons he had taken from his father, the protection of the family name was paramount. Deeds were forgotten. Personality faded like a watercolour left in the sun. All that remained through the generations was the honour of your name. You had to ensure that your name stood for something or else you and your children and their children would tarnish and rust, eventually falling into the trash-can of history, never to be brought into light again.

In a short time, of course, his name would indeed stand for something. The efforts of the last few years would bear the kind of fruit that he'd wished for when he first set out on this path, initially mentored and guided by his father and then by an older group of men who saw in him the promise that they themselves had never managed to fulfil.

The door behind him opened and he turned. Ross, in pyjamas and rubbing his eyes with a small fist, stood in silhouette.

'It's noisy, Daddy. Can't they go home now?'

Blake folded down his laptop screen and gestured for the boy to come close.

'They're having a good time, Rossy. Do you want to stop them enjoying themselves?'

'It hurts my ears.'

'What does?'

'Nanny gave me some plugs for my ears but they hurt.'

'Oh dear, I'll talk to her about that. You should get back to bed.'

'Jemmy's texting. It's noisy.'

Blake lifted the boy on to his lap. The smell of soap and clean hair tickled his nostrils. The boy's limbs were as supple and muscular as those of a cat. He couldn't believe how much he loved his children. Their future seemed to him more precious than his own. Exactly as his father had said it would be when he had offspring.

'How was school today?'

'All right. Marcus said he didn't want to be my friend any more.'

'Why was that?'

'Because I wouldn't lend him my pen.'

'Why wouldn't you lend him your pen?'

The boy shuffled on his lap. 'Because he broke my pencil last week.'

'That's very good, Ross. You must always be generous to people, but you can't let them take advantage of you.'

AFTER A WHILE he took Ross back to bed and went downstairs, knowing that he should put in an appearance before they all left.

He had inherited the house in Surrey from his father and they had added a stable block for Fiona's horses and a large conservatory at the back, looking over the acreage that stretched down to the river where he went fishing occasionally with Ross.

He stood for a moment in the dark, looking through the conservatory windows and thinking about what Steele had told him. Someone else had intervened in the retrieval of the asset. That was unfortunate. What did they say nowadays? There were more people with skin in the game. More people with something to lose.

This had been intended to be a small-scale affair with few consequences. The risk assessment that he'd run had suggested that with only one target in play, the Bressette woman, the chance of intelligence leaking out had been minimal. Now there was at least one more player – the person responsible for the recent intervention. Doubtless Steele would take care of the man – assuming it was a man. He would get the measure of him and then take appropriate steps. That was what Steele did, what he was paid for and what was in his nature – he took care of things.

The main problem was knowing exactly what was at stake. Until he got his hands on the diary, he wouldn't know what it revealed – if anything.

His wife's voice came from behind him.

'Gideon, your guests are missing your sparkling wit and your fund of amusingly sexist stories.'

Blake turned with a smile towards her.

'Have I told you how beautiful you look tonight?'

It was true – with her blonde hair swept up and coiled above her even features and long neck, she could almost be once again the svelte fashion model he had met twenty years before.

She advanced towards him.

'The sweetness of the lie does not distract from the purity of its intention.'

'Who are you quoting?'

'No one. I made it up. You like?'

He took her in his arms.

'Here's one for you – the sexiness of the wife does not detract from the absurdity of her inventions.'

She laughed, arching her back and revealing more of her throat and breasts.

'Touché. Now come and bore some of these bores so we can all be boring together.'

They began to walk towards the dining room, crossing the great hallway decked with paintings of Blake's ancestors of the last two hundred years. He pulled up short before they passed through the panelled oak door.

He said, 'We have to find a new nanny for Ross and Jemima.'

Her eyes were amused. 'Why? What's wrong with Lillian?'

'She's toast. I'm firing her tomorrow.'

'Another complaint from wonderboy? You really should start taking what he says with a pinch and a half of salt. He's eight. He's fickle. Mind you, you're forty-eight and you're fickle.'

'Finished?'

She knew when he was serious.

'All right. I'll put Melanie on to it tomorrow. Get some interviews lined up for next week.' She let go of his hand and turned towards the dining room. 'Perhaps we should let Ross sit in on the interviews, too. Let the little bugger get involved in the process, as they say.' She turned on her heel and went through the door.

Blake lifted a smile on to his lips and followed, suddenly certain that he would have to provide Steele with back-up. Whether he wanted it or not.

THE EAST COAST MAIN line had brought them close to the sea. It was too dark to make out the waves through the windows, but Sam felt the absence of land like the tug you feel on a high monument, looking down, ready to abandon your inhibitions and just fall ...

He brought his attention back to Chantal. Her reflection in the window was like a dark twin. They now had a table in the carriage to themselves and there were few other travellers in the coach.

He said, 'Tell me again.'

'Weren't you listening the first time?'

'It's not about me. It's about you remembering more the more often you tell it. Start with your grandfather this time.'

Chantal sat back in her seat and stared at the luggage rack above her head. She had taken off her jacket and her thin, bare arms rested on the table, the diary closed in her hands.

'My grandfather was Jean-Claude Bressette, a Frenchman who was born and died in the Vienne region, east of Poitiers, roughly the middle of France. What the French apparently call "France Profonde" – deep France. Very rural, very agricultural.'

'You've been there?'

'No. My father mentioned it but we never went.'

'And you don't speak French.'

'Probably the same as you. School French. My father brought me up as English and wouldn't go near France again.'

'Why?'

'He'd been a kid in America and had a tough time because of his name. He didn't speak French either and had no family there. Why would he go back?'

'Curiosity?'

'He wouldn't even watch French films, so I don't think he was curious at all. It was as though he wanted to forget France completely.'

'So let me get this right: after the war your grandfather was dead and your grandmother left France with her child, your father ... '

'Robert.'

'... Robert. Then what?'

'He wouldn't talk about it much. In his twenties he had some kind of falling out with his mother and came to England. He settled in Nottingham and in his forties finally met a woman, my mum, and married her. She died giving birth to me, so of course I never knew her. I grew up as an only child. Dad was a baker. All very boring.'

Sam thought it odd that she seemed to show as little interest in her family history as her father had done. He wondered whether she avoided it because it was painful or, as a strictly modern person, because she really had no interest in what took place before her birth.

He said, 'OK, now go back to your grandfather – Jean-Claude. Tell me his story.'

Chantal told him that her grandfather had been born and brought up in Journet, a small village in the French countryside.

She stopped and said, 'Wait,' and reached into the handbag from which she'd taken the diary, bringing out half a dozen black-and-white and sepia photographs. She splayed them on the table.

'My dad gave me these photographs years ago. I thought they might be useful for Duhamel, the translator.'

Sam leafed through the photographs. One showed a village square with a typical Norman church off to one side and two cafés on the corners of intersecting roads. There was a photo of a group of small boys in short pants and tight jackets sitting on the steps of a monument, pointing at the camera and laughing. In another, four women wore long black dresses gathered at the waist and carried baskets under thick arms. Men stood on corners with cigarettes and looked askance at the photographer. The photographs represented a life dependent on agriculture and trade and centring on markets and family.

Chantal turned the photographs and looked at them, her eyes flickering over images that could have come from a different geological era, not within the lifetime of a single person.

Sam said, 'We had photos like this in my house. What's different here?'

She looked up and gathered the photographs together. 'The war came.'

The village had been on the edge of the Free Zone, the area of southern France in which the collaborationist Vichy government had been given power by the Nazis.

Initially many French had neither approved nor disapproved of the change in government, especially when it didn't touch on them directly. But when Vichy had begun to implement more restrictive regulations the Resistance had grown in strength and in organization, helped by England and America, so that the original rag-tag groups that had argued amongst themselves in a largely ineffective manner eventually became disciplined and useful to the incoming Allied troops, even before the D-Day landings in June 1944.

Sam said, 'You sound like an expert.'

'I bought a couple of books and read online. Anything wrong with that?'

'Not at all. Tell me about the diary.'

Chantal sighed and carried on.

Just after midnight on D-Day, 6th June, five hours before the landings on the Normandy beaches, a team of SAS men had been parachuted into the territory east of Poitiers. They were the advanced team for Operation Bulbasket, a mission that was intended to hinder the Germans if they tried to reinforce their troops in Normandy. The 2nd SS Panzer Division, known as Das Reich, was stationed at Montauban north of Toulouse and it was thought that they'd head north as soon as the Allied landings were underway.

This group of men from the newly-formed SAS was there to prevent them.

The Bulbasket team, reinforced by more men on the 7th and 11th of June, set about blowing up rail links, laying mines and – astonishingly – carrying out vehicle patrols in a number of specially-adapted Jeeps, armed with Vickers K machine guns front-mounted on the bonnet. These too had been parachuted in, delighting the French *maquis* with their simplicity and robustness.

In a six week period they attacked fifteen rail targets and mined a number of important roads.

Unfortunately, they were betrayed.

Their leader on the ground, Captain John Tonkin, regularly moved his base camp in the woods to avoid the likelihood of being seen too often in one place. On the night of 3rd July, having been away on a reconnaissance trip to find a new camp, he returned to the original camp in a forest near Verrières. In his absence, someone unknown – probably a disaffected Frenchman worried about the repercussions of harbouring English soldiers – had informed the SS of the whereabouts of the group. They had subsequently put together an attack force from a division made up largely of Romanian Germans and French volunteers.

They attacked at dawn and the fighting continued until after midday. A group of 34 SAS men, together with a downed American pilot who had joined them, were ambushed and taken prisoner. One of them was beaten to death with the butt of a rifle.

The remaining men, including Tonkin, escaped and continued harrying the Germans from a new base until the end of July.

Chantal looked up at him.

'My grandfather was one of those who escaped. He told all this to my grandmother, later, who told it to my father. But it's all in the official histories anyway.'

'What happened to the men who were captured?'

'Hitler had issued a decree against anyone who was thought to be a commando and they were to be killed immediately. So this group was first taken to Poitiers to be questioned, then brought back to the area, forced to march into the forest and dig their own graves before being shot. Three had been wounded in the initial fighting and had been taken to hospital. They were given lethal injections in their beds.'

'Good god.'

'Later that year some farmers out hunting found the graves in the forest and after the war the bodies were moved to another site and given a proper burial.'

Sam leaned back in his seat.

'So this diary is your grandfather's record of that time? What he saw? What he went through?'

Chantal shrugged. 'Perhaps. I don't know.'

'But you've read it.'

She gave him a wry grin. 'I told you, I have schoolgirl French. I can read a bit. But this ... ' She waved the diary. 'This isn't exactly French.'

STEELE'S PHONE RANG ten minutes after they'd passed Gretna and joined the M6. He took it from his pocket.

'Nate, where are you?'

'We're coming into York soon. They'll have to change for Manchester.'

'Stay clear but don't lose them.'

'As if.'

'We've done it once today.'

'If I get the chance, do I take the asset?'

Steele hesitated. 'You've already asked me that.'

'I want to be clear.'

'Only do it if it's straightforward. Don't make a scene.'

'I don't make scenes.'

Steele closed the connection without further comment. He liked to keep them on their toes. And he didn't want to dwell on the fact that he'd been responsible for losing the woman and the asset in the first place.

He said to James, 'How long to Manchester now?'

'GPS says about two hours.'

'They've got to wait for a connection but they're only just over an hour away from Manchester. Assuming that's where they're going.'

James flicked his eyes towards Steele. 'Where else would they go?'

Steele didn't answer. He had no answer. He didn't know who the other man was, and that bothered him. His head still hurt, and so did his pride. He couldn't understand how he had been caught so easily – how someone had followed him out and then watched as he'd confronted the target. Then had the balls to whack him on the head ... all without being heard or seen.

And without knowing who this man was, he couldn't create a Plan B. He had to improvise. He had to find out more about the target, her background, possible liaisons or contacts who would be capable of this kind of specialised behaviour. The only information he'd received from Blake was that she worked in Manchester in a design company – whatever the hell that was – and had tried to interest the Imperial War Museum in buying property that wasn't hers to sell. His task was to follow her, find the asset and retrieve it. A three-man team was put at his disposal and they'd been watching for two days before this nonsense trip to Edinburgh had begun.

He had to think.

He had to get himself into that zone where he could sense what people were going to do. Anticipate and then prevent. That was one of the skills that Blake had seen in him.

Steele had been told, later, that Blake had read the reports on him and his exploits that had come back from Afghanistan, and then Iraq, before the trouble began and Steele's career had started to go off-piste. He was the kind of man that Blake needed in his organization and so he'd ensured that he got him. Fortunately for Steele, his problems with the Iraqi prisoners – a little light abuse on behalf of the Joint Forward Interrogation Team in Basra – had not come to the attention of the investigating group sent in by the British government. Yet.

On advice, Steele had got out and so far seemed to have escaped summons to account for himself. Working for Blake was the perfect cover, though, so he considered himself lucky. If he had to stand and explain himself to a group of old men who hadn't seen battle since the Dardanelles he was likely to tell them to lick his boots and jump through the window.

He closed his eyes, rolled his head from side to side and calmed down. Blake knew that Steele would work out what to do next. Like all expert managers, Blake had the sense to choose good people, set them tasks and parameters, then get out of the way.

Jack, Steele thought to himself again. The boyfriend. A scruffy bag of bones with tousled hair and a lop-sided grin who drove one of those new minis. They had already seen her visit his place, staying overnight. So they knew it was more than a casual affair. She would want to contact him or go to him and tell him all about the exciting events of the last twenty-four hours.

Perhaps Jack could be leveraged, as they said these days.

SAM HAD WALKED down the buffet car and returned with two over-milked lattes and two foul-smelling cheeseburgers, the cheese of which seemed to be manufactured from plastic. Chantal had peeled back the limp top of her bun, then replaced it carefully, as if unwilling to disturb whatever life she had found beneath it.

Sam saw the look of revulsion that crossed her face.

'What?'

'Apparently I'm not hungry. You might have asked.'

Already half-way through the first burger, Sam said, 'More for me. Incidentally, we've still got company.'

She sat up. 'How do you know? Who?'

Sam licked his fingers and started on the second burger.

'Guy back there. He was in the station, trying to look inconspicuous. Youngish, tall, spiky black hair, avoided my eyes when I passed through the carriage. He was good. He must have known I'd gone for the other guy and made a bee-line for this train before we got here. Took a risk.'

'So guessing other people's motives is part of being a detective, is it?'

Sam conceded the point. 'Maybe. Doesn't matter anyway – he's here and I think they've settled for following us.'

Chantal fell silent and stared out of the window. She had recovered some colour from the zoo but she was naturally pale with the skin-tone of someone who lived most of her life indoors. She was undeniably good-looking, though, and not for the first time this night he found himself questioning his own motives. Had it been a young man who had been followed in the zoo, would he have been so quick to pursue and rescue him?

He didn't know what to make of the diary. She had finally allowed him to look at it and he'd taken it from her with gentle fingers, turning the leaves slowly. The pages were filled with a spidery handwriting, in pencil, that was hard to read simply because the writing itself was small and ill-formed.

When he had become accustomed to it, though, he saw that it was in fact mostly in a French that he could understand. Jean-Claude Bressette had seemed to direct the writing towards one person – Julienne, who Chantal had told him was her grandmother. It wasn't a diary that recounted events as a record of their occurrence. It was more like a series of letters, dated and addressed just to one person, as though Jean-Claude suspected that he might not be able to say these things to her himself but wanted to get them on paper nonetheless.

From what he could understand from his minimal French, it seemed that Jean-Claude spent a lot of time apologising for being away from Julienne and 'le petit.'

'That was my father,' Chantal had told him. 'He was born during the war. His parents were practically children themselves. When I was young my dad used to show me photos of them, very prim in studio shots. Very strong, round faces. I think I inherited that.'

In the diary Jean-Claude talked about his fellow resistance fighters, many of whom he didn't like simply because they weren't from the same village. He told Julienne of the places he had been and what he had done. He described how he and his fellow *résistants* had laid mines – or, more often, simply pulled the pins that held the railway tracks together. It was much easier to cause a derailment that way, he said, and much less dangerous.

And then, half-way through the slim book, the writing changed. The handwriting was the same, but the French vanished, to be replaced by a strange language that had echoes of French but was not understandable – at least not to him.

He stared at one passage, trying to make sense of it.

"Soirce, keva zeud glaisan al rega durador. J'ouvay ceplas sifexplos lesse derail minche fer, suispe oun messo neretourn a seba. Oun onseti a zeud metrekil durador squelo oun vonsa douentend dentac de naitre."

If the diary was what Chantal's pursuers were after, then presumably the reason lay in whatever meaning the strange language contained.

Chantal turned to him.

'I've got to go to the toilet. Is it OK?'

Sam looked past her, through the carriage door towards the toilet.

'I don't see why not. They're following now. We'll have to try to lose them at some point, though. We'll be in York soon so be quick.'

'I'll pee as fast as gravity allows.'

She stood up and walked, swaying like a dancer, to the carriage door. She pushed the button and the door hissed open.

Sam watched her, moving to the aisle seat so he could keep her in sight. She was wearing her black jacket with the collar up and he watched as she stood in the corridor, not entering the toilet. He glanced at the icon over the carriage door and saw that the toilet was empty so she wasn't waiting for it to vacate. Then he noticed that she had raised her hand to her ear – what he had thought was an iPod was evidently an iPhone and she was calling someone. She stood there, still swaying, and raised her other hand to her ear. It was probably noisy in the corridor.

The train jolted and the train manager announced that they would shortly be coming into York.

A minute later Sam saw the platforms of York Station flicking past the window. Half a dozen people had already walked past him to the end of the carriage and opened the door. They stood waiting for the train to stop. His view of the corridor was now cut off.

The train lurched again and began to slow down further. He stood up and gathered together his own and Chantal's bags, then pushed into the aisle and squirmed past an elderly woman carrying a large parcel.

From this position he could now see that Chantal was no longer in the corridor but glancing up he also saw that the toilet indicator icon was still not illuminated. He pushed past the other standing passengers, muttering apologies, and exited into the corridor. The toilet door was shut. He knocked loudly on it.

'Chantal.'

The toilet was one of the old-fashioned types still found on carriages on the East Coast Main Line – push to open and slide a knob to lock. Not one of the modern variety where the door slid back and forth at the touch of a button.

He pushed the door and met resistance, but no complaint from inside. He pushed harder and managed to squeeze into the confined space.

Chantal was slumped on the toilet seat, unconscious. Her iPhone was on the floor. Her handbag was gone.

IT WAS ALMOST eleven-thirty when James steered the Touareg through the quiet streets of Chorlton in south Manchester, using the GPS to find the address. Steele knew it had become an upmarket location for commuters into central Manchester – Victorian properties that had recently been gentrified mingled with new apartment blocks boasting locked gates requiring PIN numbers. Expensive cars sat between student junk-heaps. Upmarket eateries had managed to squeeze themselves between traditional pubs whose regulars eyed with suspicion the sun-tanned upwardly-mobile IT professionals who brayed around them.

The car eased to a halt and James pulled on the handbrake. He turned off the engine and the car started to tick as it cooled down. He leaned over the steering wheel, peering at a row of terraced houses that had once been identical but had lately been renovated to individual tastes – some with double-glazed windows, others with lead quartering, some with blinds, others with curtains, some with original wooden doors, others with plastic. Steele had come from a similar environment but was appalled by the superficiality implied by the changes. What had happened to the genuine, the real?

James said, 'There's a light on. Probably waiting for the loved one to call.'

Steele was putting on his gloves, pushing stiff fingers into the yielding leather.

'Remind me what he does.'

'Creative type in the same design company as the target. Making web pages and internet stuff.'

Steele nodded. Likely to be a bit soft, then. Shouldn't be a problem.

'Any word from Nate yet?'

'Nothing.'

'Try him again before we go in. He should have checked in by now.'

James took out his phone and dialled Nate's number.

'Straight to voice mail. Must be out of signal or battery.'

A little tick of worry nudged the edge of Steele's consciousness. He hadn't known this team two weeks ago, but he knew Blake didn't give him complete idiots to work with. Nate would have had a charged battery and would have checked in by now whether he had the asset or not. The train had been due to arrive in York two hours ago and there would have been something to report by now.

He said, 'Let's do it,' and climbed out of the car. The night was cool and he could hear distant traffic in Manchester, the usual urban tinnitus, but the street they were parked on was quiet. James exited from the driver's side and stretched his neck. He glanced at Steele with an expression that he found hard to read. Concern? Anticipation?

They closed the car doors quietly. Steele nodded towards the front of the house facing them and they approached it. James pushed the white plastic doorbell and stood back.

A moment later the door opened and a young man in his mid-twenties wearing blue jeans torn at the knee and a grey t-shirt faced them. At this late hour there was an understandable look of anxiety on his face, which Steele noted was regular but still soft, without the lines and hard edges of an older man.

Steele looked him up and down.

'Jack?'

'Yes, who–'

He didn't get any further because Steele pushed out a stiff arm and thrust him back into the room. The young man stumbled but recovered quickly and stepped forward out of some reflex. Steele was the shorter man and knew that Jack probably thought he could do something to repel this invasion. But it was too late. Steele was already in the house, with James following quickly and closing the door behind them.

They were in a living room with bare wooden floors, neatly sanded and varnished, a two-seat black leather sofa, a wide flat-screen Panasonic TV and a bookcase made of tubular steel and glass shelves. Large prints of travel posters hung on two of the walls, advertising Rio de Janeiro and Bali in garish colours. The lighting was moody and came from a two-pronged uplighter that stood in a corner. Steele looked around and nodded appreciatively.

'Nice pad. Is that what you trendy people call it – a pad? You and that sexy girlfriend?'

'Who the fuck are you?' The young man had recovered his balance and was trying to appear strong, though his voice wavered as he spoke. 'What do you want?'

Steele looked at him with a certain amount of pity. He had dealt with men who were a lot tougher – physically and, he expected, emotionally – than this young creative type. It was almost no fun when there was no prospect of a worthwhile response. He had been sitting in the car for almost four hours and his nerves were stretched tight. The evening had started badly, got worse, and was now in a really bad place.

He wondered what it was in his psyche that began to give free rein to itself at times like these. He didn't particularly mind, but there was a part of him that observed these states with a kind of abstract fascination verging on anxiety. He didn't believe in any kind of religious avatar or spiritual figure except for the notion that the universe had a memory for one's deeds that it replayed to you when you least expected it. He had seen it called poetic justice or simple coincidence, and aggrandised into the idea of karma. Nonetheless, he had seen consequences of actions that were unanticipated and so realised that whatever he did was likely to come back to him at some point. It made him think of his life as a more violent version of the game known as draughts or checkers – how far could he go before something leaped over him and then reared up behind, taking him out of the game?

He said, 'Jack, have you ever heard the phrase "The ugly aunt in the cupboard"?'

'What?'

'It's a phrase I once heard someone in the marines use. It means a problem that no one wants to face up to.'

Steele saw that Jack was very young indeed. He was thin at the wrist and although he was reasonably good-looking, he wasn't particularly well set-up. No depth in the chest. Not much fuzz on his chin.

'I haven't got a clue what you're talking about. Who are you?'

Steele ignored the question, his eyes boring into the young man's gaze.

'The problem that we have to face up to, Jack, is that your young lady has something that we want. And I'm coming to believe that the only way we're going to get it from her is by ... well, not to put too fine a point on it, by threatening you.'

Jack spun on his heel and took a step towards the door that led to the kitchen. But James was too fast. He grabbed Jack around the neck and pushed his arm behind him and upwards. Jack grimaced and did well not to let out a groan.

Steele sat on the leather sofa, its surface cold and slimy, and looked up at him.

'Don't be such a cliché, Jack. You don't have to do anything but suffer for a while. So no heroics, please. James, would you be so kind?'

James released Jack's neck with his left arm and reached into his suit pocket to take out a plastic tie. Then he pulled Jack's arms behind him and wrapped the tie around Jack's wrists, pulling it tight and stepping back.

Steele nodded calmly.

'OK. Let's begin.'

SAM PREFERRED working alone.

Although his employment in Customs and Excise had meant belonging to a team, he had never felt comfortable when having to take into account other people's ideas or expectations. Even those of his boss. Now he worked as a private detective he found that there were still times when he had to be aware of the needs of other people, and it irritated him more than it should; after all, they were usually clients and they were indeed paying his fees.

But Chantal Bressette wasn't strictly speaking a client, and she definitely wasn't paying any fees. Which was why it was an irritant having to look after her when he should have been chasing the man who had stolen her bag.

Fortunately, he had been able to pass on that responsibility almost straight away.

When he had opened the train's toilet door and found Chantal on the floor, he had reversed out of the cabinet immediately and turned to face the other passengers who were waiting for the train to draw to a final halt. A sensible-looking woman in her forties was watching him steadily. She wore a black coat and her hair was neatly cut and there was a certain intelligence in her eyes. Sam reached out and touched her arm.

'There's someone in here who's been attacked. I'm going to find who did it. When we stop, can you get her into a waiting room or on a bench until I come back?'

The woman lowered her briefcase to the ground.

'How badly is she hurt?'

'I think she's just been roughed up but her bag has been taken. He won't have gone far.'

Either side of them the other passengers watched the conversation with the intensity of those for whom nothing was at stake – it was just theatre.

Before the woman could say anything more, the train shuddered to a halt and moments later the door mechanism sounded to indicate that the opening button could be operated. A young man standing nearest pushed it and the door hissed asthmatically and cantilevered back.

The woman said to Sam, 'You go. I'll help her.'

Sam nodded and squeezed past the other passengers and stepped down on to the platform. Because he and Chantal had walked to the furthest carriage on the train, he was now a hundred yards further along the platform in relation to the station exit. Dozens of other passengers were already on the platform, some milling about while they searched for their next train, others heading for the exit. Above them the vast arched glass roof of York Station echoed back the sound of their passage.

Sam moved quickly down the platform, eyes intent on finding the spiky hair and dark raincoat of the man he had seen in Edinburgh Waverley. While the passengers were a mixture of all ages, races and genders, there were many businessmen dressed similarly in dark overcoats.

He arrived at a platform kiosk selling coffee just as the flicker of spiky black hair caught the corner of his eye. The man was heading outside. Sam ran from the platform into the small commercial foyer and into the covered drop-off point outside the main entrance. He went left with the press of the crowd and came out into darkness, the old city walls illuminated above a greensward high to his right. Traffic poured past him in both directions.

Glancing left he saw the man walking briskly down the street. His head was bowed and he seemed to be consulting the screen of his mobile phone. Sam followed at a distance. There were too many people around to brace the man in public.

Ten minutes later they had crossed the river and were heading directly towards the Minster, which reared up ahead of them, lit from beneath and glowing like an orange beacon. The man had kept his head down all the time, his right hand in front of him as he worked his phone. Probably texting, Sam thought.

They passed the Minster with its twin towers and ornate decoration and veered right, suddenly hedged in by narrow lanes full of clothing boutiques, coffee shops and pubs, each of them advertising its modernity with studied restraint. Sam had been to York several times when a youngster and remembered the area well, though his sense of direction was easily confused by the rambling streets.

Finally he saw the man look up, take his bearings, and walk into the nearest pub. Sam followed and pushed through the oak door. The evening was moving on and the place was only half-full, and Sam saw that in fact it was more of a café/restaurant, with large wooden tables dressed with vases of artificial flowers and a small, marble-topped bar situated at one end of the oblong room. The atmosphere was quiet, almost clinical, with tables seating couples and foursomes talking gently over plates of pasta. There was no buzz from seasoned drinkers or the sounds of music or television. It was a restaurant designed in the New Rustic.

The man had gone straight to a table and seated himself and was still looking down at his phone when Sam sat opposite him. Sam took in the creased raincoat, the lack of tie, the shirt undone at the neck. A smart-casual look to help him blend in, but mitigated by the uncombed hair and the diamond ear-ring. The man was late-twenties and his skin-tone was good. There was some muscle there but he was probably too tall and had too much intelligence in his eyes to be merely a hired heavyweight.

The man lifted his head, saw Sam and smiled.

'Too late, buster.' He lifted the phone and waved it at Sam. 'My new spy-cam. Photos sent.'

'Clever. Shall we take this outside?'

'What?'

'The argument we're about to have.'

'What's your name?'

'What's yours?'

The man grinned. 'I asked first.'

Sam reached out abruptly and grabbed the phone, then twisted the man's arm and hand downwards on to the table so that he had to release it. Sam stood and went outside.

The man burst through the doors a moment later. Sam was waiting for him, his weight distributed evenly, his hands now empty. Two passers-by stepped off the pavement to walk around him; they had seen the expression on his face.

The man's eyes had lost their merriment.

'You don't know who you're fucking with.'

'Who? Three pricks looking for a dog to attach themselves to?'

The man frowned. 'That doesn't make sense.'

Sam knew that there was a point in every confrontation when the temperature cooled and violence no longer seemed like a viable option. He didn't want this conversation to go in that direction; he wanted this man out of the way, at least for a while. He stepped forward, into the man's face.

'You military fucks can't make sense of traffic lights. The colours are too confusing.'

The insult and the physical proximity in which it had been offered had the desired effect of making the other man attempt to punch him. He was too close for a kicking manoeuvre so he raised his elbow towards Sam's face. Sam knew it was coming, ducked and stabbed a short left-hand punch into the man's belly. As he came down, Sam met his chin with a right-hand uppercut. The fight was over immediately as the man's teeth clicked together, probably biting his tongue. His eyes swam and then his legs folded.

Sam caught him and dragged him a few yards down the street and into a gap between the shops. There were people around but they ignored him with the studied calm of modern city-dwellers unwilling to get involved. Sam knew that he had the appearance of someone acting in an official capacity – he had a serious face, neat hair and gravitas. If people thought about the event at all, they would probably conclude that he was some kind of undercover policeman. He was too old and essentially decent-looking to be a mugger or thief.

Which didn't prevent him going through the man's pockets. He found Chantal's diary and a wallet containing over two hundred pounds in cash and a Visa credit card in the name of John Smith, exactly the same as the one he had found in the pocket of the man at the zoo. It confirmed him in his belief that there was a larger organization involved in this play.

He took the money and the credit card to make it harder for the man to contact his colleagues or even spend the night in a room. He also took the phone, a new Blackberry with a sliding keyboard. Looking through the call log he found the last email that had been sent and saw that photo attachments had been added. He'd sent them in batches of three or four – about thirty pages all told. He opened one of the attachments and saw a page from the diary come into focus. He presumed the attachments would be the pages from the diary that were the most difficult to understand because of the code in which they'd been written.

Now that this group had a record of those particular pages in the diary, what would be their next step? Would knowing the contents be sufficient, so that he and Chantal were no longer in danger of pursuit?

Or would knowledge of the contents simply confirm the group in their commitment to follow and take the play to its next stage?

The fact that there were at least four participants involved in pursuing them – and probably more operating at a higher level – led Sam to believe that there was more at stake here than simply decoding the diary of a long-dead French Resistance fighter. A team of this size, and with these resources, suggested official involvement of some kind.

But how official? And what level of involvement?

The man was still out cold. Sam sat him up in the side-street, checked his breathing, and then made his way back to the railway station, thinking furiously.

BACK IN THE car, Steele's heartbeat had started to slow down. He had read that the heart rate of the best sportsmen actually slowed at moments of maximum concentration. He guessed it referred also to the notion that these sportsmen acted as if they had more time on the pitch, or behind the wheel, than average performers. But for him an increase in activity had always led to a burst in the speed at which his heart pumped blood around his body. He could feel it in his face and see it in the knotted muscles of his forearms. It was an almost Neanderthal response to adrenaline that he hated. He was trying to rise above that, to become measured in his reactions.

It would seem he still had some way to go if his response to dealing with Jack was any reference point.

He told James to drive and after a few minutes sensed the younger man looking at him.

'What?'

'You all right?'

'You and your questions. Watch the road.'

James held his look for a moment then turned back to the still-busy streets of Manchester. Twenty minutes later the Touareg pulled up opposite the apartment block that housed Chantal Bressette's flat.

THE WOMAN WAS in the waiting room. Alone. She raised a hand and smiled grimly as Sam walked through the door. His rucksack was next to her on the bench but Chantal and her Gucci bag were gone.

She said, 'I'm sorry. She went half an hour ago. I couldn't keep her here when the next train came in.'

Sam sat next to her, suddenly feeling a weariness that he had managed to keep at bay.

'That's OK. I didn't get her handbag back either.'

'She had a ticket in her coat pocket. She borrowed some money for a cab the other end.'

Sam looked again at the woman. She was smart and professional-looking, well put-together like a lawyer or accountant who exercised to stay in trim.

He said, 'You didn't have to do that. I'm Sam, incidentally.'

'Vanessa.'

They shook hands awkwardly on the bench.

Sam asked, 'Did she seem all right?'

'Frightened but OK. She'd fainted, apparently, when some man had pushed her into the toilet and grabbed her bag. What's all that about? You seemed to know who you were looking for when you ran off but she wouldn't tell me anything.'

'I can't help you, sorry. She'd been sitting opposite me in the carriage and we'd got talking, but I don't know anything else. I found her in the toilet, as you saw.'

The woman looked at him sceptically.

'You seemed pretty worked up at the time, calling her name and so on.'

Sam shrugged.

'I'm an emotional guy. I weep watching TV talent shows.'

She let out a strange laugh that was half-bark, her head tilted back momentarily.

'Right. What will you do now?'

Sam had looked at the timetable before entering the waiting room.

'There's another train in half an hour. I have a good woman waiting for me at home.'

Vanessa raised a plucked eyebrow.

She said, 'Lucky woman,' and stood up, smoothing down her coat and picking up her black briefcase from the side of the bench. Sam noticed that she wasn't wearing a wedding-ring. Perhaps she had waited for him because there was nobody waiting for her.

She stuck out her hand again and he stood up to shake it. Her eyes looked directly into his as if searching for something more than the superficial friendliness that they'd exchanged.

'I hope you have a good trip back. If you see that girl again give her my regards. She's too young and beautiful to be going through such trauma.'

'Trauma is wasted on the young.'

She bark-laughed again, then turned on her heel and left, her walk confident and direct. Sam watched her go, smiling.

AN HOUR after they had arrived, Steele shifted in his seat.

'Okay, she's not coming. Well played, Jackie-boy. You got me.'

James said, 'You want to go back to his place?'

'No, she'll have called in the police if she's got any sense. And there'll be ambulances and what not. We'll take it up tomorrow. Get us to this hotel of yours.'

James started the engine and moved off.

IT WAS THE last train to Manchester and almost empty, the other two inhabitants of his carriage sunk down in their seats and wrapped in coats as they tried to squeeze out some sleep.

Sam stared out of his window but could see only himself glaring moodily back. He felt as though he was pedalling a bicycle after it had stopped moving. His thoughts went back and forth between the zoo, Edinburgh Waverley station and the streets of York. There were apparently four men – maybe more – who wanted the diary. Chantal had told him it belonged to her grandfather, a member of the French Resistance in World War Two. It seemed to be nothing more than a record of one man's actions in a distant part of France at a particular time.

What could be so important as to need a team of four professionals to retrieve it? Obviously the parts he couldn't read would be the key – but what could they possibly say?

He took out his phone and rang Chantal. She answered on the third ring.

'Did you get it?'

'Hello, Sam, thanks for risking everything to find my itty-bitty handbag.'

'Yes, yes, thanks … did you get it?'

Sam shook his head at the phone, not sure whether he was amused or irritated. 'I got the diary but not the handbag. I think he left it on the train. I'd phone your bank and get them to cancel your cards.'

'You got the diary!'

'Don't celebrate yet. The guy took photos, so the bad guys have some of the information. Whatever the hell it is.'

'Shit.'

Sam waited a moment, then asked, 'Why didn't you stay?'

'I wanted to get back. I didn't feel safe.'

'Thanks a lot.'

'Not with you … I mean, it was late and dark and I wanted to get back to Manchester. And I didn't know if you'd be back in time for the last train. Where are you now?'

'On the train behind you.'

'Oh. I've just arrived. I've got money for a taxi from that nice lady.' She waited but Sam didn't say anything. 'Thank you for your help and everything. Will you send me the diary?'

'If you think you can look after it.'

'I'm going to give it to a lawyer.'

'And you don't know what all this is about.'

'No idea. It's an old French diary with some strange writing in it. Who's that harming?'

That's definitely the question, Sam thought as he ended the conversation with her and put away his phone. If someone wanted it so badly it was either worth a lot of money, or contained information that was useful or damaging to someone. He doubted anyone would send out the mercenary band he'd met simply because the diary was of historical interest.

He yawned and realised that he was finally able to be tired. He had been up early to check on the delegates at the conference and ensure that David Bright, the man on whom he was to serve papers, was still scheduled to arrive. He'd spent the afternoon wandering around Edinburgh and then made his way to the Zoo. He had bona fides to get him into the Mansion and had found Bright at the five o'clock gathering where everyone was given their badges and passes, along with a free glass of cheap champagne. The evening meal was to begin at six o'clock so that people had time to recover from their flights afterwards and begin brightly the following morning.

Bright had flown in from Geneva just for the conference, not knowing that his ex-wife was still in touch with his secretary, who had quietly let slip that he'd be in the UK for forty-eight hours and therefore available to receive some legal documentation. Which Sam had calmly handed over while Bright had been talking to another delegate in one of his Eastern European tongues.

He didn't realise what he'd been given until Sam had told him, at which point he had flung the envelope to the ground and looked ready to shout at the man who had delivered it ... and then realised that Sam was six inches taller and several pounds heavier. Bright's wife had told him he had a temper that often went out of control, but Sam had never thought he would be in trouble. It was what he did, after all. He didn't practise much in the way of divorce work, in fact, but Laura had convinced him that this was a good cause – especially as Joanne Bright was a friend of hers.

He thought briefly about Laura. Of late a coolness had entered their relationship, which was why he had agreed to do this for her friend. A case had recently kept him away from home for nearly a month, leaving her to deal with Dan, his son. Although Dan was eighteen he was still living mostly with them.

He and Dan – who had been brought up largely in foster homes – were still trying to connect with each other. Dan's personality demonstrated itself in behaviour that was wayward, headstrong and showed little time for authority. Sam recognised that those traits were likely to be an inheritance from himself. On the other hand, he recognised that his own behaviour could be a strong model for Dan's adolescent growth so he was attempting to include Dan in his work whenever possible, especially when it came to the increasingly important use of the internet, which was something for which Dan had developed an affinity.

When Sam was away, however, the responsibility for feeding and tending to Dan fell on Laura, which was a burden that she didn't want and hadn't expected when she and Sam had first begun to share each other's lives.

Sam took out his phone again and called her.

'It's me.'

'Hello, you. Do you know what time it is?'

'I do. Are you still up?'

'What else would I be doing at half eleven?'

'Can you fetch me?'

'I thought you were staying overnight. Where from, anyway? Crewe?'

Sam hesitated.

'Piccadilly.'

'Sam!'

'I'm sorry, it's the late train. I got caught up in something.'

Her voice calmed down. 'What?'

'I'll tell you later.'

'When are you due in?'

He told her and she eventually agreed to meet him in the main concourse, by the elevated timetables.

She added, 'Only because you went to Edinburgh in the first place for me. Otherwise you'd be in a taxi.'

LATE FRIDAY NIGHT and Manchester was full of groups of people holding out for a good time, if only they could discover where it was taking place. The air in the city was mild and the people seemed happy to take their time, clinging on to one another as they lurched between the grand Victorian edifices built to make a statement about Empire and its source of wealth. Steele looked at the people as the Touareg slid by – the young and stupid, the undisciplined ... the pointless. Girls with short skirts and showing their bellies. Boys with ridiculous hair. All of them on mobile phones, talking to friends who were probably three feet away. Stumbling along together into a future of hopeless mediocrity.

Irritated, he said to James, 'Are you actually taking us somewhere? I thought you said you knew Manchester.'

'We're almost there.'

He turned into a street that Steele saw was within walking distance of Deansgate.

He was about to comment on the location when the phone in his pocket burped. He took it out and saw there was a mail message waiting.

'About time.'

He opened the mail. It was from Nate but there was no subject-line. Instead there were three photographs attached to a blank mail. Steele directed his phone to open the first photograph and found a dim representation of a page from a diary, the writing faint but legible.

He murmured, 'Good drills, boy,' even while he wondered why Nate hadn't called. Perhaps he'd been busy. He saw from the time on the email that it had been sent two hours before – it must have struggled to get through the system. Returning to his inbox, he noted that another nine emails had arrived, each with several attachments. He looked over at James.

'Where's the laptop?'

'Boot. We didn't want anyone seeing it on the back seat and taking a chance.'

'OK. Get us to that fucking hotel asap. My man Nate has sent us some goodies.'

James glanced across curiously.

'So he got the asset?'

'Unless he's being a prick-teaser. And we don't like prick-teasers, do we? As that dink Jack now knows.'

James looked away and moments later steered the large vehicle into an entrance that led down to an underground car park. He turned off the lights and the engine, then leaned forward and put his forehead on the steering wheel.

Steele ignored him and got out of the car. He knew that James was processing the images that were in his head.

Welcome to the land of the grown-ups.

AN HOUR AND twenty minutes after its departure from York, Sam's train pulled up to platform 13 at Manchester Piccadilly, the doors hissed open and he stepped down on to the platform. As he wrestled his rucksack on to his back, his phone rang. Expecting it to be Laura, telling him she was running late, he clicked the answer key.

What greeted him was a hysterical voice that he couldn't at first make out.

And then he could.

STEELE WAS HAPPY with his room. It was large enough to have a separate 'lounge' area with a two-seater sofa facing a flat-screen TV. It also had a safe inside the wardrobe, which might come in handy. From the fourth floor he had a view of the dark street outside and was high enough to be out of earshot of any drunks or loud traffic. He liked a hotel room to be as divorced from reality as possible.

There was a knock on the door and he let James in with the laptop. He began to set it up on the low table in front of the sofa where they could both see the screen.

Steele asked, 'Do you know what you're doing?'

He had never been able to extract images from a mobile phone on to a computer – the software never seemed to work for him as it did for others.

James gave him a sidelong glance.

'Done it before. Where's your phone?'

Steele handed it over and James began to fiddle with its settings, enabling bluetooth and pairing it with the computer. After a moment he moved to the laptop and opened up a file explorer, then clicked on the first image, which bloomed to fill the whole screen – an off-white image showing two pages of the diary, its ochre writing slightly out of focus but still legible.

They stared at it.

"Nuila, messo dusren euni nezo ouaitsi ouesu du raisma lade neurbre, où esle mieurpre keums tétéon achutépar."

James shook his head.

'Bits of French in there. But also a lot of nonsense.'

Steele knew very little French and the words meant nothing to him.

'If he's got the rest of the asset then it's not our problem.'

He took out his phone and called Nate again.

'Still no answer. What the fuck is he playing at?'

'It's one-thirty in the morning, boss. Maybe he's crashed out somewhere.'

'Not without calling me, he isn't. Get all the photos loaded up on the computer then go back to your room.'

James nodded and carried on manipulating the mobile phone and the laptop until all of the photographs were in a folder on the computer. He showed Steele where he'd filed them.

'You going to send them on? Only the photos are quite big file sizes – you'll have to send several emails, like Nate did.'

Steele nodded briefly. He didn't like to demonstrate any ignorance, but when it came to IT he was pretty much a novice. He could use a word processing programme, surf the net and send emails, but that was the limit of his expertise. In the world in which he operated you left that stuff to the nerds while you did the real work.

He fetched himself a glass of water from the bathroom while James finished closing down the bluetooth connection and checking that all the photos opened correctly.

He said, 'Where did you learn all that stuff?'

James looked up, surprised to be asked a personal question.

'Always been interested in it. Liked solving problems, the usual shit. My brother even did it at university – computer science, I mean. This is simple stuff compared to that.'

'Is that what they teach you spooks these days? All mod cons. Sit in front of a screen all day playing with your mouse.'

James folded down the lid of the laptop.

'I wasn't a spook.'

'You wouldn't tell me if you were. I've worked with you cool kids before. So what were you if not Intelligence?'

James hesitated. 'ALS.'

He stared Steele in the face as if expecting him to offer a challenge. But Steele grinned instead. ALS was the Army Legal Service.

'A fucking *lawyer*. I might have known.'

James was defiant. 'I hated it, so I quit and went through training. They said I was good enough for the Paras.'

'So why didn't you join?'

'I fucked up.'

'Pray tell.'

The younger man looked away. 'Drugs. I don't want to go into it.'

Steele raised his eyebrows. 'Okay. I thought there was something off about you.'

'I was selling, not using.'

'Think that makes a difference?' He paused. 'You should have been calling me on all the shit we've pulled tonight.'

'What makes you think I won't?'

'You're in too deep now. You stood and watched.'

'I was taught to follow orders.' He stood up. 'What you did tonight wasn't pretty but I suppose there are reasons for it.'

'Spoken like a real brief. Oh yes. We always tell ourselves there are reasons. Justify the shit we do. Blame it on some kind of higher morality. But don't go thinking we're the same, you and me, just because you did what I told you to.'

'Why's that?'

'On this job I'm a civil servant. I'm sanctioned by the state's morality. You're doing it for the pay cheque.'

'Don't kid yourself, boss.' His expression suggested he'd been stung by Steele's words. He moved towards the door. 'What you did tonight was for your own benefit – you liked it.'

Steele watched the younger man's retreating back and found himself playing over in his head what he'd just articulated.

Eventually he dismissed those thoughts as the words of someone unused to the harsh realities of mercenary life. He sat down facing the laptop's screen and opened each of the photographs in turn. Nothing made any sense to him but that wasn't his role. He opened the email programme and sent Blake a short note with the first six photographs. Then he sent four more emails with a further six photographs attached to each one. At least that was one IT trick he'd learned. It took twenty minutes for the entire set of mails and attachments to leave his outbox. When he was certain they had all gone, he closed down the laptop.

He showered and went to bed, staring up at the hotel room's ceiling in the dark. What he had done that night wasn't good and hadn't yielded any useful information. Was it true what James had said? Did he enjoy it? What had James seen that even led him to believe that? Was he too enthusiastic? Did he cackle with glee as he went about his business?

A chill ran through his body as he considered his actions, remembering the sensations as his gloved fists hit flesh. The sound of fingers snapping. The sight of a tooth popping out of a mouth. He thought again about karma and the prospect of what was to come for him after his death. And he was struck by a dilemma.

Was it possible to both enjoy hurting other people while at the same time recognising that it was bad for the soul?

LAURA HAD SAID nothing after they had got into her BMW 3-series and navigated out of the car park. Sam knew that she was irritated but also angry with herself for being irritated. Once he'd explained to her what Chantal had told him on the phone there had seemed little option but to drive to Chorlton. She knew that. But he knew she would be seething that he was caught up in something he didn't understand and seemed intent on dragging her into.

Sam glanced at her profile – the shoulder-length blonde hair tucked behind her left ear, the pink blush of her cheek, her long neck rising out of a functional black polo sweater. He was suddenly touched that she cared so much for him that she would drive to Manchester after midnight to collect him. And that she would then agree to drive to Chorlton to see to a hysterical woman whom she had never met. They had known each other for a little over a year and he was continually astonished by her faith in him and his instincts, a faith expressed more in her actions than her words which were, frankly, often sarcastic. They each maintained their own houses because – they said – it was still a trial period. But in fact she spent more time at his house now that his son, Dan, was living with him. There was a pseudo-family atmosphere that he thought she quite liked, especially as Dan was often out with his own set of friends. When he had first turned up twelve months ago Laura had found him work at her company, operating as a dogsbody and tea-boy. Now, when he wasn't helping his father with internet searches or other activities, he had started working with a friend who had set up his own online company selling baby 'packages' – gift sets sourced from the Far East: soaps, towels, rubber ducks, bibs. All of which were currently stored in a warehouse on an industrial estate in Crewe.

THEY KNEW THEY were in the right street before they found the address. Three police Volvos with flashing lights, a dark blue unmarked BMW and an ambulance were parked at odd angles outside the small terraced house, whose windows bounced the strobing lights up into the sky. It reminded Sam of those days when he'd been involved in dramatic seizures, usually taking place on mundane housing estates in the north of England. Typically they had been low-key and uncontested, but occasionally there was some heightened tension and his bosses had thought it useful to bring along fleets of police vans with flashing lights and barking dogs to try to subdue the bad guys before anything stupid happened.

He turned to Laura.

'Probably best if you stay here. I'll see what's what.'

'Don't get involved, Sam. See how she is and then let's go home.'

He said nothing and closed the car door quietly behind him. The air was finally becoming cold but neighbours were still interested enough to stand on their doorsteps and watch. He couldn't blame them. Any change in routine was welcome when your environment was so ordered and calm.

He approached a policeman wearing a luminous jacket and lifted his chin towards the house.

'A friend of mine's in there. She called me.'

The policeman looked him up and down and asked for his name. When Sam told him, the policeman wrote it down, then spoke into his shoulder, got an incomprehensible reply, and nodded Sam through.

Sam noticed that the doors of the ambulance were open and there was no one inside. He pushed into the house.

The room he entered was crowded. Two paramedics were kneeling by a body on the floor while two other men in overcoats looked down on them. Chantal sat on a two-seater black sofa staring into mid-air.

One of the policemen turned to Sam and asked who he was. Sam gave his name.

'Miss Bressette called me. I'm a friend.'

At the sound of her name Chantal had looked up, her eyes like those of a child waiting to be punished, frightened and wary at the same time. They were also red from crying.

The policemen seemed uninterested in Sam, so he sat next to Chantal and spoke quietly to her.

'What happened?'

She took a long time to reply but he knew there would be several versions of events playing through her mind and she would need time to choose the right one to describe. Eventually she drew a big sigh and seemed to come back into the room. Her voice cracked with the effort of speech and was still full of tearfulness.

'He was on the floor when I came in. His face ... oh my god, his face ... ' She raised a hand to her mouth as though she couldn't say what she was thinking.

'But he's alive?'

'He smiled at me when I came in. Can you believe it? He was glad to see me. He could barely breathe but he smiled. What have I done? How did these monsters get here?'

Sam glanced up at the policemen, who still seemed to be more interested in the young man on the floor than in her. Presumably they saw her merely as someone who had found her boyfriend in this condition and didn't yet have the status of witness.

Sam asked, 'What did you tell them?'

She looked guiltily down at her hands.

'Nothing. I don't trust anyone now. I said I'd been away and I'd just arrived home and found him like that. I'm right, aren't I – this is connected?'

Sam nodded.

'Too much of a coincidence otherwise. Tell them as little as you have to. We'll get you out of here as soon as we can.'

She seemed despairing. 'Where can I go? I daren't go home. What if they're there, waiting for me?'

'Think yourself lucky they weren't waiting *here*.'

'Oh my god ...'

'So either Jack told them something that made them go away, or he convinced them he didn't know anything. Had you spoken to him?'

'Of course, on the phone. I told him when I'd be back.'

'So they could have got that from him and just waited for you.'

She turned her round eyes on him again. 'So why didn't they? Why did they go?'

'Perhaps he convinced them he didn't know anything. Brave lad.'

Chantal raised her hands to her face and wept.

Sam said, 'Of course they could still have waited to see if you turned up. Or gone to your place to see if you went there.' He paused. 'That's probably what happened. Jack will have told them you were going straight home, hoping he'd get the chance to call you and tell you to steer clear. But they beat him so badly he couldn't.'

Chantal's sobbing increased to such an extent that one of the paramedics glanced over at them. Sam nodded at him.

He said to Chantal, 'I'll talk to the coppers and get you out of here.'

He stood and approached the same policeman who had spoken to him before. The policeman looked at him with incurious eyes. Sam asked when they'd be finished with Chantal because he would like to take her back home. The policeman glanced briefly at Chantal, then back at Sam.

'Who are you again?'

'A friend. On good Samaritan duty. I take it you've got her statement, haven't you? Can she go and get some rest now?'

'Doesn't she want to stay with Mr Boyfriend here?'

'How badly is he hurt?'

The policeman looked down at Jack's thin form. 'They say some broken bones in his hands. Broken nose. Couple of teeth missing. Lots of bruises. He's sedated now so he's not talking. Not that he was doing much before.'

'Where will you take him?'

The policeman gave him the name of the hospital.

'We'll take Chantal home tonight and bring her to the hospital tomorrow morning. How's that?'

'We?'

'My girlfriend's in the car outside. I thought it best she didn't see any of this.'

The policeman nodded. He asked for Sam's address and he gave it.

'All right. We've got her statement and her address. If she wants to go to the hospital tomorrow it's her lookout.'

'OK, thanks.'

Sam turned to go but the policeman stopped him with a hand on his arm.

'Funny thing. This looks like the bad guys were invited in – no forced entry, nothing stolen as far as we can see. And neither you nor Miss Bressette have asked who we think might have done it.'

'Do you have any ideas?'

'That's beside the point. The first question is always who could have done it ... and in a case like this, which doesn't appear to be a burglary gone wrong, it might lead us to think that young Jack here knew who he was talking to.'

Sam said nothing and waited until the policeman let go of his arm.

'Just thought I'd mention it.'

Sam ignored him and sat next to Chantal again. She had been watching the conversation but Sam sensed that she hadn't been listening.

He said, 'We have to go now. Is there anything you need from here? Clothes or anything?'

'Some underwear perhaps.'

'Can you get that from home?'

'I don't want to go home.'

'OK, you go fetch it and I'll wait here.'

He stood and helped her to her feet. The paramedics had lifted Jack on to a stretcher. There was a splint on his hand and a breathing mask over his face. Chantal stopped as they carefully manoeuvred the gurney out of the room and into the street. She reached out a hand and touched Jack's undamaged hand, then ran from the room. Sam heard her feet climbing the stairs.

The policeman turned towards him again. Sam noticed that he was younger than he'd first appeared. Something about his demeanour and attitude had given him the air of someone world-weary and experienced, but in fact Sam began to wonder how much of that was a pose.

The policeman said, 'So you're taking her to Crewe.'

'She doesn't want to go home. Perhaps understandable.'

'And you know her how ... ?

'Facebook.'

'Ah.'

'Amazing the friends you can make online these days. Who'd have thought it?'

'Who indeed.'

LAURA DROVE IN silence, using the rear-view mirror to glance occasionally at Chantal on the back seat. She had brought a carrier bag with her that she clutched tightly under an arm, looking like an orphan being transported to a children's home with a bad reputation.

When they arrived at Sam's house he led her inside and took her upstairs, carrying her Gucci bag at arm's length as though it was some kind of alien artefact. He showed her the spare bedroom and went downstairs again. Laura was taking off her coat.

She said, 'Anything strike you about her?'

Sam considered. 'I'm not sure what you mean.'

'Dye her hair blonde and she could be my twin. Explains a lot.'

Sam watched her leave the room and go upstairs to bed. He had no response that didn't sound crass to his own ears.

SATURDAY

THE WALK TO L'Express on Horseferry Road had taken Gideon Blake less than ten minutes. Shepherd was waiting for him, his face pinched in the cold air and his small dark eyes watchful and without trust. He already had a black coffee. Blake gestured towards the inside.

'If it's too cold we can go in.'

'Frightened of being seen?' Shepherd's voice cracked, as though he hadn't used it for a while. He coughed to clear his throat. 'I'd rather stay out here if that's OK. I need the cold to wake me up.'

Blake shrugged and sat opposite. Eight o'clock meetings were commonplace for him. A girl came and he ordered coffee.

Shepherd said, 'You've put on weight. The good life is good, I suppose.'

Blake smiled grimly. 'You have to get past this. We're supposed to be on the same side.'

Shepherd looked away.

'Is that what you were thinking when you shafted me? Oh, we're on the same side, so it doesn't matter if I put poor old Shepherd in the shit again?'

'I had no choice– '

'You always have a choice. You're good at that, giving yourself choices. Always the choice to walk away with clean heels. That's your speciality.'

Blake studied Shepherd closely. He looked more unwell than simply having a cold. His eyes were red in the corners and his lips were flaked with dried skin. Five years ago he had worked with Shepherd almost daily, interpreting data from Eastern Europe. As one of the best linguists consulted by the intelligence services, Shepherd was used across a whole range of departments. Unfortunately he sometimes forgot which department he was supposed to be currently playing for, and he could be squeezed like a sponge to leak information that he was meant to keep to himself.

Blake had used information learned in this way to pressurise and then embarrass a political opponent in another department, and Shepherd had eventually been identified as the source. Instant dismissal from his contracts had followed and he had returned to academic life.

Blake had not been in contact since then, but he had thought a little pocket money could be a sufficient lure. The girl returned with his coffee and he paid.

He laid three A4 sheets of paper on the table. Each contained a colour image of a page of writing.

He said, 'Look at these.'

Shepherd glanced away, toward the traffic and pedestrians moving past them.

'I don't need this shit again, Blake. I'm happy doing what I'm doing.'

Blake leaned back but kept his hand on the papers to prevent them blowing away.

'Be honest with yourself, Shepherd. You wouldn't be here if you were happy. You know, I'm sick to death of you part-time academics. Willing to take our money but bear none of the responsibility. You pretend that you're doing this intel work for the good of the country, but actually it's where you get your real jollies because being an academic is so fucking dull.'

'Finished?'

Blake leaned forward until his face was less than a foot from Shepherd's.

'No, I'm not. This particular project is very important to me. Do you understand? *Very* important. On a personal level. So it can go one of two ways. Either you help me out and everything is sweetness and light and a choir of angels sing ... or I shall be very, very pissed off. And I shall make things very difficult for you at your place of work. The university administration doesn't know of your entire involvement with our little group, does it?'

Shepherd stared at him.

Blake went on, 'I didn't think so. Yes you did a little low-level translation for us ... and I suppose that would be acceptable because it adds to your credibility and, ah, kudos amongst your fellow academics. But I'm sure they'd be horrified to hear of the strategic information you were able to give us in addition to your basic translation services.'

'What strategic information?'

'You don't remember? It only recently came to light again, during one of our reviews. I'm not surprised you forgot. I'm talking about the conversations with the Serbian prostitutes that we asked you to undertake. In that hotel in Knightsbridge. It was so important you had to consult with them two at a time. Over a period of several nights. Is your memory coming back?'

Shepherd's face lost some of its meagre colour.

'This is preposterous ... there was no such– '

'Ah, but there was, you see. We have receipts. Some rather dim film. Tape recordings. It was very useful information, though I'm sure you wouldn't want the university to have the opportunity to misunderstand what exactly was going on ... '

Shepherd drew in a breath as if to continue the argument. But he caught himself and closed his eyes slowly.

'Your tiny soul must be a dark and shrivelled nugget of shit.'

Blake seemed to relax and leaned back, a friendly smile tugging at his mouth.

'Bygones.' He moved the three photographs back and forth on the table as if in a little dance. 'Come on, Shepherd, do your stuff. What does this mean to you?'

Shepherd took out a pair of expensive glasses from a designer case and peered down at the photographs on the three sheets of paper. Then he leaned back in his chair and took the spectacles off, replacing them carefully in their case, which he tucked into an inside pocket of his coat.

'Verlan.'

Blake waited but nothing else seemed to be forthcoming.

'Which is?'

'It's a kind of reverse language. French in this case. Looks like it's being used as a cryptolect. A secret language.'

'Go on.'

Shepherd sighed as though talking to a young person. 'You probably used Pig Latin when you were a kid – reversing syllables in words and adding vowels. So let's say 'coffee cup' becomes 'offeecay upcay.' It's usually a kind of argot or slang used by one group of people to conceal what they're saying from another group of people, even though they might speak the same language.'

'I'm not following any of this.'

Shepherd shrugged.

'OK. Do you know any French?'

'Some.'

'What's the French for "in reverse"? Or "wrong way around"?

Blake thought for a moment. '*A l'invers*, I think.'

He had pronounced it '*A lanver.*'

'Very good. Exactly right. Now take the two syllables of "l'invers" and reverse them.'

Blake said, '*Verlan.*'

'And there you have it. Verlan takes syllables from a word and reverses their sequence, adding bits and bobs to make words that are pronounceable. So *femme* becomes *meuf. Cigarette* becomes *garetsi*. And so on. When that gets too easy, or the words start to enter common usage, then they'll usually be verlanned again. For example *Arabe* first became *beur*. But that usage started to creep out of the suburbs and into the general media culture, so it went through another transformation and became *rebeu*. It's all about trying to hold on to power – oppressed people keeping something to themselves that others don't know about.'

'So who uses it?'

'Well it became very popular in the eighties and some people thought it had sprung out of nowhere. French rap and hip-hop singers spread its usage and so those without any historical understanding said it was a brand new style of communication. But academics have traced it back to its derivation as a kind of argot, and it seems it might have been used as a code spoken by criminals as far back as the eighteenth century. So there have probably been pockets of usage all over the place. I read somewhere that members of the Resistance would use it with each other in Paris during the war in case any Germans were listening.'

Blake leaned forward, his eyes shining. 'This is good, Shepherd, very good.'

Shepherd looked again at the paper.

'But this is more complicated.'

'How so?'

'People who use verlan usually add one or two reversed words into a sentence, words that have become standard, so to speak – so *keuf* for 'flic', which you probably know means a cop. Or something closer to your own black heart, *ripou* for 'pourri', meaning corrupt.'

Blake glanced down at the pages.

'But this is different, isn't it? Nearly all of it is coded.'

'I'd suggest this was like a secret language between two people and only they knew what they meant. Verlan is almost exclusively a spoken language, not written down. The person who wrote this had used it before and knew that his reader would understand. It's not easy to reverse a whole vocabulary on the fly – he must have practised it. So I'd guess that it was a language he was used to speaking with someone and maybe writing it, too. A girlfriend or boyfriend or family member, perhaps. Like those twins who develop a secret language that only they can understand.'

Blake leaned back, picked up the three pieces of paper, folded them and put them inside his coat.

'I'm going to send you more of these online. Do you still use your old email address?'

'I'm sure you can find out if I don't. What's all this about?'

Blake stood up and pushed his chair back under the table. The coffee that he had ordered remained untouched on the table, moving slightly with the passage of traffic on the road.

'Just answer your email. There'll be thirty pages to work on. I want them no later than tomorrow morning. Leave the context to me. It's not your concern.'

Shepherd said, 'No. Nothing ever is.'

WHEN SAM WENT downstairs he found Chantal Bressette standing outside his patio windows with a cup of coffee between her hands. Laura had lent her a thin rainbow-striped jumper that she wore over the same cream shirt as the day before. Her eyes were ringed with dark shadows when she looked at him.

'You have a pond. I always wanted a pond. Dad didn't want one. He didn't like still water.'

Sam said nothing but sipped his own coffee. It was almost the first piece of personal information she had given without it being bled from her. The day was shaping up to be fine and maybe even warm, with high streaks of pale cloud traversing the windless sky. It was one of those March days that offered a preview of the summer to come.

She said, 'If you're from Yorkshire how did you end up here?'

'I was working in Manchester and Liverpool as part of my job. But I didn't want to live there. I kept looking for houses further south, into a price range I could afford, and I ended up here.'

'Do you like it? Crewe?'

'It is what it is. It can't make up its mind whether it's industrial or rural. But a lot of industry has gone anyway. Rolls-Royce. Railway maintenance. Lot of jobs gone in the last ten years. Seems I can't get away from industrial strife wherever I go.'

'It's the same everywhere, isn't it? Politics.'

Sam shrugged. It seemed to him that although she seemed calm there was still an edge of emotion just below the surface of her pleasantries. He would have to go carefully until she'd recovered her poise.

He said, 'Tell me about your father, what it was like for him.'

'I think he was very sad, in a way. Growing up in America without any other family. Of course when I knew him he talked with an American accent, which was very strange for a girl in Nottingham. My friends thought it was exotic.'

'What happened to his mother?'

'I don't know. They had some kind of falling out and as far as I know he never saw her after he left the States. I never met her. He came over here, got a job in a bakery and eventually bought it. I was brought up over the shop, so to speak, but it eventually became quite a large franchise. He owned ten bakeries by the time he finished.'

'Is he still alive?'

She shook her head. 'He died two years go.'

'Your mother?'

'I thought I told you – she died giving birth to me. I never knew her.'

'That's tough. Any other relatives?'

She turned to him. 'Is this you detecting again?'

'Making conversation.'

'My grandmother might be still alive somewhere. Maybe she went back to France. I know the name of the village but nothing else. My dad said she probably would go back because she never stopped talking about it.'

Sam made the connection. 'Of course – the woman the diary was written for. Julienne?'

'She must be pushing ninety now, if she's still alive. Dad used to say she was very vigorous so perhaps she still is.'

'But you never met her? She didn't come here and you didn't go to the States?'

She looked away. 'Dad didn't really do family. He didn't seem that interested.'

'But he gave you the diary?'

'About five years ago. He'd been given it by his mother when he was a teenager but never really looked at it. He said it was his father's and maybe I would find it interesting. But he must have known I couldn't read it. He didn't speak French other than bits he picked up from his mother, so I never learned anything other than what any other schoolgirl learns.'

'And he didn't say anything else about the diary? Why it might be valuable or interesting to anyone else?'

She shook her head. 'There's no way he would know anything about it.' She turned her cup upside down and spilled the dregs on to the garden. She said quietly, 'I'm all right, you know. I'm not going to collapse.'

'It might hit you later. It was pretty traumatic.'

'My dad died two years ago. I'm an orphan. I have a boyfriend but not many other friends. I'm tougher than I look.'

'Let's hope that doesn't have to be tested.'

THEY WENT BACK inside and had breakfast and he asked her about Jack. She hesitated before replying.

'I've already phoned the hospital this morning. They say he's still unconscious from the drugs they gave him. What do you think I should do?'

Sam was clearing away the plates.

'Don't put me in the middle of that. You didn't want to call the police when we were in the zoo, if I remember rightly. You'll have to make your own decisions now.'

'Then why am I here? Why didn't you let me go back to my own place?'

Sam turned from the sink and folded his arms.

'Think it through. Jack was probably beaten up because he wouldn't give them any information about you. But as they knew you'd been to Edinburgh and knew where he lived, it's hard to see what else they thought they could find out. Maybe they were sending you a message. Maybe they expected to find you back there with him and wanted another go at you. Or perhaps they thought you'd spoken to him and told him where you were. Anyway, the point is they probably don't know me, so they don't know where to look next. If you go to Jack they might be watching the hospital. If you go home they might be watching that, too. At the moment we don't have a clue why the diary is important, or who it's important to, so I suggest we try to find out and then take it from there.'

'Big speech. What if I don't want to go along with it?'

'Your choice. But bear in mind this is beginning to look like a big operation. Four guys, some kind of coordination, some resources. They're not going to give up just because I put a spanner in their works last night. They're following you to see what you do with the diary and what information they can gain from it. So it's important to someone, somehow.'

'Then what exactly does it boil down to? How do we find out why the diary's important?'

'First we find a translator.'

She gestured with exasperation. 'Which is what I was doing last night.'

'I know. But this time we'll do it properly. And we don't have to travel so far.'

STEELE WAS LYING on his hotel bed watching Saturday morning cartoons on TV when Blake called. He used the remote to turn off the television and then stood up. He found he thought more clearly when he was upright and walking. He listened as Blake explained what he'd learned so far about the text in the diary. He didn't understand why Blake was telling him this because his objective had been top-level only – find the asset and retrieve it. Its contents were immaterial. Evidently Blake felt the need for explanations in order to rationalise his actions. Steele had never felt that need. Reasons were for people whose values weren't clear or strong enough. His values of loyalty and service were sufficient for him. Despite his beliefs about karma and the way in which it could return to affect his spiritual well-being, he found it hard to connect those metaphysical conceits with actual physical consequences.

When Blake had finished Steele said, 'So is my brief ongoing? Do you still want me to find the woman and retrieve the asset?'

'Until I say otherwise, yes.' Steele thought that Blake sounded tense and wondered why that would be. 'And there's another thing. I had my man at GCHQ do some research this morning. The Bressette woman used her phone last night. She contacted a man named Sam Dyke. They didn't speak for very long. I'll be sending you some information about him. We think he was an agent with Customs and Excise, as it was, so he has some expertise. He's now working privately.'

Steele took in this information while staring through his window at the pedestrians below. He felt as though some fundamental ground rule had been breached.

'A private investigator? Like a detective?'

'That's what my information tells me. Get a grip, Steele. This doesn't change anything. There's no reason for this to cause you any concern. Just do your job.'

Steele wasn't insulted. He remained calm. 'Do you think it's the man who intervened last night?'

'Use your brains. It could hardly be anyone else. You said in your email that you had no luck at the Bressette woman's house, so I suggest you find Dyke. For some reason or other he seems to have taken an interest in her.'

WHEN THE DOSSIER about Dyke came through to the laptop, Steele read it carefully and then laid it aside and thought for ten minutes. Then he put on his shoes and his padded North Face jacket, finished packing and texted James to meet him in the lobby, ready to leave. He then spent five minutes wiping clean anything he might have touched in the room. It was a precaution he always took. Finally he glanced around the room before pulling the door closed behind him. There was no door knob to wipe so he cleaned the plate containing the electronic lock mechanism instead. He put the keycard in his pocket for disposal later.

James was already waiting in the small lobby, sitting on a brown leather chair and scrolling through texts on his phone. He looked like a teenager playing with a hand-held console. He stood as Steele approached, showing an appropriate deference, Steele thought.

James asked, 'Where are we going?'

Ignoring the question, Steele turned and walked out of the lobby and headed towards the car park. When they arrived at the Touareg he swung the laptop into its boot. He glanced around the empty space and took in a breath of air. The weather was turning warm after its recent cold spell. He liked the smell of the air in city centres – there was something industrial and workmanlike in it, the promise of conflict and endeavour and frustrated hope.

'Heard anything from Nate or Clifford?'

'Clifford will be with us tomorrow. He's going to sign himself out of hospital. Nothing from Nate.'

Steele nodded to himself. 'This guy's good.'

'Who?'

'Sam Dyke. Private investigator and royal pain in the arse. Well, let's see if we can get inside his head and scramble it a bit.'

He opened the passenger door and climbed in, feeling lithe and powerful.

ANGEL WAS SIX feet three inches tall and worked hard to keep himself both muscular and agile. At the gym he divided his time equally between weights and roadwork, and though he would never be light on his feet, he could move extremely rapidly over distances of up to twenty yards, almost without noise, and then break a man's neck with the grip of his clenched arms. His skin was Mediterranean in colour – his given name was Angelo from his Italian father – and mostly smooth in tone.

On the back of his left shoulder was a knife scar where an Afghan tribesman had taken offence at Angel's apparently disparaging attitude and buried a curved knife two inches into the meat just below his shoulder-blade.

On the right hand side of his shaved head, rising like a cordillera from the otherwise smooth dome, was a ridge of scar tissue where a brick thrown by a youth in Basra had split his skull. On his left leg there were three scars, the oldest starting at his ankle, the two others just below and above his knee. These were not battle-wounds but caused by osteomyelitis, a bone-marrow disease that could have led to him losing his leg had it not been caught in time; three attempts had been needed, in fact, to eradicate the infection, leading to months of inactivity and drug treatment when he was a child.

Because he had been weakened when younger, Angel had dedicated himself to becoming strong. Mentally and physically. Lying week after week in a children's ward, staring at the ceiling and waiting for his next penicillin shot, he had decided that he was never going to be made vulnerable again. He would be strong enough to look after himself, to fight and win his own battles without the intervention of others.

As soon as possible he had left home and joined the Army. On his sixteenth birthday he no longer needed anyone's permission to sign up and had walked into the recruiting office in Aylesbury and made his commitment.

He had wound up in 3 Para and found to his surprise that he had the ability to agree with whatever order he was given. Although the Army was changing around him, becoming more focused on developing soldiers who could think for themselves in any situation, he enjoyed being a weapon. He didn't want to exercise discretion and judgement. He wanted to do as he was told, hopefully with violence.

He had eventually served in both Iraq and Afghanistan and, like many of his colleagues in the Paras, had moved to the SAS, swapping his red beret for the beige.

Three years ago he had left The Regiment and had gone on 'the Circuit,' looking for contracts with private security firms. His first job was a lucrative posting with a private security firm in Iraq, protecting oil company workers from the aggressive disappointment of their countrymen and depositing large sums in his bank while doing so. That company had eventually folded through lack of government investment and he had ended up on the open market. Which is where his current sponsor had found him.

HE LIVED IN an inconspicuous three-bedroomed semi-detached house in a commuter town on the edge of Birmingham. He practised his anonymity with assiduousness. He went for early morning runs, shopped in the local supermarket and didn't bring women back to the house. He drove a five-year old sky-blue Volkswagen Passat, the new model with round rear lights, and had no expensive hobbies. He bought music from the internet, went to the gym three times a week and liked to make his own beer, his airing cupboard often bubbling with demi-johns of brown, foul-smelling liquid.

Out at the back of the house, encroaching on a small patch of green lawn, he had built a concrete bunker that contained his weapons.

This morning he opened his back door and stood for a moment, smelling the air. He was wearing the contractor's uniform of desert-colour combat trousers, a navy-blue polo shirt and a green padded vest without a collar.

And his tattoos. They were almost as effective as an actual weapon in some circumstances. He'd started with something small before his first posting abroad but then decided to go the whole hog when he found he liked the look on other people's faces when they saw them. Now they were more than spectacular. In some respects it made anonymity more difficult, but in others it made accurate description more complex.

The sky was clear. A good day to begin a new mission.

He unlocked the door to his armoury and stepped inside. The fluorescent buzzed awake and he stepped forward so that he could close the heavy metal door behind him. Inside it was cool, the dull pearl light casting hard shadows. A shelf ran at waist height against the two long walls, with a small grey metal cabinet against the short one. A peg board on the wall to his right held his pistols – an Israeli Desert Eagle, a couple of Glocks and a MAC-10 he had brought in from the US the previous year.

Finally he came to the shelf where he kept his knives. He had both combat and survival varieties, their blades either sleek or jagged, their potential for damaging human flesh enormous. He stroked a gleaming Smith and Wesson neck knife and its cord that would keep it nestled under his tee-shirt: probably too short for what he anticipated. Then he picked up and weighed the curved heft of a South American throwing knife, its rubberized handle clammy to his fingers. Probably not accurate enough.

Then he came to his Marine Raider Bowie knife – fifteen inches in length, its trademark shape and long blade making it one of his favourites. He took it from its sheath and ran it down the length of his arm. The blade drew a pale patch on his dark forearm. This was definitely the keeper for the job he'd been asked to accomplish.

He locked the armoury behind him, then went into the house and locked the back door too. He picked up a black roll-bag from the hallway, took one more look around the ground floor rooms, then went through the front door and climbed into the Passat. He set his GPS and slid quietly into the suburban street, heading north towards mayhem.

FIFTEEN MINUTES AFTER they had left Congleton and were entering the first low hills of the Derbyshire Peak District, Sam slowed and turned through an iron gate of a modern house surrounded on three sides by neat lawns. He drew to a halt on the gravel path and switched off the Mondeo's engine. A Suzuki 4x4 was parked outside a wooden garage, with a child's colourful tricycle next to it, as though the child had attempted to mimic the act of parking. A window in the house's front aspect was open and Sam heard an old blues track thumping and scratching its way towards him.

Chantal climbed out and stood looking around her. The house was set by itself at the foot of a gently sloping hill, and the road on which they'd approached carried on past the house and down towards a sketchy village – a pub, a shop window, a couple of cars.

She said, 'I could get used to this.'

'The quiet? Jimmy can't work without quiet – and maybe a bit of blues now and then.'

They walked up the path and he knocked on the front door and after a few moments a small man with black hair curled down to his shoulders pulled it open. He wore patched blue jeans and a t-shirt promoting a tour by Seasick Steve. He looked to be in his early forties and peered over narrow oblong spectacles at them. Finally he turned round and went back inside the house.

'For Christ's sake, Sam, come in and shut the bloody door.'

Sam stood aside so that Chantal could enter first.

JIMMY TURNED THE diary over in his hands and flicked through its pages. He had expressed little enthusiasm for what Sam had asked but Sam knew that enthusiasm wasn't in his repertoire of behaviours. He also knew that a glum forbearance was more likely to be the predominant tone of Jimmy's attitude. But that was all right. Jimmy would eventually get round to the translation – that was what he lived for, after all.

Eventually Jimmy said, 'I've got to pick up Lindsay from her friend's birthday party. So you two can go down into the village and I'll see what I can do between now and then. Come back at three.'

Chantal threw up her hands.

'What do we do in the village? Twiddle our thumbs?'

Jimmy peered over his glasses at her, then at Sam.

'Impatient, isn't she?'

Sam said to Chantal, 'Jimmy doesn't want us looking over his shoulder. He works best when he's on his own.'

'It's only translating a few pages!'

Jimmy closed the diary and held it out to her.

'Here you go, then. Find someone quicker. Sorry, Sam, you know I don't do pressure.'

Exasperated, Sam stood up and pulled Chantal to her feet.

'No pressure, Jimmy. Take your time. We'll be back at three.'

He dragged Chantal from the room and out through the front door. She walked sullenly towards his car but he changed direction and headed down the gravel path to the gate and then to the main road that led down to the village.

At the gate he turned. 'Coming? Or do you want to drive the whole five hundred yards?'

She drew a sigh and followed.

THERE WAS A small shop in the village that offered tea and stale Danish pastries and a rickety table and chairs at which to eat them. The shop sold craft products ranging from scented candles to home-made biscuits, and around the corner of the L-shaped space was a floor-level tank containing several aggressive-looking fish. Sam raised his eyebrows.

Chantal said, 'Don't worry, they're toothless.'

'What?'

'It's a fish pedicure. All the rage. The fish nibble the dead skin off your feet.'

'That's the most gruesome thing I've heard in a long while.'

'The fish are usually a type that don't have teeth, so they can't draw blood.'

Sam said nothing and took a bite from his pastry. Chantal sipped her tea. A middle-aged man came into the shop and bought a box of expensive mints from the young woman behind the counter, then left.

There was no sound in the village and little in the shop.

After a moment, Sam said, 'All right, you've been itching to ask questions. What do you want to know?'

'Well first of all, who's Jimmy?'

'Contract translator. We used him in Customs and Excise when there was something we couldn't understand or was in code. Anything to do with language, he's your man. He speaks about fifteen and has a nodding acquaintance with a dozen others. Plus, he's very good at codes. Crap at people, good at codes.'

'Customs and Excise – stopping people drinking and smoking what they want?'

'One way of looking at it.'

'So what did you do?'

'I was an investigator.'

'Working for the man. Must have been exciting.'

'If your idea of excitement is sitting in a van watching a ship unload. And doing paperwork. And being polite to people I thought were probably crooks and thieves.'

'All jobs are shitty after a while. Why didn't you leave?'

'I did. Eventually. You're probably too young to remember, but there was a lot of hoo-hah a few years ago about how Customs and Excise operated.'

Chantal raised her eyebrows. 'Carry on, old man, while I fetch your Zimmer frame.'

'Okay, sorry. Anyway, there were two major investigations and in the end several cases we'd won were quashed. And several officers were suspended or placed under suspicion. It wasn't pretty. A friend of mine killed himself because he was involved in a case that was under investigation.'

'So what was going on?'

Sam sighed. The environment in which he had worked several years ago seemed to him now like the invention of a madman. The political and bureaucratic manoeuvring that had infected his day-to-day activities had been draining and reduced his motivation to such an extent that he had forgotten whatever pleasure he'd once taken in the work. To revisit that time seemed to trigger in him a physical response of revulsion and weariness.

He also knew, however, that it was good for him to talk about the events that had led to him quitting because it reaffirmed him in his choice of new career.

He looked through the shop's front window, staring at the houses opposite.

'I'll give you an example. We used to do what were called "controlled deliveries" – let's say an informant contacted one of our drug liaison officers, who were usually in Pakistan, and the informant would reveal that he'd been asked by a bunch of bad guys to smuggle heroin into the UK. That was a typical situation because they were desperate to get their goods where they would sell, and that made them less cautious than they might have been. So we'd set it all up, help the informant do the deal and make it appear that he'd smuggled the goods into the country. In fact what we'd done is brought the drugs in ourselves, through official channels, and handed the package back to him once he was here. He would then set up the buy with the *next* set of bad guys who were going to be the distributors in the UK. And we'd watch it all and then bust them. The idea was to see what the distribution channels were and rupture them. It was all perfectly legal, sanctioned by European law and so on. But there were a couple of problems with the system.'

He glanced at Chantal to check that she was still listening. To his surprise she was staring at him intently.

She said, 'Like what? What problems?'

'Well we weren't supposed to initiate an operation, just tap into one that was already in place. In other words, we couldn't set up the informants to make the contacts and make the buys in the first place. Nor set up the sales once the drugs were over here. We had to wait until they came to us with the deals. But some of our guys were a bit too ... enthusiastic. Got too involved in what was described as "misconduct".'

'So what does that mean? They'd want to make sure the deals happened so they set up the whole thing, not just watch your informant do it?'

'Yes, there was some of that. Also, we'd have to give the intermediaries some of the junk from time to time to use as samples, to lure in the distributors, and sometimes the samples went missing after the busts. Government lost property, you might say.' He paused and took a sip of his tea. 'But the worse thing was when the informants set up innocent people as buyers under some pretext, just to make sure they got their reward. Unless there was a deal when they got to the UK, they got nothing from us. So sometimes they'd try it on and use dupes who had no idea what was really happening. Our guys would bust the meetings and after a lot of fuss those innocent people sometimes wound up in prison. Some of them did years behind bars.'

Chantal looked at him for a moment as though weighing his culpability.

'And you were involved directly in all this?'

'No, but I knew people who were.'

'So you had to what – testify against them?'

Sam stared straight ahead. 'Let's put it this way: People higher up the food chain told me it would be a good idea. After all, someone had to take the fall once the papers got hold of it. And shopping people I knew would get me out from underneath it, even though I wasn't actually guilty of anything.'

'But you didn't testify.'

'No, I didn't. And so a few months later, after a decent interval, my glittering career as a private investigator began. With the emphasis on private.'

'They sacked you, the bastards.'

Sam looked down at his drink and turned his cup between his hands. Although he hadn't informed on anyone he still felt an odd kind of guilt, as though he had. Maybe it was what they called survivors' guilt, where those who'd escaped some kind of disaster felt bad for those who'd succumbed to it. Whatever, he knew that there was a place deep inside him where a good deal of anger was stored – anger that he could call on when necessary.

Chantal had leaned back in her chair and finished her own drink. Her eyes were bright and he sensed that she was opening up to him. After a moment she looked around the shop as though checking it was still empty. Then a calculation came into her eyes that he couldn't read. He found himself staring into them until she leaned forward over the table.

In a quiet voice she said, 'You do know I won't sleep with you, don't you?'

Sam felt it like a slap on the face – a rebuff for something that was nowhere on his mental radar. He felt himself frowning.

'What? Who asked you?'

'I don't want you to think that I'm all excited by being with a private eye. You must have women clients who are like that.'

He leaned forward so that he was only twelve inches from her face.

'All the time. Drives Laura nuts. I have to give her their telephone numbers so she can check up on them.'

'I'm serious. I'm just setting your expectations.'

'And you're telling me this while your boyfriend is in hospital. What makes you believe I'd think it was an appropriate time?'

Chantal coloured slightly and leaned back. 'Men seem to think any time is an appropriate time.'

'I see.'

'Do you?'

'Because you're a fairly good-looking woman you expect every man to want to get into your pants.'

'That's not it. Not exactly. I'm just saying.'

'Well let's consider the conversation closed. I have to admit I've been keeping my lust barely under control for the last twenty-four hours, but now I see that I was wrong to feel like that. From now on I'll be a model colleague. You need have no fear.'

She didn't reply and Sam didn't know whether he was more irritated or amused by her thought processes. Or whether she had been right in fact to sense something in the air between them.

WHEN IT WAS time they left the shop and walked slowly back up the incline towards Jimmy's house. There was not a breath of wind and Sam heard the shrill cries of larks across the fields as he and Chantal walked. It was the one bird-song his father had known and had helped him identify, and he thought how similar the landscape here was to the countryside where he'd been born. In his mind he seemed to have travelled the breadth of a continent since he was a child, but in fact he was no more than the length of a county away. He wondered briefly whether mental geography was a more powerful influence on behaviour than actual square miles.

They turned through the gate and began to walk up the path to Jimmy's house. Looking ahead, Sam saw that the front door was open. Suddenly alert, he put out a hand and held Chantal back.

'Stay here.'

He walked forward and into the house, calling Jimmy's name quietly. The blues music had stopped and the house was silent. Sam walked down the entrance corridor and pushed into the back room where he and Chantal had sat earlier. The room was empty. He glanced out of the rear window into a long back garden that began to climb at its furthest point, sloping into the base of the hill behind the house. A child's swing hung unmoving.

He backed out of the rear room and glanced into the kitchen. Again it was empty. He turned and through the open front door saw Chantal leaning against the garden gate, a frown pinching her eyes together.

He was about to go upstairs when there was the loud tread of shoes on the landing above, then the clatter of someone coming downstairs.

'There you are.'

Jimmy clutched half a dozen pieces of paper in his right hand.

'Just printing these off upstairs. Where's the woman?'

'Christ, Jimmy.'

'What?'

'Why'd you leave your front door open?'

'So you could come in, of course. I was upstairs, wasn't I?'

Sam stepped to the front door and waved Chantal in.

Jimmy was waiting in the entrance hall. He waved the sheaf of papers.

'I've left out the boring bits. Love-letter type stuff from Jean-Claude to Julienne. But there are some interesting bits about the French resistance and the SAS that I haven't seen before. And of course all the verlan stuff is interesting.'

'What's verlan?'

Jimmy gave him an exasperated look and explained the reverse writing in the diary.

He concluded, 'Verlan has traditionally been used as a way of saying things that you don't want non-native speakers to understand. Of course when it's written, it's easier to decipher because you can see what you're working with and have got the time to reverse it back. When it's spoken a lot of it will just sound like gobbledygook and listeners don't have the opportunity to analyse it and make sense of it. But Jean-Claude really went to town with this – the verlan sections are completely verlanned. I would almost say it's like a secret language between him and his wife, Julienne. He must have thought this was the best he could do to keep it private while actually committing it to paper.'

Sam said, 'Show me how it works. I read this passage yesterday.'

He had taken the diary and found the section that he'd pored over on the train:

"Soirce, keva zeud glaisan al rega durador. J'ouvay ceplas sifexplos lesse derails minche fer, suispe oun messo neretourn a seba. Oun onseti a zeud metrekil durador squelo oun vonsa douentend dentac de naitre."

Jimmy looked at the paragraph and rummaged amongst the papers in his hand.

'Here it is. Look, the 'Soirce' is dead easy – *Ce soir*, tonight or this evening. Then 'keva' is *avec*, or with. 'Zeud glaisan al rega' is *deux anglais à la gare*. See how it takes the zed sound from *deux-anglais*, when the words are run together, then transplants that zed to the beginning of *Zeud*. The next bit is trickier but local knowledge tells us that 'durador' refers to the town of Le Dorat, here becoming Du Dorat – the station *of* Le Dorat, then semi-reversed into durador. So in all, 'This evening, with two Englishmen to the station at Le Dorat. I saw them place explosives on the railway lines, then we went back to base. We were two kilometers from Le Dorat when we heard the train crash.'

Sam looked down at the decoded French version of the original diary entry:

"Ce soir, avec deux anglais à la gare du Dorat. Je les ai vus placer des explosifs sur les rails de chemin de fer, puis nous sommes retournés à notre base. Nous étions à deux kilomètres du Dorat lorsque nous avons entendu l'accident de train."

Jimmy was very clever, no doubt.

Sam said, 'So what's the great secret in here? Why isn't it just a diary of life in the Resistance, of which there must be hundreds.'

'Well the whole diary was obviously secret to begin with. I'm guessing he didn't want it to be found and then read by the Nazis. The early stuff is obviously very private between him and his wife anyway. But when he starts writing in verlan it seems he has something really important to hide. I think you might want to talk to someone about this.'

'Who?'

'Someone who's most probably dead.'

THE MAN AT the door had a half-smile on his face and stood with his hands folded together before him. He wore a dark blazer with gold buttons, a white shirt and a plain blue tie. His black hair was short and curled at the temples. At first she thought he was probably a Jehovah's Witness or a Mormon, and she readied herself to close the door. Another man wearing a thin windcheater over a black t-shirt stood two steps behind him. He was younger and had blond hair but wore the same alert, faintly humorous expression on a face pocked with acne scars.

Laura said, 'Yes? What can I do for you?'

The man spoke with a light voice, his eyes never leaving her face.

'We're looking for Sam Dyke. Do we have the right address?'

'He lives here, yes, but he's not around at the moment. Who shall I tell him called?'

The man reached into his jacket pocket and brought out a wallet that he flashed in front of her.

He was about to put it back in his pocket when Laura said, 'Wait – let me see that again.'

The man smiled more broadly and handed over the wallet. Laura opened it and inspected the contents carefully, noting the man's name, then passed it back.

'He's not here, Mr Steele. In fact I don't know where he is.'

'You don't mind if we look, do you?'

'Don't you believe me?'

The man said nothing but stepped forward so forcibly that Laura had to move backwards or be knocked over. The other man slipped by her too, turning sideways so as not to touch her. She followed them inside but left the door open.

The man was now in the small sitting room, looking around at the furniture as though he'd never seen anything so strange before. He went and looked over the back of the flat-screen television, then sat on the cream two-seater sofa, testing its degree of bounce. Then he stood up and glanced briefly at the books on Sam's minimalist bookshelves.

'Not much of a reader, eh? More your man of action type. Leaping to the defence of endangered females, that kind of thing.'

Laura found that her arms were crossed. The men had brought a musty smell into the room and she sensed that her face was curling into a sneer.

She said, 'I don't get involved in his work.'

The man glanced at her, then looked at his companion.

'Have a look upstairs, there's a good 'un.'

The other man left the room and she heard his steps going up the stairs and then moving around overhead.

The first man said, 'He's a good lad. He won't make too much of a mess.'

'So are you going to tell me what this is about?'

'You mean Sam didn't say? Very remiss of him. Well he seems to have got himself involved in something he shouldn't have. Something above his pay grade, as I think people say nowadays.'

'I have no idea what you're talking about.'

The man looked down and shook his head sadly.

'Please, Laura, don't be such a cliché.'

She stared at him, wondering how he knew her name.

SHEPHERD'S VOICE SOUNDED worse than usual to Blake and he was glad that he hadn't needed to meet him in person again. The last thing he wanted was to pass on any infections to his children.

Shepherd was droning on about the interesting mix of standard French and patois that he'd found in the pages Blake had sent him, not to mention, of course, the variation of verlan, which was very enterprising and not easy to understand.

'It's rare to find such a condensed version. Usually it's only spoken so to find it written down is unusual to say the least.'

Blake cut him short.

'I daresay it's a wonderful addition to the research. Now just tell me what the fuck it says. In short form.'

There was a silence at the other end that Blake would have categorised as angry – if he'd have cared. Finally, Shepherd began.

'The pages you sent me appear to be from a diary kept by a member of the French Resistance in the second war. It's not a typical diary, though, because it's addressed directly to his wife or girlfriend, Julienne. In fact, it's in the form of a series of letters, each of them dated and signed, but kept within the confines, it appears, of one book. To that extent, it's almost like an epistolary novel.'

'Please don't trace its history to Richardson or discuss the influence of Smollett. The facts, Shepherd.'

'The majority of the pages that you sent me were, as I pointed out, presented in a written form of verlan. In fact, the author makes up a good deal of the language as he goes. He writes as much as he can in a form that's not easily translated. Someone fluent in French at the time might have been able to decode it, but I'm guessing that the author was simply doing the best he could to emphasize to his wife or girlfriend the secrecy surrounding the events.'

'You're trying my patience, Shepherd.'

'The crux of the matter is that the author is part of a group of Resistance fighters operating in the Vienne region of France, east of Poitiers. When he shifts into verlan it's because of the arrival of a group of British SAS troopers who parachuted into the area on and around D-Day – the sixth of June, nineteen forty-four.'

'Jesus Christ.'

'Yes, I daresay you knew that. The British have arrived with the specific remit of hindering Nazi support to their troops in Normandy after the Allied invasion. Our author is somewhat stunned by the glamour of the Brits – they're mostly young, athletic, and they've landed with a number of armoured jeeps in which they race around the countryside.'

'Shepherd, I know all this. What else is there?'

There was another pause filled by the sound of Shepherd's breathing.

'I can hardly be expected to know what's important to you when you've given me no parameters at all within which to work.'

Blake gripped his telephone more tightly.

'Point taken. Please continue.'

Shepherd cleared his throat.

'There is an event that produces the most intense writing from our author. The SAS troopers have been hiding in the woods near Poitiers for about a month when they are attacked by a unit of German soldiers. Some of his fellow Resistance fighters are killed but he, along with several others, escape. They regroup with the SAS in another part of the forest, as Shakespeare would have said, and then they scatter again.'

'All this is known, Shepherd. It was called Operation Bulbasket. The British soldiers were later caught, executed and buried elsewhere. There's something missing. Something you've not said.'

'Well, perhaps. Our author was extremely friendly with one of the SAS soldiers, a man called Leftwich. A couple of days before the attack in the forest, Leftwich had given our author a letter to post to his own wife, should that become possible. Along with the letter he gave our author, Jean-Claude, some papers to send along with it.'

Blake sat up and felt his breathing grow shallow.

'What was the nature of these papers?'

'Actually a lot of it was personal material that he seemed to be returning to her – letters that she'd written to him, pictures of her, a photograph of his home and parents.'

'Is that all?'

'You may think that doesn't sound like much, but our author was so anxious that he went into great detail in describing the material. It appears that one of the letters that Leftwich's wife had sent him before he came on this mission was written on the back of a printed document.'

'What kind of document?'

'How on earth do I know? Our author describes how Leftwich spoke to him about it. He emphasizes its value because it came from his wife. But also, the information on the other side was important too.'

'Good god, man, what did it say?'

'Our author didn't know, of course. It was written in English.'

'Damnit!'

'But he knew it mentioned Istanbul.'

It seemed to Blake as though the world around him had suddenly become insubstantial and that he had no purchase on it. As a result, he felt the telephone handset fall from his grip and heard it clatter on his desk.

THE MAN TOOK a step towards her. He was slightly taller and looked down into her face, his hands now clasped behind his back. Laura was not often intimidated, but there was something about the restraint of this man that was frightening. He seemed to be having trouble containing his urge to be violent towards her. She felt herself trembling but stood her ground as he stared at her.

Eventually he said, 'I don't know whether you know anything or not. I can't tell. But when Sammy gets home, tell him we're on to him now. I don't know why he got himself tangled up in all this, but I've got a lump on the back of my head that I didn't have yesterday morning, and because of that I'm taking him very seriously.'

'I'd like you to leave.'

'I daresay you would. After a while I'm never welcome anywhere. It's part of my charm.' He leaned closer. 'Make sure he gets the message: keep out, give it up, drop it. It's not good for his health.'

'Who are you people? What are you after?'

The man called Steele looked as though he were about to become philosophical; his pale eyes became distant and a little vague. His small mouth pursed.

'That's a very good question, Laura, that has a good deal of politics built into it. Who are we? We're agents of the state's repressive apparatus. We're fully aware of that fact but we salve our consciences by taking money which we then use to live on. Exchange of labour. "What we're after" is a different question, of course. Defence of the realm, yes. Job satisfaction, yes. Personal salvation too, for all I know. My young colleague would probably see that as an impertinence, but he's young and doesn't understand himself yet.'

'Actually you're a thug. A thug who's read a book. A self-taught thug. Always the worse because they give themselves airs and consider themselves a cut above the rest.'

Steele tilted his head to one side, acknowledging her point of view.

'You make a good case. I do consider myself a cut above the middle-class drones, like yourself, who think that eating well, seeing the right films and reading the right books entitles you to look the other way while the fabric of society is chewed away by people who don't give a shit about it. I don't know what life's like for you. But I've seen what it's like when all this so-called culture is stripped away, leaving nothing but primitive theology and poisoned wells. The things you call culture don't have any meaning when you're on the raw edge. But I don't want my country to live on that edge, any more than you do. So I'll do what I'm asked to do so long as I can preserve my dignity in doing it.'

'Even if that means scaring women and acting like an uncivilised creature yourself?'

Steele put his hand to his heart.

'Oh, the wound. I've been called worse, and by better people than you. They were so much better they were actually able to deprive me of a living, at least temporarily.' He sighed. 'But my employment history is none of your business. Forget I mentioned it.'

The younger man came into the room.

'Nothing. The diary's not here.'

'Of course it isn't. There's nothing here, is there, darling? All gone, packed away.'

He gestured for the other man to leave and he did so.

Then he seized Laura by the elbow.

'I'm a patient man by training and disposition. But I don't like being fucked around with. And your man is fucking around with me. I'm willing to concede he didn't know what he was getting into but now he's got to get out. We know what he's got and I'm betting that he knows what we've got. But I don't care. This isn't his game, nor the girl's. And if he doesn't get out right now, there will be consequences. For him, for you, for the whole of this fucking street for all I care. Got it?'

Laura looked up at the man's grimacing face. His eyes were round and red in their corners and he hadn't shaved well that morning. His teeth were slightly yellow,

She said coldly, 'Get out of the house, you arrogant shit.'

The man continued to stare at her, then the half-smile returned to his face.

'Good. You've got it. I know you'll pass on the message because you're so scared now you can barely breathe. That's how I want you to stay. Scared breathless. Then Sammy might begin to understand.'

He turned and left the room.

Laura felt a tightness in her chest. She clutched her stomach and forced herself to take two long breaths, then followed the man outside.

As she arrived at the front door she saw Steele's retreating back and, at the end of the path, the other man talking to Sam's son, Dan. There was an angry exchange and she started to run down the path. Dan was eighteen and had for many years taken Tae-Kwon-Do classes, and considered himself able to win a fight when necessary.

'Dan – it's OK ... '

But she saw Dan begin one of his classic moves, stepping back in order to swivel on one leg, his weight transferring quickly back to the airborne foot as it approached the other man's head ...

Then the man dropped to a crouch and quickly punched Dan in the upper thigh. Dan fell over, clutching his leg.

The two men walked down the road and climbed into a large black car.

SAM WAS FINDING that Chantal Bressette was not as easy to read as he had thought. Without any evidence, he'd thought that she would be malleable and susceptible to his warnings and advice. Clearly she'd had no experience of dealing with dangerous people, but she was proving difficult to persuade. While it was true that her stubbornness might have been a sign of her naivety, he had to admit that her unwillingness to give up was admirable. She had the air of someone who was used to seeing things through and wasn't easily diverted.

They had left Jimmy's five minutes ago and were still driving through the Cheshire countryside, heading home. He had tried to convince her that visiting the woman whom Jimmy had mentioned was crazy – they didn't even know where she was, for one thing, or even whether she was still alive. She would have to be well over eighty, and while that wasn't exactly decrepit these days, there was a high possibility that she might have died. But Chantal was unmoved.

'I have to try. The diary is the only connection I have to my family and its history. Perhaps you don't know what that's like. It's the only thing that gives me any ... solidity. And the diary seems to be important in other ways, too. Don't you get that?'

'If I were you I'd be tempted to take it to the papers and let them carry the weight. Once it's in the public domain there's nothing those other guys would be able to do about it.'

This seemed to have raised her temperature. She looked at him as he drove, sighing from time to time.

Finally she said, 'I don't understand why people are trying to take the diary from me. What if it contains state secrets or something? Then the press wouldn't print it and it would all be brushed under the carpet. Whatever "it" is. I've got to follow this up myself. If you want to help, then great.' She paused and her tone changed. 'Especially as all this work seems to be a free offer.'

Sam glanced at her in the passenger seat, her hair blown back and her round eyes smiling at him.

He said, 'Cheeky bugger,' and they both laughed.

His mobile phone rang in its cradle on the dashboard.

'Will you answer that? I don't like talking while I'm driving.'

Chantal took the phone and pressed the key to answer. After a moment she removed it from her ear.

'It's Laura. Something's happened.'

'What?'

'Two men have been to see her.'

Sam slowed down and stopped the car, switching on his emergency lights and taking the phone from her outstretched hand. He felt his pulse-rate quicken, as though a dial connected to his chest had been rapidly turned up.

'Laura? What happened?'

'A man called Steele visited me. He and a younger man searched the house.'

'How? ... Why did you let them in?'

'Don't shout, Sam. He showed me an identity card, or at any rate something official from the Ministry of Defence. That's what it looked like, anyway. An official badge with his name.'

'Describe him.'

Laura did so.

'He said he had a lump on the back of his head because of you. He was very threatening.'

Sam opened the car door and climbed out. He had suddenly felt caged in and needed to move around.

'I'm sorry. This means they've found out who I am.' He stopped and pulled the phone from his ear to stare at it. Then he spoke into it again. 'Go to the coffee shop where we had lunch two weeks ago. Is Dan with you?'

'Yes.'

'Take him too. And bring the envelope under the carpet in the wardrobe.'

'That's – '

'I know what it is. I may need some protection. Don't say anything else, just go.'

He terminated the call then switched off the phone completely. No point in making their tracking easier than necessary.

Chantal had climbed out of the car and approached him. The wind on the open road blew the fringe of her pale brown hair into her face and she raised a slim hand to push it back. Sam thought at that moment she looked very young.

She said, 'Is everything okay?'

Sam fought the riot of feelings that seemed to be swarming through his body, tightening his chest and placing an iron band around his forehead. For a moment he was barely conscious that she had spoken.

Then he forced himself to inhale deeply and let the air out on a count of ten. He repeated the process and found he was thinking clearly again.

He said, 'Change of plans. They've found out who I am and they're probably tracking us.'

'How could they have done that?'

Sam took her arm, as thin as a child's, and led her back to the car.

'You phoned me, remember? If they were following you they would have had your number and been able to track anyone you phoned.'

'So what do we do?'

'They've threatened the people I love. That means anything I do now is fair game.'

The roar of the engine starting again drowned out Chantal's next speech. She flinched, surprised by the venom revealed in the way he pressed down on the accelerator, then repeated it.

'I heard you talking to Laura about "protection". Have you got a gun?'

Sam released the clutch and the car shot forward.

'Worse. Much worse.'

IT WAS HALF an hour since the woman and boy had left, and Angel felt certain that they weren't coming back for a while. They had taken bags and had left in haste.

He eased himself out of the Passat's low-riding front seat and walked up to the house. He knocked once to make sure there was no one else inside that he hadn't seen, then moved to the side and walked down the length of the house to the rear. Fortunately the house was largely concealed from neighbours by tall poplars and the back garden ran down through more trees to fields beyond. No one could see him.

He glanced at the pond and wondered why people forced captivity on to creatures that were perfectly happy in rivers and lakes.

The back door was wooden-framed and although it had a Yale lock, that would be no problem. He took out his bump key and his long knife. He inserted the bump key into the lock, pulled it back one notch and exerted a little torque, then hit the end of the key with the knife-grip. The force of the blow knocked the pins of the lock upwards and the torque pressure on the cylinder ensured that the key turned in the lock. He opened the door and took out the key. It had taken less than four seconds for him to get inside.

He closed the door behind him then stood and listened. The house resonated with that recently-vacated hush, as though doors were still settling against their jambs and floorboards were rising again after being trodden down. He had come into the kitchen and the refrigerator suddenly rattled as its motor turned off and bottles inside the door jostled each other.

Angel put his key and knife back inside his jacket and went out of the kitchen and up the stairs. There was a faint smell of pine cleanser as he passed the open bathroom door and found the main bedroom. Either side of the bed were two tables which he quickly searched – some jewellery on her side and a broken watch on his. The wardrobe contained mostly skirts and blouses of a professional cut; evidently the woman kept work-clothes here and more leisure clothing at her own house. In a chest of drawers he found plain black tee-shirts and a couple of sweaters, along with some folded blue jeans. Dyke's wardrobe was quite limited. Angel never understood why men didn't take more interest in their clothing.

In the top right hand drawer of the chest was a green box. Angel opened it. Nothing but papers – a birth certificate, driving insurance, MOT certificate for a Mondeo estate car.

He put the papers back in the box and the box back in the drawer and closed it, then stood by the end of the bed and looked around the room. He took its measure slowly, looking at angles, seeking out disjunctions. He hadn't missed anything. There was no safe, no secret drawer. It was probable that Dyke didn't keep anything at home. More likely to be in his office in Crewe.

For the sake of form Angel searched the other bedroom, apparently used by the boy. Some books and computer magazines, underwear and other clothing. A nice pair of shoes that Angel admired momentarily.

Downstairs he went through a small bookcase in the lounge, opening each book carefully and tipping it out. One yellow newsprint clipping about the miners' strike in 1984 fell out of a copy of Birdsong and floated to the floor. He replaced it and filed the book carefully back whence it had come.

In the kitchen he went through all the cabinets and the drawers, lifting the drawer lining – more newspaper – and looking carefully underneath.

Nothing.

Although he had seen that Steele and his colleague had not been inside very long, they seemed to have had the same result. Their belligerent strides as they had walked to the Touareg had suggested that they'd learned nothing.

That was good. His brief was to follow and to clean up. To check that nothing was missed.

And if it had been, he had been told specifically to ensure that it didn't lead to any unpleasantness later on. To ensure that, he had *carte blanche*.

SAM PARKED BEHIND the library in Nantwich and guided Chantal out of the busy car park and past the ornate Norman church that looked over the town square. Most Saturdays it was crowded with wedding guests in their Cheshire finery, seeing off some dashing young couple in a 1920s open-top car. Today it was locked up and forbidding.

In the square a tent had been set up and a jazz-band was playing for the shoppers and tourists who stood and watched or ambled past. 'When the Saints go marching in' drifted towards Sam and Chantal on the breeze.

Just beyond the doors of the church a narrow path led pedestrians on a back route out of the town centre. On the right were two coffee shops, and Sam shepherded Chantal into the second of these, a Costa Coffee.

Up the short flight of stairs at the back they saw Laura and Dan waiting. Laura's expression combined anxiety, fear and defiance, as though she had single-handedly seen off a horde of rampaging lions. Dan was thin with straight lank hair that fell over his eyes; he looked expectant and a little excited. He spoke as soon as Sam and Chantal drew up chairs.

'Bastard caught me a cheap shot. I'll have him next time.'

Sam ignored him and reached for Laura's hand.

'I'm sorry. I didn't think they knew who I was. I would have been more careful.'

Laura withdrew her hand carefully, a rebuff but contained in its anger.

'"Would have" isn't good enough, Sam. I was scared and I didn't know where you were and I couldn't have told him anything even if I wanted to.'

Chantal shifted in her chair.

'He's a creepy man. I don't blame you for being scared.'

'You know him?'

'He tried to ... he tried to take something from me last night, in Edinburgh. That's how Sam came across me.'

Sam had given Laura an edited version of the previous night's events to minimize her concern. She had in the last few months begun to express indifference towards his work as a way of protecting herself, and Sam had begun to censor the things he told her. Now he wondered whether that was a good strategy if it meant she remained ignorant of any danger.

Laura said, 'I see.'

She didn't seem inclined to pursue the story any further, and a silence fell between the four of them as though they'd each been asked to reflect on what had been said so far.

Eventually Laura bent down and lifted a black roll-bag on to the table.

'I didn't know whether you'd need more stuff, so I've brought some clothes.'

'How did you know I'd be going away?'

'Oh come on, Sam. If the bad guys are visiting you at home then you're hardly going to go back there. I'm taking Dan to Abigail's in Matlock. We should be out of the way there. I can work from her office for a few days, anyway.'

Dan said, 'What if I don't want to go?'

To avert an argument, Sam pointed at Dan's rucksack.

'Is that your laptop?'

'Of course.'

'Can you connect from here? Have they got wifi?'

Dan said that they had and began to start up the shiny black computer. As it booted up, Sam told him what he wanted him to research.

Dan said, 'No problem. Take a few minutes to get into the right databases but it's mostly public knowledge.'

Sam reached into the roll-bag and pulled out two passports. He opened them to check which was which. One was for him and one was Laura's. He gazed a while at Laura's photograph inside the back cover.

She said, 'Why did you want mine?'

'Something you said last night.'

Laura began to shake her head. 'Oh no, Sam, I can't let you do that.'

'You said it yourself. Look at the similarity.'

'I'm not getting in trouble just to satisfy one of your crusades.'

Chantal had been watching them with growing incomprehension.

'What's going on? What are you talking about?'

Laura seized her passport from Sam and flicked to the back, showing Chantal her photograph.

'He wants to use my passport for you if you have to go abroad.'

They saw the understanding flicker in her eyes.

'These are the weapons you talked about, aren't they? Never mind guns. You're more dangerous to them if you know what's going on, so you're going to find out.'

'Knowledge is power.'

'But it's crazy. We don't even look that much alike.'

Sam began to feel he was fighting on two fronts, which irritated him. He said, 'We'll change your hair colour first and do whatever else we need to do. More make-up. The passport photo shows Laura without any make-up, so if we beef up your lipstick and give you some eye-shadow you'll be close enough.'

Laura shook her head.

'I'm not having it, Sam. Why take the risk? Why can't Chantal here just go and get her own passport?'

'Jesus, I'm doing all the thinking here, aren't I?'

'Don't get angry.'

'Look, first of all they might be watching her house. Secondly, her name might set off an alarm at UK Border Control.'

'So might yours, now.'

'If I were using my own passport, yes.'

He opened it to the first page so they could see it contained a different name. Laura let out a sigh.

'You could just not go. Wait it out. Let all this fuss die down.'

'Do you want another visit from Mr Steele when I'm not there?'

The argument fell heavily across Laura's face and she flinched.

She said, 'It won't work. You're just being stubborn. You can't go around smuggling people out of the country.'

Sam stared hard at her, then came to a decision.

'Okay. You're right. It was stupid. We'll have to find another way.'

He lifted the roll-bag from the table and dropped the passports into its open top.

Chantal said, 'As we're here, can I buy a coffee?'

Sam turned to her as though he'd forgotten she was there.

'A one-shot medium latte with vanilla.'

Chantal turned to Laura who shook her head. Dan was still engrossed in the laptop. Chantal rose from the table and walked carefully to the serving counter as though trying not to draw attention to herself. Laura watched her go, concern etched in the corner of her eyes.

She said, 'What the hell's going on?'

'Do you think I should leave her to the wolves? You've seen Steele. I've seen what he's capable of.'

'Then take it to the police. Let them deal with it. You've always got a cause on your hands. It's wearing me out.'

Sam felt his heart harden almost like a physical tightening in his chest. They were nearing an argument that he had sensed was coming for some weeks.

'I can't help that. If these people are flashing MOD badges then going to the police will mean nothing. It might make it worse. Anyway, what would we say? It's all hint and suggestion. If we named Steele you can bet your bottom dollar he's protected in some way. The fact that he's come after me through you tells me he can pretty well do what he wants. The fact he beat up Chantal's boyfriend as badly as he did suggests he's one of the brutes they use from time to time to do their unofficial work. He'll probably be ex-forces with a protector of some sort.'

'How can you know that?'

'When I searched him last night he didn't have any official markings, just a fake identity. But he showed you his military ID with his name on it. That means he's willing to come out and play now. He's on a mission and whatever it is he'll be under instructions to complete it.'

Laura's face had suddenly grown wan and she looked on the verge of tears. Sam reflected that he hated talking to her like this but sometimes a dose of the reality in which he worked seemed the only way to influence civilians' thinking.

Laura took a handkerchief from her handbag and wiped her nose.

'You can be pretty horrible sometimes.'

'Your mother must have told you there'd be days like this.'

She shot him a look.

'Bad timing, Sam. Don't joke.'

As though he'd been waiting for this cue, Dan looked up from his laptop and pulled down his right arm with his hand in a fist.

'Yes!'

Sam moved his chair to look at the screen.

He said, 'That's her.'

BLAKE MADE HIMSELF comfortable in one of the new offices surrounding the atrium of Portcullis House, the addition to the Houses of Parliament which had been built to accommodate an ever-increasing government bureaucracy. The walls of the office looked like they were constructed of separate slabs of pale plasterboard, while the door and the two floor-high cabinets either side of it seemed to have been cheaply laminated with a pale wood substitute. Doubtless it was an attempt to mimic the panelled splendour of the Chambers of Parliament ... but it just looked cheap.

Blake reflected that these token genuflections to the past were becoming more common. They called it postmodernism in architecture – the ability to pick and choose from the past's motifs – but to him it looked like second-rate copying by professionals incapable of an original thought.

The light was beginning to fade outside and he felt a tiredness suffuse his limbs. He'd spent all day in town today and was wearying of the atmosphere. He needed to get back to the country, and home.

The door opened and Walter Lashbrooke came in. He was tall and commonly described as 'distinguished' because of his slowly-greying hair. He wore his usual dark suit and fiery blue tie, secured to his shirt with a gold tie-pin.

'The others will be along shortly, Gideon.'

'I have fifteen minutes, that's all.'

Lashbrooke raised his eyebrows infinitesimally.

'I'd prefer if you gave this meeting – and others like it – a fraction more weight.'

'Don't try to frighten me, Walter. You and I both know what this is about.'

'Do we?'

Blake opened his arms expansively.

'It's the trainer and his pals dropping by the stables to check the horse is in fine fettle. You'll be opening my mouth to check my teeth soon.'

'You always had a way with words, Gideon. It's one of the reasons you came to our attention.'

'Ah, so it wasn't my daring policy suggestions and fiery commitment to the party's doctrine?'

Lashbrooke ignored this and turned back to the door as though he had heard someone approaching. Blake had liked him since they had first met fifteen years ago, but he had to admit that the old man's politicking wasn't particularly subtle in this modern age. When Lashbrooke and the others had first approached him, Blake had been struck by their energy and decisiveness. Since then they had all grown fat on their constituents' favour and the purpose had drained from them like blood seeping from the maws of the strung-up geese slaughtered on his father's estate when he was young.

The group of his supporters – could he call them a cabal? – was now similarly enervated, but presumably gathering their forces for this last push: the ascension of one of their acolytes to the leadership of a great Office of State.

There was a sharp knock on the door and Strutt came in, carrying a plastic bag. He had lately developed a hump that seemed to ride on top of his shoulders and forced his neck downwards so that he was compelled to look up at you. It gave him the appearance of an elderly Uriah Heep, though his manner was anything but meek.

'Blake, Lashbrooke. Am I late? Where are the other buggers?'

'Sit down, George. You're not late.'

'Buggers always keep me waiting. Is there a kettle in here?'

Blake pointed him towards a side-table on which stood a tray with a kettle and several plain white cups. Blake suspected that if he turned them over they'd be 'branded' with a portcullis. Anything to make money.

Strutt went to the kettle and opened it to check for water, then switched it on. He placed his plastic bag on the round table in the middle of the room and rooted inside for a moment. He pulled out a box of tea in triumph.

'Rooibos. My brother put me on to it. Calms you down, stops you being irritable. Good for the bones, too. Anyone else ... ?'

Blake and Lashbrooke shook their heads and watched as Strutt made his tea. Finally he lifted the cup to his lips and sipped with pursed lips. He turned a sharp eye on Blake.

'When the other buggers come, Blake, we need to get down to some serious planning. It's Saturday today and the announcement's going to be made a week on Monday. We need everything in place before then. When you walk into that fucking Lego building they call the Home Office, you need to be sprinting.'

Lashbrooke raised an arm in exasperation.

'George, for Christ's sake hang on till everyone's here, can't you? It's no good going on at Gideon before we start.'

'Well those buggers should get a move on. I haven't got all day. Miriam's waiting for me downstairs – I promised I'd take her to the Ritz tonight, she wants to dance to that new music thing they have. I may have to get drunk first so let's get a move on.'

The door to the office opened abruptly and two more men came in. One was bald with two silvery tufts above his ears while the other had long fair hair of which he was notably proud and constantly brushed with the palm of his hand. Looks were deceptive, however, as the bald man was the younger of the two by five years.

Strutt raised his tea cup.

'Glad you buggers could make it. We're about to go home.'

The bald man, who was called Mcclair, grinned.

'Fuck off, George. You wouldn't miss a party for the world.'

Lashbrooke raised his hands again. Blake noticed how in later years he had become the moderator of the group rather than its driving force, as he had been at the beginning.

'Children, bicker ye not. Sit down for Christ's sake and let's get this over with.'

Eyett, the man with the blond hair, pulled out one of the faux-leather seats and sat next to Blake. Close up, the lines on his face revealed themselves like the canals of Mars seen through a telescope – pervasive, pocked and impossibly ancient. He smiled grimly at Blake and his face became like a death's head, gaunt and hollow-eyed.

'Well young man, are you up to it? I've been reading how you're the coming man. Everyone says so. And Fleet Street is agog to know whether their predictions are true – are you really going to replace the once-noble Ledyard now that his star has so mightily fallen? What do you think? Do you have the balls for it?'

Blake trod carefully.

'I'm as ready as it's possible to be. You've been supporting me all this time – what do you think?'

'What I think is neither here nor there, is it? It's whether you've got the gumption to make the changes we've been talking about lo, these many years. This is the sticking point to which you've got to screw your courage.'

Mcclair threw up his hands.

'There he goes again, mangling Shakespeare to make a drab rhetorical point. Listen, Blake, we know you won't screw up. Whatever the timescale is, you'll get things done. Given where we are in the election cycle we have a maximum of four years to get some results. We'll support you in the House, but you've got to do the pushing. Once your feet are under the table, so to speak, you've got to get the PM onside. Beef up Defence. Relax that ethical trading bullshit ...'

Blake raised his hand.

'I know the agenda. Don't patronise me. I know to whom I owe my success, and I won't forget. Now, I believe you had some other points you wanted to make.'

Lashbrooke steepled his hands.

'Gideon, we're now at a point where things are serious. While you've been Minister responsible for the Armed Forces you've been more-or-less under the radar as far as the media have been concerned. That will all change the week after next.'

'Walter, I have another meeting in ten minutes' time.'

Eyett leaned across and seized Blake's wrist with a liver-spotted hand.

'Don't be disdainful, Blake. Listen to your elders and betters. This is the endgame here and we will not be denied.'

Unnerved, Blake pulled his wrist from Eyett's grip. He looked at the men in turn and was surprised by the intensity in their eyes. No, not a cabal ... maybe a cult.

'Say what you have to say.'

Mcclair took up the challenge, his slight Scottish accent offering a softer tone to the conversation.

'As Walter has said, more eyes are going to be on you now. Already the profile pieces are beginning to appear in the papers, and so far you're coming across well. Family man, years of service, beautiful wife and two adorable children ... '

'If you only knew.'

'But you know how the press operates. They'll give you a chance. A very brief chance. They'll sit on their poisonous quills and watch for a while, waiting for the first fuck-up. And then they'll go into attack mode. It's what's done for Ledyard in the first place.'

The current Secretary of Defence had been found to have fathered a child when a student, and while it appeared that he had been ignorant of the girl's existence, the press had focused on his hardline approach to family values while apparently being free with his own oats. He had offered his resignation, which the PM was considering. In a week's time that consideration would end with him accepting the resignation and appointing the safe pair of hands that was Gideon Blake.

Strutt placed his empty cup on the table and they all turned to him. To Blake it was as though they constituted one mythical multi-headed beast, with leadership being passed between the heads depending on whim.

'We're talking about the past, Blake. We've known you for fifteen years and I think I can speak for all of these buggers when I say that we know you better than you know yourself. We were there at the christening of your children, when you made your first speech in the House, when you were given your first post. But you have a hinterland, Blake. That period before we knew you and before you stood in your constituency.'

He rapped his cup loudly on the table.

'So we need guarantees.'

'I've told you I understand my obligations– '

'Not those kind of guarantees. We're taking it as read that you'll remember your obligations. I'm talking about your past, dammit. We need to know that there's nothing in your past that will come back to haunt us. Nothing that can be dug up by some grovelling cloth-capped grubber. Nothing that will embarrass you or, by extension, us.'

Blake sat upright in his chair, feeling anger stirring in his lower stomach. It was a long time since he'd been spoken to in this manner and he decided that he didn't like it. But he pushed the anger down and forced a lazy smile to break over his features.

'Gentlemen, I understand your concerns. Truly, I do. My wife tells me that my intuition is one of my strongest points, and if I'm not mistaken you're wondering whether I have any skeletons in my closet.'

'Or your father's, or your father's father's.'

Blake took this worst of all possible insults on the chin and blinked slightly, as though a butterfly had paddled across his eyelids.

'There are no skeletons. No hidden secrets. No illegitimate children or wife-beating forebears. No slaveholders, fornicators, gamblers or thieves. For all I know one of my ancestors might have thought himself a cut above the rest, but I'm willing to forgive him his arrogance because it's what built the Empire, isn't it?'

He looked around the room at the serious, misguided faces that were earnestly searching through his words for their meaning. He rose and their faces turned upwards like flowers to the sun.

'Gentlemen, thank you for reminding me of my obligations. I'm sure we won't see as much of each other as we have done, once the announcement is made. But be sure you'll be in my thoughts as I go about my work. Good day.'

He knew they were watching as he walked around the table and left.

And he was surprised to realise that for the first time in fifteen years, he didn't care what they thought.

SAM FOUND HER sitting at a table in the bar. She looked as tired as he felt, her sandy hair shapeless and her eyes rimmed with red. That afternoon they had driven for three hours until finding a Premier Inn south of Oxford. They had booked separate rooms and he had taken the opportunity to shower before coming downstairs. He was hungry and wanted a drink and wasn't in much of a mood to babysit anyone tonight.

He saw that she didn't have a drink.

'Want anything from the bar?'

'White wine. Something dry.'

Sam went to the bar and ordered, asking for a Guinness for himself.

When he sat facing Chantal, placing her wine carefully on the table, she continued to stare through the window at the car park outside. She appeared disconnected from him, as though a story that she didn't understand was spooling through her head.

He said, 'Tell me about Jack.'

She looked at him, startled.

'What?'

'You've barely talked about him all this time. You must be worried.'

'I haven't talked about him because I don't *want* to talk about him. How do you think I feel?'

Sam sipped his drink and leaned back in his chair.

'It's not your fault. You don't have to feel guilty. Guilt isn't a useful emotion because it just makes you feel bad and doesn't inspire you towards action.'

The words seemed to irritate her, as though he could have little understanding of her situation. He realised that she was probably right but that he had an obligation to ask, if only to establish where the focus of her attention lay.

She said, 'Why shouldn't I feel guilty? I'm the one who put him in danger, aren't I? Poor thing didn't know this was going to happen to him.'

Sam ignored her pessimism. 'How did you meet?'

Chantal seemed as though she was going to continue the thread of her argument but caught herself. He wondered if she had realised what he was doing and had decided to go along with it. She leaned back and picked up her drink, looking at him over the rim of the glass.

'At work. We joined the company within a day of each other so we were both newbies together.'

'What's work?'

'Design. Being creative with computer programmes. Making adverts or brochures or web-sites ... whatever the client wants.'

'Sounds interesting.'

'Says the guy with the cool job. No, we just sit and stare at computer monitors all day, passing a bit of banter back and forth.' She stopped and looked away. 'Do you think I should have been to see him?'

Sam thought they were getting to it now – the shoulds and the oughts. Clients often wanted advice about their actions, though he was singularly unequipped to give it.

'It's risky. We don't know where Steele is. He might be watching the hospital to see if you show up. Or he might be watching your place to see if you go there. Or both.'

He had said this to her before but she seemed to want it confirming. Abruptly she turned to face him directly and leaned across the table.

'So come on, who are these people? You must have been thinking about this, getting that detective brain ticking over.'

'Best guess?'

'If that's all you have.'

'It's some kind of unit working with MOD supervision.'

'What the hell does that mean? The Ministry of Defence? Why are *they* involved?'

'Come on, the diary is full of information about the Second World War. Maybe there's something in there that they don't want us to know about.'

'You've read Jimmy's translations as well as I have. It's more of a gigantic love letter than anything containing international secrets.'

'There must be more. We've only read part of the whole thing.'

Her voice grew more intense, almost harsh, and Sam saw that her grip on her wine glass had tightened.

'Will they still be following, Sam? Are we going to be looking over our shoulders all the time?'

'You need to calm down. We've lost them for the time being, and now we've all got new phones they shouldn't be able to tap into us for a while.'

He saw that his words were having little effect. Her mood in the last few hours had darkened and she'd become more and more insular. He knew he'd never been good at giving reassurance – he didn't seem to have the right touch. There was something cool and rational in his demeanour that suggested he wasn't taking problems seriously enough. Laura had told him he had low levels of emotional intelligence. She thought he'd be wounded by the observation but he wasn't. So, perversely, perhaps he'd proved her right ...

He had to try with Chantal, though. She seemed to be getting more wound up as the day progressed.

'How did they find out about the diary?'

Through force of will, Chantal brought her attention back into the room. She glanced around as though to remind herself where she was, like someone woken from a dream which had been fully absorbing.

'Can't we talk about something else? Football or politics or something ... dull.'

'I want to pin down who we're dealing with here. We can be
dull together later. In fact I'm rather hoping for it.'

She almost smiled.

'I was tidying my place about three weeks ago and I came across
the diary in a box. I hadn't thought about it for years. I didn't want
it anymore so I thought I'd see if it could be of any use. I looked up
the Imperial War Museum online. Just to see if you could offer
them stuff. It turned out there's a form you fill in for donations and
you can attach photos of what you're donating. So I did.'

'What happened?'

'Two weeks later I got a reply saying they might be interested
but they'd have to see it first. So I made an appointment and went
to see someone at the Museum in Manchester. Did you know they
had like a branch office there?'

'Yes. It's a bit more than an office.'

'Whatever. So this young oik looks at the diary, turns it over,
and asks if he can take some photocopies. I didn't trust him,
actually. Looked down his nose at me and he was only a bit older
than I was. La-di-dah accent, you know, Oxford or Cambridge. By
this time I was pretty fed up with him so I said no. He said they
didn't think they could take it anyway because it was in French
and bits of it were in a language that was unreadable.'

'The verlan.'

'Exactly. Well I thought it was strange because on their website
they said they're interested in personal records, diaries and so
forth. And I thought they'd probably be able to get it translated if
they wanted.'

Sam nodded. 'So you thought you'd get it translated for them.'

'I was pretty mad by now, and coincidentally my firm had been
asked to produce the marketing materials for the translators
conference in Edinburgh – you know, the banners, the posters, the
brochure and flyers. I'd had it swirling around in my head for a
month beforehand and knew all the dates and the venue. So I was
pissed off and wanted to prove to the guy that the diary was worth
keeping. I did a bit of research and found there was a man at the

conference who was going to give a paper on the difficulty of translating historical documents – perfect. I went up, persuaded them to let me in so I could talk to him and arranged to meet him the next day. Then Steele turned up with you in tow and it all went wrong.'

'Why didn't you just email or call the translator?'

'I did! He didn't reply to emails and I didn't have his phone number anyway. When I talked to him at the zoo that night it turned out he'd been away from his academic email, hidden away somewhere writing the paper he was going to present. His departmental secretary could have contacted him if absolutely necessary, but I wasn't to know that.'

Sam leaned back in his seat.

'So we can presume that someone in the Imperial War Museum passed on your original contact and it triggered something. But why didn't they just say, Yes, we'll have it, then take it off your hands? Why all this cloak-and-dagger stuff?'

'Actually, I probably made it pretty clear I wasn't happy about them having it.'

'How?'

'I told him I didn't like his attitude.'

Sam grinned.

'That must have endeared you.'

'And I accidentally knocked his plastic cup of coffee into his lap.' She grinned back at him. 'Accidents do happen, after all.'

SUNDAY

JAMES SAW THEM first.

He said, 'They're here,' nudging Steele's elbow with his own.

Steele looked up through the station café window. Clifford and Nate were not walking together but were heading in the same direction at the same pace. James leaned over and banged on the window.

Steele folded his newspaper.

'Jesus Christ. Let's do a song and dance while we're at it.'

Clifford and Nate had seen James and came into the brightly-lit space. Before either of them sat down, James handed Nate a phone and a credit card.

'Don't lose these, eh, there's a good lad.'

'Fuck off.'

The two men sat facing James and Steele and folded their hands on the table. Steele reflected that neither of them would offer an apology for their stupidity. That was a feature of the younger crews he came across these days – both a sense of entitlement and a lack of guilt or remorse. If he ever had to provide official evaluations of this bunch it would be towards the lower end of the scale.

'All right, let's get this out of the way. You two fucked up, didn't you? Clifford, you let enthusiasm get in the way of common-sense.

Nate, from what you told me it sounds like you underestimated the enemy.'

Nate spoke with a newly-acquired lisp. 'So they're "the enemy". Christ.'

Steele reached across the table and seized Nate's wrist.

'Listen, hotshot, as far as you and I are concerned, Sam and Miss Bressette are the enemy. They are to be defeated in whatever it is they're trying to do.'

'Which is what, exactly?'

Steele released Nate's arm.

'Irrelevant. We have our objectives, primary amongst which is to retrieve the asset.'

Clifford was pulling the edge of a plaster that was draped across his nose. Finally it came away and he rolled it into a ball and flicked it under the table.

'We catch this guy, I'm first in line. He cold-cocked me.'

Nate said, 'Get in line behind me. I nearly bit my fucking tongue off.'

James grinned.

'Diddums – didn't he play fair?'

Clifford was unshaven and he didn't look as though he'd washed or combed his hair for a couple of days. He had spent Friday night in hospital having his nose pushed back into place, then released himself and hitch-hiked from Edinburgh to York, where he had met up with Nate on Saturday evening. They had stayed in a cheap hotel on Nate's expense money and Sunday morning Nate had bought some breakfast and the train tickets.

As with many men whose work involved physical effort, Clifford's sense of grievance was visible in the set of his shoulders and the deliberateness of his actions. He turned dark eyes on James.

'It was a fluke. He pushed me and I tripped. All right?'

James raised his hands. 'All right by me. Damned unlucky you were at the top of the stairs and his legs got tangled up with yours. That's all I'm saying.'

Steele rapped the edge of his newspaper on the table.

'Gentlemen ... this lovers' tiff can wait until we've completed our business. James, what do we know?'

'Last time I checked they seemed to have ditched their phones.'

'Dyke's smart. Any idea where he might be going? Family? Friends?'

'Doesn't seem likely, for either of them. His family is from Yorkshire originally. Father's dead, mother's in a home. His ex-wife is dead, too. We met his current girlfriend and his son. They appear to have moved out of the house. Probably afraid we'll pay them another visit. Miss Bressette doesn't appear to have any family still alive, at least in the UK.'

'OK. Then we may need some help.'

Steele stood and went outside, onto the platform. Several people were waiting for the next London train, looking both ways up the platform with that restlessness Steele associated with the world of work ... always something next on the agenda, always something needing to be done. The fact that it was Sunday didn't seem to matter. Perhaps a few less suits on view.

He took out his phone and called Gideon Blake, who answered on the second ring.

'I can give you three minutes. Where are you?'

'Crewe station. We know Dyke and Bressette are heading south but we don't know where.'

There was a pause that Steele thought was unusual. Blake was usually brusque and decisive. When he spoke again his voice was quiet.

'I think I know where they're going.'

Steele said nothing. There was now something agonised in Blake's voice, something uncertain.

'I hoped it wouldn't come to this. All these years it's what I've been trying to prevent.'

'Yes, sir.'

'I know it probably seems trivial to you, Steele, and all this effort I've asked you to put into retrieving a single object. But it's more than just the object. It's what it represents.'

'Sir – do you know where they're going? We ought to make a start...'

There was another pause, this time so long that Steele wondered whether he had lost the connection.

Then Blake said, 'I believe they're going to Hove to see my aunt.'

GIDEON BLAKE HAD recently discovered that he had habits. He had always thought that he was spontaneous, impulsive ... even instinctive. He didn't like to travel to work the same way twice. He wouldn't eat beef more than once a month. He left off deciding which tie to wear until the very last moment each morning. All of these behaviours, he had thought, meant that he was free-spirited and his own man, unwilling to be caught thinking the same way as others or following traditional patterns.

Lately, though, he'd realised that he found comfort in certain ways of doing things. He ate a biscuit in three bites. He liked his gin and tonic with four ice cubes. He did the Telegraph crossword every morning before nine o'clock.

Now, sitting at home waiting for Fiona to come back from her ride, he noticed that the fingers of his right hand were beating out a regular rhythm in sets of four on his right knee. He watched with interest and wondered where that had come from. Was it a sign that he was tense? He didn't feel it. Was it some innate musical aspiration that he'd never allowed to develop? It seemed unlikely: he could barely hit a triangle in time.

With an inward sigh he recognised that despite his best efforts, the events of the last week and of the next few days were probably beginning to take a toll. He had always appeared – and felt – languidly in control of whatever situation he found himself in. He was rarely fazed or caught unawares. He could handle surprises and reversals by simply changing his perspective. He had no need to 'act out' as they called it, to make others feel his anger or his displeasure. He would simply withdraw, re-think, then take corrective action. If people were hurt afterwards, so what. That was their look-out.

This business with the Bressette girl, though, was wearing him out. He'd thought it would be easy, that Steele would be able to deal with it quietly and return things to the status quo ante. It was his own fault. He had known something would blow up sooner or later. His aunt had told him years ago about the document and Lord knows he'd tried his best when younger to find it. Spending summer holidays in France, trudging round the tiny towns and villages where the SAS men had worked, trying to find old *maquisards* who would talk to him about the war.

But of course they wouldn't. There was a kind of silence, perhaps born from guilt or fear, amongst that older generation. It seemed that during the Occupation, some provincial French had taken the opportunity to extract revenge against old enemies and denounce them for spurious crimes, or claim they were engaged in Resistance activities when they were not. The memories of those times were still vivid for some. At any rate, his attempts to track down the document mentioned by his aunt had come to nothing. So he had sought other means of discovery. He had cultivated friends and allies in various government departments and in those institutions which were likely to come across secret wartime documents. He had developed a specific expertise to enable him to be a highly-qualified candidate for office in the Ministry of Defence, thus giving him more opportunity to find out should anything relevant be discovered.

And he had found ways and means of recruiting qualified people into teams that would work *sub rosa* for him, in the belief that they were carrying out official mandated operations. Everyone liked to be the carrier of a secret, so when told that what they did couldn't be revealed to anyone, it only made them more dedicated to the cause. Hiring them through the security firm of which he was a non-executive director simplified matters, of course, while his official status meant that he could grease some wheels from time to time by getting accreditations and documentation to give Steele and his various teams easier access.

Now his political and his personal ambitions were beginning to coincide. He was close to finding the document, he knew it; and he was close to assuming control of one of the great Offices of State. He felt a small trickle of anticipation laced with fear spike his gut – what were the implications for him? What were the dangers? What would be the rewards? What–

'Are you still here?'

Blake opened his eyes. Fiona had finally returned, her pale skin slightly moist from her exertions. She wore pale riding pants and a thick woollen high-neck pullover. Her hair was pulled as usual into a chignon that sat on the back of her head like an explosion that had been caught and expertly tied down.

Blake looked up deliberately and with an act of will stopped his right hand from drumming out its pattern. He caught the faint scent of stable that Fiona had brought in with her, the inelegant mix of excrement and straw.

'I have to go away for a short while.'

'But the announcement is a week tomorrow.'

'Tell me something I don't know. It can't be helped.'

'Is it the Bressette girl? I thought you had Steele working on it. That little shit is a little shit, but he gets things done.'

Blake filled with admiration for her. It had been a risk three years ago to take her fully into his confidence, but he had never regretted it. She had become like a right arm that gained muscle and heft each time he used it.

'It's something I have to take care of myself. It's not that I don't trust Steele.'

'Then what is it?'

Blake stood up and kissed her on both moist cheeks.

'It's family. You don't take risks with family.'

CHANTAL HAD SEEMED lighter in mood on the drive down from Oxford. She was wearing one of Laura's pale blouses today, which distracted Sam oddly and made him feel as though he'd committed some kind of clandestine adultery.

Chantal said, 'I nearly came to college in Brighton. It's very arty.'

'And that's a good thing?'

She snorted.

'You really are from Yorkshire, aren't you? Yes, it's a good thing. Arty people are nice people. We're gentle and interesting. We watch foreign films.'

'I used to watch foreign films.'

'Did you?'

'You could always guarantee a nude scene.'

She hit his thigh with the outside of her fist.

'I ought to go back to college. I fancied doing a Masters or a Ph.D.'

'So why don't you? You're still young. If you don't you might regret it later, when you've got a mortgage and three screaming kids wanting their cornflakes.'

'It's not that easy, is it? I'd have to find the money to pay for it. I'd have to find somewhere local because I couldn't afford to live anywhere else. Student life is hard these days. Did you go to college? Or was it the school of hard knocks?'

'I did some basic stuff. Didn't get to a degree, though. I had to get out and earn a living.'

'Had to?'

'I was living at home and my dad got ill – working down the mines had done him in. So I had to pay my way.'

Sam thought back to the last time he'd seen his father in the house in Thurnscoe. The pit had been closed for ten years and with it the life had leached out of the village. His father had seemed to him like a symbol of that – once vital and proud and strong, he was now weak and breathed faintly, as though lacking the energy to push the air out having struggled to take it in. His once-black hair was a coarse white splayed out against the crisp linen pillow. His watery eyes had watched Sam enter the room and now seemed to pin him, so that he stood stock still. They looked at each other for a long while as though neither knew what the proper form of action was.

Then his father did an extraordinary thing: he reached out a hand from the bed.

Sam looked at it as though it had a life of its own. Then he took a step forward and grasped it. The fingers were spotted brown and clawed with age.

'Hi, Dad.'

' 'as your mother sent you up? I asked her for a cup of tea 'alf an hour ago. Bet she's forgot.'

'She's making me something to eat.'

'Is it tea time already? Time passes quick when you've nowt to do but stare at ceiling.'

He tried a laugh but it turned into a wheeze. Sam let go of his hand, which performed a shuddering aerial dance as his father regained his breath.

'Can I get you anything? Have you got some medicine or something?'

'No, lad. Dunna bother yersen. 'ow long are ye stoppin'?'

'I've got to go back tomorrow.'

'Aye, you've got to keep your job. Don't let the bastards tek it from you.'

There was a pause. Sam wondered whether his father was thinking the same thing he was – that this might be the last time they met. He felt a pressure above his eyes and sat down on the edge of the bed. There was a musty smell of old bedclothes and something faintly medicinal, as though a bustling hospital lay just beyond the bedroom.

He glanced around at the old wooden wardrobe and at his mother's dressing-table, bought some time in the 1950s but belonging to a period fifteen years before. The mirror on the dressing-table still bore the crack on an outer wing where he had hit it foolishly practising his top-spin forehand. His mother's black lacquered box with the mother-of-pearl inlay stood where it always had, patiently guarding her meagre collection of rings and necklaces.

When he was younger this room had been a foreign land to him, rarely visited unless his parents were there. Now it seemed small and cramped and a tragic place to host his father's last days.

His father had regained some strength.

'Sam.'

'I'm here.'

'You know, I wish I'd been more places.'

'I know, Dad.'

'You can never see enough different places.'

'I know.'

'I regret that – not going places. And there's something else ... '

'What's that?'

'Don't let other folk tell you what to do. I've 'ad too much of that in my own life and I regret it now. Stand up for yoursen and tell 'em what you think. You won't go wrong with that. You dunna want to get to my age and wish you'd said things when it's too late.'

At the time Sam had thought this advice was heartfelt but somehow obvious – the kind of thing a father would want to tell his son before he died.

Now he knew how hard it was to stand up for yourself and to tell people what you thought. And he realised that the advice had been said with as much conviction as his father could muster. It wasn't in the least mundane or ordinary. It was something to live by.

HE TURNED AND looked briefly at Chantal. The GPS had wanted them to by-pass Brighton altogether, but she had persuaded him to at least drive into the town before turning out towards Hove itself. They were now heading west and would pass through Hove on the way out to Portslade and Shoreham.

He said, 'Let me talk to the woman and ask the questions. I think you're still a bit raw. We don't want to upset her and be beaten around the head by angry nurses.'

He thought she might have been upset but she shrugged.

'You're the professional.' She glanced at him. 'What do you think she'll know?'

'I can't begin to guess. Jimmy said she's mentioned in the diary. Your grandfather was supposed to send her papers from her husband if he was killed. We'll find out, won't we?'

Ten minutes later Sam turned the Mondeo through a pair of brick-built gateposts, to one of which was attached a large square board showing a frankly cartoonish image of a sunset and bearing the name, 'Golden Oaks Retirement Home.'

It was 1.55 in the afternoon.

AT 2.05 THE BLACK Touareg turned into the Golden Oaks Retirement Home and followed signs to the Visitors Car Park. James turned off the engine and looked at Steele, then at Clifford and Nate in the back seats.

'We don't know whether they're here or whether they're even coming here. What do we do?'

Steele glanced at him. 'Well you could insert your thumb up your arse and sit on it. Give us all a laugh.'

Clifford snorted through his ruptured nose. Steele turned on him.

'And you, Mr Staircase, can shut it right now. Christ, it's like taking a class of mental defectives on a school trip. Listen up, all of you. We have very good reason to believe Dyke and Bressette will come here. It's the only connection they might have to what the asset means.'

'And what's that, Boss?'

Steele took a breath and let it out slowly.

'I can't tell you that. And it doesn't matter. All you need to know is that there's an old woman here who could tell Dyke and Bressette something useful. We follow them, that's all.'

'What about the original plan – to take the asset and the Bressette woman out of the picture?'

'Plans change, Clifford, you should know that. Our task now is to find out what *they've* found out. If they seem to be getting close to the end game, then we take care of them. Those are the current orders. Everyone got that?'

There was murmured assent from the men in the car.

Steele looked through the windscreen at the other cars in the car park, which seemed to be a clearing hewn out of the woodland that surrounded the retirement home on three sides. A shale path led from the car park to a side entrance into the building that also served as a fire exit. Another path led from this door to the front of the building. The home itself was set low to the ground with large picture windows looking out towards the sea. One or two brick outbuildings were set close by, probably housing supplies or maybe a generator. Steele took stock of the situation and didn't like their position.

'This is too obvious. We can't stay here in this tank. Take us around to the front again and we'll park off-road somewhere.'

James put the car in gear and pulled back on to the tarmacked driveway. Past the main building the driveway curved for a couple of hundred yards through thickly forested woodland before hitting the main road. You could see occasional glimpses of the English Channel through the dense firs.

Steele pointed ahead, to a widening of the track where cars were supposed to pass each other if they met going in opposite directions.

'Take us off here.'

James slowed and crunched the big car off the tarmac, then turned and angled the vehicle, reversing between two large firs. They could see both ways up the drive but were largely hidden from visitors by the bushes that edged the driveway.

'Perfect. Now hunker down and try to look innocent.'

TO SAM'S SURPRISE, the nursing staff had put up very little resistance. A business-like woman with plum-coloured hair and the brisk mannerisms of a headmistress asked them their reason for visiting and Sam had lied smoothly: Miss Leftwich was Miss Bressette's great aunt, whom she hadn't seen since she was a little girl. They happened to be passing through on a rare visit to England – now they lived in Spain – and wondered whether it would be possible ...

The headmistress had looked sternly from one to the other of them as though she didn't for one minute believe the story. But then she smiled brightly as though it didn't really matter and called over a nurse in a dark-blue outfit.

'Angela, see if Jennifer has finished lunch and is up to seeing some guests.'

She waved Sam and Chantal towards some shiny leather armchairs.

'If you'd care to wait there, Angela will look after you.'

Muttering their thanks, they sat. The headmistress smiled again and walked briskly away.

Sam looked around the place. It seemed to have been built in the sixties, in a style he associated with Tyrolean houses or ski lodges – lots of orange wood and sharply angled ceilings, with tall windows and laminated floors. Footsteps clattered around them as nurses in sensible shoes moved down corridors and between rooms. Somewhere a television was showing a reality show that seemed to involve a lot of shocked booing followed by cheers.

He said, 'I expected something a little more cosy. These people must have wads of money to spend on their retirement.'

'Perhaps it goes into the food. Perhaps they dine *cordon bleu* every night.'

'I thought you didn't speak French.'

She hit him on the leg. It was turning into a habit.

Angela returned down the corridor, beaming and clattering at the same time. She stood before them with her hands folded together and smiling as though bringing the happiest news possible.

'Jennifer would love to see you. She hasn't had any guests in a while. Please follow me.'

Sam and Chantal stood and did as they were told.

IT HAD ONLY been ten minutes but Steele was restless. He was tired of looking at trees, trees and more trees. One car had passed going up and one had passed going down. Neither had contained Dyke or Bressette. It was as though he was being taunted by a universe that knew his impotence and wanted him to suffer even more. He found himself snapping at the three others in the car in a way that was both unnecessary and unprofessional. A sulky atmosphere now hung in the cabin as if he'd taken the phones away from a trio of hulking teenagers.

Finally he said, 'Clifford, go back up to the house and watch the entrance. Phone on vibrate, if you please.'

He felt the eyes of the other two men staring at him resentfully.

'Do not do anything rash. Repeat, do not. And you two, watch the fucking road. I'm about to slap the pair of you.'

The door let in a current of cold air that smelled of the distant sea as Clifford opened it and slipped out.

James lifted his chin as Clifford moved stealthily up towards the building.

'Such a good boy. His mother would be proud.'

Steele clenched his jaw and kept his silence. The time would come, though, when something would have to give. It might be later. It might be soon.

JENNIFER LEFTWICH'S ROOM was modern but had been touched here and there by the hand of nostalgia. A faded sampler hung on the wall, showing a child's view of a house with four windows and a door and complete with a beaming yellow sun in the top corner. On a small chest of drawers three black-and-white photographs in wooden frames showed a young couple in wedding pose and two other couples holding hands and squinting at the camera. Sam also noticed a heavy marble clock with a bronze plate attached to its front, an expensive-looking crystal vase and a heavy walking-stick topped by a swan's head leaning against the doorframe.

The room also contained a functional bed, an Ikea wardrobe and two comfortable chairs. He and Jennifer sat down facing each other in the chairs while Chantal perched as lightly as a bird on the edge of the bed. Through the open window they could hear seagulls and caught whiffs of cool sea air.

Jennifer had proven herself to be no fool. Approaching ninety, she had a full head of curly white hair, a straightforward, interesting gaze and the quick, precise movements of someone who has always had too much energy. Sam had expected someone wrapped in a flannelette nightgown clutching a hot water bottle, but Jennifer was smartly dressed in a dark skirt and a white buttoned blouse.

And she had caught on very quickly.

'Now,' she had said, 'I don't know you, young man, and I certainly don't know you, young lady. I am no one's great-aunt so let's stop that nonsense straight away. Who are you and what do you want?'

Sam liked her immediately and decided to be as truthful as he could. He introduced himself and Chantal, then began, 'Miss Leftwich–'

'Call me Jennifer. And I shall call you Sam.'

'OK. Jennifer, Chantal and I are researching a document that has been in her family for many years. In fact, since the war.'

'Hmm, that's interesting. How can I help?'

'The document is a diary written in French by Chantal's grandfather and passed down to her through her father. For reasons that we don't understand, there are some people who want to get hold of this diary really badly.'

Jennifer Leftwich looked at Chantal, who smiled at her. Sam thought he saw a connection pass between them, crossing two or three generations and speaking of the stupidity that men created between themselves.

'Very well, I understand. But I repeat, how can I help?'

There was a knock on the door and Sam stood immediately.

The door swung open and Angela appeared in the doorway, still smiling.

'Just checking whether you'd like a cup of tea ... ?'

The three faces in the room stared at her as though she had beamed down from an alien spaceship. Jennifer Leftwich was the first to speak.

'No, thank you, Angela dear. Very kind but I think we're all right.'

Angela broadened her smile, aimed it at each of them in turn, then left. Sam sat again and the old woman patted him on the knee as if to tell him everything was fine.

'Lovely girl but I'm sure she's here on work experience. She hasn't got two brain cells to rub together. Now, where were we? Ah yes, we were at the part where I said I didn't know how I could help.'

Sam knew that Jennifer had probably been dealing with girls like Angela all her life.

He said, 'I'll get to the point, Jennifer. We've had some of the diary translated. I should have said that it seems to have been written by Chantal's grandfather, Jean-Claude, when he was working in the French Resistance. He wrote it as a series of letters to his own young wife, Chantal's grandmother.'

'How romantic!'

'Our translator also says that while writing to his wife, Jean-Claude mentions working with a group of British SAS men who had been parachuted into the region to blow up ammunition dumps and trains.'

The old lady brought her hands together on her lap. Sam noticed the elegant slimness of her fingers – she had never done much in the way of housework during her life, he thought.

She said, 'I see. So this document is related to the war.'

Sam leaned back in his own chair.

'Yes, it is. You see, Jean-Claude also mentions that he had been given something by one of the SAS men – something that he was to send back to you, Jennifer, should anything happen to him. If you are indeed that same Jennifer Leftwich.'

The old lady seemed to draw into herself and a coldness came into the room.

She said, 'Yes, I am she. And that is my husband you're talking about. Now I will have to ask you to leave.'

ANGEL PARKED AS far from the Motorway Services cafeteria as he could – if there were any cameras he didn't want to make it easy for them.

He climbed out of the Passat and stretched. The shoulder where he'd been stabbed gave him some trouble occasionally, despite the exercise regimen that he put himself through. He gave himself another five years in this life, then he'd take his savings, find a woman somewhere in Spain and build himself a little cabin on a hill. Maybe let himself get fat and read some of those books he'd always promised to himself.

In the cafeteria he found the KFC and ordered two Fillet Burger meals, then grabbed a fistful of ketchup sachets and took his tray to a corner seat where he could look out of a window.

He estimated he was a couple of hours behind Steele and his men, but that was OK. He didn't want them to see him. It wouldn't really matter if they did at this point but it might lead to complications later, when the end game was close. He didn't want to lose the element of surprise by them catching sight of the same face twice in different locations, twenty-fours apart. His intelligence had been good so far and he had no fears about losing touch with them.

He watched the other people in the cafeteria. The day was cool and windy, so they entered with red cheeks and their hair blown about. He liked the fact that at this moment, he was just like them. There had been times when he felt separate from other people, as though he didn't respond the same way they did to the same stimuli. He had seen this most clearly in the army, where even amongst the extreme hard men he had seemed more extreme. He sometimes felt as though he was made of concrete, impermeable, unyielding. When the other guys in his unit laughed out loud, he barely cracked a smile. When they got drunk, he remained sober. When they were given an impossible order, he was first up, not last.

From time to time he wondered whether he should talk to someone about the way he felt – one of the army shrinks, perhaps. But whenever he considered talking about himself a kind of coolness formed in his gut and he knew he could never do it. He had borrowed a couple of books from the library about psychology and extreme personalities but they didn't seem to be talking about him. After all, he *did* have feelings. Quite strong feelings on occasion.

It was just that he couldn't express them or even talk about them to people. It was too ... personal. It made him feel vulnerable in a way that he didn't like.

Looking at the poor suckers around him – the families going south, the salesmen sweating in their suits, the tattooed lorry drivers – he worried for them. For their naivety. For their lack of real understanding of how the world worked. If they had been at Musa Qaleh or Sangin they wouldn't look so damn pleased with themselves. They might show a bit more gratitude ...

He drained his Coke and put it on the tray, then gathered all his debris together and put it in the waste bin. No one would ever say he was untidy.

Outside he put a breath mint in his mouth and stood for a moment looking at the car park. It was early afternoon and not too busy, except for the monstrous lorries that seemed to crowd every service station he'd ever visited.

In the Passat he checked the GPS and, leaving the car park, leaned forward to slot the device into its holder on the windscreen.

Perhaps because he was momentarily distracted he didn't see the vehicle exiting the lorry park in front of him.

He looked up from the windscreen to see the massive tyres of a huge foreign truck inches from the front of his bonnet. He mashed down the brake and skidded to a halt. He heard a loud blaring sound and realized that his own hand was pressed hard on the car's horn.

With a sigh of released air, the lorry stopped and the door of the cabin popped open.

Angel shook his head.

'Please don't do this.'

He watched as a large backside encased in denim appeared as the trucker descended. He finally reached the bottom of his descent and turned around, standing with his feet apart and his hands on his hips. He wore a stained white tee-shirt beneath a navy-blue woollen fleece, open down the front. He stared at Angel briefly then walked towards him.

Angel stepped from the Passat – it was better to be standing than have the man looking down at him. He told himself to stay calm, he couldn't afford this.

The trucker stopped advancing when Angel stood before him. He was young, in his late twenties, and was an inch taller than Angel, though heavier. Angel thought from his colouring and the shape of his face he was probably Scandinavian, maybe German. Although he generally had respect for truckers, there was a kind of blunt ignorance behind this man's eyes that didn't bode well.

The man hesitated a moment, seeing Angel's tattoos. Then he seemed to take courage.

'You blow your horn at me but it was not my fault. You should watch your road.'

'Well in this country, my friend, we are polite and we wait for smaller vehicles to pass by so that our fat arses don't obstruct the road. Understand?'

The man frowned, thinking through the insult.

'Be careful what you say to me. You are a strange man.'

'Say sorry to me and we can go on our way.'

'I will not say sorry.' He took a step forward and poked Angel in the chest. 'You make noise with your horn and it is not my fault.'

'I think you should watch your manners.'

'I do not know what means "manners". I think you should go back in your car.'

'As soon as you say sorry.'

'I do not say sorry to a strange man.'

Angel felt his heartbeat slowing even while the muscles in his arms hardened. He felt the *Zanshin* moment – that period of relaxed alertness practised in Japanese martial arts, the total awareness of one's body, the environment, the opponent. He told himself that if the man backed down, it would be OK. It didn't have to go this way.

The trucker poked him in the chest again, a small grin lifting one side of his mouth, as though he was taking pleasure in testing Angel's limits.

Angel said, 'Don't do that.'

The man poked him in the chest once more. 'Do what?'

Which was when Angel hit him. He had been trained in at least three unarmed combat techniques and had studied more. For him, the simplest manoeuvre was always the best, especially when surprise was on your side. So when his right hand whiplashed towards the trucker's neck he met no resistance. He remembered his first instructor's advice, as always: 'Hit and stick,' leaving the side of his hand against the driver's neck for a tenth of a second to allow the shockwave to travel down his own arm and set up reverberations in the man's own body.

Almost immediately, the man's eyes rolled back in his head, he juddered and fell to the floor. Angel stood over him.

'Perhaps you'll watch where you're going next time, you twat.'

He pulled down the sleeve of his jacket and climbed back into the Passat. He didn't look behind him as he exited the service station car park and rejoined the M40.

But he wondered whether he'd fucked up.

AT FIRST JENNIFER Leftwich had been absolutely adamant that she wouldn't talk to them any more.

'You must go. You came here on false pretences and now you have been impertinent.'

Sam sensed that actually she wanted to say more but it was difficult for her. He lowered his voice and touched her gently on the knee.

'I'm so sorry if this is painful for you. We wouldn't be asking if it weren't important.'

Chantal had become fidgety.

'Sam, we should go. If she doesn't want to talk then perhaps we should just leave.'

He glanced up at her and narrowed his eyes. He had more experience at interviewing people, especially those who seemed reluctant to talk. It had always been his view that people would talk if you created the environment in which it was safe.

'I think Jennifer knows how important this is. Of course we'll go if she wants us to.'

'For goodness' sake stop talking about me as if I'm not here.'

The old woman stood up and walked with surprising energy to the window. Beyond there was nothing but a vista of fir tree-trunks.

'This is very hard for me. I have lived with it for seventy years. Can you imagine what that feels like?'

'Of course not. Why don't you tell us about it?'

She sighed and put a hand on the window-sill as though steadying herself. She began talking to the window.

'It was a long time ago and I was very young. Very young. Younger than you, my dear.'

She turned away from the window and looked at Chantal as she made her way back to the armchair opposite Sam.

'My parents had died in an aviation accident. My father was from a very old family with pots of money and had had nothing to spend it on, except the occasional mistress. My brother, who was fifteen years older than me, became my legal guardian. He had a very good position in the Civil Service and just before the war broke out he was sent to Istanbul, to the Consulate there. It was only a junior position but with the war everyone got promoted quickly and soon he was very important.'

She paused and her eyes moved back and forth as though she were reliving scenes from her youth.

To prompt her, Sam said, 'What was Istanbul like?'

Her face clouded over.

'Goodness, I don't know. I was hardly ever let out, at least to begin with. But I remember the smells ... the smoke from the steamers, rotten fruit, the coffee that you could stand your spoon up in. I was very young, though, so I suppose Richard – that was my brother – thought that it would be best if I were confined to quarters, as it were.'

'What happened while you were there?'

'Oh, lots! Lots! You see, although I was told to stay indoors, there was always plenty going on. Turkey stayed neutral during the war, despite our best efforts to get her involved. So it was a real international community. The British diplomats had to keep everyone happy and there were often tea dances or little parties for visiting dignitaries. I did get to meet an awful lot of people, and I was so young ... I loved it.'

'It must have been exciting for a young girl.'

'Oh, it was, it was. Lord, I remember it more clearly than last week. The sun, the stickiness, the relentless noise.'

She had rarely seen her brother, who was often away on official business or tied up in meetings. They had an apartment in the Consulate from which she could see the Bosphorus and Asia beyond. Of course she had her own bedroom and a maid, Berna, to look after her. Richard had a bedroom on the far side of the apartment while hers opened into a large living space that was essentially an extension of her bedroom. The windows were always open and she remembered the pale curtains wafting to and fro as if unable to find rest.

'I was eighteen years old and bored silly most of the time. No television then, not even a radio in the apartment. No English-language newspapers. I rather think Richard was trying to keep the outside world away from me as much as keeping me away from it. I suppose I shouldn't blame him. I was a bit of a handful, as I proved.'

She looked at them both and grinned broadly and she suddenly had the air of someone much younger, someone who would take risks, accept dares, gamble away the contents of her purse. Sam was struck by how easy it was to underestimate older people, to forget that they might have led lives of excitement and surprise.

He said, 'So how did you meet your husband? Was it in the Consulate?'

'Robin was so handsome! He was almost as tall as you but slighter. Heavens, we were all thinner then, what with the war.'

Robin Leftwich had arrived from the Libyan desert, having taken part in one of the first active campaigns of the SAS. Slightly wounded in an attack on an airfield, he had been sent to Istanbul for treatment and recuperation.

'He walked with a slight limp that was so romantic. He had a walking cane with a skull on the handle that he swore he'd taken from a Libyan pirate ... I didn't even know whether pirates really existed.'

Chantal had become more interested and was leaning forward on the bed.

'So how did you meet? How did you get married?'

'Well, I managed to persuade Richard to let me go to an event that was being held at the Park Hotel. Very swanky. Lots of shifty Americans who one was told were intelligence officers. They sat around in the bar smoking cigarettes and drinking coffee. This event was a kind of cultural meeting – I think there might have been an exhibition of Byzantine art. I was with Berna, of course, and this dashing man who was a few years older came up and started talking to me. I remember it clearly, my little heart was beating like a wild thing. He was glorious in a white linen suit. I must have been as red as a tulip.'

Sam pointed to one of the black-and-white photos on the table. Against a dark brick wall, Jennifer wore a white blouse and white skirt and the man, presumably Leftwich, sported a field uniform and beret. He was thin and wore a pencil moustache, perhaps in an attempt to make himself look older.

'I guess that's you and Robin. Was that your wedding day?'

'Yes. I was just eighteen. I don't know how Robin did it but he managed to organize someone to marry us within three weeks.'

'What did Richard say?'

Jennifer smiled sadly.

'Oh, he didn't know. I knew I couldn't tell him. It wouldn't have been allowed. I was too young, Robin was serving in a very dangerous regiment. I was young but I wasn't stupid.'

After their first meeting in the Park Hotel, she managed to see Leftwich twice in the next week. She told Richard that she was going to the market, or to the library, or to visit friends. But each time she was meeting Leftwich and they talked for hours. When he'd recovered enough from his wounds he was set to return to his regiment in Libya for his next briefing. At that time the SAS were working with the Long Range Desert Group, driving hundreds of miles across the desert in specially outfitted Ford trucks to attack enemy airfields.

'So you see we had a deadline. His doctors had set him a date on which he would be free to return to his regiment.'

'And so you got married.'

Jennifer took in a deep breath and seemed to let it settle through her whole body.

'Yes, we did. I went with Berna to the local marketplace and gave her the slip. She was so easily distracted by any stalls selling cloth, silly girl. Then I met with Robin at a prearranged spot and he took me in a car that he'd borrowed from the hospital to a large house on one of the hills overlooking the harbour. Two men that he knew were there, and the little priest who married us. They threw some rice at us and one of them took that photo. Then we had a glass of wine – my first – and he took me back to the marketplace, where Berna was going mad looking for me. Three days later I managed to meet Robin once more in the market and the day after that he was gone. I never saw him again.'

A grim silence fell as they each considered the sorrow that lay in that statement.

Sam said, 'Did Richard ever find out?'

Jennifer cackled.

'Oh my word, did he! I think Berna must have eventually plucked up courage and told him that I'd gone missing in the market and he made some enquiries. He asked me, of course, but I just pretended ignorance. It didn't take him long to find out about Robin from other people and soon he had the whole story. I even had a ring that Robin had given me. Berna found it in my jewellery-box. I never trusted that little peasant girl.'

'What happened?'

'Oh, an enormous fight. Stupendous. We called each other every name under the sun. He wanted to know whether it was a real ceremony or whether it was just a ruse so that Robin could have his evil way with me. I told him that we hadn't actually done *that*. He said I was just a silly little girl with romantic notions, and I told him he was a stuck-up prig who was too busy to pay any attention to his own sister. It was great fun.'

In the end Richard had sent her back to Britain. The house in Surrey that had been their parents' was in mothballs and wouldn't be reopened until he came back from the war. But their mother's sister lived in Basingstoke and Richard asked her to look after Jennifer for the duration.

'Of course I was mad about that. I had less chance of seeing Robin again there.'

'And did you?'

'No, dear, I didn't. Eventually I went up to London after the war and trained as a secretary.'

'You never married again?'

Jennifer became defiant, her eyes turning hard.

'I already had one husband. I didn't need another.'

Chantal stood up and looked down at Sam; she seemed preoccupied, her eyes moist.

She said, 'I think we should go. I don't think we should bother Jennifer any more.'

'Yes.'

Jennifer looked from one of them to the other.

'Does that mean you don't want to hear about the documents I stole from my brother and sent to my husband?'

CLIFFORD WONDERED WHY he always got the arse-end jobs.

He knew that if you wanted to get ahead you had to volunteer – or at least be thought of as keen. When James had tapped him up about this job he hadn't been that interested. Working for another contractor who had some airs and graces and thought himself a cut above the rest of them. No real brief, just a vague 'objective' that seemed to change every five minutes ... It was all very well being told you were on the payroll of someone who could be grateful over the next few years; but he didn't want to think that far ahead. He wasn't considering his pension just yet.

He had found a place amongst the firs where he could see the front door of the nursing home but wouldn't be seen by anyone leaving through it. He was positioned to the side, looking at a glass fire door set in the brickwork. If he turned his head he could see the car park behind the home, where the Touareg had initially parked before going round to the front again. He had worked his way back into the edges of the woods that surrounded the home and put himself behind a couple of silver-barked trees that smelled of damp and, strangely, mushrooms. His shoes sank into the ground and he hoped his socks weren't getting wet – that would really piss him off.

He took a deep breath through his mouth because his nose still hurt.

The home bothered him a little. His father had ended up in one of these places in south London and Clifford had hated going to see him – the smell of old people's urine and old people's clothes, the air of terminal decline that settled over the place like smog, almost choking you. He'd told himself he was going to jump from Tower Bridge before he wound up like that. Whenever he had anything to do with institutions of that sort – hospitals, homes, whatever the fuck – he felt himself die a little inside. He was too intent on his own future to be bothered with anyone else's past.

He moved his position a couple of yards so that he could see directly through the fire door and down the corridor. Fuzzy brown shadows moved around inside like ghostly visitations. Smoke rose from the building's lone chimney, bringing with it the smell of burned wood and charred hope.

He heard the front door open before he saw a couple come out of the little vestibule where you could put on your coats and take off your serious face. It was a middle-aged man and a younger woman. The man wore a suit and tie, as though he wanted to get his aging parent used to the sight of funeral directors, while his presumed wife flaunted a fur coat and a skirt a couple of inches shorter than it should have been. They turned left out of the home and clicked over the tarmac drive to the car park, passing within five yards of Clifford but not sensing his presence. Chalk one up for me, he thought.

He wondered what he might have done if it had been the Bressette woman and that bastard Sam. He wasn't sure he cared enough for Steele to have obeyed his orders and done nothing but watch.

JENNIFER LEFTWICH BEAMED at them, twinkling like a Disney grandmother. Sam was beginning to revise his opinion of her. Perhaps being stuck in a home on the edge of a stretch of dark woods put twisted thoughts into your head ... she definitely enjoyed teasing them, leading them on. Like the wicked witch taunting Hansel and Gretel. So where was the gingerbread house?

'What documents, Jennifer? And why did you steal them?'

'You have to understand that Richard was a very difficult person. I say that as his sister, you know. He was terribly well-organised – I suppose he had to be, in the circumstances. There was all sorts of correspondence that he had to deal with. And of course it was all on paper – none of these emails or text messages. Everything was written down. And he would receive telegrams, of course, all the time. And some of them were in code that he was responsible for decoding.'

'What kind of messages?'

'What do you think? Secret messages. From the embassy in Ankara, or directly from the Foreign Office in London. Although we were in a neutral territory, you'd never have guessed it from all the secrets flying around. Germany had a consulate, we had a consulate. It was cat and mouse. Of course I didn't know much about it at the time.'

Chantal moved on the bed, shifting her position.

'Jennifer, are you sure you should be telling us this? You stole official documents.'

'My dear, I'm far too old to worry about things like that.'

Sam said, 'Chantal ... '

The girl stood up from the bed, her eyes brimming.

'This isn't right. One person has been hurt already because of all this. I don't want anything else to happen. I can't carry on with it.'

Sam stood up and took her arm lightly, moving her to the window and talking softly.

'It's OK. We're safe here. Nothing's going to happen to her.'

'You don't know that, Sam. Look at her, she has no idea how serious all this is. I want to go. I'm fed up with the whole thing now.'

'All right, we'll go. If you don't want to hear what she has to say, go outside. Get some air.'

She looked up at him, her large eyes still moist. He found the trust in them disturbing.

'I really don't want to hear it. I don't think I can handle it.'

She walked across the room and knelt briefly in front of Jennifer Leftwich.

'Thank you for seeing us. I'm so sorry about Robin. I'm sure he loved you very much.'

'Thank you too, dear. Yes, I'm sure Robin loved me. Are you leaving us?'

'Yes. I need some fresh air. Goodbye.'

Then she stood up and left the room, closing the door quietly.

Sam sat opposite Jennifer again.

'Speaking for myself, I'd very much like to hear what happened. If you don't mind.'

'Of course not. I've never told anyone before. Oh, apart from Gideon.'

'Gideon?'

'My nephew, Gideon Blake. You must have heard of him. He's very famous in the government now. I told him years ago because he was always interested in family and family history. He was Richard's boy, you see. When my brother came back from Istanbul and settled down in Surrey. Married a nice girl, too good for him. She died, poor thing. But Richard and she had Gideon very late. I never liked him, actually.'

Sam filed this information away. He had a sense of time speeding up around him as new information came his way.

He said, 'Please tell me what happened in Istanbul, Jennifer.'

'Well as I said, Richard was furious with me when he found out I'd got married. Cried blue murder. Told me I would never see Robin again and he'd get the marriage annulled. We went at it like cats. In the end, he made arrangements to ship me out. I remember that last day – I was ready, all packed, and I was seething. I'd never forgiven him but there was nothing I could do – I was his ward as well as his sister, so he could do with me what he bally well wanted. So anyway, I was upstairs waiting for the taxi to take me to an airbase so the RAF could fly me out. And I was steaming. I didn't want to go back to the cold and the smog and the rain. Why would I? So I stormed into his room to give him an earful, and of course he wasn't there. I hadn't realised, but he'd been called downstairs briefly, leaving papers strewn all over his desk. So I took them. Grabbed a handful, stuffed them in my coat pockets and ran downstairs to wait for the taxi outside. I didn't even say goodbye to him, I was so mad.'

'And what was on the papers?'

'I waited till I was on the plane before I looked. I was so angry and I didn't really care. But there was a very particular one that I remember very clearly. Most of it was in code, on a telegram form. But I could read the signature.'

'Who was it from?'

Jennifer Leftwich looked at Sam directly and prodded him in the chest with a bony finger.

'Our Prime Minister of the time.' She grinned wickedly. 'Winston Churchill.'

THE DAMP AIR hanging in the trees like a permanent mist had finally got to Clifford. And the cold. And the boredom. He needed to piss. Where better than amongst a bunch of trees? The old farts inside would never see him, would they?

He was zipping up when he heard the emergency door opening. The Bressette woman had come out of the door and was heading straight for him, her head down.

His senses heightened, he could hear that she was crying, a faint intermittent croak kept in check by the handkerchief she held to her mouth.

The angle she was taking meant that in a moment he'd be in her eye-line, but he couldn't move. Any noise now would draw her attention.

He took an executive decision.

Accelerating from a standing start, he was within a pace of her when she looked up. He saw the fear as her eyes widened, felt the thrill of power in his chest as his arms went around her, one hand stopping her mouth.

'Not one sound. Women bruise easy.'

He took his hand from her mouth and seized her wrist with it, dragging her towards the Touareg a hundred yards down the track.

Pain exploded across his face – he felt it as a metal taste flooding the back of his mouth. The bitch had hit him with her free hand, right across his damaged nose.

Without thinking he lashed out and caught her in the face. She sagged, almost fell. He took the bulk of her weight, which wasn't much. Down the track, he heard the door of the Touareg open up and then Steele's voice.

'You'd better have a fucking good explanation.'

Clifford bit back the pain now beginning to spread from his nose into his cheekbones. One excuse, just give him one excuse ...

'She saw me. Came out the back. Had no option.'

'That's you, isn't it? Mr No-fucking-option. Get her in the van, quick.'

They bundled Chantal into the back seat where Nate had hurriedly fashioned a blindfold from a black tee-shirt.

Steele said in a voice filled with world-weary irritation.

'All right, Team Fawlty, let's get the fuck out of here before Sam misses the little dear.'

SAM CLOSED THE door on Jennifer Leftwich carefully. After she had told him about the telegram from Churchill she had had nothing more to say. She had sat back in her seat and folded her hands in her lap as though her work was done. She could add no further details about the telegram. Its contents were unknown to her because they were encoded. But maybe the fact of its existence was enough ...

Sam had thanked her and she had nodded imperiously, which he had taken as a signal to leave.

He and Chantal had arrived with a question for Jennifer: What had Jean-Claude Bressette sent to you after Robin Leftwich was executed? But the more important question now seemed to be: What was on Churchill's telegram that you sent to your husband?

Outside Jennifer's room the corridor was empty. To his left it went past another three doors and then led directly to the emergency fire door with its horizontal push bar. He walked down the corridor and peered outside. Chantal wasn't visible. She must have gone out the front door, he thought, or perhaps was waiting in Reception for him.

He turned and walked back down the corridor to where it opened out into the reception area. An elderly man and woman had taken the seats that he and Chantal had sat in thirty minutes before; it was like a vision of their future. They looked up at him blankly but said nothing.

Sam walked to the front door and opened it, entering the small vestibule that you passed through like an airlock before entering the outside world. As he opened the outer door, he caught a flash of a black car emerging from the tree-line and turning on to the tarmac drive. He sensed immediately what it was and began to run towards the drive. The car accelerated away. As it followed the curve of the drive the front passenger's profile came into view.

Steele.

'Damnit.'

He ran back around the nursing home and climbed into the Mondeo, scattering mulch and chippings as he reversed and turned to follow. He crashed upwards through the gears for maximum acceleration but by the time he reached the end of the drive the Touareg was gone.

Left or right?

Left would take him back into the centre of Hove – more traffic, narrower roads. Right would take him towards the A27, where they could choose to go either east and then north up the M23 towards London; or west towards Chichester, Portsmouth and eventually to Southampton or even further.

He gambled and turned right, thinking that they would want to avoid the midday traffic in Hove and would prefer to head towards the motorway system. He gunned the car and peered ahead.

Five minutes later he saw them, caught behind suburban traffic and unable to overtake. He slowed enough to keep half a dozen cars between them – he could do nothing while they were both travelling.

Shortly the black car reached the roundabout for the A27 and Sam watched it indicate and turn left, following signs for Worthing. He took the slip-road and eased down on to the two-lane road. The suburban scenery of Hove fell behind and he was now driving between gently rolling hills almost mocking in their serenity. He shifted his position and tried to relax, keeping several cars and a couple of lorries between the Touareg and himself.

Fifty-five minutes later the Touareg turned on to the A275, heading towards Portsmouth Harbour and the distant feather of the Spinnaker Tower.

Ten minutes later, Sam lost them.

THE TEE-SHIRT SMELLED of sweat and a cheap deodorant and Chantal was happy when it was finally removed from her eyes.

She was in a small room in what appeared to be an ordinary suburban house. There was a bow window facing her, through which she could see other houses with the same kind of bow window on the other side of a tree-lined road. She was seated on a brown two-seater sofa with a flat screen television in one corner and a small club chair in the other. They had bound her hands in front of her with a plastic tie. They had taken her shoes. The room was warm but she felt herself shivering. She felt as though her heart had risen a few inches in her chest and was beating wildly to escape.

The man who'd accosted her in Edinburgh Zoo sat in the club chair, watching her. He wore the same blazer and white shirt he was wearing the first time she saw him, though he looked a little more ragged around the edges than in the gardens of Edinburgh Zoo.

He said, 'Need a pee?'

'Need a bigger dick?'

Steele smiled slowly.

'Yes, how is young Jack? Doing well, is he? Can he see out of that left eye yet? Caught him a nice one there.'

'What's your name?'

'You probably know by now. Your new friend isn't dumb. He'll have done his homework. And spoken to the nice girlfriend.'

Chantal stared at him without blinking. This time she wasn't going to be intimidated. She was scared, but it was almost as though she'd given herself up to whatever happened next and didn't care about consequences any more.

Steele saw it in her face and pursed his lips.

'Well this is all very lovely, accidental or not, but we've got someone who wants to talk to you.'

He nodded and Chantal realized that someone was standing behind her with the tee-shirt blindfold. It was pulled roughly over her eyes again and knotted tightly. She heard Steele get up and leave and sensed that the person standing behind her had also gone.

She wasn't going to give them any satisfaction so sat and waited with her tied hands folded on her lap like a debutante waiting to be asked to dance.

Eventually the door to the room opened again and a bigger presence came in. She sensed it was a man and he didn't sit down but stood in front of her. She felt her heart slow down as she tried to stay calm. When he spoke his voice was deep and had no accent other than a generalised southern Home Counties languor.

'Well, Miss Bressette, what a merry dance you've led us. It's all rather silly, don't you think?'

'You started it.'

'That's very ungracious of you. In fact *you* started it. You were a bit of a tease, weren't you, going to the War Museum with your little morsel. My man here tells me you didn't have it with you today so this is degenerating now into kidnapping and Lord knows what-all. I hope you're going to be sensible about it.'

Chantal heard a hint of desperation in the man's voice despite his droll attitude.

'Why do you want it so badly? What can be in there that's of interest now?'

She felt his hand descend on the top of her head and ruffle her hair.

'I couldn't possibly tell you that, could I? Give the whole thing away. Suffice to say that an old lady, who I believe you've met, was a naughty girl. She stole some papers from an important man, some very incriminating papers.'

'I have no idea what you're talking about.'

'No? Well perhaps the old lady kept it to herself, then. Perhaps she was feeling guilty, the old cow.'

'How is the diary connected to these papers?'

She felt him move away from her and his voice came from a different part of the room. He sounded as though he was facing the window.

'In some ways I suppose the diary isn't in fact connected to the documents. Except through you and ... who is it – your grandfather? Let's think it through. Your old granddad knew a man in the war, an Englishman. They fought the Nazis together in France, and your granddad wrote a diary in which he talked about this Englishman. That's what my translator tells me, anyway. Now this Englishman, Jennifer's husband of oh, about five minutes, had received a love-letter from her before he arrived in France. And this love-letter was written by Jennifer on the back of a document that she had stolen from her brother, the important man. Complicated, isn't it?'

Chantal said nothing. The man was evidently talking about the same documents that Jennifer had mentioned stealing. She had left the room without hearing any of the detail and now wished that she'd heard more.

The man in the room had come back towards her and stood so close she could smell his musk, which was slightly sour.

'Jennifer must have done it to spite him, don't you think? Come on, you're a woman. You can understand her motives.'

'Sounds like this man behaved very badly, so yes, she probably did it to spite him.'

The man paused, perhaps taking in what she'd said. She waited for a blow but none came.

'So to continue. As far as I can work out, Robin Leftwich got this love-letter, turned it over and saw something he didn't expect to see. Now, from what we understand of the verlan, Leftwich gave a bunch of letters to your grandfather for safekeeping. In the middle of a war, the dumb shit. He gets captured by the Nazis and shot for being in the SAS and your granddad hides all the letters. I spend my youth pedalling around central France trying to find anyone who knew Leftwich and might have been given something by him. And then you turn up with a diary that mentions him by name but then for some reason won't let us have the damn thing. What was I supposed to do?'

'Ask politely?'

'Are you on drugs? No, I had to be more surreptitious. I couldn't be connected to it in any way, and I had no way of controlling your actions, did I? So I had to see what you would do with it next.'

'And that worked out really well for you, didn't it?'

The man emitted a short laugh.

'Well, rather better for me than for you, it seems. Looking at you strapped up there and blindfolded, unable to prevent anything at all happening to you should I snap my fingers. Which I will do, eventually.'

HE KNEW THAT LAURA had heard it in his voice straight away. The loss of energy, the failure of the positive thinking that was so much a feature of his approach to events. Sam heard it in his voice too, which only added to his despair.

He had told Chantal that it would be OK. Everything would be fine. He'd help her ...

He'd been proved wrong. And it was killing him.

Laura's voice over the cheap mobile phone was tinny and impossibly far away. Perhaps she didn't have much of a signal in her friend Abigail's house.

'Are you sure it was Steele? She didn't just hitch a lift with someone leaving the care home?'

'I'm sure. It was the same car we'd seen before.'

'So what can you do now?'

'I don't know, dammit. I've got no way of tracking them the same way they tracked me.'

'Why not? Don't you have some names? Can't Dan help?'

Sam closed his eyes. He was parked in a McDonald's car park having toured Portsmouth for an hour looking for the Touareg. Without luck. He'd called Laura to update her and for some comfort. He usually knew what to do next but this time he was coming up short.

He realised he'd been quiet for a while.

'I'm sorry. I don't know why I called.'

'You mean it wasn't to have an argument? Weren't you missing our daily spats?'

'Well, I wouldn't say they were daily.'

'You're going to use the Woody Allen sex quote, aren't you?'

'Almost never, twice a week.'

She laughed.

'All the time, twice a week.'

It was one of their favourite shared moments from *Annie Hall*.

There was a companionable silence this time. Laura almost never gave him advice because she knew he wouldn't take it. But she had always been able to shift him out of a black mood.

She said, 'So what options do you have?'

'Come home. Or keep touring Portsmouth and hope I see the car.'

'Anything else.'

'Not really ... wait. I *do* have another name. I'd almost forgotten.'

'There you go.'

'Is Dan with you?'

'Yes, hold on.'

The telephone was placed with a clatter on a hard surface and a minute later Dan picked it up.

'What can I do?'

Sam told him, then waited online for nearly three minutes while Dan went to his computer. He came back and gave the information that Sam wanted.

'Thanks – that's great. How's Abigail's?'

'Cold. No central heating, just a wood-burner. Do you want to talk to Laura again?'

'No. Tell her I'll phone later. Or she'll see me on the television. In deep shit.'

Dan laughed and they hung up.

STEELE'S ATTENTIONS WERE beginning to unnerve her. Since the other man had left, Steele had been sitting in the club chair opposite her, his eyes rarely moving from her face. It was as though he was looking for something, some sign that would answer a question that he hadn't been able to verbalise.

Chantal was glad that the tee-shirt was no longer over her eyes but in some ways it had been better than the knowledge that Steele was staring at her.

She said, 'Can we at least have the television on?'

'It's not working. No aerial. No licence. DVDs only.'

Chantal thought about this for a while.

'Is this what they call a safe house, then? You're working for the Ministry of Defence in some way– '

Steele burst out laughing. One of his back teeth was grey. It suited the sense of rot she felt coming off him.

'Oh that's me. Mr Official. Just following orders, straight from the PM. Report directly to Number 10. Got an appointment next week to explain all this.'

'You don't have to be such a shit about it.'

'Why not? What difference does it make? If I'm nicer to you are you going to like me? Bake me a cake one day? Come to my wedding?'

'Are you getting married?'

Steele turned his head away.

'Don't be facetious.'

'Oh, hit a nerve, did I? It's all right for you to be sarcastic but not me. Those are the rules, are they?'

'The rules are what I make them. Remember that and you'll be all right.'

'What if I don't like your rules? They're pretty crap, actually. Like all men's rules, made to suit yourself but nobody else. Who was that man? Your boss?'

If Steele was surprised by her change of direction he didn't show it.

'At the moment.'

'So you're what, a mercenary?'

'That has such a cold feel to it, don't you think?'

'What do you prefer? Wage slave?'

He smiled at her again.

'Pretty clever. I can see what Loverman Jack sees in you. Why don't you just sit there and wait, like the rest of us. I'm sure Mr Dyke is right now working on a plan to get you out of here.'

This was something Chantal hadn't considered. She had thought her kidnapping was so rapid that Sam would have no way of knowing what had happened. She had guessed he probably thought she'd run off, too anxious to carry on with the search for ... for what? What were she and Sam actually looking for? The truth about the diary? So what? Were the events of over sixty years ago so important now?

She said, 'Do you know what all this is about – the diary and everything?'

Steele held up a hand.

'Can't talk about that. Not part of the brief.'

'Right, one of the rules. Well *I* can talk about it.'

She told him about her grandfather, about the diary and its contents, narrating Jennifer Leftwich's story about her husband and how she had stolen documents from her brother's desk.

'How it all fits together I'm not sure. And I have no idea why it's so bloody important now. That's all just army stuff that's so much history.'

Steele said nothing for a moment, then lifted a finger to point at her.

'You don't get to talk about the army.'

'Why not?'

'Because you haven't got a fucking clue.'

'What's to know? Lots of men with short back-and-sides running around pointing guns at each other. Always men.'

'I said, you don't get to talk about it.'

'Then you tell me. Give me the benefit of your personal knowledge.'

Steele's mouth twisted as though he was swallowing something bitter. Chantal saw that his hands clasped each other tightly between his knees as he leaned forward on the chair.

He said, 'It's about honour and tradition. What do we have as a country if we don't have honour? We're fucked economically. We don't make anything any more. We're crap at football. But we've got the British Army. And the Air Force. And the Navy. Best fighting units in the world, because we understand honour and have a sense of tradition.'

'What do you mean by honour?'

'My father and grandfather served their country. My brother was killed in Afghanistan saving the lives of two members of his unit. That's honour – doing your duty and serving your regiment.'

Chantal found that she was intrigued.

'So how does this current job fit in? How do you square kidnapping me and hurting Jack with your so-called honour? Or is it part of a tradition?'

'Don't twist my words. The work I do is for a greater good. You're seeing it at ground level. Because it happens to impact on you where you are. From a different perspective you'd see a different picture. That's what the chain of command is all about.'

'Well that's bullshit.'

'How so?'

'Because that suggests there's one picture and you can see it from different angles.'

'That's the real world.'

Chantal shook her head. 'No it's not. One of the first things you learn when you study art is that the picture an artist makes *creates* a version of the world. It doesn't represent it from one position, where you happen to be standing. You could come back to the same spot tomorrow and see what's in front of you differently.' She looked away. 'You've been told a story to keep you in your place, so you don't question authority. Your generals or colonels or whatnot don't want you to question the reality they're making up, so they've invented this nonsense about perspective. They probably tell you they have more information, don't they, so they can understand what's going on better than you. It's bullshit. They're keeping you in your place and making you feel happy about it while they're at it.'

'As I said, you haven't got a clue.'

'Maybe not, but at least I *know* that I haven't got a clue. You're so stupid you think you know it all, like a sixteen-year-old.'

He stared at her for ten seconds, then stood abruptly and left the room.

Chantal let out a lungful of air and leaned back on the sofa. She wondered if she'd set a cat amongst the pigeons or said something that was going to make things even worse for her. There had been something in Steele's face when he left that suggested he was not happy with what he'd heard. She just wasn't sure who he was unhappy with.

ANGEL STARED AT the back of the cell door. It was made of a heavy steel and was inflexible. In a way, he admired the way its form described its function. There was no escape from its brutal reality.

He had been in the cell for an hour now and still no one had come to talk to him.

But it was his own fault. He shouldn't have been so readily angered at the service station. If he had listened to his Calm Self, he wouldn't have attacked that German lorry driver and he wouldn't be staring at the back of a cell door in ... where was he? Crawley?

Instead he had allowed the Angry Self to show its claws for once. That was a realisation for him – he needed to find a way to release his aggression when he didn't have a mission in hand. His tattoos were an external sign of his angry self and he'd thought when he'd submitted to them that it would be enough ... to show people how he felt without demonstrating it through action. Obviously he'd misunderstood his own nature. There was still part of him that wouldn't submit, that needed to make itself felt. Hopefully this mission would – eventually – allow that to happen.

He thought again about his capture. They'd been quite clever about it. He had been on the motorway travelling at a respectable speed in the middle lane. They'd sent an unmarked car ahead of him and into the outside lane, and then slowed the traffic down imperceptibly, so that he was forced to slow down too. Then a police Range Rover had eased up behind him and flashed its lights until he'd been made to move into the inside lane and then stop. When they got him out and spoke to him they knew his name – or at least the name on his driving licence – so they must have radioed in his plate beforehand. And as soon as he was taken from his vehicle he'd been handcuffed and driven away. No questions.

He could only imagine that someone had seen him at the service station, some fat oik eating a burger in his car, perhaps, watching open-mouthed as he felled the kraut with the side of his hand ...

He dropped to the floor and did twenty quick press-ups. He had patience in abundance but sometimes his body needed purely physical release.

He was about to do another twenty when there was a clatter at the cell door and it opened. He stood back. A large man of about fifty with short brush hair and wearing a green sports jacket stood in the doorway with his hands in his pockets. He grimaced at Angel's tattoos, as he had done an hour ago when escorting him to the cell.

'Are you someone special, then? I don't meet many people with a get-out-of-gaol-free card.'

Angel grinned. He'd told them one phone number and it seemed to have worked.

'Do I go now?'

'You've got a lot of kit in your car. We had to confiscate it. Despite what we were told.'

'Keep it. Use it on your next victim. Easier than throwing them down the stairs – less messy.'

The policeman ignored this.

'What do you do, then? No criminal record. Been in the army. No discernible source of income.'

'If I told you, I'd have to kill you.'

The policeman seemed to understand that for once this wasn't an idle threat. He looked Angel up and down one more time, then stood aside.

Angel walked past him and a uniformed man led him out of the building and pointed him to where his car was waiting. Angel climbed inside and looked back at the station house. The man in the green jacket was standing at the top of the steps watching him, his hands still in his pockets.

Angel turned on his GPS and drove away. After five minutes he pulled into the side of the road and climbed out. In the Passat's boot, his roll bag with clothes was intact, but they'd taken a couple of pocket knives and a ball of plastic garden twine that he sometimes found useful. To the right of the boot cavity was a small well intended to house spare oil canisters or other motoring equipment. He took out the removable side and in the bottom twisted a plastic nut and pulled upwards. Beneath this was a space that he'd fitted himself. Inside, his Bowie knife was safe, wrapped in an oiled cloth. He replaced it, put back the false floor and reinserted the side of the equipment well.

Perhaps now he could get on with his job.

MONDAY

GOVERNMENT WORK WAS largely paperwork, for which Gideon Blake had no aptitude or liking at all.

In general he left it to his secretary, Pendleton, who would point out the documents that it was essential he read, or put a cross next to a space where he had to sign.

After his return from Portsmouth, Blake had walked around the many rooms of his house as though he might find an answer to his problems tucked behind a sofa or written on a scrap of paper on a sideboard. Now they had the Bressette woman she was no use to them at all. They had searched her thoroughly but she didn't have the diary with her, which meant it must have been in Dyke's car. Although they had the majority of the interesting pages from the diary – and Shepherd had come through with the translations of the verlan for all of them – Blake was sure that there was some information missing. Something that would point him towards the location of the most important document of all.

Pendleton came into the room with his usual casual arrogance. The son of one of Blake's old school friends, he didn't seem to realise that he had a grace and favour appointment. He acted as though he had earned his post on merit and, because of the old family ties, was on a social par with Blake. Nothing irritated Blake so much as the presumption of friendship. He looked up from his desk at Pendleton's smooth pale face, his blond hair quiffed artfully back and over his ears from a centre parting, and felt himself flinch with disdain.

He said, 'Haven't we finished yet? I thought you'd gone.'

'Sorry, Mr Blake. A call has just come through on the house phone. It's Sir Walter.'

One of Blake's certainties was that he wouldn't have a telephone in the same room as his work desk. Experience had taught him that the telephone would ruin a morning's thinking. He even gave his mobile phone to Pendleton to look after most of the time.

'All right. Can you pick up these papers and tidy the desk? I'll take it in the hall.'

The telephone was on a spindle-leg table in front of a mirror. Blake examined his face as he picked up the phone. Was that a line creasing his brow? He wouldn't be surprised ...

'Blake.'

'Yes, it's me. I wanted to speak to you. Are you coming up to town today?'

'What is it, Walter? Don't tell me you've called another bloody meeting. I've got a lot on my plate just now.'

There was a moment's silence at the other end and Blake wondered briefly whether he'd gone too far. Then Lashbrooke coughed and spoke immediately.

'There's been a development.'

'Of what kind?'

'George Strutt has had a breakdown. He was found wandering the streets of Hackney without his trousers.'

'Ah.'

'He was telling everyone that he was fed up with the buggers running his life. Oh, and he was giving out free packets of redbush tea, telling people it guaranteed immortality.'

Blake closed his eyes. He remembered the meeting where Strutt had extolled the virtues of the foul-smelling drink. Was it only two days ago?

'He seemed all right on Saturday. What the hell happened?'

'I've got Mcclair trying to find out. You know George, he was never the most straightforward thinker, shall we say. Anyway, I thought I'd warn you.'

'Why? What difference does this make to us?'

Lashbrooke's voice grew a little steelier.

'Use your head, Gideon. George Strutt was part of our group. Our very private group. If he's in a mental ward somewhere now, there's no telling what he might be saying to all and sundry.'

'What can we do about it? If he's in a nuthouse they won't be listening to him anyway.'

'I'm sure you're perfectly correct and the trained nurses will turn a deaf ear to anything a distinguished former member of the Cabinet might say. Not to mention his wife, Miriam. She never liked me. Or you much, for that matter.'

'Me? What did I ever do to her?'

'I don't know. Perhaps looked down the wrong side of your nose at her, as you're wont to do. Now listen. I don't know how we're going to keep a lid on this. George's people have done their best to keep it damped down, but it will only be a matter of time before the press gets hold of it. Everybody knows that you were one of his protégés, so it's possible they'll come to you for an opinion. You say nothing, except some bland banalities about wishing him a speedy recovery.'

'Can't I at least express the wish that the straitjacket shouldn't be too tight, because of course he suffers from terrible wind?'

'For Christ's sake, Gideon, get your head screwed on about this. I'm rather tired of running after you cleaning up your messes. Now don't call me unless I call you first. I don't trust telephones at the best of times, and this certainly isn't one of those. In fact, I'm going to send you another phone so that we can have some privacy. Don't give it to your man.'

He hung up. Blake stared for a moment at the receiver, then replaced it. What exactly did Lashbrooke mean by cleaning up his messes? This was supposed to be a moment of triumph for him. The coming together of several years of planning and hard work.

And it was all turning to shit around him.

'Pendleton!'

The blond haired man appeared in the office doorway, where doubtless he'd been paring his nails.

'Is my car here?'

'I ordered it this morning, it shouldn't be long.'

Government officers had now to book their transport from the Ministerial Car Service. It was a pain and thank god Pendleton took care of it.

'I want you to go ahead now. Use your own car. I'm going to spend time alone reading. I'll meet you in the office.'

'Of course.'

'And let me have my phone. I may need to make a couple of calls.'

Pendleton reached into his pocket and handed over a large-screen phone. Blake put it in his jacket pocket.

'Is it charged?'

'Overnight. It should be fine.'

'All right, go.'

Pendleton hesitated a moment, then left. His shoes clacked over the tiled floor and he opened the large front door quickly and slipped through it.

Blake went back into his office and picked up the briefcase Pendleton had packed for him. He couldn't face driving up to town with him in the back of the car so had invented an excuse, but there was no way he could spend any time reading. He couldn't focus for long enough.

He went back out into the hall, crossed the echoing tiles and strode through into the large sitting room. His wife was by the window, writing on some cards at a table and looking like a painting from some Flemish master, though in modern dress. Blake went over to her.

'George Strutt's gone doolally. Walking around spouting nonsense.'

She looked up, her eyes clear and unfazed.

'That could be difficult. They'll try to link him to you and create all kind of nonsense stories.'

'That's what Walter Lashbrooke has just been trying to tell me. I've got to go into the office. Be careful who you answer the phone to.'

'Of course. Is everything all right? You look peaky.'

'It might have escaped your notice that this is a stressful time for me. I'm shortly to be made a senior member of government and one of my sponsors has been found walking in circles in central London. So peaky is the least of my worries.'

Fiona stared up at him for a moment with a grey emptiness in her eyes, then bent her head to the cards on the table before her. She started writing a note on the first one.

'Make sure the door closes on your way out. It's started to stick again.'

BACK IN THE hall, Blake saw that the weather outside had turned foul. He fetched an umbrella from the tack room, then pushed his briefcase under his arm and unfurled the umbrella as he left the house and walked down the stone steps to the sweeping drive. His ministerial Prius was waiting and he climbed in without looking, finding the umbrella difficult to collapse now it was up. He swore briefly and forcefully and didn't look at the driver, but they were all the same anyway, cold-faced middle-aged men who never spoke in case it was thought they were being over-familiar.

'Straight to the office.'

The driver grunted and gunned the car, which pulled away with a roar and headed towards central London. Blake was taken by surprise but on reflection rather liked the attitude of the driver and glanced at the back of his head. He didn't recognise the man, which was no surprise. But he was younger than was typical and Blake realised that the man's eyes were appraising him from the rear-view mirror.

Blake said, 'Watch the road. This day will get very bad for you if you run us into a ditch.'

Sam Dyke said, 'Oh, I won't do that. You're too precious.'

CHANTAL WAS BEGINNING to understand the rhythm of their movements.

She was being kept in a chilly bedroom upstairs and there was always someone in the room on the opposite side of the corridor. Twice now she'd knocked on the inside of the door to be allowed to go to the toilet, and each time it had been a different person who answered – first the one they called James, well-spoken and with acne scars, then Nate with the odd hair. And there was the third, Clifford, the one who had kidnapped her at the nursing home – and whom she had satisfyingly whacked – and who she hoped was keeping out of her way.

Steele had put his head around the door a couple of times, the first to ask whether she needed anything for her 'lady parts,' as he'd called them, and the second seemingly just to check she was still there.

They'd brought her some newspapers and women's magazines and even a small radio, which she'd listened to until she became bored.

Now, at lunch, Steele had entered again, this time carrying a tray containing a Marks & Spencer chicken salad sandwich, a passion-fruit smoothie and a banana. He placed the tray on the end of the bed then moved back and sat on the straight chair next to the door.

He glanced around the room with a forensic expression on his face, as if checking whether she'd made any changes to the decor while he'd been away.

He said, 'Good digs, these. More comfortable than that metallic crap you and Jackie-boy called furniture.'

'I didn't realize you were an expert in modern design.'

'More of an appreciative audience. I like my arse to feel comfortable when it sits on a chair, not like it's having to balance on a razor-blade.'

Chantal had no more inclination to talk to him than to dive out of the window, but she thought it was better to appear human than remain distant. She reached over and picked up the sandwich, then began to unwrap it. The smell of bread and mayonnaise filled the room and her stomach fluttered appreciatively.

She said, 'You never told me who that man was.'

He knew who she meant but his face gave nothing away.

She went on, 'I'm going to find out eventually so you might as well tell me now.'

'You're very ... what's the word – persistent, aren't you? You can give up now because I'm not telling you anything. Don't you get it – this is a state-sanctioned operation. I'm not the bad guy here.'

'You have your moments.'

He appeared to consider this, his gaze moving inwards as though he were looking at some recessed part of his soul. When he spoke his voice was softer.

'Things have to be done sometimes that we don't like doing.'

'Like beating up my boyfriend?'

He shrugged. He had changed from his jacket and dark trousers to a tight black polo-neck sweater and navy blue jeans, and she saw the pack of muscle around his shoulders move. He seemed almost feline in the simplicity of his movements and Chantal felt herself turning cold as the inner brutality of the man facing her became evident. She realised that she was becoming sensitive to the different odours that all these men gave off – it was as though their need to portray a kind of harsh masculinity turned itself into rank pheromones that pervaded the atmosphere.

He said, 'So what do you think is going to happen here? What does the future hold for Chantal Bressette?'

'I'm going to see you rot in hell, for one thing. And I think you're going to come to a sticky end.'

He seemed surprised.

'Oh? Why's that?'

'Because criminals always do. Don't you read the papers? Nobody gets away with anything these days.'

'But I'm not a criminal. I keep telling you, what's happening to you is part of an operation.'

'What operation?'

'Protection of the realm, more or less.'

Chantal couldn't help herself laughing.

'You poor man. You're believing your own publicity, aren't you?'

'Shut your mouth.'

'That guy with the deep voice is just leading you on. This is personal to him. It's nothing to do with national security or protecting the crown jewels or whatever. He's just worried about something, and you're the lucky man who's helping him.'

Steele stood but Chantal remained where she was – on the bed with her back propped on the pillows. She continued eating the sandwich, slowly, her eyes fixed on his.

He said, 'Civilians are always the last to know what's really going on. They're on the leading edge of ignorance.'

Chantal said nothing as he turned and left. It seemed to her that she'd pushed him as far as she dared. She was willing to let him believe he'd won a debating point with a facile phrase that he'd probably borrowed from someone else.

DRIVING OUT OF Blake's extensive grounds, Sam turned left and continued for half a mile. The road was a narrow country lane overhung by oak trees and they passed no other cars. Blake was silent in the back seat. Sam stopped the car briefly to take his phone and bind his hands and he seemed in shock. His skin was white and his eyes were as dark as coal.

It had been easy to find Blake's house from the address that Dan had found, and he had known about the Ministerial Car Service because one of his former colleagues had gone to work for them. He said they often used the Toyota Prius as the vehicle of choice. He had finally found somewhere in South London where he could hire one and had spent the previous night in a nearby pub, squeezing his frame into a single bed that was too small.

This morning he had parked himself close to Blake's estate with the bonnet of his Mondeo raised.

And waited.

There had been a false alarm when a man driving an old Cortina had pulled up and asked whether he wanted some help, but Sam had simply dropped the bonnet and said he'd just fixed it – 'Dirty fuel pipe!' The man had looked dubiously at him, possibly because Sam wasn't particularly mechanical and hadn't known whether his comment made any sense. But in the end the Cortina had moved away. Twenty minutes later the Prius had turned up and Sam had been able to overpower the driver, who had shown a sweetness of nature in stopping but also a failure of professional protocol. Blake, as a junior minister, had had no security at all.

Sam turned into the lay-by where his Mondeo was parked. He climbed out of the driver's seat and opened the back door, pulling Blake out of the Prius and leading him towards his own car. Once there, he unlocked the boot of the Mondeo. Inside, the driver looked up at them, gagged and bound. Sam eased his legs up and levered him out of the boot, then took the tape from his mouth. He left the tape around his wrists.

He said, 'Sorry about that. Don't worry about your man here. I'm not going to hurt him. Now just go sit in the back of your own car a minute. I'll give you the keys later.'

The man looked up at Blake, who nodded at him.

Sam closed the boot and pushed Blake roughly into the back seat of the Mondeo and followed him in. He thought the threat of violence was likely to keep Blake in check. Although he was big he seemed soft – probably had a glittering career as the school bully, Sam thought.

He said, 'I know what you're thinking – how did I hijack a ministerial pool car? Simple – I stood in the middle of the road with my bonnet up and flagged him down. All the training in the world's no defence against basic human decency.'

Blake pushed himself back into the corner of the seat and crossed his arms.

'I hope you realise the kind of shit you're in for this adventure. Who are you?'

'You know who I am Mr Blake. I'm Sam Dyke, and your men are holding a woman called Chantal Bressette as a prisoner. Please don't argue.'

'What do you want?'

'Good, you didn't argue. Now we can talk.'

'The diary is useless, you know. There's nothing of interest in it for either of us. And besides, the whole thing is bigger than you might think.'

Sam ignored the bait and took Blake's phone from his pocket.

'Let's see what we've got here.'

He quickly found the menu for history and scrolled through the calls.

'Here we go. You should have used a better secret name than "Steele." Doesn't really work, does it?'

'I am really going to enjoy destroying you when this is over.'

'I don't think so. You've used government resources to harass and kidnap a British citizen who's done no harm to anyone. Your political career is over if only a hint of this gets out.'

Blake seemed to be coming awake slowly. Some colour had returned to his cheeks and he seemed to be gaining confidence.

'I don't think you understand the forces that you're going to be working against. I wouldn't be so cocky if I were you.'

Sam put out a hand and laid it on Blake's chest. The expensive shirt was soft beneath his touch.

'This is you and me here, in this car. Don't threaten me. I don't respond well to threats. Do we understand each other?'

Blake said nothing and Sam increased the pressure of his hand. He had been lifting weights for years and his fingers were thick and strong. He could keep up the pressure almost indefinitely.

Eventually Blake looked away.

'Yes. Now what the fuck do you want me to do?'

Sam removed his hand from Blake's chest and told him.

STEELE TOOK THE call outside the house, where the woman wasn't likely to hear his end of the conversation. To his surprise, he found that he didn't want the other members of the unit to hear it either.

He listened to what Blake said and started planning immediately.

This was the kind of thing he liked – a problem to which he'd find the solution. Put his training to use instead of having to baby-sit young wannabes who'd seen too many action movies and played too many video games.

Back inside the house, he called everyone together into the kitchen, which was the furthest room from the bedroom where the Bressette woman was being kept. He outlined what Gideon Blake had told him.

'Dyke's no fool, so we have to tread very carefully. He's not going to hurt our man – that would be stupid – but I don't suppose he'd have any trouble going for one of us.'

'And you've got the bruise to prove it.' James waggled his eyebrows like a comedian.

Instantly, Steele reached out an arm and seized James by the collar, dragging him forward over the kitchen table. His feet went up behind him as they scrabbled for purchase. Steele slowly pulled James' face closer to his own. His voice was full of icy venom.

'That was funny, wasn't it? A real rip-snorter. Remind me to laugh on my day off.'

He pushed James away and he clattered to the floor. Steele looked at Clifford and Nate intently, daring them to speak. They returned his gaze but said nothing.

He went on, 'This is meant to be a straight swap. The boss for the girl. We drive up and leave the girl in the designated spot and half an hour later go back to pick him up.'

Nate cleared his throat.

'Can we trust Dyke? What if he doesn't keep up his end of the bargain?'

'There's nothing in it for him to do that. All kinds of shit will rain down on him. It will be bad enough as it is, once the boss has got himself clear of all the hoo-hah.'

'So we just follow orders? Drop her off and pick him up?'

Steele turned to him. 'I didn't say that, did I?'

UPSTAIRS, CHANTAL HAD heard voices and then a clatter of furniture. After that, more voices. She sensed that something was about to happen and wasn't surprised when she heard footsteps on the stairs and then saw the door opening.

Steele stepped inside. He seemed a little flushed but she doubted that walking up the stairs had quickened his pulse. He pointed to her.

'Get your paltry things together. We're going for a ride. Sammy-boy came through for you.'

'How do I know that's true? You might be taking me out to a ditch somewhere.'

He stepped forward, his eyes hard and focused.

'There's a time to be coy, and this isn't it. Put your shoes on and get your bag. If I wanted to hurt you I'd do it so that you'd cry for a long time and then you'd be dead. So stop playing games and get off the bed. Go to the toilet, too. I'll be at the bottom of the stairs.'

He left the room and Chantal rose from the bed. She'd put her shoes under the chair and her coat was draped over its back. She felt herself trembling as she squeezed her toes into the shoes and wondered briefly if she was going to faint. Outside the weather was grey and looked like rain – she found that she really didn't want to go.

On the landing she turned and went into the bathroom. There was no lock so she put her bag on the floor to stop the door swinging open, then splashed some water on her face. It made her cold but not particularly refreshed. She blew her nose on some toilet paper, then threw the paper in the bowl and flushed it.

When she reached the foot of the stairs, Steele took her arm and led her to the front door. There was an air of bustle about the house, the sound of doors being shut and locked, things being put away in drawers. There was a black rubbish bag by the front door, which Clifford picked up and took outside. He brushed against her shoulder as he went past her but didn't apologise. The bruise across his nose was spreading.

When all the men had filed past her and gone out to the car, Steele placed the blindfold over her eyes and pulled her through the door. The air was chill but she already felt cold from anticipation. Steele forced her into the back seat of the Touareg and then Clifford got in afterwards so that she was held between him and Nate. More intense male odour. She sensed that neither of them was looking at her. She began to feel sick in her stomach.

Steele got in the passenger seat and James put the car into gear and moved off.

Steele turned around and touched her on the knee to attract her attention.

'Got everything? Good. Now sit back and relax. Imagine you're a parcel and you're being delivered by a nice man in a white van. Let's hope you don't get damaged, eh?'

SAM NOSED THE Mondeo into a parking slot as near to the exit as he could manage. Brighton was always busy and he knew he was lucky to find a position so close to his meeting place.

Blake sat in the seat next to him, his hands held together with white nylon rope. He had said nothing since his phone call to Steele. He seemed to have turned inward and become cold and hate-filled, like a prisoner who knew his cause was just but his prospect of escape minimal.

Sam had decided to take the Mondeo because he wasn't sure that Steele's men knew what kind of car he was driving. And the Prius would have been easier to spot than the workmanlike and common Mondeo. He wanted every advantage he could get. He had untied the legs of Blake's driver but taken the key so that the man would have to walk the mile or so back to Blake's house before raising the alarm. Sam was in no doubt that a police alert was in force throughout the country right now. But he also knew that Blake would cancel it as soon as he could, or face exposure. There would be some embarrassment but nothing like the major commotion that would occur if Blake's actions were revealed in full.

Sam took another piece of rope and attached a loop between Blake's wrists around the steering wheel, so that he was forced to lean to the right, his elbow on the transmission tunnel.

'I'm going to do the business. Don't get impatient.'

'You've crossed a line, Dyke. You do know I'm a government minister?'

'Junior minister. Don't get ahead of yourself.'

'That might change.'

'Then I'll be very happy for you. Until then, rest easy and think about what you've been up to in the last few weeks. Ask yourself whether it was worth it.'

Blake snorted.

'You're very high and mighty for a sleazy private investigator.'

'It's the way I was brought up. I was taught how to tell right from wrong. You seem to have been absent from school that day.'

'There's always a bigger picture, Dyke, you know that. You came across it when you were with Customs and Excise. Oh, hang on, that's why you were asked to leave, wasn't it? Not a team player. Too focused on individual cases and unable to think strategically. I'm quoting from memory so it might not be quite right.'

Dyke sat back in the driver's seat. It seemed that Blake had already done his homework. He had a sudden sense of how deep he was into this situation, and with very little forethought. He had always been impulsive when angered, but this was turning nasty on a bigger scale than he had expected.

It was because types like Blake irritated him. Their sense of entitlement, their belonging to worlds of privilege to which others weren't privy, turned a switch in him. He lost perspective and often found himself saying or doing things that he later regretted.

But it was too late now.

He thought of Chantal. She had been upset at the nursing home, when Jennifer Leftwich had told her story. She had reacted badly to the circumstance she'd found herself in and was then gathered up by Steele and his men as though they were plucking a flower. It had been too easy for them. He couldn't let them believe they'd got away with it. He had to keep trying or else he wouldn't be able to face himself or believe in his job any more.

He said, 'Sit tight. Enjoy the view. Don't try to get away or I won't be able to control what I say to the press when they come for me.'

This time Blake said nothing and Sam climbed out of the car, locking the door behind him.

He walked from the dark of the car park into the grey daylight. Immediately he could smell the seafront, a lingering odour of wet shingle and dead fish. Seagulls squawked loudly overhead and the buzz of traffic and people created a murmuring backdrop of sound. He turned left out of the car park and headed up towards Churchill Square. Although it was still relatively early in the tourist season, the streets were already full of people carrying cameras on their way to the Royal Pavilion and students listening through ear buds to their music players while pushing bicycles up Brighton's steep slopes. He paused and looked in a shop window but there was no one behind him or to either side. Despite the crowds of people he felt exposed. They could be watching from almost anywhere if they'd brought in the police.

At the corner of Churchill Square – a paved open space giving entrance to several shops and department stores – he crossed the road and stood by some traffic lights, sweeping the area again for signs of Steele or his crew. Some people glanced at him but no one stared. He looked back the way he'd come to see whether anyone paused or looked aside. But it was too busy to pick out individuals easily. That was the point. He needed the cover of other people.

As satisfied as he could be, he moved closer in, his pulse ticking over quickly. Outside a clothes store a guitarist had set up with a music stand. He was playing a George Harrison number and Sam paused again briefly, enjoying the guitarist's slide guitar work. He threw a few coins into the young man's guitar case and moved on with the crowd.

Eventually he took up a position in a doorway and looked across a busy road towards Churchill Square. Buses and taxis went by constantly, obscuring his view of the shop fronts opposite and the large paved area that formed the square itself. He had been here once before several years ago, following an Albanian drug smuggler as he came down from Liverpool to his distributors in the south, and he remembered the layout of the square and the roads that led up to it. The Borders book shop was now closed but the square was still the same.

Ten minutes later he saw Steele saunter on to the square with Chantal, his body language casual and relaxed. He wore a cream bomber jacket over a black polo-neck pullover and with his short curly hair and superior manner looked like an aristocrat's son being forced to run an errand he found beneath him. Chantal walked with her head up in defiance, Sam thought. Steele had pinned one of her arms next to his and was looking around keenly. Sam stepped back into the doorway and watched Steele take Chantal to one of the low walls surrounding the square. People were sitting on them eating sandwiches or just watching other shoppers. Chantal sat down as though under instruction and hugged herself. Steele stood in front of her for a moment and ran his hand over her hair and on to her neck, then looked around. If he had been closer, Sam thought he would have seen Steele grinning as if to taunt him.

There was an abrupt, loud blip from a siren.

Sam looked to his right and saw a police-car moving through the traffic, using its siren to make its presence known. He pushed himself further back into his doorway and watched as it drifted in front of him and turned, making its way towards the Steine, the square at the bottom of the hill.

He glanced across and saw that Steele had been watching too. His head turned, and for a moment Sam thought his eyes lingered on his shadowed doorway before they moved on. He said something to Chantal without looking at her.

Then he turned and walked away.

Sam moved his position to watch where he went but quickly lost him in the press of people coming up from North Street.

He waited two minutes and then approached Chantal, who spotted him and stood and then walked briskly in his direction, anger in every stride. She came to a halt before him and looked up with defiant eyes.

'Can I ask you to kill that little fucker?'

Sam grinned.

'Rule seven of private detective school – don't do what clients ask when they're angry. What did they do?'

'Nothing. Just kept blindfolding me and patronising me and talking to me about you. You've really wound them up.'

Sam took her arm gently and began to pull her down towards the car park, against the mass of people who were making their way upwards.

'People like that are easily wound up. They're all control freaks who use violence to get their own way because they're not bright enough to argue sensibly.'

'Well if you won't kill him, *I* will.'

'Jesus, I thought you'd be a mess by now, not going all Rambo on me. Let's get back to the car.'

She stopped and held him back.

'What did you do to get me out? You haven't given up the diary, have you? I'll never forgive you if you have. I don't want them to have it now on principle.'

'No, I've still got it. I had to exchange someone else for you.'

'Who? The Pope?'

Sam hesitated.

'It's probably best you don't know. You need some deniability in this.'

'Is it a man with a deep voice and a posh accent?'

'Did you meet him?'

'I couldn't see him. He talked to me in this house they had. Somewhere on the coast. I could hear seagulls and smell the sea. Like here.'

'Well it's best you don't see him now. You don't want to give them an excuse to come after you again.'

'Do you know what? At this moment I don't give a shit. Anything we can do to put the knife into him and his guys, I'm all for it. Now, where are you parked?'

FIFTEEN MINUTES AFTER he'd dropped off Chantal Bressette, Steele saw Blake emerge into Churchill Square. He looked angry, peering around at everyone as though they were personally offending him by being in the same post code.

Steele said to the driver, 'Go. Blow your horn so he sees us.'

They saw Blake turn in their direction, then hesitate before coming across the square towards the road. Steele climbed out of the car.

He said, 'Boss – any idea where they are?'

Blake looked at the car. 'What's this?'

'I'll explain later – where are they?'

Blake turned and gestured vaguely. 'Car park at the bottom of the hill. I think it's a Mondeo. Silver.'

'Okay, get in.'

He climbed in after Blake and said to the driver, 'You heard. You know where that is?'

'Two minutes.'

'Then stop talking and start driving.'

SAM ACCELERATED SMOOTHLY out of the car park and turned left, then right on to the coast road, heading towards

Portsmouth once more. Beside him, Chantal had pressed her back into the seat and had closed her eyes.

'Where now?'

Sam glanced at her. She seemed even younger than he had remembered, her skin smooth and her short light brown hair nestling in the curve of her neck.

He said, 'Are we still in this? We can give it up if you prefer. We still have the diary. We don't know what it means but neither does anyone else. We could just let those jokers crash around and worry themselves to death.'

She turned and looked at the sea and the sky through her window. Tourists in gaudy clothes walked back and forth on the wide pavement by the beach, or stood in small clusters like acolytes staring at the crashing waves. A black Labrador ran on the beach, its tongue lolling.

She said, 'It's unreal, isn't it? I feel like I'm in a film only real things are happening. Real nasty men and real bad things. What do you think we should do?'

'I'm nothing if not persistent. That's what Laura always tells me, anyway. Persistent to the point of obsessive. Dog, bone, that kind of stuff.'

'You haven't answered the question.'

'I thought I had. We stick with it.'

'Good. But what does that mean?'

'We come up with a plan.'

Chantal lay back in the passenger seat again. The sun had finally beaten back the clouds and began to warm the cabin. Sam turned up the cooling system. They drove for several minutes in silence. Then Chantal stirred and opened her eyes.

'Does Laura mind all this? Or does it get on her nerves?'

Sam didn't like talking about himself or his relationships – he hadn't learned how to do it. But then he startled himself.

'I get on her nerves. If I'm honest, I think she wants to break up with me but doesn't know how to do it.'

Chantal turned towards him. 'Why do you think that?'

'We started going out when she was under pressure, so that wasn't a conventional romance. And recently I put her in danger with something I was doing. It can't be easy for her.'

'Have you actually talked about it?'

Sam laughed darkly.

'What, and put the idea of leaving me into her head? I don't think so.'

'If it's in your head it's probably already in hers. Do you want to stay with her?'

'She's good for me even though it doesn't work the other way around. She forces me to think about other people.'

They drove in silence for a while. Sam wondered what he was doing opening up like that to a girl still in her twenties. Did he really need to talk about Laura with someone? Or was he trying to impress Chantal with his self-awareness? He felt his cheeks grow warm as he thought about it.

The sun was glinting off the sea and he put on a pair of sunglasses. They drove past Hove with its mixture of Victorian hotels and square modern apartment blocks, its rows of colourful beach huts lining the road like sentries. Ten minutes later they were passing through Portslade, its industrial skyline briefly cutting off their view of the sea.

Sam looked in his rear-view mirror.

'What's this?'

Chantal turned and saw a police-car about fifty yards behind them, it's roof-lights flashing.

Sam said, 'Let's hope they're after someone else.'

As he slowed to let the police car pass, it also reduced its speed. With a sick feeling, he pulled into the side of the road. It seemed the game was up after all. At least the officers would arrest them and he would be able to say his piece, no matter what Blake said.

The police car had pulled up behind them but now turned and moved parallel to them before angling in front to cut them off. Looking through the windows as the car passed, Sam saw Blake in the back seat waving four fingers at him and smiling grimly.

'Shit.'

Behind them, the black Touareg had pulled up close and the three other goons climbed out. They walked up to the Mondeo and one of them opened his door while another yanked open the passenger door for Chantal.

Sam got out just as Steele climbed from the police car. The police officer who had been driving pointedly looked the other way.

Sam said, 'Good to see a bit of inter-agency cooperation. Do the cops know you're a bunch of tools?'

Then Steele hit him in the face and he lost consciousness.

STEELE DIDN'T LIKE the look on Gideon Blake's face. They were in the kitchen of the house in Portsmouth, lights out, talking quietly. Even in the gloom he could see the fire in Blake's eyes – a look he'd seen before in people seeking revenge.

'What do you want to do, sir?'

'We've got to keep a lid on this. Understand?'

'Yes, sir. What do you suggest?'

'How the fuck do I know? You're the expert here.'

'Yes, boss.'

'And stop calling me that. Jesus, you make me sound like Bob Hoskins in a gangster movie.'

Steele had never seen or heard Blake acting out like this. The steadiness in his voice had vanished and he didn't seem to be thinking straight.

Blake pulled out one of the chairs at the kitchen table and sat down.

'Look, things are happening for me. Next week. I can't let this get out of hand. Can you do that for me? Can you keep a lid on it?'

'I might need to know more than what you've told me so far.'

'Well I can't. Live with it. And I want to talk to Dyke and the woman. Alone.'

'I wouldn't recommend it.'

'They know who I am, for Christ's sake.'

'You need some deniability.'

Blake snorted.

'I didn't take you for a stupid man, Steele. I'm up to my neck in this. The best I can hope for is to be in a position where I can't be touched.'

'Is that going to be possible?'

'Maybe. That's why I need to talk to them. Now.'

THEY WERE SEATED at the kitchen table, their hands tied behind their backs. Blake sat facing them, Steele standing behind them and to one side. He'd insisted on being there. James, Nate and Clifford were in the sitting room watching a movie on DVD. The sound of voices and dramatic Hollywood music drifted into the kitchen from time to time.

Sam noticed that Blake was looking tired, the overhead light emphasizing the bags beneath his eyes. His skin had lost that rosy sheen Sam associated with a public-school education and good nutrition.

Blake said, 'This has to stop. Now. I can't afford for us to keep fighting each other like this.'

'Then let us go.'

Blake shrugged. 'It's not that easy. There are issues of ... timing.'

Chantal said, 'What does that mean? How long are you going to keep us?'

'I don't want to keep you at all. But I'm not yet in a position to let you go. So I want to tell you a story. Something that might change your minds about what you think you're doing.'

'I doubt it.'

'Well, that's your privilege, Mr Dyke. I haven't forgotten the way you treated me earlier today and I'm sure Mr Steele and his colleagues will do their duty if I ask them to. But I don't want it to come to that. I'm hoping that you'll listen to reason.'

'I'm a reasonable man.'

'No you're not, but that's beside the point.'

'You've got us tied up with a house full of amoral goons with a short fuse and you expect me to be reasonable? Peddle your fantasies somewhere else, Blake.'

Steele took a step forward but Blake raised a tired hand.

'Let him rant. A creature of little intellect has to find a way to express itself. Despite my best instincts, I'm going to tell you the story anyway. Then you can make up your own minds.'

'If you're sure my intellect can handle it.'

'We'll see, won't we?'

Blake sat back in his chair and looked at them both.

'Let me think where I have to start. How much do you know about the Jews in the Second World War?'

Sam felt himself frowning. Where was this going now?

After a pause, Chantal said, 'I've seen Schindler's List. And stuff on TV. And I've read things here and there, in the papers.'

'That's a good start. Schindler was preventing his Jewish workers from being taken to concentration camps. But elsewhere in the world, the Jews were trying to help themselves. To prevent themselves being eradicated by invading Nazi armies, for example.'

Sam leaned back in his seat. It looked as though Blake was going to take his time.

Blake went on, 'Let me paint you a picture. All over Europe, Jews were trying to escape to the West or at least to Palestine, where they felt they would be safe. So in December of 1941, nearly seven hundred Rumanian Jews bought passage on a cattle transporter called the Struma, heading for Palestine and, they thought, to freedom. They'd paid a lot of money for the trip and were told it would take only a few days. They were also told that it would be a comfortable journey. But when they got to the ship they found it was too small for the number who had booked and that most of them would have to bunk down on cages that had been placed on the outside deck, not in cabins. They weren't happy, of course, but they had little alternative. They had already paid their money and the Germans were more or less at their back.

What else could they do but go on board and hope it was going to be all right. Men, women, children, whole families. Their futures depended on this boat.'

'I think we get the idea.'

'Good. So eventually it set off. The travellers were told that the trip was going to be broken up by a short stay in Istanbul in Turkey, where they'd pick up their immigration certificates into Palestine. They wouldn't be allowed into the country unless they had the right papers. With me so far?'

Sam said, 'We're not idiots.'

'Says he, strapped to a chair. Allow me to continue.'

Blake continued to describe the journey undertaken by the Struma. It was an old ship whose engine was unreliable and continually broke down, with the result that three days after it set off it had to be towed into the harbour at Istanbul. Once there, mechanics tried to fix the engine and negotiations began over the fate of the passengers.

'The British government at that time had a policy of restricting mass Jewish immigration into Palestine, which was under its protection. So they urged the Turkish government to prevent the Struma from sailing onwards. They didn't want to deal with them when they arrived. At the same time, the Turks refused to allow the desperate passengers off the ship and to set foot on Turkish territory.'

'Why?'

'Who knows? I suspect they were worried that some of the passengers would try to run away. Or perhaps they didn't want to set a precedent.'

'Or perhaps they were just anti-Semitic.'

'Perhaps. Anyway, they were held on the ship for seventy-one days. Eventually the British honoured the expired Palestinian visas held by some of the passengers, and they also allowed a pregnant woman off. In addition, there was an agreement to let children between the ages of eleven and sixteen leave, too, but the Brits wouldn't send a ship for them and the Turks still wouldn't let them on their land. So they stayed on board.'

Sam said, 'This isn't going to end well, is it?'

Blake leaned back.

'As I said, The Struma was held by the Turks for over two months, during Christmas and New Year.'

'Did they get any food or anything?'

'Yes, Miss Bressette. Some supplies were sent out to them against the Turkish authorities' wishes. Local people were more forgiving than their government. But conditions weren't good, as you can imagine.'

Sam leaned forward. 'So what happened? Don't keep us in suspense.'

'Patience, Dyke. You need to hear it all. It might change entirely what you think is going on here.'

FROM HIS POSITION in the corner of the kitchen, Steele didn't like what he was hearing. Everything he'd done for Blake before had been directly related to national security. Blake had taken him under his wing and had him working in parallel with British forces in Iraq and Afghanistan. He'd protected ambassadors, taken material that would never see the inside of a diplomatic bag in and out of countries, assassinated tribal leaders. He realised that Blake had his own agenda but that was OK – every politician looked after themselves.

But this sounded like nonsense. The Second World War was a long time ago. Fought and won. Now move on. You didn't re-fight old battles, there was no mileage in it. His own family had made sacrifices, that was for damn sure. And he understood the notion of honour and pride in your regiment and the preservation of tradition. He'd lectured the woman about that and he wasn't a hypocrite.

But where was this going? What did 700 dead Jews mean to him? What was Blake getting him involved in this time?

IT WAS NOW dark outside but no-one seemed interested in turning on the lights. Sam was aware of the other men in the house and Steele standing just behind him and to his right. Worse, his hands were tied and so were Chantal's. There was no way he could force an exit out of this. He would just have to listen to Blake and wait for an opportunity further down the line.

Blake's voice had become tired, as though telling his story had wiped him out.

'While the Struma had been kept at Istanbul, there'd been a hell of a lot of diplomatic shuttling going on behind the scenes. Remember, the Brits wouldn't let the passengers through to Palestine and the Turks wouldn't let them off the boat to go elsewhere. It was an impasse. And meanwhile, the mechanics still couldn't fix the engine. In the end, in February of 1942, Turkish agents boarded the ship early one morning and cut the anchor. They then towed the ship away from Istanbul harbour and into the Black Sea, where they left it drifting.'

A silence descended in the kitchen.

Eventually Chantal said, 'So they couldn't go anywhere.'

'That's right. Accounts of the numbers vary, but the best estimates suggest that by this time there were 769 passengers and crew on board who were left to drift. Very little food or water. Terrible living conditions. At the mercy of whatever circumstances arose. Which, you should realise, included both German and Russian u-boats.'

Chantal said, 'I don't want to hear.'

'I'm afraid you have to. The morning after the boat had been abandoned, people on shore heard a terrific explosion. The ship had blown up and sunk, with 768 people killed or drowned, including over a hundred children.'

'What happened?'

'That's an interesting question, isn't it? There were several theories. Some suggested that the passengers had blown up the ship out of despair. As they'd been towed out of Istanbul, for example, they'd hung banners over the side of the ship in English and Hebrew saying "Save us", so they seemed to know what was coming.'

'But there were other theories.'

'Yes, Dyke, there were. It was thought for a while that it had been sunk by a German u-boat. They were in the area making a nuisance of themselves. But eventually it was discovered that the Struma was attacked and sunk by a Russian u-boat, the SC-213. You'll remember I said 769 people were on board and that 768 were killed. One man survived from the sinking. A very resourceful fellow by all accounts – a young chap called Stoliar. He was blown off the ship and ended up clutching a piece of wreckage, alongside a crew-member who later slipped off the wreckage and died. Stoliar was rescued by a Turkish boat, ironically, and after some time enlisted and fought with the British Army. Personally I wouldn't have thought he'd have anything to do with Britain after what we did to him. Maybe that's why he wound up living in America.'

Sam said, 'I'm shaky on military history, but weren't the Russians supposed to be on our side? Why did they sink a ship full of civilians?'

Blake stood up abruptly.

'Well we've finally got to it. That's what this is all about. It turned out that the Russian submarine was acting under secret orders to sink any ships that could be supplying material to Nazi Germany. That is, either enemy *or* neutral ships.'

'Secret orders? Who gave them? Stalin?'

'Undoubtedly. And that leads to the second question – did Churchill have anything to do with it? People have suggested that he reached an agreement with Stalin to blow up the troublesome ship and Stalin would get something in return. East Germany, perhaps.'

'All this doesn't explain what's going on here.' Sam raised his head and looked Blake in the eye. 'It's a nice history lesson and proves yet again what racist prigs we Brits are. But there's more, isn't there? You haven't made the connection between this ship and Chantal's diary.'

Blake sighed with exasperation. 'It's not the diary. The diary is only one link in a chain.'

'Then what are we doing here?'

Blake exploded. 'It's my father, you fool!' He sat down heavily and looked at them each in turn. 'I think my father knew it was going to happen. And did nothing about it.'

SAM GLANCED AROUND the room. It was almost completely dark now. Through the kitchen window he could see the lights in the kitchens of other houses beyond. The noise from the television had lowered but he knew the men were still in the sitting room and therefore not far away.

He said, 'So what do you want from us?'

'I thought that was obvious, Dyke. It might not mean anything to you but the honour of my family is important to me.'

'So important that you're willing to risk it on a stupid business like this? With these gorillas? I don't buy it. There's something else. You're just not telling us.'

Blake spread his hands.

'It's got a little out of hand, I grant you that. But I will not see the name of my family sullied. Can you imagine the uproar if it comes out that the British were involved in the sinking of the ship? The repercussions were bad enough at the time – debates in the House of Lords and press outrage. The High Commissioner of the British Mandate in Palestine was nearly assassinated by a bomb planted by a Jewish group – his wife was injured in the explosion. It's not just me – it's our government and our national honour.'

'If we're guilty we should pay the price.'

'Well that's the kind of defeatist crap I'd expect from someone like you. Steele, can I have a word?'

LEAVING THE KITCHEN door open to keep an eye on Dyke, Steele took Blake through into what they called the dining room, though they'd never eaten there.

He said, 'What do you want to do?'

'I'm open to suggestions.' Blake seemed exhausted.

'You want to hear the options?'

'Go ahead.'

'Keep them. Kill them.'

'Nothing in-between?'

'You could use your resources to render them non-people. Or have them put away somewhere.'

Blake turned away. His body seemed to Steele to have shrunk in the last hour as the reality of what they were doing became apparent.

Blake said, 'Recommendations?'

'A question, first.'

'All right. What do you want to know?'

'Was Dyke right? Is there something else?'

'Isn't protecting the honour of my family enough?'

'No, sir. Not for you. What we've done in the past has always been justifiable. In terms of the country's best interests. This ... this Struma thing is history.'

'It might be history to you, Steele, but we're talking about reputation here – my family's reputation. I won't have it tainted.'

'What did you expect to find?'

'I don't know. I believe that somewhere out there is a document implicating my father in the sinking of that ship. I don't know how or why. When he was alive I didn't know anything about it – he never talked about the war. But my aunt told me he received a telegram sent by Churchill himself and two days later the Struma was set adrift. What if he was told to ask the Turks to cut the ship loose? What if some kind of deal was made between Churchill and Stalin and Churchill and the Turkish government? Who knows?'

'That sounds tenuous.'

'Not at all. There was a telegram from Churchill to my father. Why? Given my present circumstances I can't allow it to be found. These days the implication of guilt is enough to make it stick.'

Steele heard a noise behind him and turned. James, Nate and Clifford had trooped into the room and were standing listening to what Blake said. Steele realised now that they had been talking in the other room, which was why the sound of the movie had grown quiet.

James came forward and looked at Blake.

'Sir, we've been talking.'

Steele said, 'Didn't know you could talk, boy. Thought that was mumbling came out of your gob. Step back.'

Blake raised a hand.

'No, let him speak. All opinions should be heard.'

'Thank you, sir. Those two people out there know us. They know our names. They've seen you. We could all get in a lot of trouble. And if I can speak frankly, sir, I didn't sign up for this.'

Blake said, 'Really?' in a voice heavy with sarcasm.

'Yes, sir.'

Blake walked closer to the three younger men and looked them each in the eye. Finally he returned to James.

'And your suggestion is? Drawing on the full weight of your legal training?'

James glanced nervously at his two colleagues and Clifford stepped forward. Blue-black circles were beginning to show under his eyes now that the damage inflicted on his nose was beginning to spread. It made him look as though he hadn't slept in a week.

'We don't think we have any choice, sir. We have to neutralise them.'

Steele closed his eyes. He'd thought he'd got the measure of the three team members but obviously he'd been wrong. When you served in combat the ties you built with your team were what saved your life. You backed them up and vice versa. You had to depend on them. You couldn't be looking right and left to check they were still there.

But these three ... they'd blind-sided him. He realised now why they all seemed so young. They had probably got out of the services as soon as they could to make some money on the Circuit. They weren't loyal, they weren't schooled. He couldn't trust them.

Blake coughed.

'That's a very interesting proposition, men. I take it you meant that we should kill these two people?'

'Yes, sir. We have no choice.'

'Steele?'

'One of the options that I mentioned, sir. In principle. But might lead to more trouble in the long run.'

Only a few days before he had considered killing the Bressette woman in Edinburgh Zoo, and had had no problem beating Jack the Boyfriend. Now he was counselling caution when it came to extreme violence. He wondered what had happened to his own commitment.

Blake said, 'Yes, my thoughts exactly. Look, I have to get back home. One of you will have to take me because I have no transport.'

Steele said, 'Nate.'

Nate hesitated, seemingly caught between loyalty to his colleagues and some deeper sense of the obligations of hierarchy. Then he nodded and left the room to get the keys to the Touareg.

Blake said, 'Lord, I'm tired of all this. Steele, just hold them, all right? Till Monday. You'll understand why. I'll decide after that.'

'Yes, sir.'

James and Clifford had moved back towards the doorway, their eyes smouldering with disapproval. Blake turned to them.

'Anything to add?'

James found his courage. 'I think it's a mistake. We can't let them into the wild. It's our arses as well as yours. Sir.'

'No doubt. But in this instance my arse is a lot bigger than yours and is a more vulnerable target. Now get the fuck out of my way.'

He pushed past them and went down the corridor to the front entrance. They heard the Touareg start up outside. Blake paused at the door and gestured Steele towards him, lowering his voice when he spoke.

'Keep hold of the diary, too. I'm not sure we're going to get anything more out of it than we've already got. Scan the other pages and send them to me. I'm beginning to think it was a pointless wild goose chase. And one more thing.'

'Yes?'

'I gave you these men because I thought you could handle them. Don't prove me wrong.'

Steele said nothing as Blake opened the door and went out into the cooling air.

IN THE KITCHEN, Chantal felt that her heart was going to shake itself out of her rib-cage and explode over the linoleum flooring. There was something about the situation that she found unbearable. There was a tension in these men that she felt was bound to come out sooner or later – they were like wolves circling one another and waiting for the weakest to fall so they could pounce.

She glanced at Sam, who was sitting next to her at the table in a thin plastic chair. Their hands were bound and also linked to the bindings around their ankles. They couldn't even stand up, let alone escape.

She wanted to say something, but felt that if she opened her mouth to speak then nothing would come out but a wounded scream, like some animal whose legs had been caught in the steel jaws of a trap.

Sam turned to her without expression and then, to her surprise, winked slowly.

'All going according to plan. They don't know what trouble they're in.'

Before she could reply, the kitchen door opened and the three remaining men walked in – Clifford with the bruised nose; the well-spoken one, James; and Steele, looking grim.

Clifford was wearing a Lincoln-green polo-shirt with a Lacoste lizard on its breast. He was thick across the chest and his arms were powerful. He seemed to be leading this delegation. He had the look of someone who'd had a recent disappointment and wanted to make up for it. He came close and turned Sam's chair so that he was now facing away from the table.

James leaned with his back to the half-glazed door that led outside and Steele took up a position in the corner. Chantal felt her heart thumping even more fiercely and her pulse was now throbbing in her head. She was fearful about what was about to happen.

From his chair, Sam looked at the three men ranged around the room.

'A curry would be nice, if you're taking orders. With pilau rice and a side of Bombay potato.'

Abruptly, Clifford lashed out crosswise with the back of his right hand, catching Sam on the side of the face. His chair rocked but didn't fall. Sam grunted and breathed in deeply, moving his head from side to side. Chantal looked away but caught James grinning at her. By contrast, Steele's expression hadn't changed – he looked like the adult sent to supervise the children and make sure they didn't hurt themselves.

Sam had shaken off the blow and looked up at Clifford, who was breathing heavily and massaging his fingers.

'Better now? How's the nose, incidentally? It was nice seeing you use it as a snowboard when you went down those steps in Edinburgh. Not too good at the steering, though, were you?'

Chantal winced as Clifford hit him again, with the opposite fist. Sam seemed to have anticipated this and half-turned with it.

Clifford said, 'Just because boss man wants us to hold on to you till Monday doesn't mean we have to like it.'

Chantal said, 'Stop it! Leave him alone. I hit you on the nose – why don't you hit me back?'

Clifford's attention turned to her and she struggled against her bindings. 'Who said you're not next, you little bitch? I can't get any decent kip because of you. This fucking nose groans all night long.'

Sam said, 'You're such a wuss, Clifford. A man tied up in a chair and a woman half your size. I see now why you're a private prick – no professional outfit would have you.'

From the doorway, James said, 'He's got a point there, Cliff.'

'Fuck off.'

He hit Sam again with the back of his right hand. Sam rocked with it once more, his cheeks now beginning to show pink. Then he slowly lifted his head and grinned at Clifford.

'Sure you can keep this up till Monday? You look a little out of breath there.'

Clifford took a step forward but Steele said sharply, 'OK, enough of this bollocks. You owed him a couple of pats on the head but daddy's going to take away your bat and ball now. James, take them upstairs. Clifford, go and have a cold shower or something. Your hard-on's showing from here.'

'If I could be sure you'd pay me I'd be gone by now. I didn't sign up to nanny a couple of treasure hunters.'

'No, you signed up to do exactly what I fucking told you. Now get out of my sight. Go play Call of Duty if you want some kicks.'

Clifford stared hard at Sam, then turned and left the room. Chantal felt her breathing calm down. James came over and untied the bindings on her feet, then did the same for Sam. They both stood up and stretched their legs. Steele was standing with his arms folded.

'Boys will be boys. Let it go, Dyke, or there might be worse to follow.'

'So what happens Monday?'

Steele nodded. 'Sharp man. As far as I know, it's the beginning of the working week. What can I say? Or maybe he's set a nuclear bomb to go off in the Houses of Parliament and you two are the only ones who can save the world. I hope not, or we're fucked.'

Rising from her chair, Chantal walked up to him and spat in his face.

'Coward. You let this happen. You could have stopped it but you didn't. I hope you're proud of yourself.'

She expected Steele to hit her and readied herself to duck or raise her arms. But he wiped his face with his handkerchief and looked at her mildly.

'Proud isn't the word, Miss Bressette. We do what we have to do to make a mark in this world. James, please.'

James pulled on her arm and led her away. She saw Sam give Steele a long look as they went past him.

THEY HAD BEEN given one bedroom between them – Steele had brought up a foul-smelling z-bed that folded out onto rickety metal legs, thrown a sleeping bag at Sam and said, 'Suit yourself – bed or floor, I don't care. But no rumpy-pumpy with glamour-puss here.'

Then he'd shut the door behind him and locked it.

Chantal explained that it was the same bedroom she'd been held in before – the window was double glazed and sealed, and although there was a top-opening pane it was locked shut. The door was Yale-locked from the outside and he'd seen a couple of mortice bolts in it, too. A safe house for spooks, then, but also somewhere they might keep prize catches – defectors or people who just needed protecting for a while.

Steele had given them more supermarket sandwiches and a couple of cans of Coca-Cola. Chantal said she wasn't hungry so he ate both sets of sandwiches and drank the coppery liquid.

She watched him from the bed, her knees drawn up to her chin.

'How's the head? He caught you a couple of good ones there.'

'My dad used to hit me harder.'

'Often?'

'I was a good boy. Didn't give him any reason.'

She turned and looked through the window.

'What did you make of Blake's story?'

'I'm sure the stuff about the Struma is true. He had no reason to make it up, and the detail sounded right. Who knows about the rest?'

'Why is he so worked up about it? It was ages ago.'

'Like all politicians he thinks the world revolves around him and we should all help polish his own view of himself. Maybe his father was involved, maybe he wasn't. In any case, it's none of our business.'

'How can you say that? We're only here because of him and his father and that bloody ship. Everything that's happened in the last few days has been his fault. Everything. I don't want this any more. I don't want to be locked in a room with someone I hardly know because of something that happened seventy years ago. I want to go back to my life and my boyfriend. I want to go back to my job and looking out of the windows waiting until it was five-thirty and time to go home. I want my old life back because I'm scared and I don't belong here in your Boy's Own story. Do you understand? Do you?'

She bowed her head and Sam thought she might be close to tears. He considered her for a while.

'What do you want me to do?'

She looked up.

'Something. Anything.'

'I might not need to.'

'What do you mean?'

'Things are coming to a head. Obviously there's a deadline on Monday which is making Blake nervous. And there'll be ructions.'

'What ructions?'

'That gang are not all as professional as they'd like us to believe.'

'What are you talking about?'

'Human nature. It always comes out in the end.'

LYING ON THE bed fully-clothed, he heard Nate return in the early hours of the morning. He had thought the man would stay overnight having delivered Blake home, but obviously he wanted to be where the action was. The front door opened and closed quietly and two minutes later there was a quiet tread on the stairs as he went up to the bedroom he shared with one of the others. The four men were bunked two to a bedroom. He and Chantal were in the third. The fourth bedroom was a small box-room and through an open door Sam had seen various rucksacks and suitcases that evidently belonged to the men.

Forty-five minutes later he was still awake when he heard the locks turn in the bedroom door.

He leaped from the bed and moved silently to the far corner of the room, squeezing himself behind a wardrobe. The bedroom door itself had been hinged so that it opened flat against the wall – presumably to prevent anyone getting a jump on whoever came through.

But the door swung open leaving no one visible in the entrance.

After a wait of five seconds he heard Steele's voice, low and urgent.

'Dyke, I know you're awake. I'm coming in. I'm armed, so don't do anything stupid.'

The empty frame was then darkened as he stepped across the threshold.

In the dim glow of the street-lighting Sam saw Chantal turn in her sleep and start to wake. He stepped forward and put a hand over her mouth. Things were taking an interesting turn and he didn't want her to wake screaming. She struggled briefly before catching on, her eyes wide. By now Steele was standing in the room, his arms at his side.

He said, 'I'm going against my better judgement here, but I think this is going tits up. If you know what's good for you you'll get the hell out of Dodge and not think about this again. Blake's going rogue and for the wrong reasons.'

'In your view.'

'Don't argue. I've done things for him before and maybe I will again. But only when I'm sure it's for King and Country. Not this personal shit. He doesn't pay enough for that.'

Chantal had slipped out of the bed and was putting on her shoes and searching for her bag. Like Sam, she had been sleeping in her clothes.

She whispered, 'Come on, Sam, what are you waiting for?'

'I don't trust him. What proof do we have that he won't get us half-way down the stairs then put a couple of bullets in our back? Then tell Blake we were trying to escape?'

In the semi-darkness Steele was immobile.

'You're right, you have no proof I won't do that. And the way you tapped me the other night there's nothing better I'd like. But this is a final offer. You go now or I leave you to Clifford and the others, who'd be happy to see you placed in several bin liners and left at strategic points around this fair city.'

'You go first.'

'Okay. Walk this way, why don't you.'

He turned and went through the door. Sam grabbed his jacket from the back of a chair, then seized Chantal's arm and held her back. He followed Steele quietly, putting Chantal behind him.

There was more light on the landing because it came through the glazed front door and bounced off a mirror in the hallway. Sam guessed it was about four o'clock in the morning and there was no traffic or urban noise in the street. It made the shuffling sound of their feet seem even louder.

Steele had reached the top of the landing where it turned to go downstairs when the last bedroom door was pulled open.

James stood in the frame, dressed in shorts and a tee-shirt, his expression calm, his fair hair neatly combed.

'Thought I heard something. Going for a moonlight stroll, boss?'

Steele raised his right arm, now holding a gun with a long suppressor, and shot him. James looked down at his chest, fear crossing his face like a shadow. He said, 'Ah,' and sat down on the floor.

Directly opposite Sam, another bedroom door opened and Nate appeared, his eyes half-closed with sleep. Steele stepped forward and shot him in the chest, then stepped back again, watching Nate as he too fell backwards, collapsing through the doorway.

There was a noise in the room from which James had appeared, and through its open door Sam saw Clifford beginning to move towards them, his barrel chest naked and smooth. Sam took two steps forward, ducked beneath an outstretched arm – which he saw, alarmingly, was holding a curved knife – and punched Clifford satisfyingly hard in the kidneys. As Clifford bent double, Steele pointed and fired once more. Clifford's body jolted backwards from the shot to the head and he fell with his arms outstretched, the knife still clutched in his hand.

The sounds of the three shots had merged and now reverberated in the confined space. Sam looked at Chantal and saw she had covered her ears with her hands. He reached for her again and dragged her towards the top of the stairs. Steele held up an arm, barring their path.

'That proof enough?'

TUESDAY

OUTSIDE THE AIR was cool and the sky just beginning to show some colour.

Steele said, 'Your car's parked around the corner. We muddied the plates in case someone was looking for it.'

He handed over the keys and a plastic carrier bag containing their other possessions. Looking inside, Sam saw that Chantal's diary was also included.

'Generous of you.'

'I don't need it. Not my property. Now get the fuck out of here.'

Chantal said, 'What about those men? Won't someone have called the police?'

'The walls are lined. Soundproofed. Four o'clock in the morning. Probably not. I'll clean up after me.'

Sam said, 'Why'd you do it? Why let us go?'

Steele hesitated and Sam saw a number of options flicker at the back of his eyes. Then he made a choice and his expression hardened.

'The pay wasn't good enough.'

'Bullshit.'

But Steele had turned on his heel and was already walking back up the path to the house.

Sam looked around. There was no traffic on the street but they could hear Portsmouth waking up distantly. He said, 'This way.'

Chantal stayed a moment, looking back towards the house where she'd just witnessed the murder of three young men. Sam watched as she gathered her thoughts, then like Steele she seemed to set herself and turned towards him. He knew that in the last few days she'd been transformed in ways that she wouldn't understand for years.

But she looked up at him with clear eyes and said, 'Let's go.'

FIVE MINUTES LATER they had found Sam's Mondeo and were sitting inside with the heater going. Chantal had clasped her hands between her knees and had said nothing since they'd climbed inside.

Sam said, 'So the big question – what do you want to do?'

'What are we supposed to do?'

'Turn the lot of them in. Or forget about it all and go home.'

'Is that your advice? Is that what you'd do if you were by yourself?'

'You're the client. It's your call.'

'Is it? It seems to me I've been passed around like a package. That man Steele was right – he told me to think of myself as a parcel to be delivered and that's exactly what's happened.'

'So what do you want to do about it?'

'I want to sulk for a while, is that OK?'

Sam opened his mouth to say something, then stopped himself. She'd just seen an horrific event and was probably still thinking about it. He was a little on edge himself, if the truth were known. Sulking for a while seemed like a good option.

They were both quiet for two minutes, then Chantal said, 'All right, you've out-sulked me. What do we do now?'

'You want my professional opinion?'

'Whatever.'

'I think Blake has got something going on. This has all been desperate when it didn't need to be. Obviously something is going to happen on Monday that he's trying to protect. He wants to keep us from finding out what was on the back of Jennifer's love-letter, the telegram, but it's more than that. It's not what's in the letter that's important, it's the fact that the letter exists.'

'I don't understand what you mean.'

'Steele is a lunatic in many ways, but I think he was right about this. It's old history, what Churchill did or didn't do. Whether he asked Stalin to sink the ship or not and included Blake's father in the conspiracy. There might be some incriminating evidence about his father, but he's dead and I don't think Blake is really worried about his family honour. There's something else going on.'

Chantal was frowning. 'OK, I don't really follow but let's say you're right – the question still stands. What do we do?'

'We're in Portsmouth – we take a ferry.'

'But I don't have my passport and Laura made you give hers back.'

Sam reached into the plastic bag that Steele had given him and pulled out two passports.

Chantal said, 'I saw you drop them back into Laura's bag.'

'But you didn't see me take them out again later.'

'Oh she's going to hate you for that.'

'Can't be helped.'

'Do you really not care?'

'Of course I care but I've got a set of priorities.'

'We'll need to book tickets and I'll have to dye my hair. We'll have to get a hotel room or something.'

'It's Portsmouth – the place is heaving with hotels.'

She gave a deep sigh and leaned back against the head-rest, staring at the roof of the car.

'I have to start paying you for all this.'

'We'll talk about it.'

'You forget – I inherited my dad's business two years ago. I can afford it.'

Sam turned to look at her delicate profile, staring at the roof of the Mondeo, her throat extended and her skin tight.

'You kept that quiet.'

'One doesn't like to brag. Now, consider yourself officially hired. Do you think Blake will come after us when he finds out what Steele has done?'

'I'm counting on it.'

HE HAD MANAGED to dispose of the bodies easily enough.

It had required a little travel, and a little digging, but eventually he had buried the three in separate graves in woods around West Marden. They'd be found eventually but he'd burned off fingerprints and knocked out some teeth, so unless the police were able to do something fancy with DNA, James, Clifford and Nate would remain anonymous for a good while, even if they were found. He'd also wiped down the pistol and thrown it into a river.

Steele looked around his hotel room. He was sick of hotel rooms. Bed, TV, a desk and chair if you were lucky. A bathroom with a sink moulded from one piece of plastic textured to look like marble. Soap made for midgets. He had laid on the bed for several hours now, getting his breath back after his morning's exertions. After burying the bodies he'd been back at the safe house for nine o'clock and done his best to render it completely hygienic again. Wiped all surfaces with dilute bleach. Stripped all the bedclothes off and taken them to the local tip, along with all the knives, forks, cups and saucers. Taken the clothes that the men had left and dumped them in a bag on the doorstep of an Oxfam. Put the remaining food in a bin liner and dropped it in one of a row of wheely-bins around the corner. Hoovered the carpets upstairs and down. Wiped the bath and all the sinks.

No one had noticed a thing.

No one had called the police as a result of the gunshots last night – his pistol had done the job close-up but the small-calibre rounds hadn't made much noise, and no one had been listening at four o'clock in the morning anyway.

So he had wiped everything down as he left, then driven into central Portsmouth and took a room in a modern Ibis that looked like a wavy Viennese pastry, and where all the furniture looked like it had been cut whole from cedar trees.

What was the plan?

He had no plan.

First he had to renegotiate his relationship with Blake. That would be tricky but not impossible – Blake had too much to hide, and too much at stake, to do anything foolish. But Steele had to come up with a plausible story for Dyke and Bressette's escape, and for the fact that the three sprogs had gone missing.

He wondered briefly whether James, Nate or Clifford had family. But he doubted it. They hadn't mentioned wives or girlfriends or kids, and they had acted like they were on a big testosterone-fuelled adventure. Blake had recruited them himself through one of his shadowy security companies, so he would have ensured that they understood how secret the work was going to be ...

He realised suddenly that he was angry with Blake for putting him in the position he was now in. If he had recruited the men he would never have been forced into that action. They had been good in a primitive way, but they hadn't had ... gravitas. They didn't really *get* it. That was what had pissed him off in the end. Dyke, now ... he had got it. He knew exactly what was going on and what the stakes were. He would have been a good man to have had on the team.

If only he didn't have scruples.

Steele shifted uneasily on his bed. He'd found himself comparing what he did to what Dyke did. And, to his chagrin, not liking the comparison.

SAM KNOCKED ON Chantal's hotel room door. They'd found a Premier Inn earlier in the day, then gone out to buy supplies – more underwear, toothpaste, shaving gear for Sam.

They had returned to the hotel and had lunch, then she had gone out again to find a hairdresser who would work on her hair. She had come back late in the afternoon and told him she wasn't hungry, so he had eaten by himself that night, then returned to his room. A few minutes ago she had phoned and said, 'You should check it out.'

He had known what she meant immediately. The next day she would go through border control on Laura's passport and they had to be certain she'd make it.

Standing outside the door he realised he was nervous. He felt guilty that he was knocking on a young woman's door at ten o'clock in the evening, but at the same time he found he was excited. He told himself to get a grip. He was working, not romancing. He thought about Laura and momentarily saw her in his mind's eye – the blonde hair that floated in a curtain to her shoulders; her half-open mouth as she laughed; the roundness of her eyes. What did he truly feel for her, and she for him? They had been together almost two years now and still had their separate houses. Neither of them had pushed the relationship and he wondered why that was. Perhaps, for him, it was because his one serious relationship – complete with marriage – had been an utter disaster, ending when Tara had got pregnant and left him, telling him that she'd had a miscarriage. In fact she had gone to term and produced Dan, an outcome for which he was grateful.

Perhaps Laura's difficulty was with his work, as always. Largely it was mundane, almost bureaucratic. Researching, following, delivering pieces of paper. Just occasionally there had been the hint of danger, the last case of that type endangering her too. Maybe she couldn't get closer to him because she was fearful, either for herself or for him.

However you cut it, they were still circling each other at arm's length, without any real commitment.

He wasn't sure how he felt about that, either.

The door was pulled back suddenly and Sam couldn't help himself, he took in a sudden breath.

Chantal wore a simple black strappy thing that showed off her rounded arms and shoulders, and particularly her delicate collar-bones. And she seemed to be wearing shoes with heels instead of the flat pumps she'd worn ever since he met her, because he noticed that her weight was distributed differently. More attractively.

And the hairdresser had done well with her hair. It wasn't Laura's blonde, but it was paler – enough to surprise Sam again with the resemblance. The same sharp cheekbones but somehow more delicate. Her face was more alert. Less stressed and strained by working in a high-pressure environment.

She said, 'Hi!' and tossed her hair coyly.

'It looks good.'

'What do you think?'

Sam stepped into the room, then stood and tilted his head from side to side as he thought he was expected to do.

'Well obviously it's still darker but I don't think that's going to matter. Women dye their hair all the time. Can you do something with the make-up?'

'Absolutely. I'll make mine more garish tomorrow, that'll make it harder for them to see the differences. We're the same height. My hair's shorter but they must be used to that at the passport desk. I'm younger than Laura according to her passport but she looks great.'

'There's only five years between you.'

The smile left Chantal's face.

'I'm sorry ... I didn't mean to imply.'

Sam realised he was being defensive. He suddenly felt big and clumsy and inappropriate. He stepped to the door. 'I'd better go.'

Chantal reached out a hand and gripped his arm.

'I haven't said thanks yet. I've been so busy thinking about me I haven't thought about all the trouble you've gone to. I just wanted to say I appreciated it.'

Sam nodded. 'Have you spoken to Jack yet?'

Chantal recoiled and took her hand from his elbow.

'No. Why did you say that?'

Sam felt himself turning red. 'I don't know. He just came to mind. I just wondered ... Look, I'll see you at breakfast tomorrow. No need to rush. Nine o'clock.'

He opened the door and was in the corridor before he realised. He fumbled for his keycard and stepped into his own room, his heart beating fast.

Then he turned around, opened the door and went down to the bar.

'I'M NOT IN the mood for this, Sam.'

'Listen, just listen. I'm going to France tomorrow with Chantal. I thought you ought to know.'

'But you haven't got a pass – ... oh shit, you took it, didn't you?'

'Sorry.'

He lay on his hotel room bed and stared at the ceiling. It was twelve o'clock and he'd been drinking for two hours almost without stopping for breath. He didn't really feel drunk but realised he was talking more than usual. He felt emboldened, loose, as though what he had to say held an obvious truth.

He said, 'Where are you?'

'In Abigail's spare bedroom. Where do you think?'

'Yes, OK. I've been thinking about us.'

'Have you now? What conclusions did you come to?'

'I've been wondering why we don't live together yet. We're both grown-ups–'

'Well I am.'

'– And I think it would be a sign of commitment.'

Laura laughed ironically. He knew the laugh and knew the expression on her face as she produced it.

'A sign of commitment, he says, as he takes his girlfriend's stolen passport to France with a younger version of her. Feeling a bit guilty, are we?'

'Oh come on, you know it's a job.'

'For which you're not getting paid, last I heard.'

'That's changed. Chantal has got money after all. And the newspapers might be interested in this one.'

'Trust me as a marketing expert when I tell you that you don't want to go there. Do not get into a reputation fight with the government. You'll win but you'll feel dirty afterwards. And worse. All that DSS work you love so dearly will dry up.'

They were both quiet for a while. He imagined her in bed, like him staring at the ceiling with a cheap phone in her hand. He was lucky she had had it switched on, but then realised she'd have been waiting to hear from him for a couple of days.

He said, 'All right, you know best.'

'How's Chantal?'

'What?'

'How's she bearing up with all this cloak-and-dagger stuff?'

'All right, I think. She was scared that Steele and his mob were going to do something to her, but now she's angry. She doesn't like the way they talked to her. Put it this way, I don't think she'd vote this government in again if it was up to her.'

'That reminds me. Have you seen the news tonight?'

Sam told her that he hadn't. He didn't mention that he'd had dinner with Chantal and then been in her room admiring her hair colour.

'That old MP – what was his name ... ? Strutt.'

'What about him?'

'Well apparently he went nuts a couple of days ago and was under observation in a home. But not observed well enough, it seems. He was found hanging in his room. He'd made a noose from his sheets and managed to swing himself from the window sash. Clever bugger.'

'Well thanks for taking my expression of undying love so seriously.'

'I don't need lessons from you on how to take things seriously.'

'All right, all right, I'm sorry– '

'And the next time you call, do it in office hours.'

He made to reply but she had closed the connection.

WEDNESDAY

BLAKE PACED THE library carpet restlessly, his eyes glancing periodically towards the window and the view it gave of the entrance drive. Where was he? He said he'd arrive by eight-thirty and already it was nine o'clock.

Steele had called ridiculously early that morning, saying it was urgent that he see him. He wouldn't say why but insisted. Against his best instincts, Blake had told him to come up and gave him directions. He didn't like to mix his business interests with his home life, and he certainly didn't like to have low-lifes like Steele given the run of his estate, meeting his wife, dandling Ross on his knee ...

It was unbearable. In less than a week he would be chauffeured around the country, treated like a visiting dignitary, showered with as much respect as this egalitarian society could dare to give him. But at the moment he was dealing with cut-throats, robbers and lunatic politicians. If it weren't so tragic he would laugh. Perhaps, he thought, there will be an upside to all this. When he was Minister and more or less untouchable, he could start to really make it work for him. He already had the dummy companies lined up and Lashbrooke and the others would take care of the details, the payments and so forth ... Of course it had been about his family honour, but he had never lost sight of the fact that they were all in line to make a great deal of money when the contracts began to flow. Ten years to set up all the shell structures and commercial relationships ... He couldn't allow that to go down the pan. Christ, it had worked for Cheney and Halliburton, so why not for him?

He frowned as he saw the black Touareg turn in front of the house, scraping up the gravel. He raised his voice to call outside.

'Pendleton – let this man in, will you?'

There was a mutter from the hallway and then he heard Pendleton's precise click-steps on the parquet followed by the front door opening. A few moments later Steele appeared in the doorway. To Blake he looked gaunt, as though he hadn't slept. He seemed to have changed in ... what was it? A day and a half? Blake began to have a nauseous feeling in his stomach.

'I know this is important otherwise you wouldn't have come here, disturbing me, my family and the gravel on my drive. What do you want?'

Steele seemed to be affronted by this welcome. He stood back on his heels a little and let his eyes wander over the leather-clad books on the tall shelves. Blake felt as though he were being judged by this perusal and grew both angry and fearful at the same time.

Steele said, 'Dyke and the Bressette woman have gone.'

For a second Blake thought he had mis-heard. 'Gone? Did you say gone?'

Steele nodded. Blake wanted to lash out and slap him across the face but knew he would never finish the gesture. He turned away so that Steele couldn't see his face.

'Your employment is in very serious danger at the moment, Steele. Please explain yourself.'

'I let them go.'

Blake whirled around.

'You let them go! What the fuck do you mean!'

Steele had folded his arms. Blake was amazed that he didn't look contrite but had the air of someone who had made a decision and would brook no argument. It was astonishing.

'The others wanted to put them under ground. I thought that was a bit harsh for a personal vendetta. So I differed with them.'

'What the hell does that mean? What happened?'

'I persuaded the prisoners to leave. And took action to enable it.'

'Jesus, you should work for GCHQ – your code is worse than theirs. Where are James and the others now?'

'I've disbanded the group. They've gone to other parts.'

Blake felt his neck and lower jaw beginning to stiffen and knew – because Fiona had told him – that his face would be turning red. He walked to the window and looked out beyond the gravel drive to the row of poplars at the bottom of the front lawn. His father had planted them to give more privacy to the house. The two men he'd taken on after the Dyke incident were talking to each other by the entrance, a gap in the surrounding hedge flanked by tall stone pillars. He concentrated on their actions and slowed his breathing, recognising that this was one of those occasions when calm decision-making was going to be essential.

'So you're telling me that Dyke and Bressette are gone and that James, Nate and Clifford have been dismissed.'

'Yes.'

'I see. And what the fuck do you think we're going to do now?'

Steele unfolded his arms and put them in his pockets, almost as though he were chatting with Blake at the golf club.

'You chase them, you make it worse. Leave them to do what they want, then handle it if it blows up. You don't poke a bear with a stick. You wait for it to come to you, then throw a fucking big net over it.'

'Great – military wisdom at its finest. Do you realise what shit you've left me in?'

'You took me on as a consultant as well as a fixer. Sir. You're consulting with me. And my advice is to leave them alone. They may not even find what they're looking for.'

'Are you suggesting that Dyke is clueless?'

Steele shrugged. 'No, I wouldn't say that. But it was all a long time ago from what you were saying. He'll probably find it as hard to dig up anything as you did.'

Blake felt unbearably frustrated.

'That's not the point, that's absolutely not the point. If they make their way to France and find something – anything – that ties me or my family to a war crime, I'm fucked. And I'm not just talking about a nasty editorial in The Guardian. It will be my career, your career and the lives and reputations of several very important people. Do you *get* that, Steele?'

'I think you're wasting your effort and time. In my professional opinion.'

'Am I paying you well?'

Steele seemed surprised by the question.

'Very well.'

'I will double it ... no, treble it, if you go after those two arses and ... and ... do something so that they're kept under wraps until Monday.'

'I don't think it's a question of money – '

'Well it fucking well better be. Or else I can tell you right now that I will make sure that none of the so-called security companies that you'd like to work for in future will get any government money. And I'll tell them exactly why. If I go down, your career will go down with me. You'll be a pariah and nobody will give you work. Here or in America, or Germany or France. I even have some influence in the Middle East. So you'll be as fucked as I will.'

Steele smiled slowly, as though seeing Blake's true colours for the first time.

'You put it like that, I don't have much choice, do I?'

'None.'

Blake relaxed – it looked as though Steele would stay on track. Although he had others he could call on, none of them had the same history with him as Steele did.

Now Steele took a pace forward, still smiling. Blake didn't know what had come over the man lately.

'But I have a condition.'

'What's that?'

'You come with me.'

'What? That's not possible ... '

'You know the territory, you know what we're looking for, you know the country better than I do. With me it'd be guess work. With you along I'd stand a better chance of finding whatever the hell it is we're looking for.'

'But that's ... ' He wanted to say 'impossible', but he saw that Steele was going to be adamant on this. Then a thought struck him. It wouldn't be too bad, actually. He'd have to cancel a couple of meetings but Pendleton could handle that. And it would get him away from Lashbrooke. He would say he'd come down with some stress-related illness and was taking no visitors. After what had happened to George Strutt, Lashbrooke would probably understand.

And he quite fancied getting stuck into Dyke and Bressette. They had been a damned nuisance, like a mosquito bite in an unpleasant place that you couldn't scratch. He suddenly felt flushed with energy, as though he'd had a transfusion of fresh blood, oxygenated. For once he would be *doing* something, not just wishing for it.

He said, 'I have to make some arrangements. Pendleton!'

THEY TOOK A taxi to the ferry terminal and walked around to the foot passenger entrance. They bought tickets from the Brittany Ferries desk then crossed the concourse to check in. Sam was amazed how confident Chantal was. She had reddened her lips and rouged her cheeks, and had even added a little blue eye-liner to her eyelids. It was as though the make-up had given her a new persona.

Approaching the desk she engaged Sam in a busy conversation, as they'd agreed, so that her face was animated and not in repose. They had tested her appearance against Laura's passport photo and Sam thought there was more similarity than not. Chantal's round eyes, blue like Laura's, and her etched cheekbones gave enough of a passing resemblance. There was only a half inch difference between them in height.

There were two women behind the desk. As one of them was dealing with another passenger they were forced to head for the older of the pair, who looked at them suspiciously from behind square-rimmed glasses. She held out a hand and gave a grim smile, but said nothing.

Chantal handed over her passport and ticket. The woman clicked on a keyboard and did something with the ticket, then opened the passport. The woman glanced down at the passport, then up at Chantal, scrutinising her. She glanced down at the passport again, staring at it for long seconds. At last she folded it, put the ticket inside and handed it back. Then she thrust out her hand towards Sam, who handed over his own passport and ticket. He had been given the fake passport by his employers years ago but it was still in date, just. Under the name of Jonathan Wells. He had always been amused by the link between Dyke and Wells. He had little doubt the passport would pass inspection.

As if she had heard him, the woman gave it back to him with an outstretched arm. 'Have a nice journey.'

They walked away, towards the lounge. They bought coffee and sat with their backs to the rest of the concourse, which was surprisingly empty of people considering there was only an hour before the ferry sailed.

Sam said, 'Jesus, when I worked with Customs I never realised it was so easy to sneak in or out.'

'You should have a word.'

'Maybe after all this has finished. How are you feeling?'

'Liberated. And scared. What do you think Blake will do when he finds out what Steele did?'

'Stop his pay. Then sack him. He might send someone else after us.'

Chantal sat forward.

'Really? What kind of someone else?'

'Someone better. More literal-minded. Less reasonable.'

'Steele was reasonable? You must mix with very odd people.'

'You don't know the half of it.'

He leaned back and looked around the concourse. He hadn't said anything to Chantal but it had occurred to him last night that Blake might indeed want to take it further. With Steele letting him down so drastically he might just say the hell with it and let loose some real dogs of war. He was a junior cabinet minister, usually a sinecure without much weight. But the research Sam had done on Blake suggested the family he belonged to went back a long way and had lingered at or near the upper echelons of power for centuries. He would have wealth, contacts, intelligence and ambition.

These days people took the view that politicians were largely self-serving little bureaucrats with an exaggerated sense of their own importance. But Sam knew from his peripheral role in a government agency that the lust for power for its own sake was a critical failing amongst those who reached any prominence in government. They liked it. They wanted more of it. They didn't want to let it go.

Blake might be a junior minister at the moment, but who knew where he might wind up?

More people had entered the building now and were milling about near a nondescript door in the far wall. Young tourists with backpacks, a few families with children, several older couples, the usual mix of travellers you came across at any port. Many of them were seated on the row chairs, reading newspapers or Kindles. One middle-aged man stood to one side, talking into his phone. His eyes ranged around the room but didn't settle on any one person.

Sam thought they were probably safe for a little while. Steele would have told Blake some story or other by now but Blake would still have to get together another team, if that was his intention. Things had gone so wrong for him it was doubtful he would use official resources now – the Border Agency, telephone tracking ... it was too dangerous if he wanted to stay under the radar.

Chantal stood up beside him.

'That's us.'

The nondescript door had opened and people were beginning to file through. Sam and Chantal funnelled their way through to the far side, where a Border Agency officer checked their passports and tickets again. As before, there was no hitch.

They walked through a covered section to the outside, where the sun was beginning to grow warm after a cool start. Two long single-decker coaches waited for them on the tarmac and everyone dutifully climbed on board. When both coaches were full they set off in convoy towards the ferry, which loomed over the edge of the quay a couple of hundred yards away. It was enormous seen close up, with complicated decks and bridges high above them while off to their left they could see the trail of cars and lorries slowly climbing the ramps into the lower decks.

The ride to the ferry took less than a minute. Once there they were ushered from the coach towards a tall covered structure. This was a movable stairway, and after climbing several flights of steps in a crush with the other passengers, they eventually crossed a narrow bridge and entered the side of the ferry, which suddenly blossomed open before them. Already children were running around, exploring the various entertainment lounges.

Chantal touched his arm. 'What do you want to do?'

'Sleep for a year.'

'We haven't booked cabins.'

'This really is your first trip to France, isn't it?'

'Yes, why?'

'There are lounge seats that you can push back to sleep in. Or you can watch a film. Or eat.'

'We've got eight hours. We could do all three.'

'All right, but stay in touch. I'm going to buy a newspaper and I don't want to be disturbed.'

'Can't we go up top first?'

Sam led the way up the central staircase, past the kiosk and up another flight of stairs into the bar area. He then took Chantal through to the outside deck, where other travellers were already lining the rails or taking command of the few available deck-chairs. The air was considerably warmer now and the sky was beginning to deepen towards an azure blue. They found a place by the rail and looked out over Portsmouth, which seemed far beneath them from the height of this deck.

Chantal clutched his arm. Her blonde hair waved in the breeze. 'Like going on holiday when you're a kid. I know this is weird, but I'm excited.'

'You're right. It is weird.'

'Spoilsport.'

After a while, the engines took on a throaty rumble and the ferry edged away from the quay. In a short time they were sliding parallel to the coast, passing the dry-docked warship Victory and the immense but bizarrely delicate feather of the Spinnaker Tower. Eventually they slipped past Southsea Castle at the tip of the estuary and entered the open seaway.

It was 10.15 a.m.

STEELE WONDERED FOR the hundredth time how he'd been talked into this position. He was driving the Touareg down to Portsmouth with Gideon Blake in the back seat reading a newspaper, as if he were Mr Important and Steele was the chauffeur. Blake had said he 'didn't do front seats' because he got car sickness or some such rubbish. Steele thought it was just because Blake didn't want to talk to him. Didn't mix with the plebs.

And here they were on a venture that was bound to end in failure. How would they possibly find Dyke and Bressette now? In France? He was happy to do it because of the money and, to be fair, because Blake's threat to limit his employment potential was not a joke. If Blake dumped him and the other companies on the Circuit didn't – or couldn't – use him, he was fucked. He didn't want to end up as a bouncer on a cheesy pole-dancing club's door in East

London. But he didn't see any way in which this was going to end well.

He followed signs to the ferry terminal and then found the long-term car-park. He didn't know whose name was on the Touareg and he had no intention of going back to it afterwards, but there was no point in leaving it on a street to be picked up by the cops.

Blake stirred on the back seat.

'We there?'

'We walk the rest of the way.'

'Good. You got the tickets?'

'And passports. You're sure we couldn't fly?'

'Not between this afternoon and tomorrow morning. Flights to Limoges or Poitier are pretty limited.'

'We could have gone to Paris and driven down.'

Blake slapped him on the shoulder, now alert and apparently refreshed.

'Where's your spirit of adventure, man? We're following their route, almost certainly. You let them go in Portsmouth, they're bound to have booked a ferry. Hell's bells, we might even run into them at Hertz.'

'Couldn't you have had them tracked? You did it before.'

'Too risky. I'm trying not to leave any traces here. What's the matter, don't you want to go to France?'

Blake's cheeriness was driving Steele further into himself. He wondered how that happened – when other people were up, he was miserable; when they were depressed, he felt happy. Just a contrary bastard, he thought.

They took their bags from the car's boot and made their way to the passenger terminal. Blake had dressed down in an attempt to make himself unrecognisable – blue jeans, a pale washed-denim shirt and a thickly padded North Face jacket. And a flat cap. Steele thought he looked like he'd kitted himself out from a Littlewoods catalogue and at any moment would break into a number of male-model poses, pointing into the distance and looking at his watch. He smiled to himself.

Blake noticed it. 'That's the thing. Enjoy it. Christ, I've got a shitload of trouble coming down on my head on Monday unless I sort this out. Am I depressed? Not as much as I should be. I tell you, Steele, I've spent too long behind a bloody desk. I'm more of a field operator, if truth be told. Like my father. Representing his country in the midst of war. I'm forty-eight years of age and I feel like I've done fuck-all. My dad didn't have me until he was fifty-three because he was having too much fun. I missed out on that.'

'You missed nothing.'

'Oh don't give me that war-is-hell shit. I've read the books. Granted it's dangerous and you're liable to have your head shot off by a wandering tribesman, but you must admit it was fun too.'

'It had its moments.'

'I bet.'

'But when you're cowering behind a sandbag that you know full well won't stop an RPG shell, and you also know that two hundred yards away there's half a dozen *tribesmen* who want to blow your guts apart, then your insides turn to liquid and you start to wonder what decisions you made that put you there in the first place. And you question your life and the lives of your parents and the lives of your brothers and uncles who got caught up in this shit, and you start to question your own decision-making. And fun doesn't really come into the equation much at times like those.'

Blake had been watching him, his expression gradually turning sour.

'I'm only trying to make the best of a bad situation. I'd rather be at home nestled next to my beautiful wife in my big house with my two kids down the corridor. If that's all right with you.'

Steele said nothing, picked up his bag, and started to follow the queue of passengers through the door of the concourse to the waiting coaches outside. When Blake had started talking about his house and his wife and his children a large hole had opened up in his chest that he now knew would never be filled. It wasn't exactly envy and it wasn't exactly regret. He realised with sadness that what he felt most of all when he heard tales of others' happiness was fear.

He hardened his heart and took one slow step after another as they walked towards the coach.

It was 9.30 in the evening.

SIXTY-THREE MILES away and forty-five minutes later, on the identical latitude, Angel drove his car up the ramp into the yellow and white hulk that was the Seven Sisters, the ferry from Newhaven to Dieppe, arriving at 4 a.m. the following morning. He'd managed to book the last vehicle berth otherwise he'd have gone over on foot and hired a car. This was easier.

Until recently he'd prided himself on his calmness under pressure and simple professionalism. But this job had begun to get to him. First it had been the German trucker who'd got his goat with his sheer ... *size*. That would have been OK in itself, apart from the delay in police cells while his credentials were checked out.

But then he'd been interrupted again – the phone call that had redirected him to London.

Finding the institution hadn't been a problem – one of those wedding-cake country mansions in a suburb south of London – and thankfully the security had been practically non-existent. A private institution for the care of the elderly, it called itself.

But it was a nut-house.

He could hear the screeching before he'd even scaled the back windows to get through to the private room he wanted. Then, once he'd prised open the window and entered the room, the man was sitting up in bed in his pyjamas, watching him. Asked him if he wanted some tea – it would be good for him.

Well, it hadn't been good for *him*, had it?

Angel had stripped the bed of its sheet, wrapped it around the old codger's neck, thrown the end over the top of the high window and hauled on it. Hung on for five minutes with the old man swinging, legs kicking, grunting slightly, on the other side of the window. Then he'd tied it off and gone out the way he'd come in.

Found a pub and gone inside to wash his hands. Bought some peanuts and sat in his car for five minutes while he ate them.

He hoped to God that was the last diversion. Still, he could get a solid four hours sleep now then start the drive south to the Vienne. Hopefully his instructions would get him to the right place at the right time. And hopefully there wouldn't be any more diversions.

They were making him angry. And when he got angry, he got cruel.

Funny, that.

ARRIVING IN OUISTREHAM ferry port at just after five o'clock in the evening, Sam and Chantal had taken the shuttle bus into Caen and hired a car from the Hertz office next to the station. The office was closing and the bored man behind the counter gave them little choice in the car they could hire. It was a red Opel Meriva that Sam disliked on sight – typical quirky French 'design', he thought.

They'd driven south for an hour in fading light, then pulled off the main road into Sées, a small town that seemed to be built entirely around its large Gothic cathedral. There was a hotel on the square and Sam and Chantal took separate rooms which turned out to be at either end of a short corridor. After they'd showered they went next door to a restaurant-crêperie where they served flat French pizza and a good red wine. Lights had come on in the square and the cathedral loomed darkly against the street lamps and the incidental lights from the shop fronts.

Looking through the restaurant's window, Chantal said, 'That's a big cathedral for such a little place. It looks like it belongs in Paris or somewhere.'

'They're big on churches over here. Catholic background and all that.'

'Do you know France?'

'A bit. I travelled when I was younger. When I was a kid the furthest we went for our holidays was to Butlins at Filey, leaning into the wind to stand up straight. When I could afford to pay for my own I started coming down south, to the warmth.'

'Before you knew Laura.'

'Years ago. Dan's mother left me when I was twenty and I didn't have a family or anything, so I could do what I wanted.'

'No girlfriends?'

'Of course. Am I not an attractive and upstanding man? They were crawling all over me.'

'That would be a no, then.'

'Well, not a complete no. I had a couple of longer relationships ... hey, what's going on here? Is this Question Time or what?'

Chantal sipped her wine, her eyes laughing over the brim of her glass.

'We girls like to know who we're having dinner with.'

'I'd have filled out a questionnaire if I'd known. Save time.'

THEY PAID THE bill and walked around the square in the cooling evening air. There were no other people about and only one vehicle passed them as they walked.

Chantal had borrowed Sam's leather jacket and she pulled the collar up under her neck.

'What are we doing, Sam? What exactly is the point of all this? What if we find this bloody document and it tells us nothing?'

'Then it's still one-nil to us, isn't it?'

'Meaning what?'

'That Blake will have to lay off, for one thing. If he knows we've got some incriminating evidence then he'll keep his distance.'

'But it means we can't do anything with it. We can't get back at him in any way.'

'True. But is that what you want? To make an enemy of a big-wig government politician? A dangerous option, I'd say.'

She stopped walking and looked at him.

'I have no idea what I want. It seemed clear a couple of days ago – I wanted to stick it to Steele and whoever else was messing me about.'

'But it's bigger than that, isn't it?'

'Yes. Seeing him shoot those men without even thinking about it has got to me. Seeing violence like that close up has done something to my head.'

'I'm not surprised.'

'I've been thinking about my grandfather, working for the French Resistance. It used to be old black-and-white films or photographs, or old war films. But imagining him involved in situations like the one we were in last night ... it's scared me. I keep playing it over and over. The worse thing was the smell – the gun and the blood, all mingling together. I'm thinking differently now. I feel more cautious about ... everything. Life. Is that weird?'

'Not at all. The first time I saw something like that it changed me, too.'

'Tell me about it.'

'It's not nice. It might upset you.'

'I think I'm past caring. Tell me.'

They had started walking again and she linked her arm in his. Sam noticed it and felt uncomfortable, but put the discomfort to one side as he remembered the incident.

'A colleague and I had been sent to a scrap-yard in Preston. We thought the owner was importing and exporting stuff he shouldn't be – in fact, someone had snitched on him. Well we talked to the guy in this cabin on his yard, and my mate Frank made an excuse and said he was going for a wander around. After ten minutes he hadn't come back and I hadn't got any kind of satisfaction from the dealer. So I left him and went looking for Frank. You can imagine the place, can't you. Piles of cars on top of each other, stacks of tires, big dumps of washing machines, bikes, TVs – everything. All piled up so that there were alleys between the stacks, just like in those American cop shows. So anyway, I wander around and can't find Frank. Until finally I hear this kind of repeated knocking sound, like a hammer being bashed against a car door. Which is what I probably thought it was. So I walk down one of these alleys and turn the corner, and there are these two blokes holding Frank down. He's on his front, and one bloke is sitting on his legs while the other is bashing his head against the side of an oven, repeatedly. Frank's out of it, blood coming out of his ears, eyes as black as thunderclouds ... he looks like shit.'

Chantal's mouth was open.

'What did you do?'

'I picked up a fucking big piece of metal – I think it was a clothesline post – and started swinging. Made a couple of good connections, too. Geoff Boycott would have been proud of me.'

'Why had they done it?'

'Because they were thick buggers and didn't like this man asking them questions. One was the half-wit brother of the owner, who he kept around to keep him out of mischief. Well, it got him into more. All three went down for serious time.'

'What about Frank?'

'Deaf in one ear, sight a bit wobbly in his right eye. Lost a couple of back teeth.'

'Poor devil.'

'The point is, that was my first experience of real violence first-hand. You'd be amazed at the anger that some people find inside themselves.'

'And you have that? Is that what you're saying?'

'No, I'm saying I'm not surprised if you feel changed. Most of us don't see that level of violence at close hand, so we don't have to deal with how soft we are – I mean, as humans. When you see damage done to the human body by other people it makes you question what we're about.'

'I nearly threw up last night, right there on the landing.'

'And none of us would have blamed you. Just because Steele and I have seen violence and done violent things doesn't necessarily mean we're comfortable with it.'

'Even Steele?'

'Judging by his reaction, I'm guessing especially Steele.'

THURSDAY

BLAKE HAD HAD the good sense to ask Fiona to book a car for him. On request, Europcar delivered a small Mercedes A class to the terminal. Steele lifted the boot and put their bags inside. Blake signed the papers, then threw the keys to Steele.

'You driven in France before?'

Steele stared at him, then climbed into the driver's seat without saying anything. Blake got in the back.

Steele started the engine, then sat with the car idling until Blake sat up and leaned forward.

'What's the matter?

'First, I'm not your fucking chauffeur. You can come and sit in the front like an ordinary person. Second, I don't know where we're going. What am I to put into the GPS?'

'Jesus, you're a touchy bastard.'

He climbed out of the back and got into the passenger seat.

'We'll go to Montmorillon first. That's the largest town in the area we need. The SAS parachuted into the woods a few miles away. There'll be a hotel or something. Maybe a cosy holiday gîte for the pair of us. Better not give the impression we're gay, though. Country folk down there. Might get the pitchforks out.'

Steele started typing the name he thought he'd heard until the software found a suggestion. Blake looked at the name and nodded and when the satellites had got a fix Steele put the car in gear and drove out of the terminal car park. Apart from the impact of the ferry business, Ouistreham was a quiet and low-key town – there was little traffic and they drove on empty roads between low, creamy white buildings until they found the road for Caen, heading south.

Blake was aware of the physicality of the man sitting next to him. He'd first come across Steele when he'd helped him extricate himself from some tricky business involving cruelty to prisoners. Someone had told him a long time ago that it was good to build up deposits in the bank of goodwill, and he'd had contacts looking out for just such mavericks and bad-boys in the forces for a while. He'd used Steele four years ago when one of his security firms needed someone to take cash into Afghanistan to bribe an embassy official. He'd spoken to Steele several times on the telephone and met him just once, when he picked up the cash for the first job.

Sitting next to him now in the Mercedes he was reminded of the coarse animal brutishness of some of the people you were forced to deal with in life, no matter what your supposed rank in society. Perhaps that was why he'd found himself being more gung-ho and hearty than he actually felt – he was trying to make up somehow for a testosterone deficiency that years behind a desk had instilled in him.

As if he'd been party to these thoughts, Steele said, 'So what do you want us to do if we come across this pair? Rough them up? Bribe them?'

Blake felt something inside his chest deflate.

'Does your attitude to authority ever bother you?'

'My attitude is what's kept me alive. I don't need lessons from soft twats like you on what my attitude should be.'

'You don't have to talk to me like that.'

Steele snorted. 'I used to look up to you. I thought you were doing good work. I thought you had what it took. Always calm, the well-educated voice, the reasoned response. I didn't realise you were as morally corrupt as the rest of them.'

'Rest of whom?'

'Exactly – whom. The political class. The people who talk proper. The people who think it's their right to tell the rest of us what to do.'

'So you'd prefer a socialist wonderland, filled with proles educated beyond their capacity to understand what anything means?'

'Don't make assumptions about me based on what you think I am. I've had family members die for this country. And we're all proles. I've got no more formal education than you'd expect me to have, but I can read, and I can think, and I can draw my own conclusions. I've always known the basis of why I worked for you. It was an exchange – my dirty deeds for your money. But I think I was fooling myself that I was doing it for the country, too. Carrying on where my dad and brother left off, but in secret. Now I can see where I went wrong.'

'Which was where?'

'As soon as you offered me three times my fee to help you catch these two. A little alarm went off in my head. It's true I'd already let them go because I didn't like the fact it was becoming a personal vendetta for you. But when you offered me the extra money, I knew what was going on.'

Blake turned to him. 'Which was?'

'You thought you could buy me body and soul. The money would cover it. Your power and authority weren't enough to get me to work for you. It had to be the dosh. And the dosh trumps everything else, doesn't it?'

'Is this the longest resignation speech in history?'

Steele was quiet. Blake saw that his face – the slightly puffy eyelids, the small mouth – was set and serious.

Steele said, 'I can't resign. I'm too far in. We're all too far in. That's what money does – it drags you in. And before you know it, you're caught.'

'I'd suggest you've been reading far too many modern novels.'

'No, you soft twat. Not enough. I've not been feeding me with the right information. Perhaps that ought to change.'

CHANTAL'S iPHONE HAD a map application that they used to find their way south towards the Vienne, where Chantal said her grandmother lived. They tracked through Le Mans and crossed the Loire at Tours, passing a huge blue Ikea store by the side of the bridge, hitting Chatellerault about an hour later. Here they came off the toll road and headed east for a while before swinging south again. At Chauvigny they stopped for lunch in the square, each taking a huge French bread sandwich and sitting outside watching the fountains and the busy road in front of the magnificent Hotel de Ville. The weather had settled into a gentle warmth that was unrelieved by any breeze and with a clear sky unhindered by the prospect of any cloud.

Sam felt the sense of urgency that had driven them this far becoming more intense. His usual line of work entailed a deadline or a specific outcome that was allied to the size of his bank balance. This endeavour seemed to him like the kind of job he imagined would be commonplace when he first started advertising nearly five years ago. A young woman, an indefatigable foe, an unsolved mystery ... but now he was in the midst of it those thoughts of heroism and nobility seemed far away. He was hot and uncomfortable and the Meriva was tiring to drive, especially on the wrong side of the road and the wrong side of the car. Their goal seemed indeterminate and the outcome unknown. And on a purely practical level, it was costing him money. Ferry tickets and car hire didn't come cheap, and two rooms and meals in a rural bed-and-breakfast were not exactly a bargain these days. Perhaps he would have to issue her with an invoice after all. If either of them was still alive.

He wondered briefly what Laura would be doing. Her work as an account manager meant that she spent a lot of time travelling to meet people she didn't much care for, then spending her company's money on wining and dining them. She could be anywhere presently – in the office, at home working on a presentation, driving up to Edinburgh or down to London. Despite the travel, the work was filled with certainty. She knew two weeks in advance where she was going to be and what she would be doing. It must have made his own provisionality very trying. It probably explained her frequent irritability.

Chantal had taken their sandwich wrappers and put them in a wooden waste bin. She had asked for a glass of rosé and now she sipped it while he chugged a Coke. The conversation in the car had died down the further they travelled and they seemed to have exhausted all perspectives on the task in hand.

Looking at her map, she said, 'About another thirty minutes.'

'You know your grandmother might not be there.'

She took the implication. 'She might be dead. She might have moved away again. What do you want me to say, Sam? This could all be a wild goose chase and we've wasted a lot of our money. It was you who wanted to come.'

'Everyone tells me I'm persistent. It's about the only quality I've got as an investigator.'

'I don't know ... you've got a pretty thick head.'

'Clifford had very soft hands. He was just showing off for the big boys.'

'I don't know what to say to her – to Julienne. How do I introduce myself? How do I explain what we're here for? Why on earth am I getting her involved with these horrible men?'

'If anyone turns up, she's better off with us there. We don't know what Blake will do to find his precious document. We can protect her.'

'Really? Like we protected Jack?'

'Get those ideas out of your head. We didn't know what we were dealing with then. Now we do. Is he awake yet?'

She had phoned the hospital twice on the journey down to check Jack's progress. She had phoned again outside the café while Sam had bought the sandwiches.

'He's awake but not really *compos mentis*. They wouldn't let me speak to him.'

'But at least he's awake.'

'Will you listen to yourself? He could have died because of that bastard Steele.'

Sam stood up and walked towards the fountains playing in square pools surrounded by low brick walls. Laura had often told him that what he thought was rational thinking was just insensitivity. He'd defended himself by saying it was the famous Yorkshire 'bluntness'. She had replied, 'Call it what you want – it gets you into more trouble than necessary. Especially with people who are on your side.'

He felt Chantal beside him. She touched his arm.

'I suppose I'm angry.'

'You have that right, given what's happened.'

'But I shouldn't be angry with you. You've helped me for no apparent reason. You're a ... what did they call it? A knight errant.'

'A knight error, more like. Making mistakes all over the place.'

A dull light came into her eyes, as if something inside had just woken. 'Can we go now? I want to get this over with, whatever it is. Honestly, I feel like I've just caused trouble for lots of people, including those three dead men. I want it to stop so I can go back to work.'

'None of this is your fault. I made it worse. And this was my idea, as you said. We can still go back.'

'We're too close. Another half an hour and we might find out what we came for.'

THIRTY MINUTES LATER they drove into a small dusty village whose main feature was yet another domineering church. The sun was high and the church cast deep blue shadows across the small square, in which two boxy cars were parked. Everywhere they had driven there were boxy cars – Peugeot Partners, Citroen Berlingos, Renault Kangoos. The French seemed to love them.

On the far side of the square was a bar, apparently closed. The road on which they'd arrived carried on straight ahead, towards the next village and past a small park in which two monuments were visible through an avenue of plane trees.

Sam parked on the square and they climbed out of the car. Chantal turned and looked around. The square was empty. She could see what looked like a bar on the far side and to her left, a café that had beer advertising plates on its walls but seemed otherwise to be abandoned. The square itself was given to parking and a locked cage containing domestic gas bottles. Of the houses she could see, many of the shutters were closed and there was no sign of life anywhere, not even a roaming dog.

She said, 'So this is Journet. I'm not surprised Julienne left.'

'Farming land. Any commerce there might have been has probably been taken over by supermarkets, same as everywhere else.'

Chantal looked at him dubiously. 'You're an equal opportunity socialist, aren't you? Solidarity, brother.'

'Politics have got nothing to do with it. No, I take that back. They have everything to do with it. Farmers here, miners where I come from. All of them shafted by the profit motive and the idea of convenience.'

'Well, much as I'd like to have a discussion about ideology with you in the middle of a rural French square, I think we should concentrate.'

Sam raised his arm to point.

'There's the Mairie. A good place to start.'

They crossed the square and went inside a large cream building with maroon shutters and with the French flag snapping over its front entrance. An inquiry of 'Parlez-vous anglais?' produced a smile and slight nod from the young man who had looked up at them from behind his desk. On the wall at his back, a portrait of the President smiled at them from between two more flags.

Sam explained that they were looking for a Julienne Bressette who used to live in the village, but they weren't sure that she was still there.

The man looked at them for a moment but said nothing, though he maintained a friendly smile.

Sam added, 'This is Madame Bressette's granddaughter. They have not met. We are driving across France and she would like to meet her grandmother if possible. She has something that belongs to her.'

On cue, Chantal took out the diary and showed it to the young man. He reached for it but she withdrew her hand.

'It is private and personal. It belonged to her husband, my grandfather.'

The young man led them to the door and pointed across the square.

'En face de l'église ... opposite the church. The house in the middle, with flowers on the windows.'

'She's still here? After all this time?'

'She returned five years ago. She is old now but has plenty of ... life.'

They thanked the man and crossed the square again. He had pointed to a long building that seemed to be split into three separate dwellings, each with different sets of coloured shutters.

The house had an old wooden door, its varnish peeling off in the direct sunlight, and in the centre was a large brass doorknob that Sam raised and lowered twice, loudly.

There was no reply and Sam tried again.

Chantal said, 'It doesn't look very big – she can't be in.'

'Then we wait.'

'Do you think she's okay?'

'Probably. I don't think Blake knows this address. He knows your name and will probably track her down eventually, but I doubt he's using official channels now – he'll have taken it off the radar after his recent surprise disappearance and return. Too risky otherwise.'

'You're always so bloody confident.'

'That's what ignorance can do for you. Let's see if that bar's open, I'm parched.'

THE HOTEL IN Montmorillon was at the end of the main road and close to the bridge over the brown and slow-moving river Gartempe. Montmorillon advertised itself as the *'Cité de l'écrit et de métiers du livre'*, which Blake told Steele meant it promoted itself as the city of writing and book-related trades. Accordingly the roundabouts featured giant sculptures of books by famous French authors, and in the square there was a large model of an open book apparently made from plants and flowers shaped into pages. Beyond the square a different, older bridge, crossed the river and rose up into the old part of the town, at the top of which stood a mediaeval church with a tall steeple.

Blake had been here thirty years before, but it had changed. This City of Writing business was new, for a start. The city fathers must have dreamed it up as a tourist incentive, because as far as he remembered there was no actual history of publishing or book manufacture in the area. It was deep France and therefore agricultural in nature. But everywhere had to have a gimmick these days. You couldn't just be a nice place to visit, you had to have some kind of contrived history to pull in the Euros.

He and Steele sat on chairs outside a bar on the square, staring at the pigeons nesting high in the Office of Tourism. At eight o'clock the sun was setting, shadowing the pale cream slabs of the square and cooling the air. They were the only people out and about.

Steele had relaxed on the journey down, as though the indolent nature of rural France had somehow infected his blood. Once they had checked in, it had been his idea to walk around the town a little to get its measure. He had given Blake some military guff about always knowing the territory. Blake had agreed because being cramped in the Mercedes with Steele for five hours had made him feel as though he'd been reshaped to fit the cabin – he needed to stretch out and raise his eyes above road-level.

He said, 'Hard to think there was a lot of Resistance activity in this area during the war. They helped the British no end. In the first week the SAS were parachuted in, they guided the RAF to bomb petrol supplies at Châtellerault, supplies that were intended for the German Army's Panzer Division, Das Reich. In the following six weeks they participated in twenty-three successful operations against railway lines, fuel dumps and airfields.'

'Why are you telling me this? Have you blown a fuse?'

'The intention was to hamper the progress of the Das Reich Panzers as they came north from Montauban. Had they reached Normandy, they would possibly have turned back the invading Allies. The Division comprised over two hundred tanks and fifteen thousand men. If they had succeeded and the Allied invasion failed, it's possible you and I wouldn't be here to enjoy this fine evening in this rural French town. We would be under a jackboot.'

'And this is what's driving your actions now?'

'Don't be ridiculous. What I'm telling you is that historical events are changed by the actions of men, and that this is something that everyone who can think clearly knows to be true. The document that we're looking for has history's fingerprints on it. I can't give you details, but my position is going to change on Monday, and I can't allow anything to happen that might undermine that happy event.'

'The relationship we have is financial. I don't have to buy into your crazy world-view in order to give you an honest day's labour. Is that what you're worried about?'

Blake turned in his plastic chair and looked directly at Steele for the first time since they'd climbed into the Mercedes twelve hours before.

'I was right to take you into my confidence four years ago. You've got more intelligence than you're willing to show. You mask it with bad language and a cavalier manner, but you can think.'

Steele shrugged.

'Despite what many people think is the Army's relationship to its soldiers, it actively encourages objectivity and critical awareness. The ability to look at all sides of a problem. Then it requires absolute logic when you act upon your conclusions. When we first knew each other I admit I was grateful and dazzled by your access to power. Now I've seen the pathways that power can take you down, and the blurry thinking it can lead you to, I don't think I need it. And I don't need to look up to you any more. We can return to the old status quo, where you pay me and I act as your agent. You don't have to be nice and I don't have to be subservient. Let's keep it at that, okay?'

Blake felt that a bridge had been crossed, one that he wasn't aware existed until it had loomed out of the metaphorical mist and demanded to be traversed. He was suddenly alone again. For a few years he had felt some comfort because someone had his back. He had grown up alone and marriage to the self-serving and egocentric Fiona hadn't helped. When he'd taken on Steele it was as though a big brother had suddenly appeared out of nowhere and would make sure he was safe in whatever he did. Walter Lashbrooke and his coterie had offered political support but no emotional sustenance, rather like the emotionally-crippled but cunning boys at prep school who had induced him to run for various offices in the school social life and then manipulated him into favouring their agendas.

Now, he realised, he had no support from anyone – Lashbrooke acted like a vengeful deity who was out to squeeze from Blake whatever political and financial advantage he could; Fiona moved silkily between accommodating wife and a Lady Macbeth-like emotional absence; and now Steele had withdrawn whatever brand of brute acceptance he had formerly offered.

And here he was, in the middle of France, troubling himself with an ancient document that may not even exist; and even if it did, its ramifications might be so cerebral and historic as to mean nothing to a culture with a combined memory of about two weeks.

The mobile phone that Lashbrooke had sent him rang quietly in his pocket. It had been waiting for him in a parcel when he had returned home after talking to Dyke and Bressette in Portsmouth. He answered and walked away from Steele into the square. As usual, Lashbrooke started in without introduction.

'Your man tells me you're indisposed. I do hope the indisposition will have ended by Monday. To quote Wilde, to disappear once is a misfortune, to disappear twice would be a bloody liberty that passeth all understanding. Am I making myself clear?'

'Walter, in all the years we've known each other, have I actually given you permission to talk to me like a child? Keep a civilised tongue in your head and we might get somewhere.'

Lashbrooke was silent and Blake imagined his face reddening like that of a cartoon character immediately prior to the top of his head blowing off. When eventually he spoke it was with the contained venom of a schoolteacher pushed to breaking point by a recalcitrant pupil.

'Where are you, right now?'

'Somewhere in central France. Details aren't necessary. It's a personal matter, Walter. But trust me, I have to be here.'

'It may have escaped your notice that I've been trusting you for nigh on fifteen years. Despite little evidence to support that trust, I might add.'

'Say what you have to say.'

'Have you seen the news?'

'About Strutt? Yes. Damned fortuitous, isn't it? Didn't think the old man had the guts to do it.'

'Well, neither do the police.'

'What do you mean?'

'You may or may not know that my son-in-law has a pretty good position in the Met. He tells me there are some ... problems with the idea of suicide.'

'What kind of problems?'

'Evidentiary. Strutt is supposed to have knotted a sheet, thrown it over one of the french windows on the balcony and tied it off somehow, then hurled himself to the ground to throttle himself. But the officers are saying that notion doesn't fit. They don't see how he could have thrown it over the top of the window and tied it off on one side, then got himself around the other side. Don't press me for the details. But I thought you should know.'

'Know what?'

'That there appears to be another player in the game. You should get back here as quickly as you can. I can't protect you over there, you know.'

'Walter, I'm not going to say it again. I have good reasons for being here and I'm not coming back until tomorrow. Everything will be on track again from Monday.'

'You can guarantee that, can you?'

'I can.'

'Because I don't want to read about you being found swinging from a lamp-post somewhere with your cock in your hand. Do you hear me?'

Blake closed the phone and walked back to Steele, who had been watching him while sipping from a German beer.

'Problems?'

'When I want to share my secrets with you, I'll tell you well in advance, all right?'

Steele shrugged nonchalantly, apparently happy for Blake to take the burden of whatever distress the phone call had created. Blake raised his hand to the waitress and wondered whether to order the standard glass of wine or a large.

IF JULIENNE BRESSETTE had borne a child in 1944, Sam thought, she was probably pushing ninety years of age. But when she finally opened the door at six-thirty that night, the face that greeted them was the smiling, open and clear face of someone who knew that age was something that could be fought with optimism and youthful thinking. Her eyes were lined but clear blue and her cheeks full and rosy. She was slight and evidently still limber.

'Oui?'

Sam smiled and said, 'Bonsoir, vous êtes Madame Bressette?'

'Oui. And who are you?'

Sam was caught out. 'You know I'm English?'

'Young man, I lived in the United States for nearly twenty years. I recognise an accent when I hear it. How can I help you?'

She spoke with a strong accent herself but with no hesitation over her choice of phrase. She was evidently perfectly comfortable with English.

Sam introduced himself formally, then stepped back so that Chantal could move forward. He saw that a smile was beginning to spread over her face.

Sam said, 'Madame Bressette, this is your granddaughter, Chantal. She has come to look for you.'

At first Sam couldn't tell whether the expression that crossed the older woman's face was one of delight or of fear. Her eyes widened and she leaned backwards away from the door. Then a beatific grin widened her features and she stepped forward again with her arms wide apart.

'My dear! Oh how lovely to meet you after all this time! Oh, my dear, my dear!'

Chantal raised her arms awkwardly and stepped forward, and for a moment the two women were held together by an emotion that neither seemed to have expressed before. Seeing the easy manner in which she accepted Chantal into her arms, Sam was struck by the similarity between Julienne Bressette and Jennifer Leftwich – it was as though the war through which they'd both lived and achieved adulthood had bred something into their bones, a hardy resourcefulness that was not reliant on the goodwill or pity of others.

Julienne Bressette broke away from Chantal but held on to her hands.

'Come into the house, come this way.'

She stepped aside to let them come into the cramped hallway, which was in fact the end of a corridor that seemed to run through the depth of the house towards a lighted room at its rear. Sam noted the worn red tiles on the floor, probably dating back over a hundred years, and the plain dark wood staircase that rose up to the right of the corridor. The house was extremely old and showed its character in every beam and tile.

Julienne closed the front door and led them through to a large back room in which a wood-burning stove glowed with a dim orange fire. It hadn't been particularly cold outside, but Sam knew that older people felt the cold more keenly. The room smelled of wood smoke and lavender. He took off his jacket and Julienne Bressette took it and folded it carefully and laid it over the back of a chair.

'Sit, sit. Now tell me, why are you here after all this time? How is Robert? We lost touch with each other when he went to England. Not even a letter to tell me where he was.'

Chantal hesitated and lowered her eyes.

'I'm afraid he died a few years ago.'

Julienne sat back in her chair. The joy left her face.

'I thought perhaps that was the case. Ah, le pauvre. I took him away from here, you know. I thought we could start again in America. But he didn't like it. And the boys there, they didn't like him. He learned English quickly but they all knew he was French. That was why he left America as soon as he could. I thought he would come back here, to the family home, but no. He sent me a letter to tell me he was studying to be a boulanger of all things, in England. Is that what he did? Was it a good life for him?'

Chantal had been looking down as she talked, as though she couldn't bear to see the older woman's pain.

'He had a good life, I suppose. I was his daughter – I can't judge.'

'And your mother?'

'I never knew her. She died when I was born. I don't think my father ever recovered. We weren't close.'

By now Chantal and Julienne were sitting in chairs placed either side of the stove. Julienne leaned forward and seized Chantal's hands without embarrassment once more.

'You must have no regrets. Your father was not an easy man. He was born out of love but he didn't carry it with him. He was your father, but I'm sorry to say that I did not mind his absence.'

As the woman continued to talk, Sam took a seat at a long wooden table and glanced around the room. Dark velvet curtains covered a door to the outside and there was a wide window which was also hung with curtains that reached to the floor. There were two other doors that seemed to go to the back of the house, perhaps into the garden. The mantelpiece held a collection of pewter candlesticks and small pots, with a large plate – probably from Limoges – standing in the centre directly over the fire. An upright piano stood to one side, its lacquered top supporting several black-and-white photographs.

Sam saw that Chantal had reached an instant rapport with the older woman. They shared a son and a father, and it was as though the familial bond had reached through the man's DNA to ensure that the two women knew each other at a deep level.

He stood again and moved to examine the photographs on the piano. They were all images of Julienne Bressette standing before famous American landmarks – the New York skyline, the Grand Canyon, the Statue of Liberty, Mount Rushmore. She was always alone, always smiling, as though her purpose in being in America was to validate the existence of these famous places by inserting herself into their imagery and iconic status. Sam wondered whether she did in fact travel alone, and asked passing strangers to take the photographs, or whether there was a shadowy presence who travelled with her and whose sole occupation was to act as a recorder of the event.

After a while the conversation between the two women slowed to a halt as each perhaps remembered Sam's presence and recognised that there was a purpose to the visit beyond the re-establishment of a family bond.

Chantal looked towards him and raised her chin, as if encouraging him to say his piece. He took a padded upright chair from besides the long table and turned it so that he was facing them both.

'Madame Bressette, we're here because we believe you may know something that is the basis for a great danger directed towards both Chantal and, possibly, yourself.'

To his surprise, the older woman smiled at him.

'Monsieur, I have lived through many dangers in my time. I've learned that danger is always greatest in the anticipation, not in the event itself. Tell me more and I'll decide what exactly this danger is.'

Sam explained to her the events that had led to their presence on her doorstep that evening. When the diary of Jean-Claude Bressette was mentioned, Chantal took it from her bag and handed it over. Sam continued to talk as Julienne leafed through the pages. He talked about Connell Steele and the British politician Gideon Blake and their quest to recover not just the diary but what it might hide.

She looked up from the diary.

'I gave this to my Robert because I thought he should have it as a memento of the war in which his father fought. Now you tell me that there are secrets that I should know? Secrets that place my life in danger?'

Chantal said, 'Sam and I have discussed this. We think it's possible that you know something not actually written in the diary. We understand that most of the diary is in the form of love-letters to you from my grandfather. But there is a reference to an Englishman, Robin Leftwich, who worked with Jean-Claude as part of the Resistance effort. It's information about him that we think you may know.'

Julienne Bressette looked at each of them in turn. When she wasn't smiling, her face showed its age lines and Sam thought again of the journey this woman had lived through – her time in the United States after the war, presumably a single mother while she looked after Chantal's father. What must it have been like for her to make her way as a young woman in the world at that time? What feelings about the world did she harbour that made her come back to this small French village after so long away?

Julienne said, 'You're asking me about something that happened almost seventy years ago. My marriage to Jean Claude was brief – he survived the war but was killed in a train crash just afterwards. I was twenty-three years old. I can't remember what he looked like – I had one photograph, but I lost it in America. I don't see how I can help you. I don't remember anything.'

'Did Jean Claude ever mention the Englishman after the war was ended? Did he talk about his work in *le maquis*?'

'He never talked about it. He was not one of those who would spend his time in the bar, trying to impress other men with his actions. He did not tell them, and he did not tell me.'

Chantal looked up at Sam and he saw in her eyes a mixture of disappointment and fatigue. For himself he felt a sense of disengagement familiar to him from previous cases – when he had taken it as far as he could and there was nothing more that could be learned, he stopped worrying and resigned himself to knowing only the current truth. His years investigating the problems and frailties of others had convinced him that truth was only a transitory and impermanent factor in the lives of most people. In general, people wanted to know only enough truth to allow them to maintain their view of themselves as honourable and justified in their actions. He had always felt a deeper commitment to discovering the fundamental principles behind any particular decision, but was now practised enough to know that the version of the truth to which he could commit at any one time may not in fact represent the whole picture. While he might like to see the whole picture, it was both doubtful that one actually existed and impossible to say whose version of that picture carried most weight.

So if Julienne claimed not to remember any useful facts, then he and Chantal should accept this as the current reality and either move on or find someone who's view of reality was more complete.

WHILE WAITING FOR Julienne to return that afternoon from wherever she had been, Sam and Chantal had driven back towards Montmorillon and found a supermarket. They had bought bread and cheese and pâté, and they shared these with Julienne, who seemed to live frugally and had no food to spare other than her own meagre supplies of oily fish in oval tins. She had some *vin d'épines* that she had made herself from adding blackthorn shoots to alcohol and sugar, which she served in small glasses. They sat around her large table while Chantal talked of her life in England and how she had lived with her father, the baker.

Later, Julienne took them out into the square and walked them around the village. The street lights threw an orange glow on to the pale pavements. She described how there had been several shops and businesses on the main street when she was a child – a baker, two cafés, a butcher, a leather goods shop. 'Now the village is without life, but when I was young people lived here. We ate together. We played together. We didn't need to travel anywhere to have what we needed.' She sighed. 'Now you cannot live here without travelling. Children and old people must rely on their families to take them everywhere. And once children leave for college or work, they don't come back until they're old, like me. That is why these villages are dying. It's sad.'

Sam glanced at Chantal who saw his look and raised her eyebrows briefly.

They passed through the small park that Sam had seen earlier and which seemingly contained two monuments.

Julienne pointed to the one that was furthest into the park and, on closer inspection, was evidently a war memorial. Names of the village's dead were inscribed on a small plaque screwed into the stonework – many names for such a small village.

Then Julienne took them to the other monument. It was about fifteen feet in height and had the appearance of a round chimney placed on top of four stone steps. At the bottom, immediately above the steps, was a small opening with a pointed arch overhead making it look like a scaled-down version of a church doorway. At the very top was an opening in the curved brickwork that resembled a small belfry, but with no bell visible inside.

Julienne said, 'This is our *Lanterne des morts*, the Lantern of the Dead.'

Chantal asked, 'What was it for?'

'No one really knows.' She pointed to the small opening in the bottom of the chimney, large enough only for a child to pass through. 'Inside there are handholds so that a small person or child can climb up inside and light the lantern at the top. There are many of these scattered throughout central France, but their use has been forgotten. This one has been dated back to the twelfth century. Some have said these lanterns were lit when a dead person had been brought to the cemetery from far away and had no relationship to the church. Someone else suggested they were a meeting place for aliens, and others have said their location indicated the presence of the Holy Grail. On the other hand, it has been proposed that they were simply ovens to make tiles in. As you can see, their history has presented plenty of opportunity for fantasy.'

'Do you agree with any of these interpretations?'

Before Julienne could reply to Sam's questions, the village was plunged into darkness. Sam could not see Julienne though she stood less than five feet from him. They had been standing by the Lantern, which was illuminated by floor-mounted lamps, and the rest of the village had been lit by modern streetlights. Now the village and the houses had disappeared, not even illuminated by starlight or the creamy light of the moon. It was as though the power had suddenly been cut off to the whole village and it took time to adapt to the utter blackness. It was late enough that houses had extinguished their internal lights – or else their closed shutters had rendered them invisible from the outside – and there was no other external light. The world had become totally black.

Julienne said, 'I didn't realise it was so late. On weekday nights the streetlights go out to save electricity. They stay on Fridays and

Saturdays for revellers to find their way home. Let your eyes get used to the dark and I'll take us back.'

In the dark, Sam felt Chantal's hand find his own and grip it tightly. He became aware of her perfume and the shape of her form next to him. He wondered what it was in him that responded to such small signals and what this said about his relationship to Laura.

He held on to Chantal's hand but kept a distance between them as they walked carefully back to Julienne's house, their eyes opened wide in search of the slightest visual clue.

FRIDAY

STEELE THOUGHT that Blake was going to have a coronary. It was now Friday lunchtime and their search was still fruitless. They had started with the Mairie in Montmorillon but had received short shrift there when asking about the war and survivors of the Resistance. Nobody knew anything. They were directed politely towards the Office de Tourisme on the square, where they were given brochures for the Museum of the Resistance in Haute-Vienne and for the historic village of Oradour-sur-Glane, where in 1944, shortly after D-Day, a unit of the Das Reich Panzer Division had massacred 642 inhabitants of the village in response to the kidnapping of an SS Officer.

Blake said, 'Been there. Horrible place. The Germans shot all the men in barns, then burned down a church with all the women and children in it. Let's move on. We need to talk to someone with local knowledge. We need a bar.'

They walked up through Montmorillon, crossing the old bridge over the shifting brown waters of the Gartempe and up the steep hill into the mediaeval *Cité de l'Écrit*. Steele had to admit that the town was very pretty in a chocolate-box way. The streets were narrow and filled with bookshops, each with stands outside displaying paperbacks, comic books, photography books ... every kind of book you might want. In French.

At the top of the hill they found a bar, lined inside with full bookshelves and with a couple of tables set outside on a small patio. They sat inside at a long wooden table and when the woman came over, ordered two beers. By way of response, she handed them a long menu in a leather binding.

Steele said, 'Jesus. I only wanted a beer. They've got hundreds of them.'

'Pick one. We haven't got time for this.'

Steele pointed to one of the beers and the woman went away. He observed that Blake's usual studied calm was leaking out of him like perspiration – he had become peremptory and officious, like many of the officers Steele had known in the Army who thought a stay at Sandhurst had entitled them to respect that they'd done little to earn.

He said, 'To be frank, it beats me what the fuck we *have* got time for. What are we doing? You were impatient to get on with this yesterday but now we're wandering around a mediaeval town like a couple of feckless American tourists.'

'Nearly thirty years ago I cycled around this area looking for anybody who'd talk to me about what happened during the war. I found a lot of big mouths who actually knew nothing, and the people I really needed to talk to melted away into their hovels when they caught a whiff of what I was after. This time I'm not going to be so subtle. You and I are going to find someone who is a likely candidate and then we're going to get some answers. I need to know where this woman Julienne Bressette lives, if she's still alive. And then I'm going to find her and ask her some questions in my wretched French. Your job is to get in the way of anyone who tries to stop me. Is that all right? All clear now?'

'Was there nothing in the diary to say where she lived? All that lovey-dovey stuff from her hubby and no mention of where she was?'

'Nothing. I suppose he thought that if he was caught with the diary on him it would give his captors some leverage against him if they knew where his wife lived.'

'What about the Bressette girl?'

'She's never even been to France, as far as I could tell. Her dear daddy worked as a baker and neither of them ever came over to visit his mum. We know the granddad worked with the *maquis* in this area because of the other places he mentions in the diary. They're all in this region. But it doesn't specify where she lived.'

'Even if you know where she was in the war doesn't mean she'd still be there now.'

'You don't know the French. They pass their houses down through the generations. Nobody ever moves anywhere, or if they do they come back to where they grew up to die, like the bloody elephants' graveyard.'

Steele began to understand what was being asked of him.

'So I'm the enforcer here.'

'I didn't want you here for your report-writing skill.'

'I didn't sign up to be your torturer-in-chief.'

'Quadruple your fee.'

'Do I seem that shallow to you?'

'Quintuple. And yes.'

Steele turned and stared out of the door. The light had brightened as the morning's low cloud had finally dispersed. He was beginning to feel warm but wasn't sure whether it was the change in the weather that had induced his increased temperature or the realisation that Blake had a view of his personality and ethics which was incompatible with his own reckoning of himself.

He heard himself say, 'All right,' and wondered exactly how far he had now descended into the moral quagmire that Blake had created. And whether there was further yet to go.

JULIENNE BRESSETTE HAD suggested that they drive to the forest near Saint-Sauvant. It was a drive of a half-hour. She told them that this was where the British SAS soldiers who had been captured in June 1944 had been brought to be executed. They turned into the forest and drove for ten minutes along a sombre track between stands of tall oaks, arriving eventually at a blue-grey stone monument set back from the road and flanked by evergreens. Two rounded bushes stood like sentries to either side of the memorial. Sam was struck by the solitary and forlorn nature of the location, as though any spiritual succour that nature might normally have offered had been driven away by the events that had taken place there.

They climbed out and dutifully read the information, given in both French and English, on a plaque that stood before the monument. To the right was another post bearing the insignia of both the SAS and the Cross of Lorraine, emblem of the Free French Forces during World War Two. Julienne took them past this marker, off the track and crunching over dead leaves into the forest, where they came to a stone jagged in shape and about two feet high and hewn from the same blue-grey material as the monument.

She waited for them to join her, then said, 'This marks the first grave. Hunting dogs found it before the war had even finished. Follow me.'

She took them to two more gravestones, each fifteen to twenty yards away, and each one supporting a small wooden cross and a badge reading 'Pro Patria Mori'.

'The men were buried here. They had been captured in the forest at Verrières and then taken to Poitiers for questioning. Hitler had issued an order that all commandos who were captured should be executed immediately, so they were brought back here and shot.'

Chantal said, 'I know the story, I've read about it. But seeing it like this makes me want to cry.'

'Because you're a human being and you regret the loss of life. Now, let's get back in the car and I'll take you somewhere else. It doesn't end here.'

They left the forest and she directed them towards the nearby village of Rom, where they arrived fifteen minutes later. Once in the village another SAS insignia on a post directed them down a side-street and shortly they arrived at the walled cemetery.

Julienne said, 'Follow me.'

She took them through an iron gate and led them to the far corner of the cemetery, where two rows of white headstones, streaked and spotted with age, stood in gravel beds, each headstone bearing an engraved cross and the name of a British soldier.

'The bodies were found in the graves that you have just seen and were exhumed to be brought here. Once the investigation discovered who they were, it was decided that they should have honoured places in the cemetery. And now the commune looks after them.'

Sam walked down the longer of the two rows until he came to a specific headstone and stood before it. Chantal joined him. The cold wind whipped around their legs.

'Robin Leftwich. 24 years. Oh my god, I'm older than him. I never thought ... '

Sam said, 'Old men send young men to fight. It's always been the same.'

He looked around the graveyard at the variety of headstones and marble structures it contained, some displaying flowers, others filled with ceramic icons representing open books inscribed with dedications. In his youth graveyards had held no power over him. As he'd grown older he'd begun to feel a greater liking for their serenity.

Julienne had gone to a structure that looked like a concrete oven, set at waist height into the wall beyond the SAS graves. She reached down and opened a metal door, then withdrew a book and a ballpoint pen that lay inside.

'You can write something.'

They walked over and read the words of previous visitors to the graves. Some were from relatives or descendants, others were simply strangers who had felt compelled to offer their thanks.

Chantal said, 'I can't. I don't know what all this means to me. I'm confused.'

Sam laid a hand on her shoulder. 'That's a good reaction. At least you're feeling something.'

'And you? What do you feel?'
'I feel that we're being followed.'

THE DAY BEFORE

STEELE AND BLAKE rose early on Saturday morning and left their hotel before 7.00 a.m.

They drove out of Montmorillon as dawn broke and took the road heading to Chauvigny before turning left towards Sillars. It was a small, winding road that was initially well-tarmacked before reaching an invisible administrative boundary and becoming suddenly pock-marked with holes, as though a local government office with less available cash than its neighbour had refused to take responsibility for surfacing this section of the highway.

Blake said, 'Will you remember the turning?'

Steele turned from the driver's seat and stared at him. A headache had begun to throb behind his left temple, a sure sign that he was engaged in an activity that some part of him was resisting.

'I do this for a living. When exactly are you going to stop questioning my ability to carry out the duties you're paying me for?'

'Just asking.'

They drove in silence for another minute before Blake spoke again.

'You know what we're doing here, don't you?'

'Scaring the shit out of some civilians.'

'That's as good a summary as I've heard you make.'

The night before, Blake had decided that trying to learn anything about the Resistance by asking direct questions of old men was bound to fail. To begin with, there were few people out and about in the bars of Montmorillon. Moreover, one-time members of the Resistance were likely to be extremely old and even less likely to be occupying a seat at the back of an empty bar.

Instead he'd turned to technology. Back in his hotel room he'd used his iPad to search the internet and found a site called Vienne Résistance Internement Déportation, V.R.I.D. Blake had read avidly, moving between pages that held eye-witness accounts of Resistance members to stories of the internment of French Jews at a camp in Poitiers. Among other things, the site contained witness statements written by the sons and grandsons of Resistance fighters, including one who described the history of his grandfather's involvement in the local Resistance section, 'Groupe Robert'. In the article he described in detail the farm in which his grandfather lived and the road on which it was located. The grandson was pleased to say that he himself now lived there with his wife and his grandfather, still vibrant at the age of 93.

Filled with a cold satisfaction, Blake had knocked on Steele's door and shown him the information. A search on Google Maps found the location and using Street View they identified the route and the actual placement of the old man's farm. Blake had sent Steele out, using the Mercedes' GPS to reconnoitre it.

Now Steele said, 'Why don't you just talk to them normally? Turn up at coffee-time, say you've read his article and would like to know more.'

'You haven't dealt with these people. I spent months of my youth trying to dig up information and got nowhere. I'm not taking any chances. I need to sort this out today so we can drive back tomorrow. I need to be back in London no later than tomorrow, Sunday night. Monday's a big day.'

Steele said nothing but looked forward to the time when he could at least be beyond the politician's immediate reach.

Spending this amount of time with one person had strengthened his belief that he was a person who needed time alone, or with a group from whom he could absent himself without his absence being noted.

He said, 'It's here,' and turned slowly on to a farm track of pale crushed stone that took them around a dilapidated barn and into an informal courtyard. At the far end was a farm house of weathered grey stone, with a further barn attached to its right-hand side and what appeared to be a piggery on the left. The blue shutters on the house were closed but a light shone through a downstairs window.

'Farmers – up early.'

Blake nodded. 'Good. At least we won't have to roust them out of bed. You'll take the lead on this. They'll have already heard us arrive, but take the car out of sight so they don't see it.'

Steele reversed the car back around the ancient barn and parked. They climbed out and Blake handed him one of the black tee-shirts he'd brought with him. Steele tied it around his lower face, feeling foolish. Blake saw the look in his eyes and seized him by the arm.

'I know this probably seems stupid to your highly-trained eye, but it won't help either of us if we're recognised.'

'We spent all day in town yesterday. You're about to speak French with a terrible accent. I think even the French cops will put two and two together.'

Blake looked at him but said nothing. Steele realised he was looking into the eyes of someone who had gone far into an imaginary world, whose terms of reference were no longer the actions of sensible men and women but the desperate acts of criminals who had nothing to lose. He felt himself adopt the sensibility he had developed when facing an implacable and largely unseen enemy in Iraq, a rigorous pose of invincibility that inflated his muscles and rendered him oblivious to harm.

He walked towards the farm, feeling the hard-packed earth beneath his feet and hearing the rural chorus beginning to find its voice as the sun climbed higher above the horizon. Behind him he sensed the urgent but largely uncoordinated presence of Blake, almost electric with intent, as though he was plugged into a power source that had increased his already immense vitality and was ready to explode at the merest spark.

Steele knocked on the door and stood back, his hand reaching into his deep-pocketed trousers and grasping the handle of the claw-hammer within.

FOR THE LAST two days, Chantal Bressette had found herself almost constantly on the verge of tears. Discovering that her grandmother was still alive – and vital – had seemed to unlock a chamber in her heart that she'd never known existed. Every sensation was heightened. The linen on the bed in which she'd slept seemed crisper and whiter than any she'd ever slept in before; the air that wafted in her face when she opened the shutters in the morning held a taste that reminded her of walks in the Peak District with her father when she was young; the smell of Julienne's coffee had a pungency that struck the back of her throat and inflamed the receptors in her nose, rendering her willing to drink mugs of the caustic dark liquid that she touched only rarely in the UK.

So breakfast on Julienne's veranda, overlooking a square patio that was surfaced with creamy pebbles and shaded by a bower formed from an overhanging fig-tree, was a kind of sensory explosion that rendered her mute and watchful as Sam and Julienne talked. It seemed to her that she had been incredibly lucky to have been found and, yes, rescued by Sam Dyke. He had been forceful in a way that she hadn't encountered before, and had thought intellectually would seem brutish and without redemption. It was true that there had been times when she'd disagreed with his assessment of a situation or wished for more explanation of his position. But she knew that these feelings were the result of her own need to understand both sides of a situation, and after seeing what had happened to Jack, and how Steele had dealt with his own colleagues, she now realised that there were particular types of people for whom prevarication and second-guessing were as useful as knitting.

She also knew that she needed respite from everything she had experienced. Sam had suggested that as Julienne knew nothing of Robin Leftwich's papers or what they might contain, they should drive back up to Calais and catch the overnight ferry. She had politely refused, saying that now she had a grandmother to talk to – a new family member – she was going to take advantage of it.

Besides, hadn't he himself said that he felt they were being followed? Shouldn't they stay to protect Julienne from the kind of interrogation of which they knew Steele was capable?

Sam had made no answer to this largely because – she felt – he knew she was right. So they had slept late and were taking breakfast on the kind of bright morning that felt to her as though a slate had been wiped clean, a morning that could be the beginning of a whole new life.

Julienne said to her, 'I want to show you something in the village, but I think we should do it tomorrow. There's too much happening here today.'

'I'm happy to do whatever you want. I can't believe that you've been here all this time and I never knew you.'

'I've only been back in the village for five years. I've lived abroad almost my entire life.' She smiled broadly. 'But like all French people, I've come home to die.'

Sam said, 'You seem to have the energy of a much younger person.'

Julienne laughed. 'It probably looks like that from the outside, but it's not what I feel.'

'What is the noise outside?'

'Today is a *vide grenier* – literally, emptying your attic. A day when people sell the things that they no longer want. My American friends used to call them a garage sale.'

'We'd say a car boot sale.'

'You'll see a line of tables in the street with lots of very old things for sale – plates, clothes, cigarette lighters, coffee-makers. Would you like to go?'

Chantal said, 'It sounds delightful.'

Sam glanced at her in a way she was beginning to recognise.

'I'm not sure it's a good idea.'

'Why not? Steele and Blake aren't going to do anything in broad daylight, are they? If we've decided that there's nothing to be found here, then as far as I'm concerned, the case is closed. We rest here today and drive back up to Caen tomorrow for the ferry.'

'That's your considered opinion? That the case is closed?'

'I don't know what else can happen. We don't know whether Steele and Blake or some other gang have come after us. We don't know whether they could even find Julienne. And if they do, it seems that she has nothing to tell them. What would they do, torture an old lady? Excuse me, Julienne. It's all vanished, Sam. There's nothing here.'

Sam turned away so that she found herself staring at his profile. Her words had sounded harsher than she'd intended, as though she were an adult scolding a boy for not coming in from the playground when she'd asked. It was hard not to read his expression as a sulk.

Julienne said diplomatically, 'I'll get you a bag you can put things in. You may buy more than you think.'

She stood and left the veranda, and Chantal wondered when she and Sam had crossed the barrier that meant it was now permissible for them to argue as though they were romantically involved. She had had no indication that the line had been crossed but found it difficult to disagree with the feelings she harboured.

BLAKE STOOD BY the covered stall and drank from his plastic cup of *rosé pamplemousse*, a hybrid drink of grapefruit and rosé that was neither large enough to be refreshing nor alcoholic enough to give you a kick. The road towards the village centre ran away to his right, each side lined with trestle tables filled with – in his opinion – the most appalling tat. The sun that had risen with them this morning had now taken up position almost directly overhead and he found himself sweating copiously into his cotton shirt.

To his relief, Steele had wandered off to look at some ancient guns that were displayed on a stall near the top of the road. After learning where Julienne Bressette lived, they had decided to come directly to the village of Journet to see what they could see. Fortunately this *vide grenier* was a good cover as there were dozens of people wandering around the village.

The images from their morning's work played constantly through his head, like a film reel stuck on a loop that grew more and more exact in its portrayal as it repeated its passage. They had found three people in the house – the man who had written the original article on the VRID site, his stout wife and his ancient grandfather. The younger man was called Yves and his wife Sophie, and they shared an obstinate bravura that had irritated Blake. They had denied any knowledge of Julienne Bressette, but had done so with such evident mendacity that Steele had laughed in their faces.

The grandfather was different. He seemed to know what was going on immediately he saw Steele and Blake come through the door, the lower halves of their faces hidden by the makeshift masks. He was dark-skinned and still had a mat of white hair that was neatly trimmed and cared for. His eyes were direct and not troubled by any of the milky weakness typical of older people. He had identified himself as Patrick when Blake had demanded his name but offered nothing more. As Blake had suspected, the old man had proved tough, and it was only when Steele had gone to work on his daughter-in-law's hands with the hammer that he had given up the information about Julienne Bressette. It turned out that he had known her well during the war and that she had in fact worked for the Resistance herself from time to time, travelling by train between the Occupied and Unoccupied Zones to transmit messages between different groups of fighters.

Eventually he had told them where she lived.

It was Steele who had raised the question in the end, with the woman's hands crushed and raw, the son's mouth bleeding where his four front teeth had been knocked out and the old man silently weeping in his chair, his hands tied fast behind the chair-back.

'What do we do with them now?'

Blake had once thought of himself as decisive and able to surrender whatever conscience he might have to the demands of the real world. Confronted by three wrecked human beings he had found it more difficult to be convinced by his own moral absolutism. Steele had seen the irresolution in his face and laughed mockingly at him.

'Another armchair general. Welcome to the battlefield, sir. Do you want me to take care of it? To load your problems on my back in return for your gratitude, and your money?'

Blake had found himself unable to speak, and watched as Steele herded the three stunned people into a back room, then return to take from a glass-fronted cupboard a long-barrelled rifle that he'd drawn Blake's attention to earlier.

'They're supposed to keep these locked up. But these fucking frogs are so self-righteous they don't like being told what to do, so they don't.' He lowered his voice into a roughly-accented imitation of Arnold Schwarzenegger. 'I'll be back.'

He strode towards the rear room and in a very short time Blake heard three gunshot blasts. Steele came back in. He had an expression on his face that Blake couldn't read, but contained indications of both insanity and playfulness, and Blake realised that in Steele those two emotions were closely related, as though he was using the actions associated with one behavioural orientation to mask the deeds of the other.

Steele had said, 'Good. At last we've got some proper toys to play with. Now let's check out the ammo.'

BLAKE FINISHED HIS drink and placed the plastic cup on the counter of the temporary kiosk. He had seen Steele walking back down the hill towards him. His face glittered with animation.

'Have you seen them?'

Blake followed his gaze and his eyes caught Dyke and Bressette on the other side of the road, side by side, leaning over a stand selling second-hand electronic gadgets. They seemed somehow different from when he'd seen them last. Of course Dyke was tall and broad across the shoulders, making Bressette seem slight next to him. But she was as big as most of the French men who walked past her, glancing at her rear as they did so.

Then he realised that she'd dyed her hair so that it was lighter – perhaps an attempt at disguise. He fought the urge to go and confront them directly.

He said to Steele, who had been watching him, 'We should go. It wouldn't help us if they knew we were here.'

Steele shook his head sadly. 'Dyke already knows. He's no dummy. He'll have picked you out when they were walking up the street.'

'So what do we do?'

'You were right – we scram, just so they don't know where we are or what we're doing. Keep them on edge.'

'Then what?'

'Get back to the car, watch them. If they've found grandma they're probably staying with her. We watch and we wait. This thing's going on all day so I'd suggest we don't do anything until tomorrow, when it's all quietened down and there are fewer people around.'

'Christ, hurry up and wait. This is worse than politics.'

'Perhaps. But not as vicious.'

SAM HAD BEEN thinking about the last case in which he'd been involved that had concluded violently. It had ended when two murderous thugs, red-headed twins, had killed each other while he had watched. One of the twins had accidentally shot the other, who had in turn split his brother's throat with the curved edge of a machete. He had done it, Sam believed, because he couldn't bear the thought of society passing judgement on his brother and his delusional view of the world. They had collapsed into each others' arms and fell to earth like amoral demi-gods suddenly become aware of their mortality.

He had told himself that the effect of witnessing this fraternal immolation wouldn't reduce his ability to function should he be confronted with a similar situation again. But for the last two days he had felt in his gut a growing mistrust of his own responses. It was he rather than Chantal who had pushed to leave for England sooner rather than later; he who had expressed reservations about visiting the *vide grenier*. And now it was he who felt his nerves tighten and render his skin as sensitive as rice paper as he walked Chantal back to the house.

Having seen Blake, and then Steele, he had started to make calculations and plans for protecting Julienne and the younger woman. Where in the past he might have walked directly up to the two Englishmen to demand what they wanted, something in his psyche told him that upfront confrontation would not be the safest course of action with these two. Blake looked as taut and worried as someone whose role in life had been questioned by a higher authority. His short hair was untidy and his skin looked blotchy and pale. Steele seemed almost jovial by comparison, his small mouth twisted into a thin, cruel mockery. They seemed to have transgressed any parameters that might have restrained logical thinkers and were now entering territory inhabited by the paranoid and the confused.

In a sense he could understand it of Blake, who had no evident experience of covert work. But the notion that Steele, who had released them only two days earlier, was again engaged to hunt them down seemed to him the mark of someone whose moral sensibility had gone berserk.

He had said nothing to Chantal but ushered her around the *vide grenier* carefully, not letting his own lack of interest in French linen or jewellery lead him to walk ahead of her to a more interesting stall. Eventually he noticed that Blake and Steele had gone, probably to set up watch somewhere. He had noticed several

English license plates in the square and assumed they were cars owned by ex-pats who'd come to the sale.

Perhaps it wasn't that simple.

Chantal had bought a couple of bowls and a large multi-coloured eiderdown. He took the bag that one of the stall owners had given her for the eiderdown and with his free hand guided her back down the hill towards Julienne's house. He had already concluded that it was better to be inside than not, and it was likely that Blake and Steele knew which house it was anyway.

When Chantal turned her head to look up at him her eyes seemed as round and blue as marbles.

'Why are you pushing? What's going on?'

'Sorry. I'm worrying too much.'

'Take it easy, Sam. A girl might think you like touching her up.'

Sam took his hand from the small of her back and felt himself flushing.

'Let's just get in, okay? I don't like us being so visible.'

Chantal looked at him oddly but said nothing more as they crossed the main street and opened the door to Julienne's house. She took the bag from him and ran up the stairs to her room. Sam looked in the kitchen and then wandered through to the back of the house. He couldn't see Julienne. He went through to the outside and on to the veranda. Their breakfast cups and plates were still there.

Julienne's garden was extensive, belying the house's modest appearance from the front. It went down several levels, past a pond, through a tall hedge into which a doorway into the lower garden had been cut, opening into a large section which contained a vegetable plot and a stand of tall bamboo. Further down, the bottom of the garden was marked by a row of tall poplars. As he walked down he realised that she was not there – not tending, weeding or collecting vegetables.

He walked back up into the house and looked in all the rooms again, including the small box room in which he'd been stationed, and Julienne's own room.

She was not in the house.

He hoped it wasn't beginning. He wasn't ready.

TWO HOURS LATER the front door opened and Julienne pushed her bicycle into the hallway. The pannier over the front wheel contained several packages wrapped in paper. Her eyes were bright with exertion. She wheeled the bicycle through to the workroom at the rear of the house then came back to the kitchen, where Sam and Chantal waited for her. Sam found that he was more amused than irritated by her unwillingness to take the potential danger of their situation seriously.

'You've been shopping.'

'Yes! We have to eat tonight, don't we? I thought I'd ride into La Trimouille while you were busy at the *vide grenier*.'

'We could have fetched it in the car.'

Julienne turned to Chantal. 'Oh, were you worried about me? I'm sorry, I should have realised. I took longer than I expected because I met a friend and we talked for a while. Do you both like pork? I have some nice fillets.'

STEELE IMAGINED HIMSELF as a cauldron placed on a high flame. The actions he'd committed that morning under Blake's recalcitrant gaze had inflamed him further. He was situated both in his body and outside it, as though he could feel each footstep of the creatures that even now tunnelled and burrowed beneath the wheels of the car he sat in, while at the same time look dispassionately at himself through the windscreen, wondering 'Who is that person residing in my flesh, breathing my air?'

His emotional temperature had always been a wonder to him, a steady pulse set at low frequency that he could, at will, increase to witheringly admonish a junior colleague, or decrease to calmly plot a cunning route from a dangerous situation. Now whatever regulator might have been in place had burned out, so that he was expending energy just to sit still and not storm Julienne Bressette's house and murder its inhabitants in their beds.

His experience in the sangars of Afghanistan had taught him that it was impossible to tell from whence danger might arrive. An apparently quiet night could be split asunder by the screech of an RPG missile exploding five feet behind you and taking out a concrete wall. His experience had also taught him that patience in the service of incompetence was more dangerous than running directly at a mob of armed and motivated Taliban. For these reasons he had tried to impress on Blake the need for swiftness and surprise while being able to react flexibly when situations changed, as they would.

But working with Blake was equivalent to taking out his fingernails one by one with mole grip pliers. The pain was excruciating, drawn out and apparently never-ending. The man who he'd once thought was cool and decisive had turned out to be leery of commitment, as prone to skittishness as a goat and unable to focus long enough to propose a workable plan. He made everything up as he went along and could be argued out of it by a 12-year old using schoolyard logic. He now saw that the flexibility and willingness to adapt that he'd seen earlier in their working relationship were simply indicators of a lack of purpose and a definite goal. Blake's background and schooling had endowed him with the demeanour and rhetorical skills of political leadership while subtracting from his character any sense of values that might direct his actions.

In short, he was the same as all the other fucking 'leaders' Steele had known while in uniform, and from whom he'd hoped to engineer an escape.

Blake stirred next to him in the passenger seat and sat up.

'How long was I out?'

'About a week.'

'Fucking ha-ha. What time is it?'

'Quarter past eleven.'

They were parked as far from Julienne Bressette's house as they'd been able to manage while still keeping it in sight. This meant that they'd had to park on the square, facing the village's only bar, Chez Dom, which was still doing business. The streetlights on the square illuminated three people who sat on chairs outside the bar and talked noisily. Earlier they had seen Dyke emerge from the house and fetch something from a red car parked opposite, next to the church. And they had had their first sight of the old woman whom they'd been tracking – she had stood in the open doorway, her hand on the door, the light behind her, looking as small and unthreatening as a child. They had come all this way and done fearful things in order to ask this woman some simple questions. To Steele it appeared to be a kind of cruel taunt that she could stand there so brazenly and not understand the forces that she'd set in play against her.

Steele said, 'Any instructions, boss?'

'Do I detect a note of weary insubordination in your tone?'

'If by that do you mean I'm tired, thirsty and hungry, yes. I hope you're not going to suggest we storm the house now, with these yahoos still sitting there and living it large with the Pernod? Even if we came round the back, which we can't, it wouldn't take much to raise an alarm. This village is like a fucking toy-town, everyone on top of each other.'

'Okay, okay. We'll have to do it tomorrow. Sunday evening everyone goes to bed early. Farmers get up early to work on Monday morning. Everyone else is so bored by the game shows on French TV they go to bed just to escape from them.'

'Good decision. At last.'

'So tomorrow night we get Dyke out of the way and deal with the old woman. Find out what she knows and where the document is. Christ, I've almost forgotten myself what we're here for. Remind me if I forget.'

'If you forget I'll shoot you myself.'

Blake looked at him sharply but said nothing as Steele started the engine on the Mercedes and pulled slowly out of the square, heading back towards Montmorillon.

AFTER A MINUTE, a sky-blue Passat with English plates pulled out from the other side of the church and followed in their wake.

THE LAST DAY

BY TEN O'CLOCK on Sunday morning the sun was high enough to burn the top of Sam's head. In the last few days the intensity of the heat had grown and he had little doubt that a continental thunderstorm would arrive soon to break overhead like an upended bucket and give them respite from the scorching heat for a day or two, until the barometer started to rise again. The fields to his left contained a yellowing crop that he didn't recognise but he knew that the land was brown and hard already, as dry as an Arabian beach but as solid and unyielding as brick. That anything grew in that parched earth was to him a triumph of agricultural knowledge to which he had no access.

To his right the walls of the Journet cemetery rose a couple of feet above head height, their colour a version of the dirty white plaster that he'd seen elsewhere in the village. That morning Julienne had told them that there was something she wanted to show them. They had finished breakfast on the veranda again, then she had disappeared upstairs for twenty minutes. When she returned she was wearing a black skirt and a white blouse with a necklace of large coloured stones. She had put on lipstick, rouge and a little eye-shadow and combed her hair neatly before catching it in a barrette at the back of her head.

Chantal said, 'Should I change too? I don't have much ... '

'You look fine as you are. Now, please walk with me. It won't take long.'

She had led them out of the house and turned left, through the small park in which the war memorial and the Lantern of the Dead stood as erect and insensible as presidential guards. Within fifty yards they were out of the centre of the village and walking down an empty country road towards the cemetery.

Unlike British cemeteries, this one had a solid metal door that Julienne unlatched and passed through. It was reminiscent to Sam of the one they'd seen two days before at Rom – gravestones in a variety of sizes and colours, some heavy dark crypts – containing entire families, Julienne said – and some simple, plain headstones. On nearly every grave there were offerings – crucifixes raised on metal brackets, pots of flowers or other items of remembrance.

Sam had never subscribed to any religion but he appreciated the depth of feeling that had led the bereaved to commit such time and patience to the maintenance of their deceased ones' graves.

Julienne had scurried on her short legs to a distant corner of the graveyard, Chantal swaying gently behind her as she picked her way down the aisles between the graves. Sam had already guessed what they were going to see but he followed behind nonetheless.

Julienne was already standing with her hands clasped before her and her head bowed before a simple headstone. She looked up as Chantal and Sam drew near and he saw that far from weeping, as he had thought, she was smiling with a kind of grim acceptance.

'This is your grandfather. He died many miles from here but we brought the body back so that he could be at home. I used to visit twice a week until I left for America. He was a brave man who didn't live long enough to taste the fruits of his bravery. We would have stayed here, with your father, and Jean-Claude would have opened a little bakery and Robert would have taken it over. I expect I would have gone mad. But it would have been a good enough life.'

'You wouldn't have seen the world. I might not be here.'

'Your spirit would have come to us in some form – your father would have married a nice girl from the next village and you would have come to us eventually. Your spirit belongs here. Like mine. Like your grandfather's.'

Sam thought again of his own father's death, lying in his rumpled bed in Thurnscoe, coughing away his life force like the last gasps of a hose-pipe that has been choked off. It had always seemed to him a mistake to believe that one's identity was somehow bound up with the location where one happened to have been born. Although he had inherited certain habits of mind and personality from both of his parents, he had met people from all over the world whose behaviour was not too dissimilar to his own. He was likely to ascribe more potency to his DNA and genes than to the fact of his birth in a given square mile of land.

He could see his father now, bent over his vegetables in his back yard, his right hand digging with a trowel in the soft loamy earth, the train line to Rotherham no more than forty yards down the garden and on a slight rise, so that passengers riding by could look directly into his family's lives as though the fact of their passage gave them certain rights of trespass.

He felt no connection to that view of his father beyond a kind of nostalgia, and realised with surprise that what felt like home to him was a vision of himself and Laura sitting either side of his kitchen table. The house was dark and silent around them and they weren't even talking to each other – but he took comfort from her engagement with him and knew that his sense of personal authority and strength was a consequence of his willingness to be vulnerable in her presence. She gave him the strength to let go and breathe out, to let himself be seen, for once, as someone whose direction was not fixed.

Later, he wondered whether his absorption and indulgence in memory had blunted his awareness. Had he been more alert he might have chosen a different sequence of manoeuvres and found that the conclusion that seemed inevitable was actually avoidable if he'd taken more notice of his surroundings.

AS THEY LEFT the cemetery, Julienne threaded her arm through Sam's and walked with him. She felt as light as a bundle of dry twigs but there was a contained energy in the way she held his arm close to her side. Ahead of them the church clock struck twelve for the first time – he had noticed the peculiarity that the clock sounded on the hour, tolling the time, and then again two minutes afterwards. It also rang an angelus three times a day, just after seven in the morning, midday and seven in the evening, calling the devout to prayer. For a small village there was a lot of periodic noise.

Now Julienne reached out and grasped Chantal's arm too, so that they walked in a laboured lockstep down the road towards the village centre.

She said, 'I have remembered something. At first I didn't think it was important, but now I think perhaps it is. You must forgive an old lady her memory. Events and details swim in and out of my mind and I'm not always sure whether I have remembered something or just dreamed it. And then I think I might have told you but in fact I have not.'

Chantal petted her hand. 'We don't expect anything of you, Julienne. This was a hope, that's all. It was a long time ago.'

'You're kinder to me than I am to myself. At any rate, I have remembered that when Jean-Claude wanted to leave me a message, he would put it in the *Lanterne des morts*. This was before we were married. My parents didn't want him coming to the house because they thought he wasn't good enough for me. So he would leave *billets-doux* and little presents in the lantern. If you reach up inside you can feel steps and he would leave things there for me. Every night I would take a walk outside to see if he had left anything.'

'That's very romantic and sweet.'

'Yes, it was. Eventually he overcame my parents' resistance because it was obvious he was serious, as we say in French, and so we could meet properly. Of course, shortly after the war began he joined the *maquis* and I didn't see him regularly.'

Sam asked, 'You think he may have left something in the lantern?'

'It's possible. The diary that I gave to your father, Chantal, was delivered to me by a friend of ours after Jean-Claude was forced to leave the area. But it's possible he hid other papers and documents in the lantern for him to return to later. But he went away and didn't return till months afterwards, when the war had ended. And shortly after that he was killed in the train accident. Perhaps he simply forgot.'

A desolate quiet had descended on the road. The sky was eggshell blue and completely void of clouds, as though a cloth had scrubbed it clean and left it burnished and without a stain. He was aware of the hot tarmac beneath his feet and the shuffling sound made by their movement in the midday heat. Ahead of them the *Lanterne des morts* and the war memorial were visible through the trees in the memorial park. Sam felt his pulse quicken slightly as they approached.

He turned and saw Chantal's blue eyes on him, her irises flecked with green and round as coins.

She said, 'Do we do it now?'

Sam looked to the left as they entered the village, passing the Lantern in the park on the right. The bar was still open and two men sat outside talking to the owner, a dark-haired man with a large, rough-hewn face. The three men stopped talking and glanced at them as they came into sight. The bar owner raised a hand towards Julienne and she inclined her head. There were three cars on the square, none of them with English plates this time. A dog began to bark as though it had sensed their presence. Sam looked back towards the Lantern.

'Not now. It's full daylight and there are still people around. I don't want to be arrested for desecrating a national monument or something.'

Chantal said, 'It's only a bit of stone. Where's your sense of adventure?'

'You've never met the gendarmes, have you? You wouldn't be so cavalier if you had.'

Julienne disengaged her arms from them and took hold of their hands instead.

'We must be patient. If there is something in the lantern, it has been there for nearly seventy years. We can wait until it gets dark. The bar will shut and people will go to bed early because it's Sunday night.'

Sam had never been one to bide his time before acting, but this time he allowed Julienne to lead him and Chantal quietly to her front door. Chantal said nothing but remained tense, as though the need to comply with her grandmother had only temporarily won the battle over her desire to put an end to the mystery.

Sam said, 'Anyway, I have an idea for this afternoon. Something that will distract us for a few hours.'

'Ah, good!' Julienne closed the door behind them and stood with her feet together like a child expecting a reward. 'I like it when there is a surprise.'

STEELE WAITED IN the car while Blake paid the bill in the hotel. They had checked out before lunch but had returned to eat dinner in the restaurant, and Steele thought he'd had about as much chopped salad starter and fruit tart dessert as he was ever likely to want again.

In the fading light he watched the infrequent traffic come down the Boulevard de Strasbourg then turn and head over the bridge out towards Lussac-les-églises and points west. In the past he'd often felt a tension in his chest when about to commit to a course of action that was dangerous or beyond the common run of events. Now he realised he felt nothing. It was as though something had been subtracted from his experience of the world, like an accident victim who loses the ability to smell or to see the colour green. What the immediate future held in store for him was simply a sequence of actions for which he had a complete lack of responsibility. It had begun the previous morning with the murder of the old Resistance fighter and his family. Steele had felt a kind of fever inflaming his blood, urging him to hurt those people and then – after Blake showed his utter incomprehension about how to deal with the witnesses – instructing him to fetch the rifle from its cupboard and use it on them.

Deep inside himself he felt a giant void that made him despair for his mental health and his future as a mercenary for sale. He wasn't sure that he could continue to function if he caught sight of himself in a mirror or gave a single thought to the state of his soul. His karma was now so mortally deranged that even death held no prospect of succour.

Blake came out of the hotel and walked to the Mercedes. He threw his bag into the back seat and climbed in beside Steele.

Steele said, 'I hope you paid in cash.'

'Seeing as I took out five hundred Euros from the cash point down the road, I don't suppose it will make much difference. I'm still traceable if anyone's serious about it.'

'Thank God you're not famous.'

'Yet. Rather depends on what happens later today. Are you going to start this car or are we supposed to push it to Journet?'

Steele set the car in gear and they headed down the narrow road, through a set of traffic lights and followed a bend up and out of the town centre. The setting sun angled through the pale stone buildings and burnished them a rich gold. It was early evening and there was no one on the street and barely any traffic. After a few hundred yards there was another roundabout which Steele slowed down to traverse.

Blake said, 'Look! It's them.'

On the far side of the traffic island, beyond a large, moulded representation of the book Colomba by Prosper Merimée which occupied its centre, Steele made out the red Meriva they'd identified as Dyke's hire-car. Dyke was driving with the old woman in the passenger seat. No doubt Chantal Bressette was in the rear.

Blake said, 'Keep the island between us and them, then go round and follow.'

Steele drove slowly around the island, keeping the slightly raised mound at its centre, topped by the statue of the book, between him and the Meriva. It continued down towards the centre of Montmorillon from which he and Blake had just driven.

They followed Dyke into the square in the centre of town and watched him park in the tarmacked slots set aside for cars. Steele drove straight through the square and pulled into the parking spaces on the other side of the Office of Tourism, out of sight of the square. They climbed out and walked back to a position where they could observe.

Dyke and the two women were already out of the Meriva and were walking slowly towards the narrow road that led up to the old bridge. Steele and Blake had taken it two days before when they had walked up into the *Cité de l'Écrit* looking for old *résistants* to question. There were only so many routes available once they were up there, so Steele signalled Blake to stay put. Dyke and the women would have to come back down again.

They watched the trio amble slowly up towards the bridge over the Gartempe, the older buildings of the mediaeval city rising ahead, many of them showing their original beams, and looked down on from above by the old church and its tall grey spire. There was nobody else in the square, nobody on the bridge, and not a sound from the pigeons that fluttered above them in niches let into the back of the Office of Tourism building. Steele wondered at the complete absence of sound. At other times a strange muzak had been present in the town, issuing from old-fashioned speakers above shop fronts and broken up from time to time by what sounded like bursts of advertising. Now they were silent. There was a golden sun on the horizon and three figures on a bridge. If Steele had been an artistic man he might have seen in the tableau an opportunity to capture an image redolent of desolation and abandonment. But in fact to him it was merely an opportunity to observe the strengths and weaknesses of an enemy who were themselves ignorant of the danger they were in.

Abruptly, Dyke broke off from the trio staring over the bridge at the river and walked back down the hill towards the square. Blake and Steele hurried back to their positions on the far side of the Office of Tourism and peered around the side.

Blake whispered, 'What's he up to?'

'I've left my mind-reading kit at home. Maybe he's fetching something from the car.'

He shifted so that he could see Dyke walking towards the red Meriva, his broad shoulders visible in a dark polo shirt above the other cars in the square. Steele watched as Dyke paused and looked back towards the bridge, as though waiting. Then he climbed into the car and drove off.

Steele laughed and prodded Blake in the arm.

'He's only gone and fucking dumped them. He probably thinks they're safer here. That's the first stupid move I've seen him make.'

'So we take the women?'

'How are you with rope and blindfolds? That farmhouse this morning was a real treasure-trove of nasty-looking stuff.'

Blake turned and looked him up and down. 'Sometimes I can't read you at all. Just when I think you're getting tired of all this cloak-and-dagger play-acting you surprise me again.'

'My karma's fucked, so what do I care? Now let's go and have a word with those bitches on the bridge. I give you that as the title for your autobiography, when you've done with politics and turn to fiction.'

'I'm already there. Horror section.'

CHANTAL BRESSETTE HAD allowed herself to worry a little about their situation, but Julienne was so blithe and carefree that she found it hard to maintain a sour demeanour. She recognised that Sam thought he was doing the best thing by keeping them out of the way. And it was true, there was nothing that she or Julienne could have done if it came to some kind of physical confrontation. Nonetheless, she felt obscurely chided by being left behind, as though it was a comment on her abilities or commitment.

Julienne had taken her further up into the old town, past bookshops – open but devoid of customers – and past a bar that was also closed. At the top of the hill they'd turned right, climbed a few steps to a small courtyard, and were about to enter the church that faced them when a hand gripped Chantal's arm. She turned in shock.

Blake looked at her, his face mocking, his mouth twisted into a callous grin.

'Thought you'd seen the last of us, did you? You should have given it up when my insubordinate colleague here gave you the chance.'

She noticed Steele standing a little behind his superior, his arms folded as though he was bored.

Chantal felt herself begin to tremble as though seized by chills. But before she could say anything, Julienne stepped forward.

'I think you're looking for me. I'm Julienne Bressette, Chantal's grandmother. Is there somewhere we can go and talk? Then we can go back to Journet and see Mr Dyke. I'm sure he'll be waiting for us.'

AS SAM DROVE back to Journet, the sun behind him throwing the shadow of his car ahead like a jittering silent movie, his heart seemed to swell and fill his chest so that he could barely breathe. He thought again of the story he'd told Chantal about his friend Frank, beaten by the scrap-metal merchants. He hadn't told her of the guilt he'd felt, the days he spent visiting Frank in hospital, the nights he'd woken up in a foetid sweat. He had taken up running and lifting weights after that to get fitter and stronger but the memory of Frank's head striking the side of the rusting gas oven had never left him. Violence had become something he was good at, but only because he gave up something essential of himself when he engaged in it. He became less than the man he wanted to be. He had a sense that people like Steele became fuller versions of themselves when they acted with violence – it expressed a fundamental aspect of their character. And he was fearful that his own relationship to violence would render him hesitant because he found it difficult to give himself over to it completely.

Arriving in Journet he parked opposite the house and let himself in. He had earlier offered to hold on to the key so that it was in his keeping when he returned. He had suggested to Chantal and Julienne that they all spend some time in Montmorillon and perhaps have something to eat before coming back later at night to inspect the Lantern. They'd been willing enough and walked together up into the old part of Montmorillon, with Julienne intent on showing them around the church and the older monuments higher up. When they'd reached the bridge and were looking down at the river, he'd turned away with the excuse that he'd left his wallet in the car. He had the feeling that Chantal had not believed him but she'd stayed with Julienne rather than follow him to test her doubts. Now they were alone in the town. Montmorillon was a ten minute drive from Journet and while they might compel one of Julienne's friends to drive them back, he hoped that they'd realise why he'd done it and just wait for him to return.

The house was cooling as Sam walked down the central corridor to the large dining room which ran crosswise at the back. He intended to check out the aluminium ladders that he'd seen in her workroom. He'd wait until it was dark and then go down to the Lantern and see what he could find. If he needed to look at the top of the Lantern, he'd have the steps with him.

He came to a halt when he saw a package on the table. It hadn't been there when he left the house with the women earlier.

But then he remembered that he hadn't been last to leave the house. Julienne had stepped back inside, ostensibly to fetch another coat. Looking at the package, he realised why she had done so.

It was wrapped in oilskin, but was unmistakably in the shape of a small pistol. There was a note resting on the package, which he picked up and read.

'You might find this useful.'

The package was held together with string, which he slipped off the oilskin. Unwrapping the pistol, he saw at once that it was an old Walther PPK. He knew that the handgun had been issued to German military officers and police during the second world war, and was in fact the gun with which Hitler had eventually killed himself. He could only imagine that Julienne had got hold of it at some point and kept it hidden in the house for all those years. He picked it up and pressed the magazine release button below the slide and pulled out the magazine. The single stack was full – seven cartridges ranged and ready.

He said, 'God bless you, Julienne.'

THREE HOURS LATER he was ready. Stepping outside the front door he saw that the village was asleep. The streetlights glowed orange and were shaped like old-fashioned lanterns. They were for the most part attached high up on the sides of the houses that lined the road, except for a couple on posts in the square. They gave the village an eerie yellow glow, their shadows stretching deep into the crevices behind the church and between the rows of dwellings. There were no other lights showing from the houses along the road or on the far side of the square. At a few minutes to eleven, the village was asleep.

A screech owl passed overhead, sending its forlorn cry into the night as it hunted its prey. Sam looked up. The sun of the earlier part of the day had eventually been swallowed by thunderous clouds, and now he could see no stars and there was no moon.

He turned off the hall light behind him, stepped outside and swung the door closed. Facing him the massive front of the church of Saint Martin loomed overhead. Julienne had told him it was only built in the nineteenth century as a replacement for one that was falling down, but it had the aura and gravitas of an edifice that was centuries old. She had also told him that the entire area around the church, including her house, was built on land that had served as a graveyard centuries before. Everywhere he walked he was likely to be stepping on old bones.

He pulled his jacket tighter and did up the zip against the brisk night air, then picked up the light aluminium stepladder, hinged at the top, and walked towards the small walled park that was named the Square of the Priory of Saint-Jean and in which stood the ancient Lantern of the Dead.

At the entrance to the park there were two stone pillars and beneath each one a large square flower pot. Sam stopped and looked around briefly, then went in and bore left towards the Lantern. Inside the park the Lantern was illuminated from beneath by three lights set into the gravel on which it had been placed. There were four steps up to the Lantern itself, which was constructed of stone that had been hewn from a quarry and shaped into a round chimney over eight hundred years ago. It was nearly three times Sam's height, topped by a stone cross. Just beneath the cross was the opening in which he presumed the actual lamp would be placed. At the base of the chimney was an arched doorway about two feet high, just enough for a small child to climb inside. Cut into the stone inside there were semi-circular holes for a child's feet. He would have been expected to climb inside with a torch of some kind and then ascend to the top to light the lantern itself. Julienne had said that the exact purpose of the Lanterns was still unknown, except that they were usually associated with cemeteries or churches, and so seemed to be part of a ritual associated with death. The most likely explanation, she'd said, was that they alluded to the myth whereby the dead were enabled to see their passage as they travelled from terrestrial gloom to heavenly light.

Beyond the Lantern was a plane tree of enormous proportions, towering overhead, its leaves rustling ceaselessly in the wind. The lights from beneath the Lantern also illuminated the near side of this tree, turning its leaves a parchment white, a ghostly apparition against the black of the sky. To his left was a small stand of shrubs just higher than the height of a man.

Sam put down the ladders and prepared to look inside the Lantern.

A voice came out of the darkness to his left.

'I like a bit of old architecture, me.'

Steele stepped forward into the white light rising from the lamps buried in the gravel at the Lantern's base. He had been concealed behind the bushes to Sam's left. He held a long rifle in his right hand while his left pushed Julienne Bressette forwards. The older woman was a little unsteady on her feet but she smiled gamely up at Sam. There was a movement to his right and he saw Chantal heading towards him with Blake at her back. He was also holding a rifle. They had been hidden behind the broad trunk of the plane tree.

Blake said, 'These Bressette women have more backbone than anyone I've met in all my years in politics. I don't know whether that says something about them or about politics. What do you reckon, Dyke?'

'I think your political career is about to come to an end for the sake of a historical misunderstanding. I think you have no idea what you're doing and are thrashing around like a stuck pig.'

'Brave talk. In many ways you're right. I am making this up as I go along. I have so many pressures on me, you have no idea. Have you ever been married to a woman with a sense of entitlement so great it beggars belief? Have you ever had a team who were supposedly on your side, working for you, but constantly making demands that are impossible to fulfil?'

'I don't think you're one to talk about entitlement. This whole escapade has been about your sense of entitlement.'

'Escapade? I've never heard anyone use that word in speech before. You're an interesting man, Dyke, and it's a shame that we're on opposing sides.'

Steele coughed and both Sam and Blake looked at him. He raised his rifle and pointed it at Julienne's back, then gave a small shrug.

He said, 'What are we doing here? Am I supposed to be issuing threats or something?'

Blake said, 'Just hold on, take your time.'

Steele glanced at him, said, 'Ah, fuck it,' then pushed Julienne out of the way and walked up to Sam, resting the barrel of his rifle against his chest.

'You had your chance, big guy. I let you off the hook once. Why should I do it again?'

Sam said, 'Charity?'

Blake seemed galvanised. He pushed Chantal forward and came closer himself.

'I wouldn't argue with him, Dyke. He's in a bit of a foul mood this weekend.'

'So am I. Tell me, what happens tomorrow? What has all this been about?'

'I'm afraid that's government business. You'll find out in good time.'

'If we all get to tomorrow.'

Steele prodded Sam in the chest with his rifle. 'Worried?'

'Curious.'

Steele grinned. 'So are we. Blake?'

'Yes, of course. Dyke, Madame Bressette has told us that you had plans to investigate this ... this lantern. She seems to think that if her husband did leave anything, it might be here. Now we've been very nice and waited an hour in this cold for you to turn up so that we could all be together for this little party. So could you do the honours and have a look? I see you brought the ladders.'

Sam hesitated. He had to get the timing right.

'What do you expect to find?'

'Oh good lord, we've been through all this before. I expect to find a love-letter written by my aunt on the back of a highly sensitive telegram. If I have the telegram I burn it and save my family – and myself – a lot of shit. If you had found it, I daresay the press would have soon got hold of it and my career would have nose-dived. At this particular moment that would have been disastrous for me and my colleagues. Not to mention the almighty hubbub created with our Israeli allies.'

Behind them the church bell began to toll eleven o'clock for the first time. The deep bass of the clock bell boomed around the village. After a pause of two minutes, it would repeat the toll. Sam began to tense, waiting it out.

When the clock had finished its eleven strikes, Steele said, 'I don't see any movement, Dyke. You know what I'm capable of.'

Later, Sam wondered whether he could have done anything differently. There was a premeditation in his actions of which he wasn't proud, but he had known that dealing with someone like Steele was likely to draw on all his reserves of commitment. The brutality that resulted seemed to him something from which there was no escape if he wanted Chantal and Julienne Bressette to emerge unharmed. The fact that his own actions depended on precise timing and a willingness to take risks with their lives was something he didn't like to contemplate afterwards. If it had gone wrong, he would only have had himself to hold up as the guilty party.

Steele had stepped back, and he and Julienne Bressette were now standing more or less on top of one of the three lights that were buried in the ground and pointed directly upwards, illuminating one side of the stone Lantern and casting them in an eerie blue-green glow that shadowed their faces. Blake still had Chantal Bressette in front of him, his rifle pointed at the ground. Sam placed a bet with himself that Blake would not have the ingrained speed of thought to act calmly should the situation develop. His first thought would be one of self-preservation. The bravado he was exhibiting now would vanish once he was in the position of victim.

Now Blake said, 'Come on, Dyke. We've had a root around inside the bottom there, but we needed the ladders to get up on top. You're all tooled up, as they say, so let's see some action.'

Slowly Sam picked up the step-ladders and opened them out. They were the sort that would bend against the hinge to straighten out and act as a normal ladder. He snapped it into place, then took a couple of steps forward and positioned the now straight ladder against the side of the Lantern.

'Up you go.' Blake had turned, dragging Chantal around with him.

Steele had not moved but craned his head to watch as Sam climbed the steps.

When his head was parallel with the top of the Lantern, he paused. Not long now. He looked down on the four faces turned up towards him with varying degrees of trust and hope etched on their features.

He took another step upward and then reached into the opening at the top of the Lantern, beneath the stone cross. The brickwork was cold and rough as it brushed against his fingers, feeling damp in the evening air. His hand found and then gripped a small object, as he knew it would.

And then everything went black.

IT WAS THE moment he had been waiting for, when all of the lights in the village went out. They stayed switched on overnight on Friday and Saturday but on Sunday they reverted to their weekday timetable and went out at eleven o'clock.

The blackness was instant and shocking. Sam could see nothing, but neither could anyone else. His sole advantage was that he was anticipating it, between the first and second tolling of the hour, and so he was able to act.

He grabbed the Walther PPK from inside the top of the Lantern, where he'd placed it two hours earlier, and slid down the ladder. Perhaps two seconds had elapsed.

He looked towards the sunken light where Steele had held Julienne. Although the power had been cut to the lights they still glowed with a fading orange illumination and he could see the vague form of Connell Steele. He seemed to be turning the rifle towards him. There was a deliberation in the action and Sam knew that Steele was trying to guess where he would be.

Sam fired, aiming for Steele's body mass. There was a grunt and Steele's rifle went off, flashing briefly and scattering gravel at their feet. Sam saw him fall to the ground. He took two steps and grabbed the rifle from Steele's hand.

Perhaps four seconds had elapsed.

He turned back to where Blake had been standing with Chantal. He could see nothing. Although his eyes were starting to acclimatize and make a distinction between the black of the land and the dark grey of the sky, he still could not discern shapes. It was a bizarre sensation, the darkness having a depth and weight of its own, like a shroud thrown over the world.

Then Chantal called out.

'Sam! He's running!'

Now Sam could hear steps moving away. The ground beneath them was dry and hard and Blake's footsteps were just about discernible. And then they became crisp as Blake's feet found the gravel path that ran through the park from one set of stone gates to the other. The only thing that lay in that direction was the road out of the village. But there was a single light down there coming from someone's bedroom window. Blake seemed drawn towards it, his steps coming faster as he broke into a run.

There was a noise behind him and Sam turned.

He sensed that Steele was struggling to sit up.

'Julienne, come towards me.'

She said, 'I'm here,' and he realised that she had already come close. He pushed her gently behind him, then stepped towards Steele and bent down.

'You should have put it down. I wouldn't have fired.'

Steele was struggling to breathe but said, 'Pussy.'

'Is it bad?'

'Fucking lucky shot in the dark.'

'Don't insult me, I can leave you here.'

Steele took several more short, urgent breaths.

'So tell me, pussy, where's the paperwork? You took it, right? Hid yourself a shooter up there and took the paperwork.'

'Sorry, there was nothing there.'

'Ah, shit. Done my karma in for nothing. King and country, all that bullshit. Defence of the realm. Didn't even get a result.' He paused and in the silence his breathing was harsh. 'I've got a long hard swim coming up, haven't I?'

'What swim?'

'Across that river. What those old Greeks talked about.'

'It was a boat. They went across by boat.'

'Oh, got that wrong too, did I? Never mind. I've got one of those, a boat. Not here, though. Never here when you need it. So it's a swim for me. Time to make up for all the shit I've done. Make amends. Get my karma right so I don't come back as a fucking fly.'

Sam nodded, then realised that Steele probably couldn't see him.

'Someone will have called the gendarmes with all that shooting. Ambulance will be on its way.'

'Fuck off. They're all hunters round here. They'll think it's a wild pig got its due. Ha, not far wrong.' He paused and breathed hard again. 'So did you know we were here? All a game to set us up?'

'A wild guess. I didn't know you'd have the women. My fault. That's going to fuck up my karma, too.'

'I should have let Clifford do you in. He really wanted to.'

'But you didn't let him. That's a brownie point for your karma. Shorten the swim.'

Steele seemed to calm down, his breathing becoming more shallow. He began to make a noise that Sam thought at first was a drawn-out moan. But then he realised Steele was crying, a high, keening note that pierced the air. He reached down and touched him on the shoulder and the noise stopped at once. Steele took in a long breath.

'I suppose this is no more than I deserve. Anyway, he's gone down to the cemetery. We parked the car outside so you wouldn't see it in the village. Stupid bastard's forgotten I've got the keys.'

Sam thought that Steele had begun to laugh at his own irony, a haunted croaking sound coming from the back of his throat. But then he shivered and went still.

Perhaps a minute had elapsed.

Despite himself, Sam felt his spirits rising. So far he had survived, as had Chantal and Julienne Bressette. Perhaps it would be all right in the end. He had known when he left the house that he was running risks at a number of levels. He had thought that the women were safely out of it and had been shocked to see them in the park. It had complicated all of his thinking.

But even while he rejoiced in his good fortune, he wondered whether Steele had in fact sacrificed himself. There had been something welcoming and exhausted in the way he had talked of the transition into death. And Sam suspected that he had been simply a means by which Steele had found a way out of a life that he found increasingly stultifying and without merit. It wouldn't have been the first time that he had seen surrender masquerading as bravado.

At last he was beginning to make out shapes as his eyes grew accustomed to the pitch black. There were a couple of bedroom lights showing through closed shutters and the light that they threw over the park seemed to grow more intense as the receptors in his eyes worked to pick up whatever illumination they could.

He said, 'Are you two ladies all right?'

Chantal and Julienne confirmed that they were.

'Nobody hit?'

'No.'

'Good. Can you go back to the house? Here, I've got a torch.'

He handed over the rubber torch he'd kept in his pocket, clicking it on as he did so. The light flared intensely as Chantal took it and pointed it at the ground.

She said, 'What about you? Don't tell me you're going after that lunatic? If you find him, tell him he's lost *my* vote.'

Sam said, 'I've not finished detecting yet, have I? Remember what I said about persistence?'

BLAKE WAS THIRTY yards from the car before he realised Steele had the keys.

'Fuck fuck fuck!'

He turned round and could see virtually nothing in the centre of the village. Whatever residual glow had remained around the streetlamps had now subsided and only the shaft of light from the bedroom that had guided him down the road was still visible, throwing a white mark across the tarmac like a ghostly finishing line.

He still had the rifle in his hands but had never fired it – or any other weapon, for that matter. Without Steele he felt naked. He wished abruptly that he had followed through on his idea to have someone pursue Steele to tidy up after him. He could have called out a code word or sent a text or some damn thing ... he needed someone to look after him and make all this unpleasantness go away. He realised yet again that he had sailed through his life and his career like a yacht without any ballast, barely touching the rough and unforgiving waves that might have made him look down to gauge the depth. He had no idea what he was doing when he had to do it for himself. His whole life had been a reaction, not based on a clear direction or set of values that he had decided to pursue. Even this misadventure, searching for a mythical document snatched from his father's desk, was becoming increasingly fanciful, a quest that he'd followed because he could, and because he didn't like the idea of anyone having anything to hold over him.

Well that was all up in the air now. Whether the document existed or not, its pursuit had seen him off. He felt a wave of self-pity rise in him, followed almost immediately by a surge of anger. Damn it, he *would* see it out ...

He thought he heard footsteps coming down the road after him.

It would be Dyke, of course.

He had never been a man prone to considering his fate as an abstraction, pre-ordained and incapable of mediation. But Dyke's doggedness and unwillingness to let things drop was beginning to seem to him like an embodiment of Nemesis. It was both annoying and wearying to keep coming up against Dyke's square, blunt features and his square, blunt mode of thought.

He rounded the Mercedes, glinting dully in the blackness, and pushed through the white metal gates of the cemetery.

SAM HEARD THE gates of the cemetery turn on their rusty hinges as they opened and, moments later, clanged shut. He slowed to a walk and moved so that he could approach the gates along the concrete wall that formed one side of the graveyard. The dark bulk of the Mercedes was parked directly outside the gates facing the village and on the other side of the road he could make out another vehicle, parked facing in the opposite direction.

He turned back to the gates. That morning he'd seen that the cemetery was in the shape of a square about a hundred yards on each edge. The walls extended a couple of feet above him and the white metal gates, hanging between two rough concrete pillars, were as high as the walls. There was no way he could scale those walls without a boost. He would have to go through the gates.

He remembered that immediately on the other side of the gates was the central aisle, a gravel path that went straight down to the far end of the cemetery, where there was a curved building of some kind – a sepulchre, perhaps. Steps rose to the right, onto a higher level. Other paths were cut crossways with the graves laid regularly either side on a grid pattern. Thankfully it was still dark, and while he would show up briefly against the white gates he should soon be lost in the darkness. Having said that, his own night vision was working efficiently now and he had to assume that Blake's was too.

Treading carefully, he approached the gates and looked at how they were locked. There was a simple metal handle that turned, opening a latch. The noise of its sliding would be the first indication to Blake that someone was following him in. Sam thought that he was more likely to have moved to one side to aim with a clear shot than to be standing behind the gate – close to the danger point – and ready to fire when Sam came through.

But Blake was an amateur. You couldn't know what he would do.

Slowly Sam reached out his hand and felt the handle. As he thought, it had been turned completely, Blake making it as difficult as possible for someone to follow without giving himself away.

Sam turned the handle, pushed the door open, and stepped back.

There was no response.

He called out, 'Blake, give it up. There's too much to lose now. Don't make it worse than it is.'

Blake's voice was muffled, as though he was at the far end of the graveyard and possibly behind a headstone.

'How can it possibly be worse? Is my wife having an affair, too?'

Sam didn't hesitate. He rammed the door open and rolled inside the cemetery.

BLAKE FIRED AND was startled by the noise made by the old rifle. He was grateful it even worked. Steele had given him a lesson that morning but they hadn't found the opportunity to actually fire it. The recoil nearly tore the old piece out of his hands. He ducked down again. He'd seen Dyke roll into the cemetery but then lost him behind all the headstones and catafalques standing between him and the entrance.

When he had come into the cemetery he had stumbled his way around the outside walls, tripping over low graves and colliding painfully with marble headstones. He was sure he'd have a bruise on his forehead the next morning where he'd slipped and banged himself on a hard stone cross. For no reason that he could fathom, he summoned an image of the house back in Surrey, and taking Ross down to the stream to fish. The grass was always lush and green down there because the stream flooded periodically, making it ideal for picnics in summer and nice to sit on a couple of collapsible chairs with a bent rod in your hands. He thought of Fiona standing in the veranda waving at them, her hand idly resting on Jemima's blonde head. It was the kind of rural idyll he had wanted for himself, but realised with a pang of regret that it was an experience he'd rarely engineered. Too often he was up in London with Lashbrooke and his gang, plotting, manoeuvring, discussing details ... he didn't take care of the important things. Again he felt a rush of self-pity rise from his stomach up to his eyes and begin to sting.

He looked down to wipe his eyes and saw for the first time the name on the gravestone behind which he'd taken shelter.

Unbelievable. Un-fucking-believable.

Jean-Claude Bressette.

The little toe-rag whose diary had set all this in motion. Here he was at ten past eleven on a Sunday night in a small village in the middle of France ... and he was hiding from a ruffian behind the grave of a man whom he'd never known but who had brought down all this grief on his head.

He knew that he needed to keep quiet, to hide himself from Dyke and try to get one over on him if he could.

But he couldn't help himself. A dry, caustic, ironic cough emerged from the back of his throat. He swallowed hard and held it back as best he could. But he felt it coming again ... and this time let it out – a hard, cold and defiant burst of laughter.

What did it matter, in the end? What did any of it matter? His reputation was now down the toilet. Fiona would leave him. He doubted he'd ever see the children again.

The laughter caught in his throat and he found himself standing up, his vision misted. Before he knew it he'd taken several steps towards where he'd last seen Dyke.

He raised the rifle before him and called out.

SAM WAS CROUCHING behind a large tombstone when he heard Blake call from barely three yards away. As he looked up he saw the vague outline of the other man.

And he was facing towards him, looking down, the rifle barrel pointing towards the top of his head.

Blake said, 'Stand up. Look me in the eye when I shoot you.'

Sam rose to his feet, the Walther still in his hand. Blake gestured with the rifle.

'Drop the gun. Jesus, I sound like a cop show.'

'I'm not going to drop it.'

'Are you mad? I'll kill you anyway.'

'No you won't.'

'Why won't I? Look.'

He raised the rifle and fired it into the air. The noise was tremendous and echoed around the enclosed walls of the graveyard.

Sam said, 'You killed some air. Well done you. It's different when it's a person.'

'Aren't you afraid to die? Or are you just stupid?'

'Tell me about Monday. What happens?'

'I get important, famous and then rich, in that order.'

'So it's a political thing in the end. Nothing to do with honour.'

'You're being simplistic. It's possible to have both – riches and honour.'

Sam paused as a new thought came to him. 'You can't change the past.'

'I don't want to change the past. I just want to control it.'

'Trust me, you can't. I've tried. It's inside you. And that's the place you can control least of all.'

Blake laughed. 'What bollocks you talk.'

'So have you said goodbye to your family?'

'Why should I say goodbye to my family? Things will carry on as before.'

Sam said, 'I doubt it.'

Then he dropped the gun.

And raised his hand to point.

BLAKE WAS CONFUSED as he began to turn his head to follow the direction in which Dyke was pointing. Then he sensed a movement and whirled around quickly, bringing the rifle barrel with him.

A monstrous figure towered over him. A man, yes, but built on a large scale. He was a head taller than Blake, with a shaven scalp and broad shoulders. And he gave off a brutal male musk that filled Blake's nostrils.

But his face – his face was awful to contemplate, and Blake felt his mouth drawing back in a rictus of horror.

Although the dark of the night still surrounded them, Blake could see that the entire surface of the man's face was tattooed.

And the design was that of a skull.

It was as though the man's skin had been torn from the muscle and bone beneath, revealing the mechanisms, the joints and tendons, the groups of nerve and muscle that worked the jaws and eyes. Like a *trompe l'oeil* painting, the tattoo imitated the lipless grin of a skeleton, the bared teeth rising up into the jawbone. The eye sockets were black and the nose had been tattooed as though it was a pared-back bone with gaping holes either side. Above the forehead, the top of his skull had been inscribed with the whorls and curls of an exposed brain. The man looked as though every line and wrinkle in his skin had been inked. It rendered him monstrous, almost inhuman, and for a moment Blake wondered what ghoul he'd raised from the graves around him ...

Inside the dark circles that surrounded his eyes, the man's pupils glittered.

Blake felt a chill of ice form in his stomach and trace a path down through his bowels. He barely noticed when the man raised a long knife and held it before his eyes. He heard his rifle clatter to the gravel beneath him.

The man spoke in a voice that was deep but without accent, a plain and ordinary voice in the end.

'Walter Lashbrooke sends his regards. He says if you can't clean this mess up, then he has to. He says, tell Gideon he was a bloody fool. He came so close. Message over.'

Then he whipped out his left hand, seized Blake by the neck, spun him around and drew the knife across his throat, where a thin line of blood grew thicker and began to spill down the front of his jacket, taking with it Blake's hopes, regrets, failures, and life.

SAM WATCHED THE tall figure stoop to gather up the lifeless body of Gideon Blake in his arms. He stood for a moment looking at Sam, then spoke.

'None of this happened. Go home.'

Then the figure turned and strode towards the exit gates.

Sam waited a moment, then followed. As he approached the gates he heard a car start up and drive away. When he looked outside, Blake and Steele's hired Mercedes was still there but the car on the other side of the road had gone and in the distance a pair of red rear lights was receding on the road out of Journet.

EPILOGUE

AFTER THREE DAYS of discussion and argument with the French authorities, Sam began to wonder whether the French had invented the notion of bureaucracy to give a polite gloss to what seemed to be sheer incompetence. Everything had to be touched by the hands of at least three people – ostensibly to ensure that processes were followed exactly, but in fact simply increasing the opportunity for human error. However, he acknowledged the fact that he'd smuggled Miss Bressette into the country on a false passport and, what's more, that he had shot and fatally wounded another person. For that he was accountable.

Fortunately, it transpired that Chantal's grandmother had some powerful friends in the local hierarchy. Her bravery during the war, transporting messages between groups of Resistance fighters, and her willingness to come back to the area after so long abroad had given her a *cachet* that she had nurtured during the last five years. She answered the door to several important-looking men over a two-day period and sat with them in the back kitchen while Sam and Chantal remained with a friendly gendarme in the sitting room.

It seemed also that Blake's colleagues in London were prepared to pull some strings on his behalf. He was visited by a serious young man who'd driven down from Paris and talked to him in hushed tones in the garden. Sam was advised to say as little as possible about Gideon Blake – in fact, his whereabouts were still unknown. Without Steele to explain his own and Blake's movements over the last few days, any knowledge that Sam or Miss Bressette might have would be best, it was explained, kept to themselves.

ON THE THIRD day they were told they were free to go. It was evident that Chantal and Julienne had been taken prisoner by Steele and that Mr Dyke had acted to save them both. Why Steele had done what he had done was immaterial at the moment. Investigations would continue in Paris and London but for the time being, no further action would be taken against them.

THE FOLLOWING MORNING, Julienne Bressette spoke to Sam and Chantal and instructed them to be ready to walk across to the Mairie. There was something they had to see.

Sam and Chantal met in the hall five minutes later and shrugged at each other. When Julienne arrived she was as neatly dressed as always, her hair pulled back from her strong, radiant features.

She turned to Sam. 'That evening, you knew, didn't you?'

'Knew what?'

'You knew that there was nothing in the *Lanterne des morts*.'

'Of course ... I'd been there earlier to hide that gun you gave me. I wanted an advantage.'

'No, before that. You had seen the book.'

Sam grinned at her. 'Ah, the book.'

It was true that when he had come back from Montmorillon on Sunday evening he had a few hours to spare and had remembered something. On the train from Edinburgh, Chantal had shown him old photographs of Journet, including one of several young boys sitting on the steps of a monument of some kind. At that time he had no idea what it was. But the memory had piqued his interest, and he had looked at Julienne's shelves and found a blue-bound paperback that described the history of the village. His French was rudimentary, but the image on the cover had drawn his attention at once: a black-and-white photograph of the *Lanterne des morts* apparently standing on a street corner. Flicking through the book he had found the section on the history of the church and the graveyard, and references to the Lantern itself. Translating slowly, he realised that the Lantern had in fact been moved to its position in the park only in 1980. Prior to that it had been located on the corner of the street where they now stood. Chantal's photograph had shown it there. If it had been moved so recently, then anything that had been concealed inside it would have been found. Steele had been right, in a way – Sam had gamed them, tricked them into believing there was something important to be found in the Lantern when in fact it had already given up any secrets it might have had.

But then a thought occurred to him.

'Of course I found the book very easily.'

Julienne smiled at him but said nothing.

Sam went on, 'In fact, it was on top of a pile standing in front of the shelves, wasn't it? You intended me to find it, the same as you wanted me to find the gun. You're a tricky little fighter, aren't you?'

'I'm eighty-eight years of age. Do you think I've got here by accident? Now, come.'

She led them out of the house and across the square towards the Mairie, its flag still snapping and waving in the wind. Sam felt as though it was the first fresh air he'd breathed in three days. At his side, Chantal put her arm through his in a comradely fashion. He was moved by the gesture and squeezed her hand with his arm.

Inside, a small committee was waiting for them – the mayor, his female assistant and the young man who'd given Sam and Chantal directions when they'd first arrived. The mayor was a small man with thinning grey hair and spectacles, and he looked grave as he shook Sam's hand and gave the women the traditional kisses on the cheek. Then he raised an arm and guided them round to the back of a row of storage cupboards. He took a key from his female assistant and ceremoniously unlocked a drawer in one of the cupboards, taking a metal box about twelve inches by six from inside. He moved to a table then opened the lid. Sam and Chantal craned forward to see what was inside. Julienne stepped forward and pulled out a handful of folded papers, brown with age.

She said, 'I wasn't here when the Lantern was moved but these were kept for me. I only found out yesterday when I made enquiries.'

It seemed to Sam that she had been deliberately restraining herself from looking at the papers, but now she did so. Everyone else stood still and watched.

After a while, Julienne said, 'Yes, they're from Jean-Claude. He tells me he's going away because the Germans are looking for any member of the *maquis* they can find. He also tells me to send on these letters.'

Amongst the small pile there had been a bunch of letters tied together with string. She reached out and gave them to Sam.

'You can have these.'

Sam unknotted the flimsy string and began to look through the letters. He saw at once that they were written by Robin Leftwich – signing himself 'RL' – and were addressed to Jennifer Blake. He looked through them quickly, seeing that they were all conventional love-letters written on lined paper he'd no doubt cadged from the French *résistants*. When he'd finished leafing through them he turned them over and went back through them slowly.

He looked at Chantal.

'It's not here. Letters from Leftwich to Jennifer written on ordinary paper. Nothing like a telegram or anything written in a hand other than his.'

'Nothing from Churchill, then? Nothing to make all this palaver worthwhile?'

Sam grinned at her. 'If there was, Leftwich probably lost it or burnt it. Or maybe it never reached him. Jennifer sent it in the post to him while he was in the new SAS – perhaps they intercepted post for fear of spies.'

Chantal sighed and pulled a face.

'I feel cheated. Don't you feel cheated?'

Sam gathered the papers together and put them in his pocket, then nodded at the small French gathering, who had been watching with incomprehension. He took Chantal's arm and led her outside. The day was brightening again and though the wind was brisk he felt the air was tending towards warm.

He said to Chantal, 'That's the eighth rule of private detection: Never expect to receive the answers you want. It would make life too easy.'

PORTSMOUTH SMELLED OF petrol fumes and of a dank misery that he couldn't identify. In the end he thought it was just the way the atmosphere smelled in Britain and decided to ignore it. He picked up his car and drove back via Jennifer Leftwich's nursing home. She regarded him coolly when she came into the Reception area, but when he gave her Robin Leftwich's letters her face crumpled into a kind of teary gratitude. He sat with her while she slowly read through the dozen or so letters, smiling at a phrase or a thought now and then.

Eventually she looked up and he saw a kind of peace settle into her eyes.

'Thank you, Mr Dyke. It's very kind of you.'

'You're welcome.'

'I can put these with the others, now.'

Sam sat up straight. 'You have others?'

'They came after the war. I don't know who sent them. Perhaps it was Chantal's grandfather. Perhaps somebody found them.'

'Where are they?'

'Oh ... safe. They'll be burned when I'm gone.'

Sam didn't know how to ask the question he most wanted to ask, but she saw it in his face and said, 'Yes, the telegram is there. After all these years I don't remember what it says. It didn't seem important at the time. I was looking at the other side.'

'I understand.'

'Do you? You have to realise it was all I had left of Robin, until you brought these. Yes they were my letters to him, but he had touched them. He'd scribbled little notes on some of them. I wasn't going to let my brother or his awful wheedling brat of a son get their hands on them.'

'Why didn't you say you still had the telegram when Chantal and I were here?'

'My dear, you never asked. You seemed more concerned about Chantal's state of mind and hurried from the room. Very courteous. But did I understand correctly – you're a private detective?'

Sam said, 'Allegedly.'

Jennifer Leftwich grinned at him mischievously.

That's a rule they don't teach you in private detective school, Sam told himself: Always ask one more question.

LAURA SAID NOTHING when he handed back her passport. She rapped it twice against her other hand, then turned and went upstairs. The weight and speed of her steps on each tread told Sam a story he didn't want to hear. He went out into the garden and peered down into his fishpond. He didn't know anything about fish but had thought it would be a Good Thing if he had something other than himself to look after.

He heard a footstep and looked up. Dan was standing in the doorway, watching.

'I cleaned it out the other day. Getting a bit mucky.'

Sam was surprised. 'Are you supposed to clean them out?'

'I looked it up.'

Sam nodded. 'Ah. Good job's somebody's got some brains around here.'

'Where's Chantal?'

'She's staying with her grandmother for a couple of weeks. Going to learn some French, I think.'

'And how's whatshisname, Jack?'

'Getting lots of rest.'

They looked at each and a smile passed between them. Then Dan looked away.

'Laura's really pissed off with you, you know. You should say something.'

'If there was anything I could say, I'd say it.'

'So you're just going to ignore it, as usual, and hope it goes away.'

'Usually works.'

'No, it doesn't.'

After a moment, Dan turned and went back inside. Sam took a turn around his garden, bending down, touching plants he didn't know the names of, picking up bits of rubbish and leaves and putting them in a green plastic compost bin. Eventually he went back inside. Something was cooking and he wandered over to the hob to see what it was.

Laura came in behind him carrying a wooden spoon. He turned to face her.

She said, 'Sam, I'm leaving you.'

He said, 'Yes, I know.'

Final Note

Thank you for reading this book. Reviews are lifeblood to authors, so I'd be grateful if you could write a review wherever it suits you best.

Thanks again.

Keith Dixon

Other Works

The Sam Dyke Series

Altered Life
The Private Lie
The Hard Swim
The Bleak
The Strange Girl
The Secret Sharers
The Innocent Dead
The Lonely Grave
The Second Guess (short story)

Standalone Novels

A French Darcy – a Romance
Actress – a Contemporary novel

Essays on Writing

The Idle Writer
Crime Writing Confidential

Blog

www.cwconfidential.blogspot.com

Webpage

http://www.keithdixonnovels.com